Novels by Breakfield and I

MW00789991

The Enigma Factor	*The Enigma Beyond*
The Enigma Rising	*The Enigma Threat*
The Enigma Ignite	**SHORT STORIES**
The Enigma Wraith	*Out of Poland*
The Enigma Stolen	*Destiny Dreamer*
The Enigma Always	*Hidden Target*
The Enigma Gamers A CATS Tale	*Hot Chocolate*
	Love's Enigma
The Enigma Broker	*Nowhere But Up*
The Enigma Dragon A CATS Tale	*Remember the Future*
	Riddle Codes
The Enigma Source	*The Jewel*

Kirkus Reviews

The Enigma Factor In this debut techno-thriller, the first in a planned series, a hacker finds his life turned upside down as a mysterious company tries to recruit him...

The Enigma Rising In Breakfield and Burkey's latest techno-thriller, a group combats evil in the digital world, with multiple assignments merging in Acapulco and the Cayman Islands.

The Enigma Ignite The authors continue their run of stellar villains with the returning Chairman Lo Chang, but they also add wonderfully unpredictable characters with unclear motivations. A solid espionage thriller that adds more tension and lightheartedness to the series.

The Enigma Wraith The fourth entry in Breakfield and Burkey's techno-thriller series pits the R-Group against a seemingly untraceable computer virus and what could be a full-scale digital assault.

The Enigma Stolen Breakfield and Burkey once again deliver the goods, as returning readers will expect—intelligent technology-laden dialogue; a kidnapping or two; and a bit of action, as Jacob and Petra dodge an assassin (not the cyber kind) in Argentina.

The Enigma Always As always, loaded with smart technological prose and an open ending that suggests more to come.

The Enigma Gamers (A CATS Tale) A cyberattack tale that's superb as both a continuation of a series and a promising start in an entirely new direction.

The Enigma Broker …the authors handle their players as skillfully as casino dealers handle cards, and the various subplots are consistently engaging. The main storyline is energized by its formidable villains…

The Enigma Dragon (A CATS Tale) This second CATS-centric installment (after 2016's *The Enigma Gamers*) will leave readers yearning for more. Astute prose and an unwavering pace energized by first-rate characters and subplots.

The Enigma Source Another top-tier installment that showcases exemplary recurring characters and tech subplots.

The Enigma Beyond the latest installment of this long-running technothriller series finds a next generation cyber security team facing off against unprincipled artificial intelligences. Dense but enthralling entry, with a bevy of new, potential narrative directions.

The Enigma Threat Another clever, energetic addition to an appealing series.

the Enigma Broker

Breakfield and Burkey

BOOK 8: Award Winning Techno-Thriller Series

The Enigma Broker
Charles Breakfield and Roxanne Burkey
© Copyright 2023 ICABOD Press
ALL RIGHTS RESERVED

Published by

ICABOD Press

ISBN: 978-1-946858-34-4 (paperback)
ISBN: 978-1-946858-69-6 (ebook)
ISBN: 978-1-946858-23-8 (audiobook)

Library of Congress Control Number: 2016915892
Cover, interior and eBook design: F + P Graphic Design, FPGD.com

Second Edition
Printed in the United States

TECHNO-THRILLER I SUSPENSE

Acknowledgments

We are grateful for the support we have received from our family and friends. We look forward to seeing the reviews from our fans. Thank you in advance for your time.

Specialized Terms are available beginning on page 379 if needed for readers' reference.

In the very near future conventional wars will be replaced with Economic Wars designed to cripple a target population, rather than a geographical target. The difference being, Economic Wars will leave the infrastructure intact. As the weapon of choice, computers will lead the charge. Winners will advance their goals, while the losers will struggle to eat.

...The Enigma Chronicles

Lost in the Blink of an Action

TEN YEARS EARLIER

Darkness had settled over his dreary dorm room. He hadn't bothered to eat after answering the university chancellor's endless questions. He was too stricken with the deep fear of being expelled from school and, worse, the humiliation it would bring to his family. Nothing had been threatened or decided when the conversation ended, but a promise of a disciplinary decision before the end of the weekend had been suggested.

He reviewed the consultations and joking that had led up to today. It had been one of those days where events begged to be changed and forgotten. Choices that seemed so innocent in theory had turned so horrible after the fact.

He had been a loner for the three years he had been in the program, with no social life. On the rare occasion that he worked with other classmates, he'd found that he had been responsible for most of the work to complete a given project. It really had not bothered him because it was during this semester the poor students and laggards had been weeded out. The remaining students were all Type A personalities with an unyielding drive to succeed. He had finally felt he was with men who had equivalent capabilities in logic, reasoning, and forward thinking, even from their different disciplines.

From the beginning, he had focused on database programming, using logic and forward views of the times to leapfrog the generally accepted thinking. The thought leadership that was coming out of the Ivy League schools or newly emerging technology businesses was dwarfed by visions he and the few classmates he considered near equals had roughed out. His late-night studies and conversations with these men had allowed him to lower his guard, as he thought about being accepted as one of them. He had honestly believed that he could step out from his old, structured world and easily move into this new one. He was confident that this new world was filled with people who spoke and understood the possibilities of the digital realm.

Sadness with the weight of his choices caused him to shake his head in disbelief. How would he be able to honor his family name with this hanging over his head? Even though the others had laughed it off and cried 'college prank', he would clearly not be able to make this excuse the focus of the upcoming discussion with his uncle. Guilt had slowed every thought, action, and response today.

He had not spoken to his co-conspirators at all since they had been taken away from the hospital, even though, as he passed, one of them grinned and quipped, "It will all work out. Keep a stiff upper lip, old chum, and your inscrutable face intact."

At that moment, regardless of the punishment meted out by the university, he knew he needed to plan how he would make amends. He practically choked every time he considered how he had come to the university robed in honor but had now replaced it with unendurable shame.

As the oldest son of the patriarch of a long line of an honor-bound tradition, he had no excuse for tainting the family name. True, he was thousands of miles from home in a culture that usually shrugged its shoulders at college indiscretions, but he knew distance was not a safety net as it might have been before telephones, fax machines, or even telegrams. He had been given the opportunity to gain advanced education at a European university. His uncle and other family members had sacrificed to meet the costs even though he had qualified for some scholarships. Those might even be at risk after this stunt.

If he were able to complete the program, he needed to increase his course load and finish faster to save the family any additional expenses. In the forthcoming discussion with his uncle, he planned to lay this out as one in a series of steps in his path to forgiveness. He also had been outlining for months a series of programs, a bit before their time, which could gather information in new ways and use his yet-to-be-completed programs to make deterministic decisions. He had the brains, he had the dreams, and he had the tenacity to use what technology was available, stretching it to the limits, or to create the rest. The cruel luck of this escapade was what made the focus of his next avenues become clearer.

Armed with the confidence of his plans and cash to pay for the privilege of using a semi-private telephone, he went to purchase his cellular phone. Until this time he had been confident enough to send long letters home at the end of each semester, along with his grades and class standing. Now a private conversation was needed, and to hear the voice of his uncle was critically important. Getting the device, some instructions, and a plan that afforded international calling with a controllable cost element, he placed the call to his uncle's offices, which were just beginning their day. When connected to the receptionist, he formally asked to be connected to his uncle.

His uncle answered quickly with concern in his voice. "My esteemed one, are you ill or in danger?"

"No, my uncle, but I am in trouble and need your forgiveness." With all the concern removed from his tone, he sternly

3

replied, "Why would my ward and the son of my deceased brother need forgiveness? What have you done?"

He could feel the stern iciness in his uncle's voice but was determined to petition for a second chance. As had been outlined in his head in his dorm room, he related his activities, point by point. There was no soft-pedaling on his culpability in the matter at hand as he related the activities to his uncle and sketched his go forward plans. After thirty minutes of one-way conversation, he went silent.

As the seconds stretched into minutes, concern heightened in the young man's chest, threatening to crush his heart and stop his breathing. He finally could take no more as he begged, "Uncle, can you not speak to forgive me?"

"Silence!" his uncle demanded. "You have disgraced your family and your ancestors. There is no amount of planning you could do to rectify the steps already taken by you. You will never call here again or show your face to your former family. You are dead and gone. The funds you have in your account as of now are all you will get from me, ever. You will never amount to anything good or pure again. Do not embarrass this family again by using our name from this day forward. You chose dishonor as a life's course, so make the transition complete and answer to another name. You are a ghost in shame and will be alone for eternity."

With that last remark, his former uncle disconnected the call, as well as cast him out alone into the world. Each of the statements made by his uncle replayed in his head, growing colder and harsher each time he rewound the conversation. He made his way slowly back to his dorm room and replayed all the events that had led to his demise. As he finished packing his bags, turned out the light, and shut the door, he completely accepted that his past was now gone.

Those simple activities, coupled with the realization that

his past had been stripped from him, had helped him reach a decision. As he stared into the night's darkness, a new resolve grew within him. He announced loudly and with deep-seated conviction as he strode through the darkness toward the bus stop, "I will show you all! I have the patience to endure this obstacle, but I will win back my honor even if it is only for myself! A man without a past is free to reinvent himself into the image of his choosing! I will become the ghost, not mourn the loss, and I will win for my new family of me."

CHAPTER ONE

Number Crunching Issues

Mike Patrick was looking at the big wall screen in his opulent office overlooking the recently expanded Suez Canal as data streamed in. His tailored shirt strained at the buttons following his typical oversized lunch with his cronies. As the head of ePETRO, Inc., he felt he could eat daily at a five-star restaurant and never have to work out. He was too important to have anything look amiss, even though his valet was constantly letting out the seams of his tailored suits or simply buying larger sizes. An outsider might consider him powerful, rather than simply full of himself.

Mike behaved as if he was at the limits of his patience as he ran his hand through his salt-and-pepper hair and demanded, "How in the hell is that possible? We have agreements…uh, I mean understandings, in place that oil production quotas should not be overrun. Roslyn, are you actually telling me that world oil production is hovering well above its allowance? Who's violating their understood production limits?"

Roslyn had worked with Mike for several years as his number two. She had more incriminating pictures and reports than he even knew, though he was aware of some. Roslyn was a large woman and slightly taller than Mike at 1.83 meters. Her red silk suit, though quite expensive, had been sat in for way too long and looked like no amount of pressing would remove the wrinkles. Her hair was well cut, but its color of old wheat was not attractive against her sallow skin.

Roslyn opened her eyes wide in obvious bewilderment and, through her generous lips painted red to match her suit, stated, "According to the report, no one, Mike. That's what doesn't make any sense. If this report is correct, then no oil producing country or corporation within our organization is violating their understood quotas."

Mike was grinding his teeth in anger as he complained, "At this price point we can't make back the cost to drill for, let alone bring up, the damn stuff. And, Roslyn, if you try and tell me that stupid old joke about losing money on every barrel of oil but that we can make it up in volume, I will box your ears!"

Before Roslyn could offer anything else, Mike practically hollered, "Get everyone on the phone! We are going to get to the bottom of this. I want to know who is violating our agreements and why."

Roslyn was hesitant and her eyes were awash in reluctance, but she finally managed to respond, as non-offensively as possible, "Uh, sir, I have been fielding calls from all of them already, asking us the same question. The last few phone calls were from people as agitated as you are, sir. I think we need to do a little more homework before we round everyone up on an encrypted video call."

Mike rolled his eyes as he asked, "So, what are you saying? You don't believe anyone is lying about boosting their numbers?"

Again, Roslyn shifted uneasily as she sat in her chair. She blinked as she searched for the right word choice and offered, "Sir, I believe everyone is holding firm on their oil production numbers because our satellite surveillance cannot confirm the extra forty percent of oil from any of the known locations. That suggests that this increase in product has to be coming from somewhere else.

"Even if someone was sneaking out that much extra oil, my question is why and how would we not have known of additional production areas? If it is a new entrant to the market, they would be as hurt by selling prices that are lower than production prices, just as we are. Or, if someone is bringing up oil with newer, lower cost extraction technology, we would have already heard about it."

Mike, now calmed down to a just seething level, queried, "Okay, so let's just say, for argument's sake, no one is fudging on their quantities. The only other possibility is…"

Roslyn finished his sentence. "…the numbers have been tampered with."

Mike rolled his eyes at the remark and was about to respond when his personal line rang. Not wanting to waste any effort, he answered it on speakerphone, and his administrative assistant quickly began, "I know you told me not to disturb you, but the chairwoman of the Board is on the line with what is most probably the rest of the Board as well. She's not taking no for an answer and did not provide her usual jovial greeting to me. When I complete the connection, I suspect you will be on with all the Board of Directors, sir."

Mike didn't get a breath to respond before he was on live with the chairman and likely the entire board. Using the speakerphone and trying to buy a little time to realign his thought process, in his cheeriest voice he offered, "Good day, Chairwoman, and of course to all the other conference call attendees. I rarely get a social call from the Board since I know you all to be quite busy.

"I am confident that I didn't miss a regularly scheduled meeting, so I am wondering…"

Marge, the chairwoman, promptly broke into the monolog. "Cut the crap, Mike! I called this emergency meeting with the rest of the directors because I want some answers. To be on this

Board of Directors you have to own stock in this company, and right now all the market players are heading for the exits and dumping our stock like it was radioactive.

"Now, when I see my investments heading south in this nuclear winter without a heads-up from the president of our company, it makes me think he's asleep at the wheel. I expect you to immediately tell me who has gone rogue on our oil production agreements. I also want to know the plan and timeline to get them back in line for oil at our agreed fair and profitable price point so our stock price will stop screaming *Dive! Dive! Dive!* like it was a U-boat commander under attack!"

Mike muted the speakerphone. With a sour look on his face, Mike turned to Roslyn and flatly stated, "Marge the Barge on a rampage again. Glad I'm not there to see her 140 kilos of body mass fighting to overwhelm the buttons on her tent dress."

Roslyn struggled to suppress her laughter at the vulgar but humorous description as he took the phone off mute.

Mike put forth his most diplomatic, well-practiced voice as he offered, "Madam Chairwoman, we understand the gravity of the situation. I am rapidly evaluating all our informational resources to quickly get to the bottom of the situation. I propose…"

Marge barged into Mike's oily speech. "Am I hearing you don't have a frosty, fricking clue as to how this situation arose? We hired you to have timely answers for our pointed questions. All I'm seeing is a soon-to-be ex-oil company president with no pointed answers but clearly a stupid pointed head. I don't pay you so I can be uninformed about something as dramatic as this. If you don't want to be back earning a living rough-necking out in west fencepost Texas, pull your head out of your backside and give me answers now. I don't want a bit of the mealy-mouth doubletalk you give to the reporters!"

Mike had to mute the phone again to bring his breathing back under control. He shot a stern look at Roslyn and pointedly asked, "Are you going to let her talk to me that way?"

Roslyn, completely on the spot and with a puzzled look, responded as naïvely and sincerely as possible, "Uh…what way, sir?"

Seething at the dressing down he was getting and more that was about to come, Mike unmuted the phone and evenly stated, "In looking at all our data, documentation, and numbers of all partners, rivals, and peers that produce oil, no one can be accused of overproduction. Our shipping to market, our insider information, and our satellite imagery all point to the same piece of information. No one is overproducing, Madam Chairwoman."

Marge sputtered for a second, then boomed, "What? Are you insane? At forty percent over-capacity production, prices on the commodity markets are dropping to fire-sale pricing, and you claim no one is flooding the supply chain?

"Mike, you aren't stupid enough to think I would believe the entire planet is lying about its production numbers just to make us look bad. Since you truly have nothing else better to do, why don't you find out who or what is playing this little joke on us, hmm?"

Mike could feel the ice from Marge coming through the phone with her last comment. Marge was a thoroughly unpleasant woman, but with her enormous bulk and intimidating manners she usually got her way. Her management style was a combination of coercion, threats, and psychological beatings until she got the answers she wanted. Marge the Barge was a formidable opponent in the business world, and it was better to stay clear of her. You couldn't really call her cruel because that would have meant that she enjoyed her brutal effect on others. She cared for nothing – not pets, not family, not her community, and probably not even her life. Her rise to the top had cost her all of her human emotions, save one. She had to win at all the global business games she wanted to play in. Nothing else mattered. And, like any psychological addiction, the momentary rush didn't last long enough before a new rush was required. She was a very sad excuse for a human being.

Mike, feeling calm again, realized that she would have her way. If it meant that he was out of the way, then so be it. He smiled at the corporate combat barrage that was being shoved at him as he countered, "Madam Chairwoman, we are working this issue with all due haste. If that is an unsatisfactory answer to you and the Board, I shall, of course, tender my resignation. Will that make the situation more palatable for the Board?"

Without the benefit of a video to observe the impact of his statement, Mike was sure that all the board members were staring at Marge and waiting for her answer.

After a long pause, she finally conveyed, "You are one of the few people who can get me to reel in my temper when it gets a little out of line. I will not accept your resignation but will charge you to get to the bottom of this mess. I want order restored in the marketplace as rapidly as possible. To do that, I am prepared to offer additional resources to make sure you are successful. Do we understand one another, Mike?"

Mike muted the phone and retorted to Roslyn. "Oh good, we aren't going to reenact the Jonah and the Whale story." Roslyn smirked slightly.

Mike unmuted his phone and stated, "As usual, Madam Chairwoman, you have not understated your position. I understand completely. Allow me to disengage from this call so that I can return to my analysis. Good day."

After he disconnected from the call, Mike studied Roslyn for a moment, then questioned, "How is it that markets have different production figures than the producers of a raw material?"

Roslyn added, "We know who all the players are and we know within three to five percent how much they can pull from the ground. I am working to discover how and who could be distorting those numbers."

Mike asked, "Why can't we just publish our numbers to the markets? That should be enough to make this go away and get oil back to where it should be priced."

Roslyn offered, "Our word against the commodity traders and brokers that make this economy go round and round? Their numbers are usually quite close to ours. At this point, our figures would mean a huge jump in oil futures and probably lots of angry people decrying the big bad oil producers of rigging the supply figures to raise the price. I'm sure we would be painted as self-serving opportunists trying to squeeze the average consumer. How big of a private army would we need to surround ourselves with to survive?"

Mike clucked his tongue and said, "Yeah, I can see that as a classic run-for-your-life moment. I don't think those are the kind of resources Marge the Barge was suggesting we call on.

"This is just great. We can't tell the world their numbers are wrong for fear of starting a firestorm, but if we don't, we will be out of business selling our product for less than what it costs to bring it to market. Let's run the numbers one more time to see if we missed anything. If it comes up the same, then try to set up a full video conference with the others to discuss potential solutions."

Roslyn nodded her head and said, "Yes, sir."

CHAPTER TWO

Board Games

The office was suitable to the man who had been ensconced in it for several years. Old European styling of the desk and chair was tastefully offset with a tile floor and an area rug that displayed woodland creatures and birds. A high-definition screen was mounted on the wall, and a simple keyboard was accessible on the desktop. Papers were neatly stacked with a clearly determined order of priority. A matching filing cabinet was modest in size due to most information being maintained digitally in the secure data center adjacent to this office. Quiet music was playing lightly in the background with infrequent interruption by the chimes of the antique wall clock.

Otto lifted his head from the documents he was reviewing and smiled broadly as he noted the incoming caller ID on his cell phone. He warmly greeted the caller, "Thiago, my good man. How nice to hear from you again. I know we haven't had a chance to chat, but I had noticed on my calendar that our semi-annual business call is coming up next month. I wouldn't want you to think that I am remiss in our discussions. I trust you are well, and that delightful daughter of yours, Lara, is prospering with her fashion endeavor. How can I be of assistance, kind sir?"

A sullen Thiago asked, "Otto, do you remember those 13th and 14th century maps of the world where Europe was thought to be the center of the universe? The fear of the times was if one sailed a ship too far in any one direction, one would fall off the world into the abyss."

Somewhat taken aback by the tone of Thiago and his odd introduction, Otto cautiously confirmed, "Yes, I recall pictures of those maps, as well as the associated fear of the times.

"Tell me, is there a subtle parallel to ancient but wrong impressions of the world and your present state of affairs?"

Thiago lamented, "It feels, Otto, like my business world is sailing off into the abyss. Do you have a few minutes to visit? I know I sort of sprang this call on you, but I feel I need to talk to someone if for no other reason than just to hear it stated out loud."

Otto responded, "My friend, I actually do have other activities scheduled, but if you hold for a moment, I can move a few things around so I can visit for a while." Otto put the phone down and quickly rescheduled a few things on his calendar and then stated, "Okay, now can you net this out for me so we don't have to revisit the last six hundred years of history to get to your issues?"

Thiago chuckled slightly and allowed, "Point taken, Otto. How well you know me. Where to begin?

"For years, we Brazilians have tried to build a business portfolio that operated on the different cycles of commodities, up or down. Our energy holdings, mining operations, and, of course, shipping businesses have come close to being an ideal model until recently. We were about to sink several offshore oil wells here in Brazil when we watched the floor pricing buckle under the oil oversupply problem. We were also planning to sign a deal with the Chilean government to launch a new copper mine when that commodity's price began to flatline as well.

"With no demand for raw materials or oil to ship, I now have so much excess shipping capacity that I am going to have to do layoffs and idle my shipping fleet."

Otto listened sympathetically to Thiago and offered, "My friend, we both know that business cycles come and go. I'm sure you are not overstating your position, but in every business, there are ebbs and flows for products, whether finished or raw materials. I am confident that we can provide some useful guidance on how to weather this business storm, as well as be properly positioned during the next upturn."

Thiago countered, "Otto, I was fairly sure that this would be your position on the matter. Before calling, I and my staff played a little game of *Let's Pretend to be Otto* so we can see what our options are. Now, what we found as a result of that exercise is really what I'm calling about."

Otto, somewhat perplexed, responded, "Please, Thiago, go ahead. I'm decidedly interested in hearing how the Otto game went."

A slight grin blossomed, transforming Thiago's initial scowl. He explained, "We began digging into our numbers, trying to understand how we missed the oversupply issue of both oil and copper, when we discovered something, I can't explain.

"In each commodity area where we were planning to invest, we had diligently analyzed each of our competitive producers. We came up with a figure that simply doesn't match what is being stated on the world markets. We even discovered that production figures from my organization are being advertised as well, even though none of what is being attributed to us is, in fact, accurate."

Otto did a double take as he asked, "Thiago, how is that possible? You seem to be suggesting that your intended commodity production values are being input into the world commodity markets, but you did not physically have the materials up for sale.

"Hold on there! If your materials were being listed in the commodity markets and a sale was transacted, then it stands to reason that you had revenue coming in but no corresponding outflow of goods. Wouldn't that show up on your corporate books?"

Thiago grinned a little more and continued, "Ah, good, we are tracking to how the pretend Otto would think. We reasoned that as well, but, alas, no free money. I come to you with this issue to see if you can make any sense of it.

"I'm not out anything, except my future. I'm even considering new investment in offshore drilling. I've plenty on my plate to worry about. I'm hoping you and your team can look at this anomaly to see what can be done about it. Because, right now, it appears from the outside looking in that we are selling commodities onto the world market, yet not recording the income. If the government saw this, they would accuse us of income tax evasion and become most unpleasant. At least more than usual, anyway. If we found it, then someone else is bound to find it and start pointing fingers. I need your help sleuthing out an answer, my friend."

Otto thought for a moment and then queried, "Do you think we can turn your exercise into a board game? We could name it *Being Otto*. A board game of strategy that does combat against intrigue, with financial digital crime. I bet we can make an online subscription version as well.

"I know you thought of it, but since I'm Otto, I want a 70/30 split for the revenue. My favor, of course."

Thiago clucked his tongue and replied, "You're right, I shouldn't have teased you about being Otto. But the rest of the story is true. Can you and your team work this for me, please?"

Otto chuckled slightly and admitted, "Yes, of course, old friend. But, in the meantime I need you to design some swell board pieces for *Being Otto*. Don't tell Lara, though, as she'll want a share of the royalties. Maybe one of the pieces could be a commodity trader getting ready to jump out of the window. Or maybe one of your oil tankers loading up an order of tennis shoes. Oh, and hey, how about turning one of your offshore oil drilling platforms into a water park slide?"

Thiago chortled and stated, "Now I remember why we only visit twice a year and do lunch. Good day, Otto."

CHAPTER THREE

May I Have This Dance?

The dark walls of the room were made more somber by the minimal amber lighting that circled the edge of the ceiling and the candlelit sconces at wide but equal distances along the walls. Floor and ceiling were covered in mahogany with darker stains pooled along the floor. No carpets muffled the sounds of the heavy chairs as they moved with the occupants sitting and shifting. Table lighting fanned out from the leader's position of power, minimizing the view of his features.

The meeting leader and organizer gave a slight smile as everyone took their respective seats and waited quietly for him to begin. No idle conversation or whispers came from the attendees. Before they were all seated, a large black female enforcer approached the leader and quietly whispered, "The room has been swept. No unauthorized electronics are present."

She took up her post behind the leader and stood at attention, aware of every movement made by everyone in the room. She looked quite menacing as she stood still as granite.

The leader seemed tall even while seated. His dark, straight, thick stock of hair was well groomed, if a little long. His eyes appeared black and dead in the muted light. His hands were sculpted, with long fingers. No jewelry adorned his hands or neck. His dark suit nearly blended with the color of the massive leather armchair.

After a few moments, he finally offered, "I appreciate everyone breaking free from their daily routine to attend this meeting. I know you find travel to this monthly meeting tedious, but I do not trust the importance of our meeting content to encrypted voice/video tunneling controlled by the very people we seek to, uh…re-orient.

"I wanted to advise you that monies from our standard business practices are being funneled into our newest project. We need to have clear milestones at the computer-projected intersect points so that our goals can be achieved while we remain an anonymous entity. Let's go around the table, and give me short, crisp bullets of each of your assigned projects."

Before the third attendee could begin their report, the leader interrupted him, "Moncrieff, can you explain your failure to the group? Your actions in the copper commodity area were picked up by a most dangerous adversary who has been scanning for other examples, which could potentially expose our carefully orchestrated plan."

Moncrieff tried to swallow, but his dry mouth would not cooperate. After several deep breaths, he managed to regain control as he haltingly offered, "I, um…saw an opportunity, rather, that is, a trading anomaly which would let us, um…I accelerated our earnings with that trade. I thought that…"

The leader raised his hand to gain silence. Moncrieff struggled to keep his terror under control as the leader stated, "We have very simple rules in this organization. That way, when someone doesn't comply with them, we have very simple solutions."

The leader cut his eyes over to his other enforcer who, in an instant, was behind Moncrieff. The enforcer's bulk had pinned Moncrieff between his chair and the massive mahogany table. His large, powerful arms quickly wrapped themselves around Moncrieff's head and abruptly twisted it 180 degrees, producing a sickening crack loud enough for all to hear. The large black man then dispassionately stepped back to let Moncrieff's body slump to the floor.

The leader, moderately pleased with the demonstration, stated, "For the group's consideration, I need someone in this role who can be trusted to follow instructions succinctly. As you all are aware, we want to discourage independent thinking that deviates from our plan or risks our detection. If there are no objections, I would like to appoint LJ to immediately step into the role and responsibilities so recently vacated."

No one dared to do anything except nod their heads in agreement. LJ, the enforcer, smiled broadly, revealing several gold-encrusted teeth, then promptly took the seat at the table which Moncrieff had occupied. LJ's head to shoulders had no clear neck delineation. He too wore no jewelry, and his black leather slacks and black satin long-sleeved shirt completed the look of the enforcer turned player. The other enforcer kept her smile in check, even as she gave a barely perceptible congratulatory nod to her associate.

The leader added, "LJ, you have a week to determine the extent of the possible breach into identifying our team. All available resources transfer immediately to you, including housing and vehicle arrangements."

LJ nodded agreement. He recognized time was of the essence in complying with his new task. He would use all his own computer resources to make certain the breach was obliterated. He thought back to those he had worked with as he considered the best way to make the data shifts remain untraceable. All his work had been to achieve this point of power, and one misstep would end more than just his career. If his faith had ever been real, he might have prayed. But prayers would not keep him alive or on top of this crowd.

CHAPTER FOUR

How Do We Get There from Here?

Quip nodded thoughtfully as Wolfgang and Otto briefed him on their findings.

Wolfgang commented, "I don't understand the copper commodities anomaly, which started me looking into this area of finance. It flared up, begged to be noticed, and then resumed normal trading. Most peculiar activity. Almost like a misbehaving child who just had their parent correct an improper behavior."

Otto and his longtime associate, Wolfgang, were the oldest colleagues of the family business, with Quip being the third core member. The business had been founded after a rather frantic escape by their families from Poland at the beginning of World War II. They had made good on their government's promise to deliver the Enigma machine, captured from the Germans, but had copied it before delivery to the British.

Their acquisition of the Enigma machine had become the basis for the financial protection and restitution they began as a service to friends and family in Europe. The family business, coined internally as the R-Group, had been long diversified with banking, portfolio management, real estate, shares in various thriving businesses, and the most relevant these days, the cyber security and information division. The closely held family business had customers everywhere on the globe but still maintained the lowest profile of any company. Discretion was a key operational goal for their organization. Without a reference from someone they knew, you didn't find them, they found you.

Quip, the more colorful individual of the three, was well educated in the field of computer design and machine intelligence. Quip had spent most of his youth and early adult life in education, earning his doctorate at a very young age and creating computing inroads when he wasn't into some kind of mischief.

Until recently falling in love with an intelligent communications specialist named Eilla-Zan, he had only focused on building the technological capabilities of the R-Group. Quip was the brilliant creator of the core computing resource of the R-Group functionality known as ICABOD, translated as the *Immersive Collaborative Associative Binary Override Deterministic* system. Over the years, Quip had expanded the capabilities of ICABOD and was constantly increasing its computer power and artificial intelligence capabilities.

He and Jacob, grandson to Wolfgang, had both added programs and routines that allowed ICABOD to consume and analyze huge amounts of data that helped to expand the artificial intelligence limits of ICABOD. From time to time, it was difficult to remember that ICABOD was a computer and not a human being who had just dialed into a conference call. The heavy ethical grounding and the humor tutorials that Quip had been administering had pushed ICABOD's capability to the point that he was a critical member of the team, with insights built from the enormous amounts of information gathered.

The R-Group business was controlled by the family members, with voting conducted to accept or reject potentially too high profile or risky work orders. The fundamental mission of the R-Group began with fighting the Nazis in WWII. In the decades since that war, the team had learned that there was always someone or something that would step up into the role of the next adversary. Quip liked to say they had taken the Robin Hood operating parameters and added digital content to keep the wealth intact for those who actually earned it. R-Group assignments supported individuals' and even governments' fights against human injustice as well as helped maintain a level of balance between powers.

The services provided over the years to its discreet customers had allowed the wealth of the R-Group to grow. As such, no one in the group needed to work, but their ethics and conscience compelled them to stay at it and remain vigilant against the world's cyber enemies. Sometimes they walked a very fine line in fighting the evils they encountered yet remained ethical to a fault. Over the years the team had increased their financial prowess and exhibited insightfulness into humanity, and thus were adept at staying farther ahead of the technology curve than any entity, including well-funded governments.

Otto asked, "Wolfgang, I've known you a long time, and I sense you are going to add more observations that will convey your annoyance at this situation."

Wolfgang chose his words carefully before he answered, "Someone or something is driving commodity prices down to the breaking point. At this rate, world order will be irrevocably changed in six months.

"Otto, you and I have discussed this already. However, we needed to bring Quip up to speed and add any new information to what we currently know."

Otto asked, "Do we know who yet? Any new development since we spoke last?"

Wolfgang cautiously continued, "We only know what is happening, not who is driving it.

"What we are seeing, Quip, is a very old, yet very simplistic, business model called predatory pricing. A company or a group of like-minded companies band together and offer goods at a lower price that market leaders can't match. The incumbent begins to lose market share if they hold their price, or they match the predatory pricing, thus causing them to bleed red ink on their income statements. The initial market leader either exits that market or they implode against the onslaught.

"Television sets, stereo equipment, and computer chips all have these types of business casualties covered in textbooks. It took a lot to get Western governments to see the problem for what it was, and then pass legislation to help safeguard their home industries.

"The predatory pricing model looks like it has been dusted off, freshened up a bit, and is now being used in the commodity markets. The difference today being whole populations and nations appear to be the targets. In several cases, the issue is affecting multiple countries in waves. The commodity building blocks of our civilization are being destabilized to the benefit of the consumers yet the detriment of the producers. The world depends upon orderly markets behaving in a predictable manner. At present, I am seeing just the opposite."

Quip nodded, then questioned, "But, Wolfgang, isn't a lower commodity price a good thing? Doesn't cheaper commodity pricing lower the per-unit cost of the outputted item, which means you and I pay less for finished products?"

Otto interjected, "Yes, it does…for a while. When the producing entities can't match the unprofitable price that the commodity is being traded for, they are forced to exit the business or sell to their former competitors, now market leaders, at greatly reduced prices. In time, the market-makers for the commodity become oligopolies or monopolies that are capable of commodity price extortion to the buyers, then ultimately you and me."

Wolfgang agreed but added, "While Otto is correct in his statement, it actually goes farther than that. Dropping a commodity price to a very attractive level also puts financial pressure on competing technologies that could be used instead.

"For instance, with the price of oil so low, transportation and heating utilities are not investing in competing technologies like renewable energy. As a knock-on effect, companies in those industries stop investing in their products and either sell or exit into bankruptcies. This process is very shortsighted, and while the buying public gets a cheaper price on their petroleum for transportation and heating their homes, their future is being mortgaged right under their noses. This can also have a chilling effect on their investment portfolio, though they might not realize it for an extended period with mutual funds."

Otto offered, "We are beginning to see signs of political opportunism where some commodity producing countries are starting to feel victimized in this process.

"My friend in Brazil, Thiago Bernardes, has reached out to us for some help in understanding every side of the issue. Brazil's economy is very much built upon the commodity prices they receive in the world market. Drive the price down and revenues shrink. Too low and it can prematurely drive companies out of business, which also reduces the government revenues from licensing and taxation. That then has a chilling effect on the economy as a whole, throwing people out of work, which drives political unrest. The social programs of each government, designed to create a financial safety net under its citizens, is now unsustainable, which also adds fuel to the fire."

Quip, not completely convinced, asked, "Gentlemen, the world's commodity production and trading markets are fairly well self-governed, due to known supply and demand models. What you seem to be suggesting is a deliberate effort to disrupt several commodity markets so someone or something can step in and take them over without regulation.

"Businesses explore for natural resources, make estimates of how much could be at a discovered site, the raw product gets mined and then processed for market. There are several advanced, complex models that are used to estimate to a very close approximation of how much is going into the market and how much that future market is worth to the producer. This is a fairly well-developed science, and they all behave the same way. I simply don't see how anyone could derail one of these models, much less all of them."

Wolfgang hypothesized, "Unless the mathematical model for those industries has been tampered with. By that I mean, either their inputs into the model have been altered or the computer models have been rigged to deliver production numbers high enough to drive the future prices down."

Quip rocked back into his chair and studied both men for a moment before responding, "You would need a top-notch group of dedicated evil types, with a fantastically complex mathematical model, to keep track of all the pieces in play. The data processing requirements would be staggering."

ICABOD politely interjected, "Dr. Quip, are we at the point in the discussion where you ask me if this is a supercomputer task? Because I can confirm the necessity of having an enormous amount of processing power to plot the activities in play, as well as what the results should look like at different points in the future."

Quip clucked his tongue and stated, "Just when I think it's only us in the conversation, ICABOD reminds me of the correct contribution to the discussion."

Otto chuckled and added, "Usually it's me complaining about ICABOD finishing my sentences or predicting my next thought."

Wolfgang said, "Gentlemen, I believe we need to bring in our other team members and examine this topic with all present. Any disagreement?"

Quip asked, "Are we going to include Julie and Juan? We still haven't resolved Juan's open issue with his last indiscretion."

Otto lowered his head and quietly offered, "Even though she is my daughter, as well as a member of this group, I'm reluctant to pull them in on this discussion until we can get to the bottom of what we are dealing with here. Besides, Juan is out for a while. Julie has her hands full with their CATS business and the twins during Juan's absence."

Wolfgang nodded and said, "I don't believe it is necessary to bring them into this yet. I think we can just add Petra and Jacob."

"I'll set up the meeting then," confirmed Otto.

CHAPTER FIVE

Settling In, then Right Turn

Petra woke slowly, aware that her surroundings were different yet familiar. The embers in the fireplace glowed and enhanced the burgundy color of the drapes. The early morning light peeked through the center from the window. The bed was comfortable and warm as she laid silent and still. The soft sheets, which she knew were striped burgundy and cream Egyptian cotton, retained the warmth while hardly adding any weight. She smiled to herself as she caught the sounds of Jacob's even breathing to her left. As her eyes adjusted to the dim light, the images of various statues and paintings confirmed they were, in fact, in their old room in Wolfgang's chateau in Zürich.

Bowen, Wolfgang's manservant and houseman, had retrieved them late yesterday at the airport and delivered them to the chateau. They'd eaten a light meal in the kitchen, with Bowen serving personally, then retired. So much had happened since the last time they had slept in this room together.

Petra had finally overcome the mental hurdles of her injuries from a mission gone wrong in Argentina, and Jacob had offered to give up everything to prove to her how serious he was about making their life work. Most things had been talked through, and they had realigned their plans together. Petra had admitted there were still things that she needed to work on, but further admitted she wanted him right beside her for the journey.

Petra needed to get up and move but didn't want to disturb Jacob. She carefully slid the covers over and slipped out of bed, snagging a lavender silk robe from the adjacent chair and donning it in a practiced fluid motion, almost like a dancer. She glanced at the resting face of Jacob with his dark wavy hair, almost too long, highlighted against the lighter sheets. She turned to move toward the attached bathroom.

Jacob's deep voice pierced the silence as he quietly noted, "What a shame."

Petra froze, then turned and asked, "What's a shame? Our being back in this home?"

"No, sweetheart. That you made it so easily out of bed before I could wrap my arms around you."

Petra chuckled, "I'll be right back. Go back to sleep. It's early yet."

Petra turned and continued on with her initial mission. As she walked the short distance, she realized her muscles were sore from the long flight, and she knew her hair was desperately tangled. They had been so tired when they retired that she had not taken the time to redo the braid of her long blonde hair. After she closed the door, she turned on the light and took a critical look at herself in the mirrors. Her body looked trim and well-proportioned as she dropped the robe. As she suspected, the hair needed work, and she righted it in short order. She washed her face and noted that it still showed some scarring, though it was healing and wasn't as horrible as it had been. Best of all, it simply didn't matter to Jacob.

While Petra attended to her morning routine, Jacob had quickly added logs to the fire and coaxed it into a gentle burn. He returned to bed and extracted her ring from the bedside table. It sparkled and glimmered in the firelight, making the purple of the amethyst stone even richer in color. They had talked about so many things, and Jacob was nearly confident that Petra would agree. He just would feel so much better if she would ask for the ring back. He had debated it with himself over and over, including on the flight home and even after they had retired last evening. Petra had fallen instantly to sleep while he contemplated what the right steps would be to get their whole life back on track.

Petra watched Jacob play with the ring from the doorway and noted how warm and appealing the room was with the glowing fire. He was unaware of her presence so she took the time to just look and enjoy his being. His mussed hair suited his strong jawline. Though he was nestled against the pillows, she still could appreciate the sculpted muscles of his arms and strong hands. Hands she knew from firsthand experience were strong and capable, yet also gentle and sensual. They had shared so much love in this room, and she had nearly ruined it with her thought-lessness. She knew exactly what she wanted and refused to waste any more time with ridiculous doubts.

Petra made her presence known as the silk robe swirled as she approached the bed. Petra smiled and exclaimed, "Jacob, thank goodness you found my ring. I think it will match my robe perfectly, don't you?"

She extended her hand, palm up. He looked momentarily startled by her comments and then pleased as he grabbed her hand and tugged her onto the bed with him. "Yes, my darling, but I dare say it will look wonderful, even without the robe, on your beautiful fingers."

Jacob began kissing and sucking each of her fingers on her right hand and then continued with the fingers of her left hand as he gently slipped the ring onto her finger and pulled her into an embrace. Kissing her thoroughly, he asked, "How does that feel, sweetheart?"

Petra groaned and murmured, "The ring is perfect, thank you. But I think more kisses are definitely in order, maybe without the robe."

"As you wish, sweetheart," Jacob spoke gently into her ear. In one practiced motion he removed the robe and brought her under the covers.

Their lovemaking was a generous giving and taking until they were both at the brink. This was perhaps more erotic and sensual as the barriers between them had been completely removed, and they were moving together as one. As the man, Jacob was stronger and more insistent. Yet Petra was lithe and wild as her body dictated her desires, which only fanned their passions higher, until they noiselessly fell off the edge of the mountain and floated on seemingly endless clouds of satisfaction as the sensations engulfed them. They pulled each other closer, totally absorbed into their cocoon of endless dreams filled with passion.

When at last they awoke, they both seemed pleased to find one another so very close. They resettled into the pillows, kissed and gently caressed until Jacob broke the silence. "I am so glad you are with me. Thank you for claiming your ring again."

Petra smiled. "Thank you for waiting for me to get it together. I love you, Jacob. I'm not certain how I will face each of our work assignments, but I will tell you when I am not comfortable with something."

"Good, then we can figure out how to fix it. For now, let's go downstairs and eat, then we go work out. I suspect you kicking my ass in the gym will keep those fears at bay!"

"You're on, mister. Let's go."

They had eaten and were headed down to the gym on the lower level when they saw Wolfgang. Petra hugged Wolfgang in greeting, and then Wolfgang hugged his grandson.

"Glad you two are back. Hope you rested well. We are having a meeting at the operations center this afternoon. I would like it if you could both attend."

Jacob looked at his grandfather and noted a bit of concern behind his eyes. "What's up? Please tell me we don't have to travel today?"

Wolfgang smiled faintly and remarked, "No travel, but something is definitely afoot, and I want all the input possible. Please?"

Petra patted his arm and reassured, "Of course. Just let us grab a quick work out and we'll meet you there."

CHAPTER SIX

Tell Me You're Kidding

Thinking back to yesterday, Juan felt fortunate to have called Julie and checked in. It provided him a bit of time before she would grow concerned. With any luck he'd have a really good story and solution ready before they spoke again. Julie and he had been married for such a short time, yet it felt like they had faced and conquered challenges most couples take many years to face. Julie was a true family member of the R-Group, as were his daughter and son, he supposed. He missed the twins, almost as much as he missed his lovely wife at this point, but knew Julie was taking care of their fledgling but thriving business.

Juan had fallen in love with Julie during a situation his brother Carlos and he had worked out of with their friend, Jacob. Juan had recently been allowed more visibility of the inner workings of the R-Group when he'd had taken off to locate his missing Uncle Jesus. He had followed so many leads and knew this absence would force him to regain the trust he had earned with the R-Group members. Juan was a pilot by trade, and passion, devoted to his wife and children. But he considered his uncle the black sheep par excellence and the last of his pre-Julie family. This feeling of loyalty moved through his mind as he focused on the conversation.

Juan listened intently, without interruption, to his Uncle Jesus as he recounted the story. A couple of times Juan started to say something but caught himself and motioned for Jesus to continue.

Jesus offered, "I know what you're going to say, nephew, but I didn't break my word to you and your brother Carlos. When you two got me out of the drug trafficking trade, I took my money, with the new identity, and went to ground. I've been lounging in the Caribbean for most of the time since I last saw you two, just taking it easy. But I got bored, with nothing much to do except order fruity chick drinks while moving from one seaside resort to another.

"I started to take stock of myself and realized I needed some gainful employment other than subsidizing the top-heavy female waitresses who all claimed to be going to school to justify the heavy tips they felt entitled to receive. It was fun for a while, but it became obvious that my money wasn't going to support me and my following of co-eds. While I was studying the silver frame on my prized Velvet Elvis painting, it struck me that I could be investing in precious metals, like maybe silver or gold even.

"Don't laugh, but I did me some research on the subject and was amazed at how familiar I was with some of the mines. I located, in Mexico's Bajío region, the largest silver mine in the world. Guanajuato is one of the leading centers of silver mining, and it's not far from the village of La Valenciana, which is a little north of Guanajuato. I decided to take a look. As I was touring there, I found an advertisement for the El Tigre Company that boasted of being able to place investors into their mining operations.

"You and I both know mining is a rigged game in Mexico, a lot like the drug trafficking business. To succeed, one needs a legitimate company that is on the take with the local government to be able to buy-in."

Jesus looked at his nephew and could not see any hint of how this was being received. Juan had a talent, as did Carlos, of not showing his emotions, but the wheels were turning, regardless.

"It seemed my luck had changed for the better when I met this Paulo character. He claimed to be with the Collective Holdings of Assets Reserved for Denomination, I think. CHARD, he called it. He said he could get me a seat at the table with the folks mining these precious metals. Turns out that when you find silver you usually find gold and copper. I was only really interested in the silver, but old Paulo claimed that I had to do some copper in the commodities market before he could get me into the precious metals. Thinking back on it, I should have been a little dogged on my silver exposure and walked, when all they would let me play in was copper.

"Anyway, I put down my earnest money to do a trial to see if it was for me. I made up my mind a few days later and went to get back my earnest money and go hunt for something else. Upon reflection, sure wished I hadn't done that. At first, I couldn't find him. Then when I start making inquiries, I got a whole lot more attention than I was looking for.

"Anyhow, I am right glad you came looking for me, nephew. You and Carlos have always been the best of family for me."

Juan clucked his tongue and offered, "Uncle Jesus, you say that because we are the *only* family you have. You mean to tell me you strolled back into Mexico, after we hauled you and your loot out, looking for high-profile silver mining investments? Did it occur to you that the federales might still be looking for you?"

Jesus made a sour face and stated, "Who'd of thought that the infamous Mexican government would clean up their act and actually abide by the law? I mean, after decades of corrupt practices they have to up and grow a conscience. You just can't trust anybody these days!"

Juan closed his eyes and shook his head back and forth in disbelief. Then, sizing up the situation, he very subtly pulled out a tiny cell phone, which had been concealed in his boot, and placed a very quiet call to his older brother.

Carlos answered quickly and demanded, "Juan, where the hell are you? I've been trying to get ahold of you. Do you have any leads on our missing uncle? And don't tell me you've gone *bozotic* on me!"

Juan blankly stared off into space and absentmindedly asked, "Bozotic?"

Carlos snapped, "Yes, *bozotic*. You know, that's where Bozo the Clown has a colossal idiotic moment and goes *bozotic,* for all intents and purposes!"

Juan, with a very annoyed tone, responded, "No, Carlos. I have not gone *bozotic.*" Then in a hushed tone, he triumphantly proclaimed, "But, yes, Carlos, I have found our uncle."

Carlos did a double take and, somewhat relieved but puzzled, asked, "That is good news. Where did you find him?"

Juan somewhat dejectedly offered, "I'm in the cell next to Uncle Jesus."

CHAPTER SEVEN

For the Meeting, You Bring the Donuts...

Jim Hughes, aka Stalker, ambled into Eric's office with one of his usual conversation starters, a box of assorted donuts. Jim plopped himself down into one of Eric's chairs that could almost be classified as comfortable and sipped his coffee. Grinning, but without saying a word, he pushed the box across Eric's desk so as to indicate a gesture of friendship and to confirm their age-old ritual.

Eric's office was somewhat larger than most in the three-letter security agency, due to his job grade. The office was typical, low-budget government with mismatched furniture and high-end technology. This one was unimaginatively outfitted with early World War II furniture that actually might have been in service in the Spanish-American war. The drabness of the office surroundings was a blatant contrast to Eric's work ethic, yet not his outlook on life.

Eric looked up from his work with the same look of annoyance one would display if you had discovered gum on the bottom of your shoe. After studying Stalker and eyeing the box, Eric flatly asked, "So, I can have any one of the donuts I want, except the jelly filled ones. Right?"

Stalker grinned from ear to ear and offered, "Oh, I know the rules. You can pick anyone of them that you'd like, but for you it's only enjoyable if it's the one I prefer. Go ahead, you choose first."

Eric somewhat tersely stated, "Well, at least you have some real variety to choose from for a change. It used to be that none ever made it into my office. Now that they are showing up again, I distrust them, so how can I pick them?"

Stalker chuckled slightly while he suggested, "You'd have to admit that the thieving of my prize jelly donuts ceased after the perpetrator was exposed. So, if you don't want to trust them, then I guess they are all mine."

Eric quickly snatched one of the prized jelly donuts from the box, raised it to his mouth, but stopped short of taking a bite. He asked, "Alright, I have to know. Is this one filled with petroleum jelly, like the one you used to smoke out the thief?"

Stalker chortled slightly and offered, "She was certainly clever at stealing them, but old Arlette never knew what hit her when she bit into all that petroleum jelly. Woohoo, what a yelp and torrid confession that was. She was going to report me, until I asked her who she thought they would write up, the petroleum jelly donut maker or the thief? We never got along after that, now that I reflect on it."

Eric almost smiled as he bit into the donut while watching Stalker. Then Eric stated, "I'm glad you whacked her that day. What a piece of work she was."

He seemed far away as he savored the jelly donut.

Eric softened a little and continued, "I'm glad you're here, old friend. We have a new situation that has been brought to me by our think-tank people."

With something of a puzzled look on his face, Stalker asked, "Uh, the Quants?"

Eric clucked his tongue and flatly corrected, "No, those are the mathematical wizards of mass destruction on Wall Street.

I'm talking about a bunch of highly cerebral Asperities that seldom venture out of their backroom. The backroom that is fully lined with whiteboards and where all their meals are brought in so they don't have to socialize with anyone. You know the kind; if you try to talk to them, they stare at their shoes until you ask them about something they care about."

The blank look on Stalker's face amused Eric, who continued, "What our think-tank has come up with is a high correlation between the sinking commodity market prices and some highly influential but as yet unknown *Dark Matter Organizations*, or DMOs, as they have now been dubbed. These are nefarious organizations currently undetected but presumed to exist based on cause-and-effect quantum economics. Just because we can't see them doesn't mean they don't exist. It is theorized that they are manipulating the commodity market status quo to further their own agenda. I need you to talk to the people at the Chicago Mercantile Exchange for any additional details on their processes for brokering commodities."

Managing to reel in his disbelief, Stalker finally responded, "Gee, Eric, I haven't used a slide rule in years. Worse, my knowledge of quantum mechanics was, at best, underwhelming. I have no idea what quantum economics is, so I'm not sure what any of this has to do with me. I hunt for bad guys or good guys that have been nabbed by bad guys. I don't navigate through economic theory. To be honest, I am simply uninterested in what comes back from your Quants. Frankly, I was going to ask for some more assignments in Europe where I can be with Mercedes."

Eric frowned and responded, "That's still on between you and Mercedes, huh? Well, not to disappoint you, but we're being told to curtail all foreign assignments due to budget cuts again. Almost all the work I am going to have for you is within our borders."

Stalker was a little irked at the response and countered, "Only hunt for the bad guys within our borders? That must mean all the bad guys in foreign lands have been grabbed, and there is no need for international travel. Gosh, I feel safer already!"

It was now Eric's turn to be irked. "You may not have excelled in mathematical computation, but I'm sure you earned a straight A for sarcasm and insubordination. So, get this straight, we're in budget-cut hell again, based on the near fatal incompetence of our elected officials. However, we still have a job to do.

"Why can't Mercedes relocate to this country for a while? She must have earned some seniority by this time, based on her abilities and value."

Stalker studied the comment for a few moments. He quietly replied, "You know, every once in a while, you actually come up with a good idea. Worth exploring with her. But let me ask you this, mister penny-pincher. What if my hunt for these bad guys points me to distant lands? If you want the job done thoroughly, then I may have to hammer them in their nest. An email saying in English or any other language, 'Now stop it,' is just not going to work."

Eric turned his head while nodding in annoyance. He finally offered, "I should have eaten both jelly donuts while I was in a good mood. Look, Captain Obvious, I know we have to follow the bad guys to their nest to get the job done. I just don't have the latitude to have you based outside our boundaries. I can approve international travel for the right reasons.

"First, I want you to work something out with Mercedes so you two can be together. However, I don't have to fund it. Second, I want you on this case of falling commodity pricing, in particular the price of oil and coal. Third, I will loop in our friends at the R-Group to do the mathematical side of this assignment, so there is no need to get your panties in a wad about having to use a slide rule again. And fourth, make sure you get raspberry jelly next time instead of sour cream cheese. Got it?"

Stalker, grinning from ear to ear, smirked, "Oh good, you did enjoy it. How nice."

That afternoon, Eric launched a call on his secure international line to Zürich.

A friendly male voice answered, "Eric, what a pleasant surprise. I always enjoy hearing from friends associated with my favorite three letter agency. How can I be of service, kind sir?"

Eric smiled as he greeted, "Good afternoon, Otto. I trust you and your organization are doing well and are profitable. Do you have time to visit on another assignment? I need some colossal brain computing power to augment my brawny top agent in a new game of cat and mouse."

Otto grinned and asked, "Ah, would this be about the think-tank report on falling commodity prices which are being artificially manipulated?"

Eric sat blinking, almost unable to respond, while he listened to Otto lightly chuckling on the phone.

Finally, Eric admitted, "Otto, I guess I should not be surprised that you have already accessed my source of information, but I am annoyed. You could at least have pretended to be intrigued by the potential of a new assignment."

Otto, still smiling but removing the tone from his voice, offered, "But, Eric, you contract with us because we have our finger on the pulse of what's important. Who would need us if we were constantly behind on our intelligence gathering? Of course, a new assignment with you would be welcomed."

Half smiling and half annoyed, Eric responded, "Okay, point taken. I need you to assist Stalker in his assignment. He has national security clearance, and you have the digital intelligence to help point him in the right direction. I have him here with me so the two of you can begin the process. Our regular terms, I assume?"

Stalker leaned into the conference phone and remarked, "Good day, sir. I am glad to be working with your team again. May I use the special cell phone for our communications, per Eric's instruction?"

Otto agreed, "Yes, when do you want to begin the discussion on the DMOs?"

Eric and Stalker looked at each other in silent awe of Otto's foreknowledge of the situation.

Then Stalker, not missing a beat, asked, "How about now?"

Otto smiled to himself and offered, "Let me round up my usual suspects and call you back on this number. I believe it will take me thirty-eight minutes. That should give you time to freshen up your coffee and procure some fresh raspberry jelly filled donuts. Talk soon, gentlemen."

After Otto had dropped from the call, both Eric and Stalker eyed each other.

Stalker promised, "I swear there are no electronic listening devices in here. I had it rechecked."

Eric sighed and admitted, "This is why I call them."

CHAPTER EIGHT

The Top of My Game

EZ sighed heavily, which was designed to get Quip's attention. They had been resting comfortably in bed. But now it was obvious to Quip that something was on EZ's mind, so he asked, "Why for the big sigh, my love? Remember, I am a man, and without contextual clues of what is behind the big sigh, I will again be oblivious to what is troubling you. For my part, I'm wonderful. We just had mind-blowing sex, I'm still full from breakfast, and I'm resting comfortably. Sweetheart, I recognize that women have a list with two to the nth power of happiness requirements, so can you tell me which one is unfulfilled?"

EZ frowned at Quip's subtly disparaging comments, then remarked, "We need to change the sheets on this king size bed, and I'm tired of always having to do it myself. Will you help me, please?"

Quip, somewhat chastened, responded, "My darling, please forgive me for not being a better partner and for being so insensitive to our household chores. I, of course, will lend all manner of assistance in said activity.

"In fact," with a gleam in his eye, he continued, "allow me to introduce you to my championship status as a world class Sheet Toss competitor. I am known to rank in the top one percent of my age class and only recently have retired from active competition."

EZ looked across the pillow at Quip with a blank look that provided him the motivation to demonstrate his sheet tossing prowess.

Grinning ear to ear, he leaped out of bed and commented as he was retrieving fresh sheets from the linen closet, "Honey, be a dear, hop up, and pull the soiled sheets off so I can recreate my last winning competition show."

EZ, not quite comprehending Quip's highly animated activity, complied. She kept a wary eye on Quip, not completely sure that he hadn't started some new medication that he had failed to alert her to. She got out of bed and complied. "Okay, honey, the bed is stripped, but I don't understand…"

Quip motioned for her to stand on the other side of the bed. He then assumed his new persona in the form of the world class Sheet Toss competitor on the other side. Part of getting into character was to also provide the running commentary of a non-existent announcer, as if broadcasting the event live.

Quip said in his now dual role as announcer, "Good afternoon, ladies and gentlemen. We're here ringside at the Sheet Toss competition finals. The front runner, as has been the case many times in these dramas, is the Quipster who has been relentlessly piling up points and sending competitors home in tears. One has to ask themselves; just how long can this winning machine stay on top of his game?"

EZ stared in disbelief at Quip's narrative.

He continued, "This is the final competition. The fitted sheet has been preplaced for the entire competitive field. The crowd behind us is obviously awash with emotions of awe and respect. The Quipster signals for silence as he completes his final positioning movements. One cannot help but admire the sinewy build of this man and those powerful muscles that have tossed sheets onto king-sized beds for nearly a decade, rolling up win after win. That determined look in his eye and his rippling muscles indicates that he is ready once again for combat. Here is a man who no longer has to call for do-overs after a poor throw. I've watched him over the years, and he has told me that at this point his concentration is such that he no longer hears anything from his surroundings."

EZ stared in cautious amusement as Quip drifted farther into his Sheet Toss persona.

"Folks, he has grasped the edges of the sheet, letting them drape through his skilled hands with shifts and folds deftly being controlled effortlessly so that the top sheet is ready for the go point. His breathing quickens, he sways the sheet edge back and forth, and there. It looks like a perfect snap and…look at that. The sheets have fanned out to a perfect parallelogram and are now lazily landing perfectly, covering all four corners of the bed. There aren't even any wrinkles in his sheet toss.

"Let's see what the judges say. OMG! No one can match him! A perfect TEN! The look on each of the competitors' faces says it all. They simply cannot catch him. The crowd is now roaring with acclaim for the Quipster. Listen to them."

EZ's suppressed a giggle as Quip danced around with his arms held high in the air, hollering.

"…Quipster! Quipster! Quipster!" Quip continued his narration. "But, for all his wins, ladies and gentlemen, he is still humble in his magnificence. The crowd is now trying to push past the security team that has been hurriedly deployed to protect the Quipster. This is always a tense moment for the champion Sheet Toss competitor as he…"

Finally laughing at Quip's antics, EZ pulled off her panties and used the elastic to propel them at his face, thus silencing the narrative monolog. She bounded over to him and, pulling him on to the bed, took over the announcement speech.

"Whoa, ladies and gentlemen! We have a Sheet Toss groupie who has made it through the security team to the Quipster. It is clear that her intent is to mate with the Sheet Toss champion on the winning sheet toss demonstration. We'll be right back after these commercial messages!"

Quip and EZ were now rolling around again in bed when he complained, "Ah, honey, you messed up the sheets again."

EZ stopped and stared at Quip with a mischievous smile and responded, "Yeah!"

Quip suggested, "I also have world class skill in the Pillow Packing competition. Would you like to see my skill at pillow packing, as well?"

EZ offered in a sultry tone, "Packing, yes, honey, but not with pillows."

A while later, after an extensive sexual encounter, they snuggled together, with her fiery red hair spread out in all directions. Quip ran his fingers through a thick hair group, enjoying the texture.

"EZ, I just love you, honey. You put up with me so sweetly."

EZ smiled and agreed, "I do, don't I! So how many times have you run that gag with the ladies?"

He pulled her close and whispered, "Don't believe all the nonsense of the crazy announcer, honey. You know they are just trying to sell something. Why I…"

The phone rang that insistent tone indicating work, and they both groaned.

Quip reached for it, knowing full well it would not cease until answered. "I guess Otto scheduled that meeting…"

CHAPTER NINE

Too Far to Help

Carlos had been searching for two days to isolate the signal from Juan's phone. Ever since the abrupt disconnect, Carlos had grown more and more concerned, not only for his brother, but also his uncle. He reminded himself for the umpteenth time that he was a telecommunications specialist able to capture and leverage satellite communication signals, bending them to his will.

His employer, Andy Greenwood, had let him open up this office in São Paulo in order to live with his love, Lara. In the business of telecommunications support for clients all over the world, it didn't matter much where they worked from, providing it was secure. Andy had divided the customers, with Carlos focusing on support for those in the southern hemisphere. They had recently updated their customers to some of the latest and greatest versions of software and were in a few months of monitoring and responding to trouble tickets. Luckily, it was a slow time.

Carlos had taken advantage of the slow time to see if he could determine where exactly Juan was incarcerated, if that was really the case. With all the tools and computing power at his fingertips, Carlos couldn't isolate the exact location, but had narrowed it down to a region. That region of Mexico was fairly heavily populated and had several jails, none of which advertised their guests. The only good news was it would take weeks for the officials to process the paperwork to cross check with any other in-country regions.

He angrily cursed the screen and ran his fingers through his thick black hair. His powerful muscles flexed with the effort as he thought about all his options. The operations center was in Lara and Carlos's home, so he could still be close to the action. Lara wasn't fooled a bit. She knew that something was up, though, like always, she didn't question his actions. She just folded her loving arms around him and nuzzled his neck.

Lara ran a highly successful fashion design empire that challenged the fashion houses of Europe and America. She was a beautiful woman with dark auburn hair, brown eyes, and a shape that often-left Carlos panting from their enthusiastic love-making. A woman who was smart, beautiful, artistic, business oriented, but who had also captured his heart and soul. He had only just settled into their life a few months ago and hated the idea of leaving to return to a place he knew would only be trouble. Lara wouldn't hold him back, but he hated to place her into a position of worry after they had finally agreed their destiny was together.

In a month, give or take a week, he could possibly go into Mexico hunting while Lara and her crew went to their next photo shoot location in St. Thomas. Maybe he could join her a little later, and they could take the few days of vacation, which they had discussed. He didn't think he would be able to wait out another couple of days, let alone several weeks. Most of his ties in Mexico were off limits. Sure, there was a slight residual income from his investment in the Chihuahua desert venture, but there was no way to communicate with any of them. They had not contacted him for some time.

He closed his eyes and ran all the options through his weary mind. Then a slight possibility started to take shape. There was one person that he knew who had no ties to Carlos and Juan's prior lives or even his Uncle Jesus. This man could be trusted, and they had toasted more than once with high quality cerveza. The good news was the man was already in Mexico and had already spent nearly a month with his friends and family. Perhaps he would like some extra pesos to help his family.

Carlos pictured Manuel Sanchez in his mind. Manuel was a wiry man with a quick smile and an eye for anything he could capture on film. He was a good man and attracted ladies easily and, just as easily, became distracted when he held a camera. Manuel had demonstrated more than once that he could capture more emotions in a single shot than most people experience in a week. His set designs and well-balanced photos had helped Lara with her Destiny Fashions and her meteoric rise as an industry leader. Manuel had also spent time here in São Paulo where Carlos and he had done that male bonding thing.

Carlos worked for a couple of hours more after downloading files from one of his sources. This data helped isolate Juan's phone identity and was cross-checked to the limited positioning data he had originally captured. He had further narrowed the search field down to three cities and their three jails. One of these, Carlos's research revealed, had a history of successful bribery efforts reported by Americans.

Carlos called Manuel's number and waited for the connection.

Manuel answered in Spanish with an annoyed tone. "Hello, this better be important, I am very busy in my favorite bar."

Carlos, leveraging the Spanish of his youth, calmly replied, "Manuel, it is Carlos. I need a favor, please."

Manuel's tone changed to concern as he asked, "Carlos, is Lara and the rest of the team alright? How can I possibly help you?"

"Lara is fine, though a bit annoyed with me for not explaining any of this to her. Manuel, it is not for me I ask so much but rather for Juan."

"Your brother, Juan? The man who stole the girl of my dreams and married her? The beautiful JAC should have been mine, you know. She is so pretty, and that magnificent smile. My heart was captured the moment she smiled. I will never be able to give it to another."

Carlos breathed, then chuckled and asked, "If that is the case, how come you told that beautiful model on the beaches of Florida during the last shoot that she was the only one for your heart, just as you put her on the plane to fly to her home?"

Manuel laughed, "Alright, you would remember that. She was a pretty girl, but not as pretty as JAC. What do you need, Carlos? Make sure you mention how it will make JAC happier with me, and I will be sure to help."

Carlos sucked in a breath and related, "JAC actually doesn't know all the details, and I, for one, would like to keep it that way. You know, between us men. Juan was looking for our uncle and apparently his search took him into Mexico. Our uncle is a bit of a rebel and may have done some regrettable things in his life. Those things may have followed him when he returned to Mexico. Can you believe a rich old man with girls at the beach fawning all over him might give that up in a momentary lapse of judgement? I don't exactly know what took my uncle to Mexico, only that I received a call from Juan that indicated they were in adjoining cells. Then the signal died and he, well, um, never revealed the city of his captivity."

Manuel was astonished. His head barely wrapped around the idea of Carlos calling him for help, but the kind of help he was suggesting in Mexico had big risk written all over it.

Before Manuel could respond, Carlos continued, "I have isolated the location of his last transmission down to three cities. I was hoping that you might do a bit of investigating for me. I would rather not worry Lara, as she is so busy planning for the next season. JAC is busy with her household and new business. I was hoping since you were at least in the country you might want to help. I will, of course, pay you handsomely for your time and efforts." Carlos held his breath as he waited for a response.

Manuel balked at the request momentarily before he queried, "Why ask this of me? While I do kind of like you two, this sounds more like a family issue and I'm not family. Why aren't you doing the sleuthing and rescue of your own brother?"

Carlos shifted uncomfortably in his chair as he delicately stated, "Uh…well…you, ah see…uh, my past isn't much better than Juan's. I figure, if they grabbed Juan, then they are probably still looking for me too. The fact that you are not family helps us in the hunt for him. I'm not asking you to break him out, just to help me find where he is…um…being stored."

Manuel considered the proposal and wondered if he would even want Lara or JAC being involved. Carlos was wise to call him rather than involve them. However, he needed to think of a good excuse to do the sort of prying into affairs of this sort.

After some long moments of silence, Manuel agreed, "Carlos, I'm not sure if I've had enough tequila to buy into this scheme of yours, but I will try to help. I will need you to wire me some money to grease the way and send me all the information you have to my email. Just don't expect me to swallow a poison capsule if I get caught too!"

"Agreed. I will send the funds to the account Lara deposits your funds into and the information is being sent now."

"Carlos, it will take several days to arrange anything. I will be in touch."

CHAPTER TEN

The Smallness
of the Digital World
...The Enigma Chronicles

Jacob was sitting in his area of the R-Group's Zürich operations center, reviewing several of the programs and intrusion traps "he had installed in various areas of the data center over recent months. All was behaving as designed to optimize data gathering, sorting, storing, and analysis. The operations center contained an enormous amount of computing power and state-of-the-art technologies that allowed the R-Group to support their customers. Jacob was a highly skilled programmer by education and by practice. Petra, a world class encryption guru, had tutored him in the finer points of those practices since he had joined the R-Group.

Unlike Otto's space, Jacob's work area was highly task driven. ICABOD had sorted through the numerous log files and provided these to Jacob in hierarchal order for consideration. Three high-definition screens, integrated to a single black surface-mount keyboard, responded to his every keystroke. *The Adaptive Polymorphic Input Command and Kinetic System*, or APICKS, was a black polymorphic surface engineered to ergonomically respond to hand size and finger length as well as hand angle of the individual, so they didn't need to adjust anything in order to enter data from the keyboard.

The command lines of the console could just as easily take verbal commands rather than keystrokes, but Jacob preferred different modes of operation based on the task at hand. Using the keyboard allowed him to structure the logic internally before issuing the commands through keystrokes. The molded black surface had a toggle switch which allowed him to move quickly from one screen to the next, and the adaptive console responded by re-orienting its passenger to the proper screen if the action took more than a few seconds. Jacob had found it a little creepy at first when the normally flat table began puffing up to fit his hand, but once he was immersed into machine-code character, it seemed to suit him nicely.

The sounds that resulted from the interactions varied slightly from one screen to the other to help him correctly interact with each work area. His work surface was clear of papers outside of the current task sheet he referenced. When the task was completed, Jacob provided electronic notification, then slid the task sheet into a shredder. He was working to eliminate the paper in total, but the requests came from too many places and he refused to use email. That refusal to deal with email, along with prioritization and mid-task shifts, was sometimes best resolved with the paper at hand in his interrupt-driven role.

The speed, accuracy, and efficiency of his work results amazed both Petra and Quip to the point that, as long as his fingers were moving, they avoided bothering him unless an emergency arose. Instead of a door to his work area that he could close for privacy and quiet, he had amazing glove-soft leather-covered earphones that allowed quiet intimacy with the machine response, on top of soft music in the background. Distractions were consequently non-existent for him, as well as for the others in the operations center. The leather on the earphones happened to match the color and texture of the chair he used. After a stint where he and Quip had worked on a problem for almost twenty hours straight, Quip had provided each of them with customized body-contoured chairs, complete with environmental controls for heating, cooling, and massaging. Jacob's seating was the color of aged whiskey, Quip's was buffed mahogany, and Petra's was light pink as in a beginning blush. If needed, each chair could access instant messaging without destroying a workflow or task.

Each of the workspaces, with their white noise walls, offered privacy for the team, yet was very open. If they felt inclined to work together, they could do so inside of any of their designated spaces or in one of the conference rooms. Each of the conference rooms resembled a high-tech spacecraft bridge, yet each was furnished appropriately for group meetings.

Jacob had just completed another task when he was alerted to an inbound call on his cell phone from a United States based number. Before he ignored it completely, ICABOD provided a text on the screen he faced.

This is not a spam caller, Jacob

Jacob smiled at the proactive ability of the supercomputer yet again and cautiously answered, "Good day."

"Is this Jacob Michaels?" the male voice gruffly demanded.

That last name was one he had used what seemed like a lifetime ago, well before finding out about the R-Group. He was immediately on guard and suggested to ICABOD in the IM window to do an extensive origination of the call and the background of the owner of the number for him. He glanced at the inbound number, which had been manipulated and masked as it was sent to his phone. That was a clear indicator of the potential relationship of the caller.

Jacob responded, "Yes, sir, it is. Who are you, please, and how can I help you?"

"My name is Mike Patrick, and you did some work for me on my corporate network security systems several years ago in New York. Your former boss tried to help me, but he doesn't have anyone that can work on my current project and suggested I call you. When he mentioned your name, I recalled our meeting and your abilities."

Jacob accessed the history of his work as a pen-tester in New York City. He had provided services and recommendations to many financial institutions and several large management firms during his tenure. ICABOD prompted him in the IM window with background on an organization named ePETRO, and its top-ranking executives included this caller. Other information about the company was also offered to him for reference; however, the company name did not ring any bells.

Jacob replied, "Mr. Patrick, I worked for many organizations when I lived in New York, but I do not recall working with ePETRO. Did you have a merger or acquisition that would have changed your firm's name?"

Mike, at least five to ten years senior to Jacob, had been a new CTO at the time for MaraOil and had been impressed at the speed in which the young man had accomplished the systems review and updates to their internal workflows over a six-month period. The detail-oriented service he received then was what he felt he had needed for employees to find the root of the problems, as well as get Marge the Barge off his ass. Apparently, access to information was still a part of this young man's skillset.

"You worked on some network testing, certifications, and security issues when I worked at MaraOil. I have since moved on in essentially the same field but as a CEO for ePETRO, which is a multinational commodities broker.

"I am having some issues with data analysis and potential data corruption of the partner production information. I am typically found these days in London, but we have offices in several countries in which we do business. Do you still work in security and data handling, or have you moved on to some other field?"

Jacob recalled the man and the operations he had run at MaraOil. At the time, Mike had been a jerk to his staff and to his help. The guy had a way of belittling his staff and definitely did not have the knowledge for operations for the company. Jacob had to return for fast training segments several times one-on-one with Mr. Patrick. The guy was a weasel, but the project sounded in line with the issue Wolfgang had related. Premium pricing though, definitely the big bucks to work with this guy.

"Mr. Patrick, I do work in the information systems profession and provide contract work for customers all over the world. I can send some of our team members to take a look at your issues, and then assess a project cost to you. Possibly as early as next…"

Mike's panic was instantaneous as he interrupted, "No. I need you, specifically. I have seen you work, and your former boss says you hold the highest confidence levels for your customers' business issues. My problem is very immediate, and I am more than willing to pay top dollar to get you onsite. I can put you up in the finest accommodations and provide you with a driver, anything you need to meet my timeline."

The desperation of the man was quite evident. Jacob knew that sort of attitude was usually because other avenues had failed, and a boss above was screaming. Sounded like a hornets' nest. Jacob started a slow grin. It was exactly the kind of situation he worked best in, but contracts were typically handled by Otto. Almost as if on cue, an IM window hit Jacob's display with:

I am sending you a dropbox and secure email account for his information. It is now the current work item on your screen. You can provide a briefing to the team. I can add the work order to this afternoon's agenda if you wish. ePETRO is having serious investor issues at present, they control about 40% of the oil distribution markets. The summary of this information is now in document ePETRO.1 Standard premium rates are currently at 500 Euros per hour with a PO guaranteed for a 25,000 Euro minimum (or three days including travel costs)

Jacob smiled as he read ICABOD's IM and said, "Mr. Patrick, I will need information background before I can commit to tomorrow. I will need a PO for a minimum of twenty-five thousand Euros, which covers the first three days of my time at your locations. I need details of the issue, when it began, steps you have taken to date, my contact while on site, and, of course, administrative access to your systems."

Mike was stunned. The price was high, and the access would take some time. He mentally reviewed the risk of not taking this action.

"Mr. Patrick, are you still there? Did you hear what I said? Do you want to continue?"

Mike gathered his thoughts and found his voice as he responded, "Yes, Mr. Michaels, that will be fine. Please send the total request of what you need to my email, *mpatrick@epetro. net,* and I will get right to work on it. You seem more confident than I recall, Mr. Michaels."

Jacob chuckled. "I have had a great deal more experience and larger customers to work with since we met. And, please, just call me Jacob, Mr. Patrick."

"I will, thank you. Please call me Mike. I look forward to our working together." Jacob sent back:

ICABOD, send along the email and the details we need. I will work on the briefing for the team.

Oh, and I will update the agenda. You know we promised Otto.

CHAPTER ELEVEN

The Lair of the Beast

LJ was a little intimidated by the inner sanctum of the organization's director. The incessant flashing lights and low, dull rumble of the computer equipment always reminded him of the dark forces lurking just below the surface, ready to be unleashed upon the world. LJ, the powerfully built enforcer for Takeru, was not easily intimidated by much of anything. But ever since he had joined the organization, he'd always felt uneasy inside Takeru's planning center.

LJ's tactic had always been to enter a room quietly to gain perspective of the situation. It had provided an advantage as an enforcer, but the oppressive tension in the sanctum was difficult to ignore. He imagined that this must have been what it felt like for the lone champion as he advanced into the lair of a beast. LJ was favored at present, but he recognized one's personal collateral was always a fleeting whim with someone like Takeru who hated so completely, but so objectively.

Takeru turned his gaze to aim it at the large black man, who immediately stopped dead in his approach. The malevolence of the room and the man were unmistakably projected around LJ, but not at him. LJ swallowed hard and was mentally trying to speak his carefully worded statement, but couldn't seem to offer up his thoughts to the director. As it turned out, Director Takeru took the speaking initiative, consequently driving the discussion where he wanted it to go.

While intently studying LJ, Takeru flatly stated, "People in my organization should know what I'm thinking so they don't have to ask what's next. Not only do I expect you to solve problems, so as to fit into my streaming plans, but I also expect you to correctly anticipate my next need. Moncrief wasn't able to do that.

"Now I sense hesitation in you as well, or am I mistaken?"

Takeru never raised his voice much beyond the low background hum of the server equipment, which somehow only made the conversation harder on the visitor, adding to their anxiety. LJ had experienced that manipulation in prior meetings in this sanctum. He was now caught in a dilemma. Should he discuss his original issue, or say that the director was wrong?

LJ took a deep, calming breath, recalled the teachings of his religious youth, and then respectfully offered, "You are not wrong, director. As you perceive correctly, I have a problem, and I'm unsure if my solution will meet with your approval. I don't seek to burden you, but I do seek your guidance with the overall plan.

"I recognize that you need people who can execute properly, not whiners. My concern is that the ebb and flow of this issue could destabilize other areas of your plan."

Takeru, in a rare display of near human emotion, stated, "If I only had eleven more like you, LJ, I could achieve world dominance without all the missteps my people make. I feel generous at this moment, so ask me your question. Your sizable contribution to our ongoing operations and new endeavors has earned you the right to petition under certain conditions.

"As the director of CHARD, I am in a position to grant reasonable requests. What do you have in mind?"

LJ was somewhat relieved that he had not sparked the wrath of Takeru, yet he was still cautious of the situation and the line he balanced upon. He petitioned, "I want permission to use Alisha in my operation. This is only to have her in an adjunct position and not to take her away from her normal duties on your behalf.

We have worked well together in the past, and, well, she is some-one to be trusted. When we were allowed into your organization, I always had it in my mind to work with her on my portion of the overall agenda. Will you grant me that latitude, Director Takeru?"

Takeru, being the emotional cripple that he was, could not laugh or enjoy human emotions in himself or those expressed by others and so was unable to respond with a smile. His only internal response was to process the situational request to see if the action was a benefit or a detriment to his planning.

After a few seconds, Takeru dispassionately replied, "Should my needs go unfulfilled, I will consider the arrangement null and void. Recall during our next scheduled meeting how I expect to see more ground gained with your additional resource. You may go now, LJ."

Takeru returned his gaze back to the pulsing lights and multiple monitors that seemed to provide sustenance as well as visual updates. LJ turned to leave the room and noticed that, as he reached for the door to let himself out, his hands were shaking fitfully.

HMX ↓ -7.50
CMX ↓ -9.33
HCC ↓ -3.90
SOX ↓ -7.74

Alisha was a large, black woman with carefully cropped hair. She had a diverse background of nursing, wrestling, and religion. She had been on again, off again with this bouncer-turned-enforcer-turned-power broker for years. They drifted together for sex and to support various criminal activities. She would have liked to change how they lived but realized that was a false dream.

Her expression reflected doubt as she questioned, "Lordy boy, are you sure this is a good idea? My feeling is this situation is about like the time my brother stirred up a fire ant bed, and then him and some of his friends pitched me on buck naked for wrecking his shiny new bicycle. I'm here to tell you that I got bit in areas that I only let you nibble on. So here I am again with that awful feeling in my…"

LJ cut her off. "Honey, will you stop worrying? We took some of our seed money to be properly positioned for our next gig, which got us brought into a good business proposition, and now we have a seat at the table, which means a promised share in the profits. Yes, I admit he is a little creepy, but we needed a new venue from which to work. I told you, this one would get us into some even greater financial freedom than what we had."

Alisha looked at LJ skeptically and admonished, "We didn't even get a chance to enjoy our last gig's profits before you signed us up for this one. I was looking forward to enjoying some nice parasol-topped fruity chick drinks at the beach while you were scheming to try and get my skimpy bikini top off and make it look like an accident. You know there is something naughty about you when we are in public places. You're always trying to show off my girls!"

LJ had always been partial to his Alisha. At one time, early on, she did have an eye-catching figure, but now her 115 kilos of bulk didn't really show off well in a bikini, and so the *girls* were always going rogue when she least expected it. Even though LJ continued to work out daily, his weight had gotten away from him as well. To be honest, his 135 kilos of male bulk weren't such that he believed they should be on a public beach slugging down their favorite adult beverages. That was a sure recipe for overhyped amorous intentions, which drew way too much attention. After a few drinks, she magically slimmed down, and his friskiness tended to get them too much attention for the kind of work they did. He believed that until they could afford their own private island, he didn't want to run the risk of exposure, being as it were.

LJ admonished, "Sugah, we are on the right track, so trust me on this one. I can deal with this situation, but I need you with me on it. Okay?"

Alisha, not willing to let it go, insisted, "That's what you said when we began to work with Xavier. You saw how that turned out, or have you forgotten? Sure we got money, and lots of it, but at what cost?

"Just for the record, I'm with you, but I've got a bad feeling about it. We've never had to deal with someone that nearly makes you wet your pants every time you have to go see him!"

LJ somewhat indignantly responded, "Oh, so you don't think I'm on top of my game here? Listen to me, sweet-chops, you may be finger-licking good, but your fortunes weren't so hot until we got together. My dreaming-n-scheming works best if you are with me one hundred preeecent, so don't be doubting our future together!"

Alisha was somewhat taken aback by LJ's statement and after a few moments asked, "You kind of like having me around? And I mean not just for riding the pony but because we be a team? When you put it like that, you almost sound romantic, sugah."

LJ smiled and offered, "Honey, stick with me on this one, and I promise it's our last gig before retirement. We'll buy our own island and have the waitress blindfolded when she is delivering your FCDs with their little parasols. Deal?"

Alisha giggled a little bit and asked, "So is my man ready for some dinner and maybe some of the old fireplug hopping action from your woman that you like so well?"

LJ's smile showed off all the gold in his teeth, and he replied, "Yes, honey, just as soon as I change into some fresh underwear. These got soaked again."

CHAPTER TWELVE
Railroading Commodities

Roundhouse practically shouted, "What do you mean, don't bother? We got a fully loaded train of coal here in Wyoming, ready to bring it back to Texas for power generation, and you're telling me don't bother? Even if the value of the cargo is slipping by the minute, which is not my problem, the biggest issue here is how the hell am I supposed to get home if we don't move these hundred-eighty cars of coal?"

The caller on the other end of the line tried to offer in a conciliatory tone. "Now, Roundhouse, I wasn't going to strand you there in Wyoming just because they said, 'Stop what you are doing.' The problem is our buyers in Texas have multiple fuel options they can use in their power generating plants. With oil and gas so cheap they have opted not to buy this load of coal, so we need to hold you up while I try to find another buyer."

Roundhouse was a huge man who had worked the railroads all his life. It had been his passion to be a train engineer for as long as he could remember. His hands were so huge that a quarter would easily slide through the center of his wedding ring. When he had married Mildred, she said that he could follow his dream and found a ring that would fit, not bind. They had spent their lives in Cut 'N Shoot, Texas, raising three girls, who were all the apple of his eye. They all successfully wrapped him around their fingers. It actually pained him to see his beloved railroad being hammered by a heartless commodity market-driven world.

He had been called Roundhouse for so long, almost no one remembered his real name, Timothy Standour. Until direct deposit came into his life, his small-town bank gave him trouble cashing his payroll check because it didn't say "Payable to Roundhouse". He was well liked and respected for being a solid family man who looked out for his girls.

The dispatcher continued, "It doesn't help that the public is putting pressure on coal-burning power plants to do something more environmentally friendly. With cheaper fuel alternatives, the buyers are playing their politically correct environment cards and taking their business elsewhere. You need to sit tight until I can find a place to sell this load."

Roundhouse, now seething with anger, questioned, "So how long, Henry? Will it be twenty minutes, a few days, or 10:00 o'clock next summer?"

Becoming annoyed himself, Henry tersely offered, "It won't be 10:00 o'clock next summer."

Roundhouse stated, "I don't understand. It takes days to get here, days to load up, and days to get back, but it sounds like we didn't have a legitimate buyer locked into a contract before we started rolling this train. If we had a legitimate contract in place, then let me go deliver it and let the lawyers fight it out. If we didn't have a contract, then give me the name of the bonehead who has me stranded here, at risk of missing my granddaughter's birthday party!"

The dispatcher sighed and explained, "Commodity pricing works both ways, old friend. If the price of coal had doubled overnight, we would be putting the screws to them, and if they wouldn't accept the new higher price our contract would allow us to sell that load of coal on the open market for more profits. The contract was only agreed to by the buyers when it contained a condition that if pricing fell, they could decline to pay the negotiated price, and we would again sell on the open market.

"Trouble is everyone is seeing the same thing. The price of coal is still dropping due to oversupply, and frankly, the buyers are waiting to see if the price will fall further. You need to wait until we can find a buyer, even if they are located in Europe. If that happens, you will get to move, but not back to Texas. The train would route to a depot on the West coast to load a freighter. I'm sorry, old friend, but this one is beyond our ability to control."

Roundhouse yelled, "Oversupply? Who are you kidding, anyway? My train is the only one scheduled in or out of here for weeks. From what I'm seeing, there can't possibly be an oversupply, because almost nothing from this state is being loaded out. I've talked to all the rail coordinators. They are asking me to turn out the lights in the coal mining pits after I leave because no one is ordering. I'm no genius at economics, but let me ask you this, how can there be an oversupply when no one is mining anything?"

Henry calmly offered, "The supply damage has already been done, and people have simply quit buying. That signal was the cue to the producers to stop mining and furlough everyone. Which is what will happen as soon as you get back, Roundhouse."

The harsh statement quickly pulled Roundhouse up short. It never even crossed his mind that his job would be a casualty as well in the commodity price wars. He felt very hollow and lonely now that the weighty statement had been made about the lifestyle he cared so much about.

After a few sobering minutes of reflection by both men, Henry quietly consoled, "Me too, old friend. I am fairly sure I won't be here when you get back. In fact, I was let go yesterday, but I wouldn't go until I got you home safe and sound. Based on how things are going around here, I may not make it down to your granddaughter's birthday either."

It took a lot to pull Roundhouse up short in a conversation, but that was exactly what had happened. His eyes filled up with tears, but he refused to let them overrun as he quietly replied, "I'm sorry, I didn't know how bad it was. Forgive me for getting so angry at you when they have already dismissed you. Thanks for trying to get me back home. I'll wait here for your call, my friend."

Henry could only nod his head and then silently disconnected from the call.

NMX ↓ -7.50
CMX ↓ -9.33
HCC ↓ -3.90
SOX ↓ -7.74

Henry ambled into Mr. Tomkins's office and, without an invitation to sit down, plopped himself into the chair closest to the desk. Mr. Tomkins was a senior VP for the train dispatch group, was well connected with his commodity buyers, and the most up-tight stickler for appropriate employer/employee protocol interactions. A person never showed up just to speak with Mr. Tomkins, because he only ever talked about business and his rarified mathematics.

He never socialized with anyone, never discussed family, since no one believed he had anyone. While he was always polite to people, he was never friendly. The attitude everyone had towards Mr. Tomkins was that he was probably dropped on this planet by aliens, based on his inability to deal with people.

Mr. Tomkins raised his eyebrows several seconds after Henry was seated, then commented, "I'm fairly sure we had no scheduled meeting for this morning. May I know the nature of this visit?"

Henry was unimpressed with the terse comment and took his time to respond, which made Mr. Tomkins's jaw muscles flex, indicating annoyance.

Finally, Henry asked, "What are we going to do about the trains we have parked in Wyoming and Appalachia? More specifically, I have engineers wanting to route back home, and we don't have a bill of sale from a bona fide buyer to even give them a destination to head towards."

Mr. Tomkins dryly remarked, "Well, they should have realized that working extra hard to diligently add to the oversupply problem would create additional problems for us all. The extra hauls that are showing up on my reports contributed to our oversupply problem. But, to your point, I'm in contact with all my domestic buyers and some new foreign ones to try and find a home for these extra loads of coal. I've got some new contacts in the Netherlands, but they are currently offline, based on their time zone.

"I appreciate our engineers' work ethic to bring in extra runs for us, but right now tell them to stop and breathe. All the extra runs they made have us buried in product that is consequently dropping daily in value."

Henry did a double take and was unable to contain his astonishment. He exclaimed, "What are you talking about, Mr. Tomkins? They haven't been doubling up on their runs. In fact, these engineers, to a man, are grousing about how little work they have had. I know all our engineers and their work ethic, but I am here to tell you they have not exceeded their standard quota runs based on our expected sale rate. What numbers are you looking at, because it sounds like the numbers you are looking at are wrong?"

Annoyed that anyone would question his math or his precise calculations, Mr. Tomkins spun the display terminal around to show Henry the extra four runs of coal that were shown to have been made in the last six weeks, two extra by each of the currently stranded engineers.

Mr. Tomkins calmly offered, "See there? These engineers have been exceeding our contract commitments since late last year. Frankly, all it has done is drive down the price for our product on the open market. I'm sure you feel justified to demand we do something for them, but bluntly stated, we are in this pickle because of them."

Henry stared incredulously at the loads being delivered at the stated rate shown on the display. Henry had an incredible memory for details and statistics. Once seen they were always available for recall. He was one of those people who could accurately quote, off the cuff, sports statistics for the last twenty years or more, populations of cities they hauled in and other trivia statistics. Though not a mathematics wiz like Mr. Tomkins, his recall was almost never questioned.

After the information sank in, Henry looked up from the screen to Mr. Tomkins's face and slowly said, "These numbers can't be right.

"In 2013, Powder River Basin pumped out 407,566,885 short tons of coal, which was down from the peak of 462,600,212 in 2011, or a drop of 12% in three years. If the demand for coals continues to fall as we were seeing at that time, we expected to see about 359,080,608 short tons of output. Your numbers are going in the opposite direction.

"I don't remember the Appalachia output figures like Powder River Basin, but what you are showing in this spreadsheet are almost what the entire U.S. market shipped in 2013, which was 641,190,957 short tons of coal. Where are you getting your numbers from?"

Henry typed in the website without a pause. The numbers came up.

Growing somewhat alarmed, Mr. Tomkins pointedly asked, "I guess I shouldn't be surprised by your memory of coal output in this country, you and that recall of yours. But what you seem to be saying is that our train engineers are not making multiple runs to our suppliers. If that is the case, then my numbers have been polluted somehow."

Henry then added, "It is 1,222 miles one way from Powder River Basin, Wyoming to Austin, Texas. The maximum train speed allowed is 60 mph on a class 4 railway line. However, we classified them as only class 3 which means max is 40 mph. You know our average speed due to city traffic, curves, and grades is only about 25 mph. If you do that math," he emphasized, "then it's about 50 hours one way.

"Further, the trains would have to be loaded and unloaded multiple times at each end. That can take up to three days. The best you could hope for is for a train to load in two days, travel without incident for 2.5 days and unload in another 2 days for a total one-way pickup and delivery of 6.5 days or one full week. Add on the return run of another 2.5 days and that has a full cycle of 9 days for a coal train.

"Those are the simple physics of rail transport with no delays, which never happens. For your spreadsheet to be right, we would have to be turning trains around in 5 days which means we would have to shave almost 40% of the transport time off."

Mr. Tomkins silently ground his teeth at having been pinned by his subordinate on mathematical computations, which he felt were beyond Henry's ranking in the company.

As the two men stared at each other, Mr. Tomkins questioned, "Weren't you let go yesterday? Why bring this issue to upper management after you have been laid off?"

Henry boldly stated, "That's the difference between you and me. I care about other human beings that I have worked with for so long. They become part of my extended family, and when they need my help, well, that's what I do.

"Back to my original question, what are we going to do about my two engineers who are stranded?"

Mr. Tomkins uncharacteristically smirked and then allowed, "Please issue instructions to bring both of them back with our trains of coal. I don't have a buyer for them yet, but it is reasonable for the coal to sit in Texas, devaluing, as easily as it would in their current locations."

Henry almost smiled at having gotten Mr. Tomkins to allow the trains to roll home. But before he could go call his two engineers, Mr. Tomkins stated, "Oh, and please shred the layoff notice that was issued to you. It occurs to me that we need more level-headed thinkers around here like yourself. Don't worry, you can continue to tell people that I'm an alien here on my adopted planet. It will help to maintain my mystique."

Henry grinned sheepishly and simply nodding, left to make his phone calls.

CHAPTER THIRTEEN

Numbers Don't Lie, Do They?

Jacob had called a team meeting in the central conference room in the Zürich operations center of R-Group for the bottom of the hour. He'd assembled the information that Mike Patrick had sent, along with the background information ICABOD had found. Jacob had found it interesting that this man had been able to track him down.

On the screen was an assembled timeline displaying photos of Mr. Patrick that dated from college, with long hair and odd shades relevant to the time. Not at all the same looking man Jacob had worked with in New York. He had dropped out of Stephen F. Austin University in the final year of his advanced graduate program for no documented reason. Later he had completed two degrees, apparently while working for a Texas-based company during a boom time in oil. It seemed he'd gained a bit of professional polish, elevating both his positions and titles as he'd moved from one organization to another. He had been based in New York City for several years but traveled as needed for the positions he held.

Jacob sipped his coffee and mentally tried to determine the reason that Mr. Patrick had called him. When their paths had crossed several years ago, it had been event specific. Admittedly he'd done a thorough job, but there had not been a relationship between them. Closing the presentation, Jacob waited for the team to arrive and thought about how this might map to other crazy events. It was never dull in the world of information security.

Petra and Quip entered and sat on the far side of the conference room table. Petra passed along a covert half-smile as she crossed his line of sight.

Quip commented, "Don't think I didn't see that, Petra. I'm wise to you two. So very glad you are back here and together. Now, I can tease you both again. Right?"

Jacob grinned and replied, "You can try, Dr. Q, but I'm not the same guy I was my first visit here. I have learned a lot and I believe you have as well."

Quip's grin widened as he stirred his coffee and grabbed a cookie off the ever-present plate centered on the table. Quip was responsible for the cookies being available each day, and though he always shared, he would grumble if he wanted one and the plate was empty. Haddy, Otto's wife, had made certain there were always spares available in the kitchen.

Jacob's mind quickly assessed the crazy events that had first brought him to Zürich. The secrecy of the location, the history, and the why of it all. Petra had been a big driver in his coming as they'd started a relationship in New York City, which neither of them had expected, but once he'd found her he had no intention of letting her slip away. Then he had found out that the mother who had raised him and supported his education in technology was really the daughter of Wolfgang. When she was killed, Jacob thought he was the last of his family until he discovered the truth that Wolfgang was his grandfather. As if on cue, Otto and Wolfgang both entered and grinned at the assembled team as they took their seats on the near side of the conference room table.

Otto grinned, and his eyes twinkled as he assessed his daughter, spotted her ring, then gently accused, "What, no hug, my dear Petra? You have been in this building most of the day and couldn't seek me out?" He looked almost put out, then grinned again.

Petra smiled and demurely responded, "We have been trying to catch up on the notes provided by Wolfgang. I promise we will sit down and talk soon. Things are good!"

Wolfgang nodded at the comment and added, "Jacob, would you like to start?"

Jacob looked over the group and offered, "I received a call earlier and wanted to brief you, as well as get a bit of perspective from each of you." With that he dimmed the lights and launched the presentation from the back wall as though the wall was alive. The images of the man appeared as well as the years under each of the photos. None of the photos showed his entire face, and certainly no smiles or professional headshots had been available like for most corporate executives.

"This man is Mike Patrick. He called me earlier today asking for help with his group's commodity trading anomaly. This time-line represents his life from a late start in college based on his age, until present. He currently heads up a group based in New York City called ePETRO. ePETRO is a group of petroleum-based holdings that has historically been very prescriptive in their product's production and distribution.

"Mr. Patrick is the son of an Asian mother and an American father of Irish descent, both presumed dead. He was sent to boarding school from an early age for education and to presumably make something of himself. His father was killed during his early military career and never saw his son. There was, however, a death benefit from the military paid to his mother. That is when he was sent to boarding school. He kept out of trouble through high school, and his records indicate he was always in the top of his class. There are gaps between his exit from boarding school and when he attended college in Texas. Possibly he was finding himself. There is a hole in this time, but that could be due to a number of things, including poor data retention practices which are common for these years in many areas outside of government.

"I met him when I worked in New York as a pen-tester. He had a problem in his data center that I traced. I found him to be a particularly annoying man in his treatment of the staff. A bit overbearing, likely accentuated by his large build, yet almost inscrutable in his facial features. He liked my work and was very forthcoming about how he located me when we spoke.

"He has asked for help in finding out the production count inconsistencies that are being reported as a part of the ePETRO collective." Jacob changed to the next slide, which showed numbers and production graphics. He waited for the team to review them when Wolfgang stood and walked a bit closer.

Wolfgang pointed as he commented, "This shift right here, three months ago, is the point where the downward pricing started. Can you overlay that with the pricing in the same increments?"

Touching the wall, Jacob pulled in the next slide and paused for it to be viewed.

Wolfgang continued, "See what I mean? Jacob, how did you know to assemble this presentation in that order?"

"I guess I have been around you long enough. This also lines up with the problem as Mr. Patrick outlined it. What I see as really interesting however, is the global buying over the same period that ICABOD assembled."

With that he changed the slide, and there was indeed an inconsistency with this new information.

Otto intervened, "I see the differences, and it does look like a problem, but this modeling is only for the last four months. In any of the commodity's markets, four months is like a breath, not totally indicative of a trend. Or have I forgotten my economics?"

"Otto, you are correct!" Wolfgang agreed. "However, the lines during the same period should track, and these are like polar opposites. Something is odd in the numbers. A further study of these numbers over a longer period of time, along with other factors mapped into here, is definitely warranted.

"What does Mr. Patrick want, Jacob?"

"He asked that I specifically come to his headquarters and take a look at his data systems and verify that he has no issues. He refused me remote access and has removed any external access from all the database sources and all applications. If there is a trail, he wants me to find it. All staff has been given an unexpected holiday with no access to the office whatsoever until the issue is identified, and a solution put into place. He wants me on site tonight or first thing in the morning.

"I suspect his Board of Directors is not happy, but the frozen state will stem the asset shrinkage for a few days."

Quip had been somewhat distracted during most of the session up to the point where the four months of commodity was discussed. He interrupted, "Could this be connected to any of the railroad issues that the U.S. government has us looking into?"

Otto shook his head and replied, "I don't see how that would work, but we cannot discount it. I have been checking while listening, and Thiago's current interests do not have any relationship with ePETRO. When you look at it historically, Wolfgang, it might be a prior business cross point that we can keep an eye out for."

Petra suggested, "Jacob, I think you should go and take me along."

Quip snickered but quickly looked away as he stifled it.

Petra, with her eyes on the screen and totally composed, added, "If this is a programmatic issue with the data, you might need some added encryption breaking support. Two pairs of eyes would likely be better than one."

Quip started to make a smart comment, but thought better of it as Otto said, "I agree. Both of you go take a look at the situation and see what there is to capture.

"Quip, I think you can start to add in some data sources for us to use. As usual, I would hope that you would be the central project manager."

Wolfgang volunteered, "Let me look at the numbers, and I think going back several years might pull out a view of the trends over time, which should prove interesting. Quip, I will coordinate the use of ICABOD's resources with you."

Quip nodded, all business now.

Otto finished, "You two go ahead after you do some of the preliminary research. Call him and delay for at least a day, and let us know if you think of something else you need. I will get an update from Stalker and start reaching out to our other sources. Perhaps Thiago and his associates know more than they realize. I also need to get with Eric's team and find out how much they have been able to uncover in their investigation. If for no other reason than to rule that out as a link into this issue."

Quip asserted, "I will set up some daily calls and the usual location for our findings as they are uncovered.

"Thanks, Jacob, for the briefing."

CHAPTER FOURTEEN

Futures Trading – The Long and the Short of It

The smiling lady extended her hand and offered, "Welcome to the Merc, Mr. Hughes. My name is Claudia, and I will be your liaison while you are here at the Chicago Mercantile Exchange. Your organization only advised us this morning you were on your way here to assess this commodities market phenomenon. One would guess you were an overachiever in school, based on your eagerness to help us get to the bottom of this pricing freefall."

Claudia was none too subtle about scoping out Jim's powerful build in case something could be arranged later. Jim immediately caught the sexual undertones and indiscreet looks at his bottom, which completely turned him off to her. *Ah well*, he thought to himself, *either people are annoyed when a federal agent shows up or they are undressing you with their eyes.* At least this one is female and relatively easy on the eyes.

Claudia was tastefully dressed in a business casual dress that was a full size too small. Dressing to distraction was part of her game plan in a meteoric climb up the corporate ladder. *Business Seduction*, she liked to call it, when futures traders and potential business partners came calling. It was rumored she seemed to do quite well with the men, but oddly enough it was suggested her business seduction skills also worked on the female futures traders just as well. For Claudia it seemed to be the finesse of the game. Jim bet she loved to play, and played to win.

Jim easily maintained his professionalism as he responded, "Miss Claudia, I have a particular interest in Powder River Basin and Appalachia coal futures. In particular, I need to understand how the problem occurred."

Claudia sensed that Jim Hughes would be a difficult candidate but, unable to resist the challenge, said, "Well, we have a saying here at the Merc; the best thing to cure high prices, is high prices!"

Claudia laughed at her insider joke humor while Jim looked on dispassionately. Realizing the joke didn't translate to non-futures traders, she quickly added, "As prices go up and up, the lure of profits brings more entrants into the commodity production business. That then adds to the supply, which then leads to downward pricing pressure. Usually, the high-cost producer is the first to retool their business model, or exit the business. The survivors return to business as usual, or almost. This time, however, it appears that no one is blinking at the game of corporate chicken. The supply numbers are stubbornly high, and everyone is suffering."

Claudia offered Jim a seat, then turned around to seat herself. She allowed her dress to ride up farther than necessary to properly seat herself. Jim, somewhat disgusted with the flagrant display, was nonetheless unable to turn off his scoping abilities, so he readily enjoyed the show. Claudia went on to re-cross her legs in such a way as to have Jim focus on how high up her legs her nylons traveled. Claudia seemed to be spending a lot of unnecessary time straightening herself and the tight-fitting dress, in Jim's estimation.

Finally growing tired of the display, Jim asked, "If your clothes are so uncomfortable, why don't you go change them? I'm sure your antics play well for the futures traders trying to get ahead, but, frankly, I am here on government business. And only that. Your packing the goods in a spray-on dress act doesn't contribute to our information exchange. Please let me be clear; I am ONLY here to exchange information, understand?

"If need be, I can have your supervisor take a call from my supervisor with potential results. You can be selling your goods as SPAM email offerings for lonely Russian girls seeking male companionship. Now, is the floor show over?"

Claudia was somewhat taken aback by the no-nonsense attitude of this impressive man. She really didn't want to give up trying to engage him in the seduction, but she didn't want to test his character any farther since his threat sounded legitimate.

She tugged her dress line down and quietly offered, "You must have a very special lady back home to resist such an easy invitation, but alright, have it your way. You see, we get two kinds of people in here: people wanting an advantage and those offering help. My job is to find out which kind of person you are and then engineer the next step. Frankly, we don't get many in here to help."

Claudia studied Jim for a few brief seconds before she stated, "Let's talk about how commodity prices are set and why they are not working correctly now. You had asked about coal production in this country specifically, but coal is produced globally. That can help or hurt domestic prices. We watch all markets, but something is wrong – really wrong."

CHAPTER FIFTEEN

That's All I Know About the Shipping Business

LJ gave his biggest grin to the agent as he stuck out his hand to shake hands as a show of respect during this first meeting. LJ had played this role before, using his affable personality and pretending to be a country bumpkin who was way out of his league. The booking agent studied LJ for a moment, then reluctantly accepted the handshake.

LJ began, "As I said over the phone, I'm wanting to charter some of your boats."

The booking agent stared uneasily at LJ, expecting this to be some practical joke that was being played. When the rube in front of him didn't admit to it being a come-on, he finally asked, "Are you sure you know where you are? You're asking about a boat charter, and all my charters are for hauling petroleum in ships classified by Dead Weight Ton. We don't charter sport fishing boats here, sir."

LJ laughed uproariously, then he slapped his knee as he exclaimed, "Oh, you think I be here looking to charter some shrimping boats like that black feller from that movie a while back. Har! Har! Don't that beat all? I show up to charter your fleet to move thousands of barrels of oil, and you think I'm some hick from the sticks wanting to do some sport fishing while slugging down my favorite beer."

The good-natured laughter put the situation at ease, but the booking agent was still mortified beyond belief and could not hide his beet red face.

LJ finally caught his breath and added a smile. "No need to be embarrassed, son. You're probably new to the job, and this is likely only your second week. No matter, I took your comment as great sport. Now, let's get down to business, shall we?

"Your inventory of ships looks to be a right promising fleet for the amount of oil I need to transport. Since almost all of them are moored and not working, I'd expect a very attractive rate over the coming months. Now, I want to focus on the very large crude carriers of your fleet since I'm taking delivery of a lot of oil futures. Oh, and also, my computer technician needs to install some software to ensure that my loading and unloading meets the taxing authority's requirements. The last time we did this, they didn't believe my numbers and wanted to argue about what I was claiming. My new auditing software program will eliminate that sordid discussion before it can occur!"

The booking agent began to voice some concern about loading out some new unsanctioned software into their computer systems.

LJ offered, "Now, I know what you're thinking, so I'll have my people work with your people to get it installed. Then you don't got no need to fret yourself at all. Let me get my checkbook out, and I will begin the bidding on your tankers at $7,000 US a day for each of your largest crude carriers."

The booking agent sputtered and questioned, "What? Are you insane? These units ordinarily bill out at $50,000 a day!"

LJ grinned as he shook his head and offered, "The last time you saw that figure was in 2007. With all the new shipping that came online since then, coupled with the oversupply but low price of oil these days, you're lucky I don't go to the other charter service that is next on my list."

LJ stood a little straighter and seemed a bit less backwoods as he suggested, "Now you've already insulted me, questioned my software tracking needs, and then grew belligerent during our pricing negotiations. No wonder all your ships are moored and going nowhere. I guess I best be off so you can enjoy no revenue stream to offset your interest payments. Maybe you ought to consider offering sport fishing charters 'cause you ain't gonna get much business with your attitude. Good day!"

LJ had every intention of collecting his things to move out of the offices when the booking agent made an anxious move to intercept him and begged, "Sir, please forgive my shortsighted approach to our negotiations. I meant no disrespect. Please, if we could start our meeting over, I'm sure that your decision will be different and well worth your time."

LJ smiled broadly and happily sat back down.

The booking agent started again, "Hi, my name is Alonzo and I am here to help you, sir."

LJ grinned and, extending his hand again, replied, "I'm LJ, kind sir. I am here to charter several of your carriers at $7,000 a day. Additionally, I need some special consideration on top of our transaction. Do I have your attention, and can we do business?"

Alonzo swallowed hard but quickly responded, "You do, indeed, sir."

HMX ↓ -7.50
CMX ↓ -9.33
HCC ↓ -3.90
SOX ↓ -7.74

Takeru motioned Alisha over to his terminal without taking his eyes from the screen. Once there she gave him a crisp salute and said, "Sir?"

Takeru recounted with very little emotion, "Alert LJ that he has surfaced on the grid. His actions were picked up by the SABOTAGE program. *Sequential Algorithms Based On Timely*

Assessments to Garble Eavesdropping is key to my organization for flying under the radar of those who would try and stop us. If my Big Data program can recognize his efforts, in concert with our ancillary efforts in this commodity, then so can others. Put a call into him to terminate his exposure. There must be no trace, am I clear?"

Alisha was already pulling out her cell phone to dial the stored number as Takeru dispassionately finished his sentence. LJ felt his phone vibrating in its holster and quickly took a look to see who it was. He might have ignored it, but it had a famous Lonnie Lupnerder song for a ringtone that caught the attention of Alonzo, who promptly added the lyrics to the ringtone. At that point, LJ figured it would be a good time to excuse himself to take the call outside. LJ got up and offered, "Apologies, but I need to take this call. I'll be right back, kind sir."

The Lonnie Lupnerder ring tone had put Alonzo in a good mood, and he continued to hum along with the tune in his head as he, from time to time, made air drum gestures as though he was part of the band.

LJ stepped outside the offices and asked, "Hon, whatcha doing calling me at this precise moment? I'm teeing up the bulk of the oil tankers I need for my project, and we are down to the final paperwork that needs to be filed electronically. Hope this is worth the interruption."

Alisha cut right to the point. "You got famous quick, LJ. Your current activity surfaced moments ago on that fancy program called SABOTAGE, and the director of CHARD said for you to terminate all actions, and I do mean terminate."

She moved to an area that had the additional ambient noises of more servers and lowered her voice as she continued, "Now, he didn't ask, but I'll bet you needs to go speak with him ASAP about this so you don't end up like Moncrieff. Understand?"

LJ ground his teeth and slowly shook his head back and forth in anger. He took a couple of deep breaths and replied, "Well, dammit! Looks like I ain't any better than old Moncrieff. The only thing I got going for me is that he can't have me sneak up on myself from behind. Argh!"

LJ took a few more deep breaths as he psyched himself into his enforcer role. Then he quietly replied with no nervousness in his voice, "Alright, let me tidy up things here and do a digital wipe-down before heading out. It is a shame though, 'cause I kinda liked the kid. Don't bother telling the director I'm sorry, since it won't do no good. I guess I'm going to have to come at this a different way. Thanks for calling me, babe. Talk soon."

Alisha walked back to the area where Takeru sat, staring into his terminal screen, and offered, "LJ has been alerted, and the wipe-down is being initiated, sir."

Not taking his eyes off the screen, Takeru simply nodded and commented, "Let's see how well he can cloak an exposed position. That will be all, Alisha."

CHAPTER SIXTEEN

Foresight or Hindsight?

O tto had assembled all the bullet points and questions he wanted to discuss with Thiago. This was standard business in advising his customers on what they should or should not do. Otto had learned a long time ago that customers always say that they want to see all the options, but every time he ever did show them all the options, they fell into paralysis by analysis. Nowadays, two choices were all he would offer. But on this pending discussion, he felt something unidentifiable prickle at the back of his mind, as if he'd overlooked something significant. It was not like him to have anything left nagging, but something was off. He simply was unable to pinpoint the what. He placed the call, leaving the video element unconnected.

"Thiago, my old friend, I wonder if you might have a few minutes for me to offer an update to our last conversation?"

Thiago frowned at the unexpected call, but he wanted answers. "Yes, Otto, of course. I just wasn't expecting your call. You typically provide notification so I can get it into my schedule. Let me send off a quick note to my admin to let her know I need to move my next appointment."

"I do apologize for the lack of notice," Otto allowed, "but I thought you would benefit from a bit of an update, and I had a couple of areas I wanted your thoughts on for clarity."

"Otto, it's not a problem. I know you are working in my best interest, so I, of course, will make time for you. Now, please, tell me of your findings."

Otto's face took on a very serious expression as he related, "We took a look at the numbers on oil production from a different starting point. We still have not determined where exactly the numbers became inflated, but we know they are. As you suggested, the reporting of the numbers was significantly higher than the reality. What we found interesting is that several producers in the region had numbers that seemed inflated as well. The data seem to ramp up in an almost predictable manner as if they are reaching a predetermined target."

Thiago sighed and anxiously replied, "Why is it I hear a good news/bad news tone in your voice. What you're saying was what I suggested to you."

Otto slightly cleared his throat, then continued, "Don't start dancing yet, my friend. When the investment in anything seems too risky, businesses like yours shift from one thing to another. As you stated, your investment in offshore drilling may be poorly timed, based on the inflated supply of oil. At this new, unexpectedly low price for oil you would not be able to earn enough to cover your sunk costs. Offshore drilling is the most expensive and highest risk opportunity you could pursue, but without a clear view of prices soaring, this investment strategy is ill-advised."

Thiago's enthusiasm deflated. There would be no fast cure. He knew that, but he had still hoped.

Otto added, "I know this is disappointing news, but nothing you weren't already aware of, I'm certain. The only way to pursue an offshore drilling endeavor would be to defer part of the risk by bringing in some partners so the risk is not all yours. However, there is a growing movement of unrest in your country which I suspect you are feeling as well. With this kind of political uncertainty, finding enthusiastic partners for a risky venture would be highly problematic."

Thiago sadly replied, "Yes. The economy overall is unhealthy, and businesses I have worked with for years are closing locations or moving out to some of their foreign offices. The business community that I participate in is trying to bring home the jobs and revenues. People are voicing their opinions, louder every day, on the need for more jobs.

"Brazil is a proud country with a rich heritage of diverse wildlife, innovation, immense resources from the land and the sea, and a traveler's paradise, regardless of budget. We have always had pockets of unrest, some even brought on by Carnival or all the other festivals we host. We are even questioning our government officials and their honesty as a whole. It is a hard time.

"My Board of Directors recommended that we further distance ourselves from the government contracts and cut corners now to lower the possible perception of any improprieties."

Otto perked up and asked, "Surely, my friend, your firm is not involved with any of the problems the press is relating about your elected officials."

"No, of course not!" emphasized Thiago. "Our firm is not political. As you know, we do not back any elected officials nor contribute to campaigns at even the most local levels. My firm simply helps to fight over-regulation initiatives which have risen greatly in the recent two years. We were asked to contribute to some campaigns to help reduce these, but we refused any involvement in the political sidings. It is actually against our business policies. As a fair play corporation, we want appropriate rules and regulations that we can all fairly compete in for profitability. We do not subscribe to having the playing field skewed in our favor to everyone else's detriment. There is no honor in that."

Otto felt a bit calmed with this response. He had known this was the policy, but he wanted to have his client acknowledge where their business philosophy was today.

"I knew that was the policy, but it does me good to hear the conviction in your voice.

"Now, Thiago, the good news. After a review of your cash position, investments, and costs streams, I am recommending that you increase and diversify your investment exposure during these uncertain times. Those investments should be tailored to add new revenue streams to your organization."

"Otto, my company's cash position is very poor at this point. Yes, I have cash, but the ratio is far lower than I would like with the economy dropping daily. I might do some foreign investments, but in this political climate it would look like we are taking our capital and fleeing. The people are in a state of unrest, fueled by the economic downturn, and one more corporation pulling up stakes and running will only exacerbate the population's attitude toward government and large corporations."

"Thiago, there are two schools of investing thought at play here. If you believe all is lost, then sell out and run. If you believe in the future of your country, then invest locally to take advantage of the good times when they return. This will prove to your fellow countrymen that you are part of the solution. Any investments, foreign or domestic, which would drive some jobs locally would be good, and people will remember that your company stayed to fight for a better Brazil. How about some investments in solar energy to help develop the aspects of going green? This would create some jobs and allow some dependencies on oil and natural gas to be replaced with renewable fuels, like solar. The reason I mention that as a possibility is that the renewable energy industry has been hurt by the oppressively low oil prices, and several companies are closing their doors or simply selling off their intellectual property very cheaply. One day the price of oil will go back up to make energy alternatives a necessity for a growing population. Do you want to be properly invested for that next series of events?"

Thiago thought about the possibilities of shifting investments and how he might be able to sell this to his Board of Directors. It actually had some good potential for his company and for Brazil. Even with his current cash reserves, he was able to cover his costs with excesses for at least three years, but he was not totally sold on the idea.

Thiago suggested, "What do you think, Otto, about my selling off some of my ships to cover the additional costs for such a venture? I think the Board of Directors would applaud the diversity, just like they did when I insisted upon investing in Destiny Fashions. That resulted in the huge influx of cash reserves. The revenues of that venture will flow into my company for at least three more years, with an option for more based on the economy at that point. It was a great diversification strategy, thanks to you.

"It seems like your advice is usually right, and I'll formulate the plan and take it to the Board. Even if I sell my ships for a fraction of their value, it will be better than the costs to maintain them. Thank you, Otto, for your perspective as always." Thiago chuckled and added, "It is why we will continue to play the Otto game here."

Otto interjected, "Thiago, I would rethink selling your ships. You don't need the cash, and when oil productions shift you will need those ships to maintain your leadership role in commodity shipping. The real or misquoted numbers in oil production and resulting lower prices to consumers is having an adverse effect on transport to market, which is depressing the fees charged for chartering your ships. If shipping demands increase, you will be forced to buy new ships at far higher prices, right? Additionally, you will be fighting to buy ships precisely at the same time everyone else will be. I suggest you lease them out for temporary storage during this slow time so that they can contribute to the debt service you owe on them. If anything, look to buy more ships at pennies on the Real and lease the space back to oil producers who can't sell their oil currently. Remember the buy and hold strategy of Buffy Worthington. Buy quality and hold until good times return!"

"Yes, Otto, of course. Who could argue with the success of that investment genius, the oracle of Anchorage? She was dogmatic in her teaching but is to be admired. But I do not see that happening any time soon as the oil production numbers overall indicate several years of surplus. The Arab nations are continuing to produce at very high levels. If I sell the ships now, I can use the funds for some of this alternate investment you speak of."

Otto gently tapped his fingers on his desk as he reminded, "Thiago, you do recall Buffy's basic lessons on investments? She always taught buy low, sell high. Everybody is selling so now is the time to buy. You are in a good cash position, consider following that strategy. I will send over the entire findings and recommended investments for your review. Call me with any questions, my wise friend." As Otto disconnected, he still felt an annoying tingle at the back of his neck. He hoped he could find the answer to that unasked question soon.

CHAPTER SEVENTEEN

Can You Be Cheated if There is No Thief?

...The Enigma Chronicles

Otto's third attempt finally was able to break into Wolfgang's deeply focused analytical probing exercise that always appeared to onlookers as if he'd slipped into a coma with his eyes wide open.

Otto smiled and said, "Ah good, we don't have to bury you sitting up. Well, I can only assume that you have been highly focused on our newest challenge and that all your cerebral neurons are close to becoming neutrino particles capable of penetrating our data center. I hope you won't think me impertinent, but after four or five hours of your laser-like attention on the computer screen, don't you think a short respite for food and oxygen are warranted?"

Wolfgang blinked a few times and then asked, "What day is it, Otto?"

Otto chuckled a little and replied, "You know what's funny? I know you well enough to understand that you may not be kidding. Now, if it were Quip, I'd say his intensity was due to re-indexing his porn collection. So, what is it that has you focused so deeply, old friend?"

Wolfgang spoke thoughtfully. "I haven't seen him re-indexing his adult content collection much since he and Eilla-Zan moved in together. I expect there is a cause-and-effect relationship there."

Otto stared at Wolfgang in disbelief. "Am I given to understand that you assisted in the re-indexing of Quip's porn collection? You? Mister prim and proper? In all the years I've known you, I have never ever heard you say anything harsher than 'poop' and that was because you tripped, fell down, and got a mouthful of it. I mean I have asked – okay, begged – to help with the re-indexing, but you?"

Wolfgang smirked slightly and commented, "I always know when ICABOD is sorting through a large data set or processing a Big Data project, because the systems become very slow. Our illustrious Dr. Quip's porn collection is one of the biggest data set re-indexing jobs ICABOD does. Ever since Quip and Eilla-Zan have moved in together, the system has remained quite responsive."

Both men chuckled at their deductive reasoning exercise. Then Wolfgang offered, "Otto, I am working from the statement that Jacob got from Mike Patrick about their systems. I had told the group during our briefing that I would look at the numbers going back a few years. I actually went back across several boom-and-bust cycles to see if there were similar supply/demand pricing activities that I could parallel with our current set of circumstances. I wanted to do all the transportation/energy commodities, but just settled on doing oil first."

Otto remained attentive during the monolog as Wolfgang continued, "I found that with all the new sources of oil that came online in the U.S., there was indeed a large surplus being reported in the oil traders' databases, as well as the government numbers. I find a couple of troubling issues in what I'm seeing. Not only is there a plethora of new companies coming online with their inventories, but all the regular producers seem to be boosting their production as well. The extra production of the existing oil producers, coupled with these new oil sources, is very easily the culprit in this windfall for the consumers."

Otto stared at Wolfgang for a moment and then asked, "But you didn't stop at that, did you?"

Wolfgang nodded slightly, gave a knowing grin, and stated, "No, it looked too easy. So I dug through everyone's production umbers and tried to match it to actual shipped product. I found I couldn't. Then I started questioning the source numbers, and that's where things start to get interesting. An event occurs which allows new technology to be introduced to the harvesting of some raw commodity that drives the cost to produce downward, thus luring new participants into production. This seems to have happened in many boom-and-bust cycles for oil production. New harvesting techniques bring in new competitors, and soon there is too much product and the price drops. Only companies with strong balance sheets survive until the next boom. Because of this repetitive soar or dive market, people typically set up special purpose corporations to shield themselves from risk spilling over into their other holdings.

"Apparently, several shell corporations were set up to complete this new surge in drilling, known as fracking in the U.S., which is where approximately 60% of the oil glut was coming from. I found it curious that the amounts from these new companies, plus the inflated numbers from the regular oil producers, exactly matches the 40% oil global oversupply that is driving down the price."

Otto's eyebrows were arching up to his hairline at the discovery. Otto interjected, "Are you going to tell me that these new shell corporations are, in fact, that? Just shell corporations, set up to pump up the numbers that couldn't be done by doctoring production numbers from the existing producers?"

Wolfgang offered, "I found some legitimate shell corporations that did, in fact, produce some actual oil. However, by and large, most of them were empty corporations with no real assets save one attribute: they dutifully reported producing oil. While I have only done a statistical sampling of all these new entities, even the legitimate shell corporations seem to have wildly inflated production numbers."

Otto stared incredulously at Wolfgang and asked, "Are you actually suggesting that this oversupply of oil is a carefully engineered sleight of hand to drive down oil future prices and current spot pricing on a global scale? The next thing you'll tell me is that nicotine ingested in large quantities is good for you!"

Wolfgang remained quiet while Otto asked, "Okay, let's just say for argument's sake that this is what is going on. Who or what is making a killing in the oil commodity markets based on this supply/demand manipulation? Who are the bandits?"

Wolfgang seemed a little frustrated as he answered, "That's what I don't understand. The answer is, no one is making out like a bandit on this. All the big players are making their usual bets, and the galaxy of small traders are either making modest profits or losing their pants and ponchos just like usual. There is no single big winner out there. The facts, at this point, do not conform to the theory, Otto, and I find it frustrating."

Otto smirked a little and offered, "Well, if I know you, old friend, you'll find that missing piece just before you have to admit defeat. I am glad I just finished suggesting multiple diversifications to Thiago, who at least has a cash surplus.

"I will say that you have done some very impressive work on this, so far. My counsel is not to give up on your theory. As far-fetched as it sounds, I think we are on the right course. We just need some more evidence."

Wolfgang nodded. "Agreed."

CHAPTER EIGHTEEN

Railroad Romance and Driving the Train

Roundhouse sat in his favorite low back chair while Mildred, his wife of 30 odd years, rubbed his tired aching muscles that began at his neck and cascaded down from there. He sipped on his locally brewed craft beer. This brew was bringing craft beer drinkers to Cut-N-Shoot, Texas from all over the Southwest. Between the neck massage and the wonderful creamy beer, the difficulties of the last five days on the railroad began to ebb away.

As Mildred expertly worked Roundhouse's tired muscles, she also began working him for what had happened. She asked, "Hon, why did they try and strand you there in Wyoming?" Then she teasingly added, "You weren't trying to cross-train one of those young fillies who's always trying to move up the ranks, were you?"

Without choking too much on his beer, he sarcastically responded, "How well you know me. You know a man can only resist so long those five-foot tall, two-hundred-pound beauties in their grimy overalls and coal dust-caked hair, as they spit out part of the chaw that has been carefully stored in their sagging jowls. I mean, what a turn on to see a toothless smile beaming out from a face that has been carefully made up with coal-based mascara so that no skin shows through. You're lucky I came back, honnnney!"

Mildred made a gagging gesture to confirm her feelings about the all too vivid mental picture Roundhouse had described. After a slight smirk and grin, she persisted, "Okay, what I want to know is, what is going on with the price of coal? I don't understand why they have cut back on your hauling runs. Heck, even with those cutbacks there is still an oversupply. I've been talking with the other engineers' wives and sweethearts, and their story is just like ours. Less work because of the oversupply. I even posted on my social media to see if it was the company's competitors running ninety to nothing. But nope, they've started to flame me and your company about hauling out too much!"

Roundhouse, trying to stay in the numb zone, appeased, "Mildred, we have some savings, so we aren't going to starve. Besides, if things get really bad you can always go back to being a massage therapist again, just like when I met you."

Mildred made a sour face and retorted, "Funny how when we talk about making ends meet, I always get volunteered to going back as a massage therapist. What if I wanted to be a high-class call girl pulling down a six-figure income? I mean, think about it. You can make a fair bit of money just having your clients naked. But if I up the ante and get naked too we could really bring in some money!"

Roundhouse sat blinking and was unable to respond to his wife's outrageous comment. True, she was still a looker and had kept herself in shape. Why, at the last dinner dance event in town, all the guys were clapping him on the shoulder and offering their praises for his having such a fine woman. Realizing Mildred was overwrought, he decided to soothe the situation and smoothly speculated, "A six figure income? Boy, I could pay off that new bass boat in no time. Would we have to set up our own brothel? I don't know much about running high class call girls, but I'm willing to learn. But before we get started in our

new joint adventure…get it…*joint adventure*…perhaps you best
show me some of the inventory you're going to be renting out?"

Mildred's annoyed mood softened greatly as her rose-shaped
mouth gentled into a grin. She ran her fingers through his hair
and quietly whispered, "We don't have grandkid duty tonight.
If that offer is real and still good, then let's skip supper and go
right for the dessert. What do you say, handsome?"

Roundhouse smiled longingly at Mildred, and with more
grace than expected from someone of his large size, he swooped
her up into his arms and promptly marched them back to the
bedroom.

```
HMX ↓ -7.50
CMX ↓ -3.33
HCC ↓ -3.90
SOX ↓ -7.74
```

ICABOD commented to Quip, "Dr. Quip, I have uncovered
new information about one of our target commodity oddities,
that being coal. It is not one of your usual sources, but it should
not be surprising that social media can be very informative in
the posting for current or top-of-mind events. In the more than
four hundred current top running social media applications I
am interrogating globally, I have observed some basic parallels
to the rural party-line telecommunications that use to exist before
landlines became common, and way before cellular technology
allowed everyone to have their own phone.

"Social media is an excellent vehicle for sharing, in real-time,
the important life events that people experience. Depending
on the age of the users, their friends and family, as well as the
media of choice, it offers some insights. The users can distribute
in a one-to-many fashion rather than tell each person in sequence.
However, as an emotional outlet for perceived unfair or unjustified
circumstances, social media has evolved to become a stage or
forum to air grievances, and it can invite disinterested parties to

the conversation. As a monitoring tool, social media can be leveraged to aggregate similar information and distill it into quite useful reconnaissance without alerting the advertising parties."

Quip blinked at the excessive diatribe that ICABOD had launched into and abruptly offered, "What you are saying is that the plummeting coal commodity price chapped somebody's ass, and they put their complaints into social media de jour?"

ICABOD remained silent for a moment, then suggested, "Dr. Quip, there isn't enough Big Data arrays from the past and present for me to sift through to come up with your rather vulgar but succinct situational analysis.

"I am willing to wait for some more of your pithy evaluations, or I can continue if it would please you. I know of your dream of being a late night talk show host, so I would judge that this is good therapy for you."

Quip groused, "ICABOD, you don't have to boil the ocean every time we are looking for clues in our information searches. I have you sift through mountains of data so I don't have to. In those areas where we are looking for obscure clues that are needles in the proverbial haystack, it is unnecessary to tell me all about the haystack. Just net it out so we can take that information to our next decision point. When we need more background on the information point, I will ask. Understand?"

ICABOD acknowledged, "Understood, Dr. Quip."

About that time Wolfgang joined Quip in his office and proudly stated, "Well, I've finally got some financial leads on the coal commodities problem. It looks like it all started back in 1880 when they first began hauling the product to market. There was a high affinity with hauling oil as well. The financial dealings with both of these commodities apparently lends itself to weight shorting, delivery irregularities, and some financial sleight of hand.

"Brokering commodities seems to be a good ol' boy network that is quite resistant to proper weights and measures, which suggests a high correlation to organized crime. With the growth in populations and settlements into communities and cities, the demand has increased. With that demand, the control over a given commodity has centered on those that seized the opportunity early on. From there, the industry created a significant lever for control. The resulting back-room deals lend themselves rather handsomely to income tax evasion and price setting as a way of life."

Quip's eyes glazed over as Wolfgang's offering closely approximated ICABOD's earlier monolog. Wolfgang continued, "Now these Dark Matter Organizations don't appear to be part of the commodity gaming institutions that are in current operation. My beginning assumption was that the financial footprints of these DMOs must be as cloaked as these operators are.

"I built a reverse financial algorithm to only look for non-associated money movements, but only on a parallel and not necessarily parabolic course. And *voila!* A pattern emerges that is almost identical to these commodity anomalies. So now what I want to do is ..."

Quip, unable to take any more, barged into Wolfgang's analysis. "Wolfgang, stop it! I now know what's wrong with ICABOD. He's been listening to you. I no sooner get done lecturing him on just netting out his research, when you come in here boiling the ocean right behind him. For God's sake, I'll trust your methodology if you two will just tell me what the answer is that you have found."

Wolfgang was about to comment on Quip's complaints when Jacob and Petra strolled into Quip's office, oblivious to the turmoil.

Petra happily announced, "We've run our background analysis on the ePETRO company and their falling oil price with some important success.

"It all started back in the 1880s when…oh, Jacob, you give them all the background information leading up to our discovery of…"

Quip was ready to call emergency services to ask for a defibrillation device and an antidote for caustic background research from one's associates.

He loudly proclaimed, "Can someone in this room just provide the net-net statement of their research and spare me the endless soliloquies on how you got there?!"

Otto showed up at the door to the office and blandly stated, "I can. Lunch time!"

Otto smiled at everyone's silence. "I could hear Quip's anxiety from all the briefings, so the answer is, let's all go eat and I will fill you in."

CHAPTER NINETEEN

Smooth Talking While J-walking

Otto briefed the team following a conversation from Eric and Stalker. "Stalker interviewed a lady at the Chicago Mercantile Market and feels something else is behind the dramatic shifts. He forwarded the data the geeks in his back office discovered which you can review."

The team sat quietly reflecting on what they had heard from Otto and quickly scanned the documents.

Jacob was the first to respond. "Stalker's digging yielded the view into the environment which believes that trading on dubious numbers is immaterial so long as you do it faster than your competitor. Is that too simplistic an interpretation?"

Wolfgang added, "It is what we have suspected. Skillful data tampering that people are simply not used to questioning. We are seeing the old habit of doing it the same old way and not questioning the outputs. Because no one ever questions the inputs is the exact vulnerability that is being exploited here.

"I don't know what is more frightening. The fact that an exploit is being conducted in plain sight or that no one is willing or capable of questioning the integrity of the source information. Even the big companies with their own production group and a sister commodity trading group are out of sync with each other. You'd think they would at least be talking to one another, but they don't!"

Quip, in his normal manner, contributed, "You know what they say about computers? They make very fast and very accurate mistakes. When you shovel garbage in one, you cannot expect anything less than garbage out in return. Our technology has but made fools of us when we can no longer discern the proper path of the enlightened. Computer, heal thyself and offer but to enrich our lives, not enslave us with your digital lies."

Amused by the old joke and nonsense commentary, Jacob added, "And he who lives by the sword dies by the sword. So, he that soweth bogus numbers into the commodity markets, looking to juiceth the system for profits, shall reap bags of crap for his underhanded toil.

"Yay, but the righteous programmers and data specialists shall turn the tides of the evil doers, and the profits will turn to ashes in the mouth of the vanquished. Let me rail with furious anger upon those toads who would steal from my brothers. For I and my legion of followers will smite thee in thy crib, if we catch you asleep, and the world will know justice and peace. *Jacobs Psalm 4.096.*"

Otto and Quip's blank stares were more than enough to goad Petra into a similar soliloquy, and she delivered, "Oh, woe and boils to the evil doers that bring us to the precipice of digital Armageddon, where no truth can be had from the wondrous computing power of posting our private lives on social media websites.

"I would have you lie down in rich data mining sets of marketing research and point the way of the righteous person in quest of the lowest price point on the Internet. *Petra's Pithies 2n power.*"

Before anyone could pull themselves back from the fire and brimstone sermons delivered by Jacob and Petra, ICABOD sermonized, "I will follow you, my brothers and sisters, down through the shadow of the valley of dead processors and outdated operating systems. Though I fear no 1.0 release, I will travel with you shoulder to shoulder in this wilderness. If need be, I will drink from the bitter cup of roll back of the upgrade to the previous release. I will not shrink from a hazardous backup and restore, for I am one with my creator's disk drives. Let no one stay us from our quest for the truth. *ICABOD's Sundries* $\Sigma \infty \pi$."

Even Otto joined with the others in the uproarious laughter that ensued. Once everyone's composure was restored, Wolfgang suggested, "Let's investigate some of these data sources to see where the false data is being injected. From there, we should be able to work backwards to see who is doing the injection. However, I suspect that it is not going to be as easy as that. It is fairly obvious that this is not just your common hacker looking for a few coins. Because if it were, we would have already been trapping on their activities, but as it is all we have to go on is the supposition that it is a DMO, quite clever at covering their motives."

Otto nodded and added, "Agreed."

CHAPTER TWENTY

The Lesson

LJ practically blew past Alisha in order to see Takeru. Knowing that he couldn't appear too adversarial with the director, he recognized he had to restrain his manner, yet convey his annoyance with how the shipping incident had been handled. As far as LJ knew, no one had challenged or confronted Takeru and lived to talk about it. He felt this was like a fork in the road, in that he couldn't just meekly accept the orders to terminate everything for his own self-esteem. This would also prove to the director that he was a driven associate not to be trifled with.

LJ had played the situation over in his mind several times and felt that an aggressive posture about the event, tempered with restrained respect for the director, might convey loyalty but mild indignation at how he had been treated. An apology to Takeru would be seen as weakness. He had decided to be bold. The stage had been set, the verbiage well-rehearsed, and LJ was firmly into character. The problem was that the audience had come to see a different play.

Takeru had actually taken his usual stare off the computer screen to watch LJ's approach. In a flash, the director had correctly assessed LJ's mood, judging from his quick breaths and aggressive posture during the approach across the data center into the open offices. As LJ came to a stop in front of Takeru, he almost had enough time to begin his protest but never got a word out.

In the blink of an eye, Takeru had quickly unsheathed a beautiful *katana* from its handcrafted wooden display in one single fluid motion. As with most activity done by Takeru, he dispassionately wielded it so as to drive it downward straight at LJ's neck. The *katana* would have cleaved him down to his lungs if the effort had continued. Takeru stood, hardly breathing, with the sword blade resting on LJ's shoulder.

Alisha had maintained a respectful distance from the two men, knowing that they were going to exchange words, so she was able to witness the near-fatal display. Even though she was a powerful enforcer in her own right, she could just only contain her astonishment. Nevertheless, she expelled a short, low-volume shriek of fear. Takeru stood motionless as he gently rotated the finely polished blade to catch, then reflect, the dim computer light into LJ's eyes while he had the blade on LJ's shoulder.

LJ had always been good under pressure, whether it was selling spiritually blessed glassware to unsuspecting religious types, playing a role as a chauffeur to kidnap someone, or even dealing with powerful criminals. This time seemed different to him.

Not breaking a hint of a sweat, he rotated his head to gaze at the blade and remarked, "Now that's a right fine-looking sword, Mr. Director. I'm probably not wrong in saying that you wouldn't use something that nice to carve up a Thanksgiving turkey. And I'm right glad you didn't chip that fine blade by hacking into my tough, hard bones."

Takeru almost smiled and cited, "I'm glad we had this talk. You probably thought that I only ever have someone else to do the unpleasant things in my business. Rest assured, I'm quite capable of being my own enforcer when the occasion demands it. And by the way, I can speak from experience, this blade doesn't chip when it hits bone."

LJ, a little more emboldened, suggested, "I'm guessing that this here sword is not your standard flea market offering and probably has some history to it. I'd be right pleased to hear about this mighty fine sword and that carved display you keep it resting on."

Takeru pulled the sword back. Then, with all the finesse of a ballet artist, spun the sword around each arm and, as one revolution was complete, he seized the hilt with the other hand. Almost as if in a carefully choreographed scene, he whirled around and expertly returned the sword to its sheath in one fluid movement. After returning the elegant weapon to its display rest, Takeru let his gaze fall on LJ and quietly replied, "Some other time about the sword's history.

"You came in here to confront me about your clumsy approach to securing the oil tankers for our project, correct?"

LJ replied, "You know, it occurs to me that if you had really been pissed at me, I'd be LJ cutlets by now. Okay, so I was upset for how the situation unfolded. What I don't understand is, if this really bothered you, then why did you let me live."

By now Alisha had wandered closer to the two men. She struggled to quell her anxiety about LJ nearly being cleaved in two by Takeru. Noting her proximity, but not taking his eyes off LJ, Takeru said, "Sometimes the best lessons are the harsh ones. I am not prepared to replace you two because of your unrestrained enthusiasm. However, a few lessons in digital stealth will be necessary for us to be successful. You are like so many I bring into my organization. You are in a hurry; you want to do everything in one fell swoop. That causes you to neglect the simple truth that exceptions get flagged in the digital world.

"For our purposes, small moves look like other events, which allows our activity to fly under the radar of those looking for the anomalies. Hiring all the tankers at once, from one company, when no one else is contracting is like taking an advertisement out on the Internet saying 'We be doing questionable stuff here.'"

LJ protested, "But I couldn't get them at the price I wanted without hiring all of them. Otherwise, I'd have to…"

Takeru interjected, "Yes, go to multiple places. A clever man, which I think you are, would realize a smart man would use different aliases. Your big single score of chartering their whole fleet at once, with your traceable company, would be far too obvious to go undetected.

"Understand, I saw your clumsy activity in real time with my SABOTAGE software, correct? I aim it at a generic area of interest like oil future prices, and it shifts through mountains of Big Data in real time looking for unexpected and illogical activities, cross references them for validity, and then postulates what you Americans would call WTF."

LJ grinned slightly and offered, "Ah, yes, the old *Whiskey, Tango, Foxtrot* event. I know of it and have been known to exclaim it myself when the occasion demanded it."

Takeru looked as though he might have to suppress a smile but continued, "I wanted you to go back at this project with a fresher understanding of how to accomplish our objectives without exposure.

"Do not expect me to hold the sword back from our next forced discussion. Are we in agreement? No more mistakes?"

LJ slightly nodded and stated, "Thank you for my lesson, Mr. Director. There will be no more mistakes."

LJ gathered Alisha to go as Takeru took up his normal operational mode and returned his gaze to the monitor. LJ couldn't help but cast one more glance at the beautiful sword as they left the area.

CHAPTER TWENTY-ONE

Even Heavy Fog Can't Hide the Truth

...The Enigma Chronicles

Petra felt excited as their flight attendant, Cathy, wearing her crisp suit, bouncy red hair, and engaging smile, welcomed them onboard for their flight to London. Jump-Jets was the preferred charter carrier used by the team to minimize the traditional airport hassles. The seats were glove-soft white leather, with all the trim done in gleaming mahogany accents. It was definitely one of the more elegant charter carriers, ready to happily accommodate any passenger need or request. The last time she and Jacob had taken the charter, Petra had been recently released from the hospital after a savage attack. Cathy had been the attendant on that flight and was absolutely delighted as she remarked several times on how Petra had made a full recovery.

Jacob took the window seat. After they both buckled up, he held her hand in the most charming way, while turning it slightly to watch as the light refracted off her lovely ring. The rainbows created had a rich purple color he seemed fascinated with as he gently strummed his thumb across her fingers. Nothing much needed to be said, as he was content with her joining him. They worked well together, the encryption guru and her programmer sidekick, as he liked to tease. He was ready to relax and enjoy their flight since all the prep work had been done before they'd left.

Once they reached cruising altitude, Cathy provided some refreshing adult beverages and a nice selection of fruit and cheeses. She offered to provide even more substantial fare if they wished, but they declined. One of the things they enjoyed on a flight with Cathy was her ability to relate stories of other travelers. She was always quite careful to reserve the names but had quite a way with words. With very little prompting, Petra had convinced Cathy to take an adjoining seat and tell a story.

Cathy thought for a moment and started, "Not too long ago, I was on a flight with Angelina, the celebrity, and her entourage. There was the press guy, the accompanist, the costume designer, and the dog. The dog was a riot, about three pounds of determined female puppy, named Hope, who bossed everyone around. Heck, I even had to provide liver pâté for the little thing. And I don't mean just chopped liver. Hope detested not being next to her master continually. She ended up being quite the howler when her master had to take a bio break or change her outfits and makeup.

"I was impressed at how patient this celebrity was with Hope. She finally explained to me that she had rescued Hope when she was very little and abandoned at the side of a road in the country. Anyway, there was a new costume which needed to be finished for the performance that night, all blingy with sequins everywhere. It was a size that I couldn't wear even when I was six but looked beautiful when she came out strutting in it. Even Hope thumped her tail in appreciation of the dress. The sequins scattered lights everywhere, almost like hundreds of fairies.

"Hope had stopped eating to admire her master and thumped her tail to the song she would performing when she wore the dress. I was permitted to capture the song on my cell phone. I can promise you it was rocking at thirty thousand feet. Everyone clapped and whistled as the song ended. That was when Hope became agitated or more likely so worried that her master would disappear at the rear of the plane again. In a nanosecond that dog jumped onto the seat arm, then up onto the top of the seat back, where she launched into her master's arms.

"I barely suppressed my giggle as remnants of liver pâté covered the front of that white and silver dress from the whiskers of that dog. The costume designer screamed, the dog wailed, and the press guy tried to take my phone, then thought better of it. I did help clean up the costume, but it was a lost cause. The celebrity whispered in my ear while I was working on it to not work too hard as she really hated the way it pinched her, and the sequins scratched."

They all chuckled at the story, then really laughed as Cathy actually showed them the video after extracting promises of their silence outside of this group.

Cathy asked, "Where are you staying in London? It is one of my favorite cities, especially for shopping."

Petra replied, "We are staying at a bed and breakfast located not too far from the Tower of London."

Cathy couldn't help herself as she inquired, "Are you on your honeymoon? I couldn't help but notice your lovely ring."

Petra blushed and became a bit tongue-tied. Jacob would explore that reaction later as he smiled and clarified, "No, this is a business trip. We are meeting with the head of ePETRO to review some of their systems and make some recommendations based on our findings. A lot of technical stuff."

Cathy nodded and turned her head as if trying to retrieve a memory. She finally said, "Would that be with Mr. Patrick? I think he is from ePETRO and has flown with us several times."

Petra was curious and asked, "Is there anything you can share about him that would help us be a little more prepared?"

Cathy pondered for a moment and then realized it would be kept between them, so she relented, "I don't like to talk poorly about my passengers, but he and his group are usually very difficult. A really picky, demanding, not fun passenger, if you know the kind."

Jacob filed that little background fact away as he probed, "Does he fly with you often between London and New York?"

Cathy added, "Sure, that route as well as to their other primary offices. He often brings along the big wig customers, and they are almost as demanding, but not nearly as bossy. The last time he was on the flight, he not only overate, like usual, but was on the phone to several people complaining about this inadequate production report, that out-of-line partner, and all of it noted down by his secretary, Roslyn, who is another piece of work. I hope you two nice folks watch yourself around them. That woman made the most awful faces whenever she thought he wasn't looking. What a pair! If there is trouble with the company, I bet she is at the root of it."

Cathy looked at Petra and then knowingly said, "You know the kind of woman, Miss Petra. She would rather stab you in the back and walk over you on her way up? I would bet that she is capturing every bit of dirt she can on that man, to take him out at some point."

Petra smiled and thanked Cathy for the great information. She didn't want to press Cathy any further and take advantage of their growing friendship. Petra redirected the conversation to the best places to shop. Cathy was only too willing to relate the places she enjoyed. After a bit, Cathy excused herself to tend to flight duties and meals for the crew.

Jacob leaned over and kissed Petra's cheek. "Sweetheart, we are going to have to make certain we look under every stone at this facility, from server room to every laptop."

Petra grinned and nodded.

HMX ↓ -7.50
CMX ↓ -3.33
HCC ↓ -3.90
SOX ↓ -7.74

Mike Patrick greeted Jacob and Petra in the reception room and escorted them back to his offices. His office was nicely appointed with a huge window view of London. The conference table was marred by repeated use, as were the chairs. The chair cushions were worn leather and surprisingly comfortable. When the weather was clear, one could likely see quite a distance, but today's view was thick with fog. A rather imposing figure of a woman entered and smiled as she reached out to shake hands, while simultaneously appraising and categorizing the guests. Petra was too thin, too pretty, and too self-assured to be anything but an assistant.

She grabbed Petra's hand and stated, "My name is Roslyn. Mike can't do a thing on his own without me. I'm sure you can relate."

Petra matched the grip and quietly replied, "I am not certain how I might relate to that, but nevertheless you may call me Petra. I specialize in solving encryption algorithms and creating encryption processes and routines. Jacob thought my skills might prove useful in this effort."

Roslyn frowned at being outmaneuvered by a woman she had underestimated. She dismissed her error and turned to Jacob. She extended her hand and greeted, "Jacob, Mike mentioned how instrumental you were in solving an issue he worked on when he was in New York. A pleasure to meet you, sir."

Jacob shook her hand and gave her a cursory smile. "Nice to meet you, Roslyn."

Then he turned toward Mike and asked, "Mike, you indicated you had some problems reconciling the oil supposedly being produced and shipped versus what the summary reports are stating. Petra and I, as I mentioned in my response to you, need administrative access to the servers and any login and password information that is used by the members of your consortium. I believe that…"

Roslyn let out a screech and protested, "No way. I will be happy to work with you and give you access to the necessary accounts, but if I think it is not relevant, then you won't get access."

Then she turned to Mike and firmly stated, "These people are unknown to me, and I have no way of validating their intentions. I would be doing a disservice to you and ePETRO if I allowed any of this to take place. Marge will stand…"

"Roslyn, shut up!" Mike stood to his full height and, with the extra weight he was carrying, looked very imposing. He leaned toward her and continued, "You may think I can't do a thing without you, but this outburst of yours is one of the reasons I requested Jacob's help. It is my ass on the line here. Marge gave me full authority, and frankly, I don't need your permission. Now you either turn over full access to every single piece of information and show our guests where the systems are located, or I will have to escort you to the door as well as dismiss you. Your choice!"

The red of her current power suit actually dimmed compared to the blush that blossomed on her pale skin. She appeared to have sunburned right before their eyes. Jacob and Petra, ever the professionals, turned away slightly to pretend to admire something on Mike's wall. Roslyn struggled to regain her composure while Mike stared her down. She swallowed rapidly but, to her credit, did not shed the tears brimming in her eyes. She squirmed a bit and then cleared her throat.

Mike, unwilling to give up his advantage, demanded, "Well, what's it going to be, Roslyn?"

Taking a deep breath of composure, Roslyn quietly replied, "Mike, I see what you mean by access.

"Let me get that information for you two right away. Would you like me to get you something to drink or perhaps a snack?"

Petra felt a little sorry for the woman. She quietly replied, "No, thank you, Roslyn. I think we will be fine for a while. Let me follow you so you can show me where we will be setting up. Jacob, why don't you and Mike finish talking, and I'll be back shortly."

Jacob turned toward Mike and confirmed, "Mike, we will be looking at everything. I got your message, and Roslyn seems to be on the up and up, just protecting you. But we will check it all. Petra and I did review what you sent. We prioritized which files to review and in which order. Petra is an expert on encryption."

They continued a discussion on the files and the access required. Jacob reassured Mike that they had their own laptops and clarified network access. Mike had set them both up with guest access but promised Roslyn would come through with full access. Petra showed back up at the doorway and waited.

Jacob gave her a private smile, then turned back to Mike and promised, "We will find out why the numbers are off and provide the data, regardless of who is to blame."

As they settled into a small but private office and began to access the systems, Petra commented, "Wasn't that interesting?"

"Yes, it was different than I expected. I thought they might come to blows."

"Jacob, she could be hiding something big to protest so loudly."

Jacob nodded, then said, "Then let's locate the proof and go back to the hotel for some rest..."

Petra laughed aloud, play slapped his shoulder, sighed, and then muttered, "You have such great ideas, and now I am distracted."

CHAPTER TWENTY-TWO

Dressed for Success

Lara had busied herself all morning with the designs for the fall line-up for her Ladies of Leisure line. This entire week they had focused on each of the women's clothing venues, from business to the swimming pool, with the final look wrapping up everything she had planned. Her papá had invited her to lunch three times this week, and she'd had to cancel each time. This was Friday and there would be no cancelation. She was ready for a change of scenery and conversation. She wondered if she should invite Carlos to join them but then decided to put that off until later. Something was distracting him, but she'd not had a chance to do anything but finalize these designs.

A quick glance at the clock informed her she had ten minutes to freshen up and head out for lunch with Papá. They had agreed to meet at Speranza for one of their favorite indulgences, pizza. Her papá, Thiago, had been eating pizza there since they had opened more than fifty years ago. Even though Thiago had been overcoming some health problems, which included eating better, he had somehow talked his physician into allowing pizza now and again. The bigger problem with Thiago's health had been poor resting, stress from running a hugely successful business, and high quantities of traditional Brazilian coffee. He tended to like it strong and thick enough to butter his pastry with it. To be allowed his pizza, he willingly ceased coffee and actually only had a couple of cups of tea now in the morning.

Fluffing her hair, touching up her lipstick, and taking a serious look at her dress, she smiled. This dress was one of her designs from her spring collection. It had the bright shades of yellow, orange, and red flowers loosely outlined with black brush marks. The top displayed her bust in an elegant yet unmistakable manner. The shirt was cinched in at her narrow waist with a leather belt of red which was the same color as her earrings and lipstick. Her well-manicured nails had a similar shade of red gracing the ends of her long, tapered fingers. Her only piece of jewelry was a hammered silver necklace Carlos had given her when they were in Mexico and first getting acquainted.

She turned on her toes and headed out of her office with the intention of walking the short distance to the restaurant. The walk would do her good while she watched the people strolling through the business district of São Paulo. Lara noticed her papá patiently waiting just outside of their destination. He looked fit and trim in his off-white linen suit and his graying hair, trimmed but on the longish side. Lara noticed the women admiring him as they passed and turning their heads to get the alternate view, but they were not being too discreet about it.

Thiago clucked his tongue as Lara gave him a quick hug and a brief kiss to his cheek. He murmured, "Do you have to look so spectacular, causing all these men to stop short when they see you reach me? Where is that delightful man of yours? He would certainly minimize your entourage."

Lara laughed and retorted, "Me! You are the one that the women are getting whiplash from, trying to capture your attention as they crane their necks to see you from all sides.

"I wanted a nice lunch with you, Papá, and Carlos has been busy working on something he has refused to share thus far."

As she frowned slightly at the statement, he took her arm and tucked it into his. Thiago negotiated the door for them as they waltzed inside the building and zeroed in on Speranza. Thiago was greeted by name and shown to his reserved table. The noise level was tolerable, with random laughter in intermittent intervals. During the business day, there were, of course, no children, which also kept the noise levels subdued.

"I love this place, Papá! I was thinking of the pizza I should order all the way here. Do you think they still make the cheeseburger kind you introduced me to when I was younger? I haven't had it in such a long time."

Thiago grinned at that fun memory. He had taken care of Lara for so long and they had shared so much. He once thought she could take over his business, and she still could, but Destiny Fashions kept her busy as she won award after award. He was so proud of her.

"Yes, my darling daughter, I am certain you can have that and even a bowl of ice cream if you wish. Now though, what would you like to drink?"

At that moment, the waiter appeared and they ordered their beverages and pizzas, which they decided they would share. Moments later the waiter returned with their drinks, and Thiago offered up a toast to a good day. Lara smiled as their glasses touched.

"Do I need to call Carlos and ask him to join us? I was not trying to be remiss."

Thiago waved her off with a gesture and smiled as he replied, "Not necessary. I just feel he may want to help you if you agree to take on my small task. It should only last a Friday and possibly into Saturday morning."

Lara wrinkled her brow in confusion and asked, "Why do I get the impression you are trying to set us up for something."

Thiago laughed as he answered, "Because I am, of course. To be honest, business is a bit down, and instead of selling some of my boats, as I first thought, I have advertised for leasing them. Six people will be coming to the docks on the coast Friday to put bids in on leasing six of the tankers. I was hoping you and Carlos might meet with them and negotiate the contracts."

"But, Papá, why do you need me to do this? I have no idea of this side of your business." Her eyes narrowed as she looked pointedly at Thiago with a frown and asked, "Are you ill again and unable to travel? Did you forget to tell me about something? You have withheld that sort of information before. I can call your doctor as soon as we are finished. He will tell me."

Thiago held up his hand and quietly said, "Stop! I am not ill. I just wanted you to stay with the business a little and get Carlos to go with you so you both could romance one another. I'm just a meddling old man."

Lara grinned and asked, "Really? Is that your total story? But you must have internal people far more familiar with the shipping portion of your business than me."

"Well, yes. I wanted this activity handled quietly, and my normal team subscribes to the premise, *no sooner done than said*. So, yes, that is the whole truth and nothing but the truth.

"More importantly, I have noticed that you both seem to be going in different directions, and I prefer it when you are glowing and he looks less distracted. I think you chose well, Lara."

Lara nodded and smiled. Their food arrived, and they both savored every single bite of the delicious pizza in between continued conversation and storytelling. After they finished up their lunch and hugged at the door, Lara promised to help with the ships and take Carlos. Thiago promised to cover a very fine hotel close to the docks.

HMX ↓ -7.58
CMX ↓ -9.33
HCC ↓ -3.30
SOX ↓ -7.74

Lara finished up her shower and evening rituals, then waited for Carlos to return to their bedroom. He had promised he would be up shortly after his rush to his downstairs work area. She had applied the lotion he liked best and carefully dried her hair. The pillows were fluffed on his side as she leaned against hers, reading the latest romance novel from her favorite author. The steamy scenes were just what she needed to ensure she would remain awake awaiting her love.

Carlos finally entered the room and was surprised but pleased that Lara was awake and welcomed him with a smile. "Sorry, my darling, to be longer than I thought. Are you enjoying your story?"

"Not as much as you will enjoy my story, when you finish your shower and come to bed." Lara smiled that delightful provocative smile he knew so very well.

While Carlos removed his clothing, Lara related the request from her papá, which he readily agreed to. He even apologized for neglecting her and promised to hurry. Carlos vanished into the shower, leaving the door ajar and showing off his muscles in the mirror. The angle of the mirror provided Lara with a voyeuristic view of her man with his sinewy muscles and black hair. The slight steaming from the hot water dimmed but did not obliterate the view. He was powerful, handsome, and extremely sensual.

Lara could feel herself get moist at her core. Between reading her saucy novel with its graphic descriptions and looking at Carlos as he toweled off, the hunger in her eyes was clear as Carlos emerged from the bathroom. His desire was evident in his hardened erection and the dark desire in his eyes. He noticed that the sheets had slid down, revealing the dark area of her aroused nipples.

In his most seductive growl, he whispered into her ear that the novel must be very interesting and asked if he had a chance of capturing the desire he saw.

Lara leaned into him and pressed her naked body against his length and suggested, "My prince, you are the only man for me. I would like to show you some of what I read to see if it meets with your approval."

He held her close and offered, "By all means, take the lead and show me all the details you wish, my love."

She began by kissing his wonderful mouth and outlined his tongue with hers. While he stroked her gently from hip to breast, caressing first one then the other, she pressed him onto his back and straddled him, pressing her moist curls against his hardened shaft and sliding up and down. Their mouths touched, and the kiss deepened until her body took over and took him deep inside.

Slowly yet deliberately she slid up and down his entire length, controlling the tempo and getting him more and more excited. She pressed him deeper into her with each thrust and rubbed her most sensitive core against him until she came apart, shattered, and took him over the edge with her. Her body continued to enjoy the pleasure until their hearts returned to normal, and he pulled her a bit closer as they shifted onto their sides.

A while later, her eyes fluttered open, and she saw he was watching her. "My prince, did you like that chapter from the story?"

He pulled her closer and offered, "Maybe I should read a chapter or more of your book. Perhaps I can pleasure you better."

Lara sighed, closed her eyes, and whispered, "You'll likely wear me out, but I am willing to risk it, my prince."

CHAPTER TWENTY-THREE

I Was a Prince

LJ remained standing, almost at attention, while Takeru gazed into his computer screen. LJ had learned early on that the director always knew he was there but would only engage once he was ready. So LJ waited to be acknowledged.

Just about the time that LJ was going to leave, as he dared not speak or clear his throat to gain an audience, Takeru spoke, though he did not turn his gaze from the screen.

Takeru softly stated, "I was destined to inherit much from my elders. Then in the blink of an eye, all changed, all was gone. I remember how cold I felt at that point in my life."

Takeru turned to face LJ and insisted, "I will win back all that was denied to me and more. I have given you an important piece of the puzzle, as I have to others in this organization. Understand – your role, along with the others, is to complete your assigned tasks in the way I have prescribed so that our actions fly under the radar of those who would try and stop me. Once we hit critical mass, it will be too late to intercept the things I have set into motion. Then the dominoes will fall, one right after the other."

LJ contemplated the statements for a moment and then offered, "I can see our movements pushing and pulling raw commodity prices globally. There is the obvious benefit to this organization of profiting from a large upswing as soon as the errant data sources are corrected. Manipulating commodity prices in this manner is nothing short of brilliant, my director."

Takeru merely snorted lightly and responded, "What a disappointment. I see that you too are as shortsighted as everyone else. You believe that my end game is merely profit in manipulating commodity prices. I guess, in a way, I should be pleased rather than disappointed in your level of comprehension."

LJ was somewhat taken aback by the comment. He tried to discern what more the director had in mind as he mulled over the comments.

Takeru appeared to be enjoying the unsettling effect his comment had on LJ. It even drove him dangerously close to actually smiling. In this very rare moment of human pleasure, Takeru couldn't help adding to LJ's moderate level of understanding as he added, "The dropping of commodity prices has a sidebar effect of offering profits to us which do help fund some of the other operations that I have fingers in. It is not the end game, my large associate. How well versed are you in global economics and finance?"

LJ, unsure of the conversation's direction, took the good ol' boy route and offered, "I know that Canadian bacon, English muffins, and French fries have to be ordered differently in other countries, if that's what you want to know."

Takeru smirked and then changed into teaching mode. "Falling commodity prices affect the two things I want to drive. The first is falling government taxes, and its companion, reversing the inflation every bloated government needs to survive. Those are the two weapons I can use to crush governments.

"That being said, why are you not out pounding down the price of oil as we discussed?"

The startled look on LJ's face was the revelation of the director's statement. Astonished, LJ slowly commented, "With falling commodity prices, such as oil and lower price points for consumables, that means lower tax collection, doesn't it? And with falling consumable prices, one sees little to no inflation, which is a built-in multiplier for increasing revenue for governments, isn't it?"

On the verge of smiling, Takeru smugly revealed, "And with falling tax revenues the over-leveraged governments have been printing money to finance their bloated budgets. We can now crater one right after the other. The result then makes room for a new ruling order, my CHARD group."

LJ was unsure if Takeru's plan was the result of brilliance or insanity. After a quick reorientation of his thought process, LJ cautiously ventured, "My director, you must have great faith and confidence to confide your plan to me. Some of the plan's dynamics seem beyond reach. Take for example…"

Takeru merely waved his hand at LJ to end the conversation as he simply stated, "My proof of concept began with Japan while I studied under my former mentor. The result is now called their second lost decade.

"If you look around today, Brazil is already in economic ruins and is busy rounding up their elected officials for trial and execution. I made sure that there was plenty of evidence for an execution by the outraged citizens. Russia and Saudi Arabia are the next easy targets because of their dependency upon oil sales, but with them, it will be a crushing outcome. But not before all the other bloated western governments are set in motion to begin defaulting on their so-called "sovereign debt". At present the worst offender is your country of birth, the U.S.

"When that has been set into motion, they will frantically try to intercept the downward spiral which will, in fact, accelerate it. The arrogant banking and finance community will be forced to write down huge losses based on their exposure to their archaic lending practices and beg for help from their government as they did in 2008. Predictably, the government will help the situation to death in typical bureaucratic fashion. Basically, the government itself will finish what I started. Then it will be my time."

LJ became a little afraid of the obvious global collapse which he clearly had a hand in. While unsure of *his* feelings in this matter, he was, however, certain that the attack plan for the CHARD group had every possibility of succeeding. Somehow, as greedy has LJ had been his entire life, there was something troubling about having his home country, the U.S., being targeted as well.

CHAPTER TWENTY-FOUR

Shared Secrets
Are a Group Crusade
...The Enigma Chronicles

arlos was careful to maintain a guard on his enthusiasm when he saw the incoming call. He cautiously surveyed the area to ensure Lara was not within earshot of his pending conversation. Once he had confirmed Lara was out of the area, he answered, "Hi, EZ. Thanks for ringing me back so quickly."

EZ was a little puzzled as she replied, "Since when do you need to send an email requesting talk time with me? After all we have been through together. I mean, we may not have ever been lovers, but we damn sure are close friends. So what is this nonsense about 'please give me a call when you have some personal time alone so we can chat?' I know we work on cloak-n-dagger stuff all the time, but call me so we can talk in private? Seriously? I made this a video call just so you can see how annoyed I am."

Carlos slowly closed his eyes at the dressing down EZ was giving him and knew he deserved it. Carlos pulled together his carefully rehearsed spiel and promptly discarded it for an impromptu discussion with a lady who never had trouble expressing her thoughts or feelings.

He admitted, "You're right. In Yaqui speak, I'm being a big Üῷ╤Ż╳ again. Let me just put the giant burrito on the picnic table so we can both carve on it. I know that you and Quip were there that night I called Juan. I suppose everyone thinks he has slipped back into a previous lifestyle we had agreed to give up. Plus, knowing Juan, he wouldn't defend himself against such a harsh opinion, but I have to ask for help on his behalf. It's my fault that he is in this mess. If you want to keep your hands clean, just tell me to go away, and I won't bother you again."

EZ, now just plain annoyed, shot back with all the anger of a mama tiger defending her cubs and their den. "Hold on, buster! I haven't said anything other than just deal straight with me. That's all! I haven't told you to go pound sand or hung up on you. But, yes, Juan left us wondering what was wrong and why we got no explanation, so what are we supposed to think? In fact, this conversation is shaping up to have the same result with you, unless I get some straight poop. What's it going to be, mister stoic Yaqui Indian?"

Carlos, now a little bit annoyed himself, tersely retorted, "Our Uncle Jesus went missing. I called Juan to leverage him and his new sleuthing organization to help find Jesus. I called him, rather than do it myself, so I wouldn't worry Lara just as things were beginning to normalize between us.

"In hindsight, if I had gone looking for Jesus, it would be Juan now calling you asking to help find which jail in central Mexico that I was being held in."

EZ rocked backwards at the statement and nearly dropped her phone. After a few deep breaths, she flatly stated, "Well, crap! Why didn't we simply start there, Carlos? I mean, it's not like we haven't had to work at pulling his bacon out of the fire before, so why should this time be any different? Right now, I want the particulars so we can begin to work this, hmmmm?"

Carlos was pondering his life's choices and wondered out loud, "You know, EZ, I'm not sure which is more unsettling; you knowing and dressing me down, or Lara not knowing and me deserving a dressing down for that which has yet to happen."

Before any more dialog could occur, Lara stepped into his field of vision with her arms folded and a cross look on her face. Momentarily disoriented, he was unable to respond to EZ.

Always flexible in odd situations, EZ quickly saw on her end of the video call that Carlos was not alone and stated, "Why don't you put this on speakerphone so we can all hear?"

Carlos grudgingly complied.

EZ stated, "It's a good bet your loving Lara has just joined us for an explanation as well. Hi, Lara. Let's get you caught up on current events. Just for the record, Carlos is asking for help in locating his accident prone brother, Juan, whom he thinks is locked up with his also missing Uncle Jesus somewhere in central Mexico. And the funny part is that he is concerned that you might be upset at the current events, so he was trying to get help without you knowing.

"I suspect he is also trying to hide the fact from Quip, Jacob and, oh my goodness, does Julie know?"

Carlos rolled his eyes and with a sweeping gesture of his arms, loudly stated, "Geezus, why don't you just tell everybody?"

Then it was EZ's turn to be dumbfounded as Quip announced over her shoulder. "Hey, that's a great idea. Why don't we all get to the bottom of this little drama?"

EZ slowly looked over her shoulder and as innocently as possible greeted, "Hi, honey. How long have you been there?"

Quip, somewhat indignant, stated, "Long enough to also be invited into the call. But, in all fairness, Lara, you were invited first for an explanation, so I can wait my turn. Please, go ahead."

Lara was stunning with her dark wavy hair, currently on the longer side with a fullness and a shine that brightened up her entire face. Her womanly shape continued to keep Carlos mesmerized. Her eyes darkened to almost black, but Lara's anger was quickly being displaced by hurt feelings. She hesitatingly stammered, "How could you possibly think I would not want you to hunt for Juan? He is not only your brother and my trusted pilot, but he has also taken a bullet for me. How dare you think we wouldn't marshal any and all resources to bring him back?

"EZ, can you help us find Juan? I suppose that means we need to get the black sheep uncle out too, but hell, he would be a bonus to the main prize."

Smiling sweetly into the video, Lara asked, "Quip, do we have your permission to use your fabulous lady in locating him? I would understand your reluctance to allow your great love to be sullied in such a sordid endeavor. I know he is a wanton rogue of questionable judgement sometimes, but I care, we all care, about Juan. I'm sure Julie would concur."

Lara looked sternly at Carlos and then added, "And, let me guess, she doesn't know either, right?"

Carlos looked like he wanted to crawl under the desk. Quip and EZ were both giving him the hairy eyeball, and Lara was making him feel like a whipped dog.

Lara was shaking her head as she added, "We will call her after this and bring her into the loop as well. Right?"

Carlos swallowed hard and nodded.

EZ looked hopefully at Quip for his agreement on the request. Quip could feel everyone's eyes on him, even those on the other end of the call. After grinding his teeth momentarily, he clucked his tongue in annoyance and proclaimed, "It would sure be tough to go through life as me if I failed to acquiesce to the group's request.

"Just as well, I've noticed how hard it is to hold a grudge against the lad anyway. So now that we have all done full disclosure here, what is our next step?"

Carlos offered, "We need to discreetly find which jail they are in. He made a call to me with a smuggled phone, I assume, but I couldn't get the location before the call ended. I was hoping to get EZ to help triangulate his location from the cell towers in the area.

"I also asked a friend of mine in Mexico to make some inquiries about him, so I have two things in play."

Lara rotated her head around to look at Carlos and incredulously asked, "May I know who in Mexico you asked to help look for Juan? Please tell me you didn't ask Manuel Sanchez to help out!"

Carlos again felt all eyes on him as he admitted, "Well… yeah…I sort of did."

Now it was Lara's turn to loudly proclaim, "Geez. Why don't you just tell everyone then? Do we have a social media website up that proclaims *Help Free Juan*?"

Quip, now somewhat enjoying the much deserved dressing down Carlos was receiving, chuckled and recommended, "Madam, let us try from our side first before we ask a novice to wander into this hunt for our lost friend.

"Carlos, can you intercept him and ask that he stand down before we fill the Mexican jail with all our friends and relatives?"

Carlos, humbled, voiced a weak response. "Yes, I will intercept him."

After they had all disconnected from the call, Lara tenderly pushed Carlos's hair back behind his ear and, gently kissing him, whispered, "Thank you for trying to spare me this worry. But as your partner, promise me from now on we share all problems. Agreed?"

Carlos nodded and, gently caressing her face, offered, "Yes, my love."

Lara smiled and reminded, "Now we call Julie. You better do a better job of explaining than what you just exhibited, Mr. Üφ̄ƵжК"

CHAPTER TWENTY-FIVE

Waiting Again at the Wrong Bus Stop

...The Enigma Chronicles

Julie studied the number of the incoming call and an uneasy feeling came over her. She asked Maude to handle the twins while she took the call. When she finally answered, she swallowed hard and asked, "Hi, Carlos. What's wrong?"

Carlos cut his eyes quickly to Lara and then calmly responded, "Hi, Julie. Can't your dear brother-in-law just dial you up to say hello and ask about my niece and nephew?"

Julie now suspected something was indeed very wrong. She flatly added, "Carlos, the last time you called me unannounced or off the weekend of your standard inquiries on our family, I believe you had Lara and Juan conferenced in, and his plane was in trouble. So if Lara is on the call with you that is strike one. Who all do you have on the call, please?"

Carlos gave Lara a sour look and dutifully replied, "Did I ever tell you that with your intuition you could easily be a Yaqui Indian?

"Yes, there are others on the call. I have Lara again, but this time I have EZ on instead of Juan. And yes, my brother is standing, yet again, at the wrong bus stop!"

Julie closed her eyes and slowly shook her head. Her anger began to build as she came back onto high alert. Her logical approach immediately kicked in as this was now all business. "Carlos, can you give me something more useful than his choice of mass transportation?"

Before Carlos could answer, EZ barged in. "Boss, what we know so far is that he went hunting for their favorite uncle, Jesus. When Juan and Carlos last spoke, both men were thought to be incarcerated in some Mexican jail.

"Carlos brought me in to help geo-locate the last signal so we can then create the plan to get them out. Lara is on the line because Carlos was trying to hide all of this mess from us. He thought we would worry too much if we knew. Now that we are all up on current events, do you want to take a turn at yelling at him too?"

Before Julie could respond, Carlos blurted, "Just so you know, Julie, Lara has my favorite walking stick and would be happy to use it again on your behalf if that will make the situation more palatable. You just have to give the word."

Julie's temper greatly subsided at Carlos's statement, but her anxiety was soaring at the present events. She chided, "Well, here we are again, looking to retrieve Juan from harm's way. I should never let him out of my sight. If I'm not laundering his identity so he can disappear, I'm heading a hunting expedition for him and his downed plane in the Australian outback, or dragging his beaten and bruised body back from a dungeon where he's been..."

Julie began quietly sobbing, interrupting her rambling tirade about her beloved husband.

EZ finally interjected as she also soothed, "Julie, I know just how you feel. We all realize he has a penchant for trouble, but you being with him on some of these assignments is simply not the answer. He is very adept and resilient, thankfully.

"Julie, don't think for a second that, under your personal aura, everything will be perfect for Juan on some of these ill-advised adventures. Look at it like this, we are on the outside and in a position to help. If you had gone, then who would be caring for Juan Jr. and Gracie?"

Julie smiled to herself and replied, "Alright, I'm done being mad, so let's get into character here and begin the search. I need to do a little homework to see just how we can get him out since these are legitimate law enforcement people holding him and not just your run-of-the-mill thugs.

"EZ, are you at risk with Quip by working on a Juan-related issue, since Quip is already mad at him? Oh, and thanks all for caring for mister accident prone."

Quip, quiet to this point in listen only mode, interjected, "Nah, I'm not mad, Jules, just concerned he returns so I can get Jacob to throttle him."

CHAPTER TWENTY-SIX

The Challenges of
Unbalanced Equations

Petra could see Jacob's head shaking out of the corner of her eye. She sensed something was amiss. They had been working for hours checking log files, firewall rules, and root access files on all the key servers and secure edge devices. His posture clearly indicated that he was seeing something wrong.

Petra turned toward him and stated, "I know that when your head is on a swivel and the oscillator mechanism is driving your cranium back and forth there is usually a discrepancy between what we are being told and what you are seeing. So, do you want to talk about it, Jacob?"

Jacob smirked slightly as he replied, "Are you insinuating I look like a cheap electric desk fan when I'm working? No wonder I can't get a date over the Internet. Ah well.

"What I'm seeing is nothing. There is nothing wrong. No firewall rule anomalies, no unauthorized login attempts, no brute force login attempts in the log files, no tampering with the log files to cover up any bogus activity, no out-pulsing of large data files at the wrong times of day, or any escalated admin privileges for anyone who doesn't already have them. Basically, the club-house has only admitted regular members."

Petra puzzled over Jacob's laissez-faire attitude towards his research and asked, "Then the color of the sky in this picture is a proper blue, or am I missing something?"

Jacob continued, "Either we have come to the wrong place of the time/space continuum in this part of the galaxy, or everything had a wholesale makeover of the environment just before we got here. I mean, it's fuzzy where I would expect stuff to be, but no one has tampered with the personality of the environmental log files. I am going to dig a little more in a couple of areas, but it appears that Roslyn is right about everything being locked down and tamper-proof."

A satisfied tone from the person behind them offered, "I told you everything was as it should be. Now you two have been at it for hours without a break. I've ordered in a light snack for your consideration. This permits you to disengage, but not have to go off premises. I know how it is to get wrapped up in something and not want to leave the building. Oh, before you go, let me get a photo of you two for my scrapbook."

Before Jacob or Petra could move away from the computer screens or stage a nice couple's pose, Roslyn had taken several photos with her cell phone.

She shooed them into the kitchen area and stated, "Not to worry, I'll log you out of the computer while you go snack."

As they moved into the kitchen area, Petra again could see that Jacob was contemplating something, so as soon as they were out of earshot of Roslyn, Petra asked, "Jacob, you have that look again that suggests you are trying to solve a programming problem. However, let me interrupt your thought processes long enough to say that, as an encryption specialist, it occurs to me that you are looking exactly where they expected you to look, which is why it appears pristine. Which suggests…"

Jacob nodded and finished her statement. "We are looking in the wrong place. How did you get to be so brilliant and pretty, my dear?"

Their flirting touches with their observations did not escape the watchful eye of Roslyn, standing at the doorway of the kitchen, as she announced, "How do you feel after your break? Do you need an evening break for dinner, or do you want to prowl some more on the systems I've provided?"

Jacob was somewhat irked by Roslyn's smugness but politely responded with a slight knowing smile, "You know, Roslyn, I think after ten hours of this we need to relax for the evening and start again fresh tomorrow. I have some ideas about a different attack vector that we can launch tomorrow."

Roslyn was uneasy with Jacob's disarming attitude toward tomorrow's exercise.

NMX ↓ -7.58
CMX ↓ -9.33
HCC ↓ -3.90
SOX ↓ -7.74

Jacob and Petra arrived the next morning to a facility in turmoil bordering on chaos. A different administrative assistant greeted them but was very distracted. The admin deposited them not in their workroom, but in Mike Patrick's office.

Mike was slightly disoriented and seemed to have trouble focusing on the discussion at hand. After a few rambling sentences, Jacob raised his hand to halt the discussion and bluntly asked, "Mr. Patrick, it doesn't take a genius to figure out something is desperately wrong. The bobbies boiled past us on our way in with very agitated looks. Can you share what the problem is?"

Mike was nearly speechless as he blankly mumbled, "She's gone...so much left unsaid...um, I wouldn't have let her go...I can't believe...no one should have to go like that...it's all over so quickly and before you're ready."

Petra was the first to grasp the situation and softly offered, "I'm sorry for your loss, Mr. Patrick. The bobbies were here to tell you about her untimely demise, weren't they? You were lovers, weren't you?"

Jacob had trouble hiding his astonishment at the statement.

After a moment, Mike volunteered, "We went to a lot of trouble to camouflage that relationship. How did you know?"

Jacob, moving his astonished gaze from one person to the next, was watching the dialog going on as though it was on a daytime soap opera and wondering what the next outrageous statement would be.

A single tear ran down Mike's cheek as he tried to pull himself together. He looked at Jacob and challenged, "You probably think our relationship was funny, don't you? Two large mammals, trying to mate for some desperately needed affection not offered from anyone else? It's all my fault. All of it! If I hadn't pressed her on the access rights issue for you two, she would have ridden home with me. But instead, she took the underground tube because she was in a snit." Mike's voice trailed off as he absent-mindedly added, "...jostled and fell in front of the incoming train.... No time left to say sorry."

Jacob and Petra glanced at each other and then back to Mike repeatedly during the ensuing silence. Then, almost as if he had just woken up from a trance, Mike stated, "Well, you have your work that is still waiting. You have a new administrative assistant, Laurie, to help you conclude probing this problem, so don't let me slow you down. Let me know when you find the source of the problem."

Almost on cue Laurie showed up. Early twenties, dressed in business casual in grey tones, short black hair, just over one and a half meters and trying for trim, she ushered them to their work area. As they were getting settled in, Jacob turned to Laurie as he matter-of-factly stated, "I'll need a copy of the accident report and a phone number of the officer investigating Roslyn's accident when you get a chance."

Laurie's look of astonishment told all, and she was about to protest the request until Jacob lowered his head and gave her his *I'm not kidding* look that preempted any discussion.

After she left, Petra asked, "Why do you want that? We are supposed to be looking in their data systems, not into underground rail accidents."

Jacob pondered her comment for a moment and then thoughtfully offered, "We now have an unbalanced equation. Yesterday, we had all the pieces but were looking in the wrong place, as you said. Today, we were going to look in the right place, but one key piece is missing. My hunch is that something rebalanced the equation for us, so we would continue to look in the wrong place. It all looks too convenient."

Petra caressed Jacob's face and smoothed his hair back behind his ear as she said, "How did you get to be so brilliant and handsome, my dear?"

CHAPTER TWENTY-SEVEN
Point Taken...

Wolfgang shook his head in disbelief as he continued to review the digital update provided earlier by ICABOD. The news couldn't have been more poorly timed. Otto and Quip poked their heads into his office and invited him to lunch but received no response.

Otto and Quip looked at each other, and then Otto remarked loudly to Quip, "Looks like another later-than-usual lunch for us. I would have liked for all of us to leave for lunch on time, but, nooooo, we're going to have to disconnect Wolfgang from his information feeds, and that can't happen until he tells us all about it. Well, go ahead and spill it, old friend. We're hungry."

Quip, not anxious to relive all the gory details leading up to Wolfgang's mind meld with the monitor, hurriedly asked, "Can you just net it out for us, so we don't have to start again in the 1880s, like everyone has been doing here of late?"

Wolfgang moved his field of vision to rest on them. Then in an annoyed tone, he stated, "Of course, it can wait while I enjoy the munching, crunching, and smacking noises you share with everyone at the table while you power down the animal fat required to further harden your arteries!"

Again, Quip and Otto exchanged glances between themselves. Quip sarcastically asked, "So, what's your point? I do not subscribe to the overused *eat right and exercise* approach to a balanced lifestyle, because you die anyway!"

Otto intervened as he gently offered, "Old friend, I see you are over-amped on some of these assignments, and it pains me to see you all-consumed. Please, come join us for a relaxing lunch, and we can discuss your latest discovery. It would please us if you would join."

Wolfgang smirked lightly and confirmed, "You're right. ICABOD has been scouring the planet looking for useful information feeds to help with my analysis. Frankly, the problem is that he is too good at his job. I'm being bombarded with more than I can process. Yes, it is time to take a break."

Quip cheerfully suggested, "Wolfgang, perhaps we could augment your current cranial processing capacity with some neural implants to boost your thinking horsepower. I'm not talking about vacuum tube technology here. I recommend the high-grade silicon baked in gallium arsenide and thoroughly coated with some highly effective but greasy olive oil derivatives before bolting them onto the back of your skull. The battery pack you can wear when mobile like a backpack, or just lean it against your desk when you are working.

"ICABOD and I have been desperate to try this on someone, so how about you? I'm sure that you would then be capable of easily keeping up with…"

Wolfgang, rapidly tiring of Quip's insane ramble, clucked his tongue and cut off the monolog. "What's on for lunch, gentlemen?"

NMX ↓ -7.50
CMX ↓ -9.33
HCC ↓ -3.90
SOX ↓ -7.74

Over lunch Wolfgang tried to articulate his latest discovery. He explained, "The economic sanctions that the EU and the U.S. had against Iran have been lifted in their latest round of talks. Consequently, Iran can now legitimately offer its oil on the world markets, just as the oversupply of oil is at its worst. This puts that much more strain on suppliers, with more downward pressure on the price of oil. No multinational corporation would have dared to do business with Iran with the sanctions in place, but now with them being lifted Iran is in a position to flood their oil into the marketplace for badly needed hard currency.

"Even though the price of oil per barrel keeps dropping, they will be unable to resist selling into the marketplace. From their perspective, of course, some money is better than no money for their only marketable raw resource."

Quip added with his usual comedic observation, "Yeah, I see what you mean, since no one is interested in buying extreme religious beliefs or terrorism, which are free exports anyway. They really do need some more viable products that are desired exports. When your only marketable raw resource is oil, you get branded as a one-trick pony."

Otto and Wolfgang rolled their eyes as Wolfgang resumed, "This turn of events has added legitimate quantities of oil to the world markets, not just bogus numbers. However, after being ostracized from the international markets for so long, their accounting practices have deteriorated, and they do not have the appropriate measures of financial governance to participate with other international entities. Basically, their financial checks and balances, required to play in the global marketplace, would be like having an uneducated teenager from some backwater farming community show up at a high society gala dressed in overalls while everyone else is in tuxedos and gowns. Their size may allow them in, but they would be hopelessly outclassed in participating with the others."

Otto puzzled that comment for a moment and then asked, "I admit that they may not be as sophisticated as the others of the world market, but they have legitimate product to offer. Where are you going with this, Wolfgang?"

Wolfgang responded, "If the so-called sophisticated oil commodity traders are being maneuvered with bogus figures, how can this fresh entrant into the marketplace expect to compete? I believe that their systems will be so porous that whomever is boosting the other world producers will do the same to Iran, and inflate their production numbers with yet another quasi-legitimate oil source. Moreover, they won't have the financial discipline to resist selling for an ever lower dollar per barrel price. I see them playing right into the hands of this DMO."

Quip mused, "It's as if this conspiracy is growing legs and walking off on its own. With everything you are seeing, perhaps we should just turn around and float downstream with the current instead of fighting it."

Otto and Wolfgang both turned to give Quip a hard look as Wolfgang tersely stated, "That is exactly what happened when the Nazi party came to power in Germany in 1933. No one contested their illegal activities because the economy was getting boosted by the flagrant disregard of the laws.

"Now, here we are again, things are being manipulated inappropriately, but because the results favor me currently, why should I complain? This situation is no different, because the laws of civilization are being violated with the end game that we all lose. Individuals, corporations, nations, and belligerents must be made to play by the rules, or we all end up in a world war like 1939. We are here in this place and in this time with knowledge of history that clearly illustrates that flagrant disregard for the law cannot be tolerated. The answer is always the same; either stop it early, or stop it later. The only difference is how much more effort it takes to stop it later."

Quip nodded thoughtfully and quietly stated, "Point taken."

CHAPTER TWENTY-EIGHT

Sometimes All You Get
Is a Smile and a Nod
...The Enigma Chronicles

Stalker cautiously extended his hand as he greeted the two men. Henry warmly shook his hand while Mr. Tomkins only nodded with a slight, halfhearted smile. Henry offered refreshments to Stalker as they moved to the conference room with Mr. Tomkins reluctantly bringing up the rear of the procession.

Once seated, Stalker offered, "Gentlemen, thanks for taking time out of your schedules to meet with me. As indicated over the phone, I am investigating the coal price collapse and the associated important field research. What can you tell me about your supply overages?

"Claudia, at the Merc, showed me the results of your work. She also assured me you were historically timely and ethical in your reporting. Frankly, I'm quite interested in how you were able to contribute to the understanding of the supply problem."

Stalker listened to Henry's recounting of production numbers, while at the same time he noticed an increasingly icy, detached attitude from Mr. Tomkins. The more animated Henry got the more withdrawn Mr. Tomkins became. Finally, Henry paused enough for Stalker to ask a few questions.

"Which one of you is the commodities broker and which one is the rail coordinator?" Stalker inquired. "Henry, based on your spirited discussion and number quoting, I would have guessed that you were the commodities broker, but that isn't the case, is it?"

Henry was puzzled by the comment and clarified, "No, Mr. Tomkins here is the commodities broker. He is the funnel for everything coal related going out and dollars coming in. I thought I said that over the phone. I'm sorry if I gave you the wrong impression, Mr. Hughes."

Stalker suggested, "You can call me Jim, Henry. Let me play back what I understand so far. You're saying this organization has not made the huge productivity gains that your numbers going to the Merc suggest. You have made a very good case that you could not have made a 40% gain in coal runs and that what is hitting the world market is simply not possible with the equipment and people you have in production. Have I misstated or misinterpreted what you have told me over the last forty minutes?"

Henry quietly stated, "That is precisely what I am telling you."

Stalker pointedly looked at Mr. Tomkins. "For the discussion going on, Mr. Tomkins, you don't seem to have much to say in this matter. As a matter of fact, for someone handling all the transactions for this organization, you have been remarkably quiet. May I know why?

"Specifically, can you explain the discrepancy between what is actually being moved and what is being reported?"

Put on the spot, Mr. Tomkins hesitated before responding. Stalker noticed the man struggling to formulate a response while keeping his emotions in check.

Finally, Mr. Tomkins cleared his throat and with a monotone voice replied, "I report what I am given, nothing more, and certainly nothing less. If this is going to be an inquisition, then I suggest you bring back a warrant so we can address these accusations with our corporate attorneys present."

Jim coolly pulled out his identity badge again for Mr. Tomkins to view a bit closer as he clarified, "I'm a sworn legal representative of the U.S. government, but you should understand, I'm not here to help you but to get to the bottom of a problem.

"Let me restate my position. I do a couple of things quite well. The one thing I truly excel at is finding bad guys doing bad things in good places, and right now you are doing everything to convince me that there are bad things going on in a good place. Now, is the rest of the equation true? Are you part of the problem, or are you going to be part of the solution?"

Stalker's words caused Mr. Tomkins to shiver. Henry stared at Mr. Tomkins and shrank away as far as the chair would allow. The look of fear on Mr. Tomkins's face was clear to both men. Stalker slowly moved his hand inside of his coat to reassure himself of access to his weapon, if necessary.

Finally, Mr. Tomkins blurted out, as tears began rolling down his cheeks. "I have to tell someone. Do you understand? I have to tell someone, but they will kill them if I do! I don't care what badge you pull out or how you threaten me with your federally sanctioned, strong-arm tactics.

"If I say anything, they die. If these brutes even think I've said anything, they die. If they think I helped you, they die." Then, almost under control and rapidly wiping the tears away, he flatly stated, "Do what you want, I cannot help you."

Stalker was not surprised, but Henry was dumbfounded.

Finally, Henry was able to gather his wits again and asked, "You have loved ones being threatened? My God! You had us all believing you were from an alien planet, which is why you never spoke about your family. I may have to change my opinion of you, but first you need to help us.

"Hell, I'll get Roundhouse in here, and we will all go kick some serious caboose here. Now open up so we can help you, dammit!"

Stalker quickly interceded, "Oh, let's hold on here. He's already told me what I needed to know. All I need now, Henry, is the mechanics of how it is done. Then I will watch and listen."

Now, each clearly studying the other, Stalker asked, "Are you okay with me watching and listening? Understand, you will need to act like I'm simply not here. All your communications, both voice and email, should go on just as if there is nothing different. Otherwise, they will sense something is wrong, and that we don't need. I'm not leaving until I get to the bottom of this, so nod your head since this is the only communication we will exchange."

Mr. Tomkins, clearly somewhat heartened by Stalker's words, nearly smiled as he nodded his head. Stalker cut his eyes between both men as he smiled confidently.

CHAPTER TWENTY-NINE

Run, Don't Walk

Alisha remained at attention waiting for Takeru to grant her an audience via his inaudible contextual clues. After several agonizingly long minutes, he turned and focused his cold stare upon her. Then he questioned, "Was London successfully executed? The links on this side have gone dark for the time being, so I am surmising you were effective."

Alisha struggled slightly to suppress the grin that threatened to erupt across her face. Under control she, in the most business-like manner, stated, "The loose end was intercepted with no serious breach in security."

Takeru almost displayed a look of pleasure with his cruel smile. He further asked, "And her cell phone? Was it retrieved as well?"

Alisha's good mood was immediately replaced with anxiety, but she managed to respond. "No, Director Takeru, but the unit was effectively destroyed under the wheels of the train. The authorities have already written the event off as a full-blown accident. If her phone had been missing it might have looked like a robbery, which would have left the case open for further investigation. I deemed it best to leave it behind, but totally inoperative."

Takeru's expression confirmed his approval of her decision. Takeru was ready to turn back to his monitor and resume his emotional feeding, but Alisha, somewhat emboldened with his approval, decided to push the envelope one more time. "Director, sir, I was in position to deal with the two investigators that were there. I believe they are still a threat to your operation, so I still don't understand why you wouldn't let me..."

Takeru snapped his head around and focused his now burning black eyes on Alisha with such murderous intensity that the look threatened to have her soil herself. In a terrifying tone and volume, he recounted, "I have you here to tidy up loose ends, not for assassinations. If I wanted two more quickly eliminated, I would contract with the Clock-Stoppers out of Argentina. They are efficient and expendable, and now that their organization has collapsed, very cost effective.

"Besides, these investigators are NOT the primary target, so I want them jostled, not executed. They will be taught suffering first, so they must remain alive. They may yet have value, depending upon who they are really connected with. At present, they are providing me with breadcrumbs to get into their inner sanctum. They're collateral damage to our overall project. It is possible they could help resolve a puzzle I have worked on for many years. My ability to listen to some of their communications has been only temporarily, I trust, interrupted.

"Your job is to carefully follow my instructions, so everything will converge the way I have planned it. As you well know, there is no room here for undisciplined actions or thinking!"

The only thing keeping Alisha's terror under control was the thought of LJ and how his cavalier attitude might handle the situation. Sensing that Takeru had finished his uncharacteristic tirade, Alisha offered, "Understood, director. I am prepared to meticulously follow your instructions, so my cell phone is not also placed under a train. I still have twelve more months on my carrier contract, and they won't let me upgrade early without a huge cost impact."

The cool response had a calming effect on Takeru which returned the usual unfeeling gaze to his eyes. After a few seconds, before returning his gaze to the monitor, he stated, "At this point in your service to me, you may count on getting your cell phone upgrade. That is all."

Alisha struggled with her emotions as she turned to leave the area as quickly as possible without running.

NMX ↓ -7.50
CMX ↓ -9.33
HCC ↓ -3.90
SOX ↓ -7.74

Quip asked in an annoyed and whiny tone, "Honey, why don't you remember to set the sensors, cameras, and alarms when you go out? I have them set to send full information feeds to ICABOD in case we get someone who believes he is more entitled to our possessions than we are. The system is also there to make sure we are not ambushed by someone when we return home. If someone who takes a fancy to you – and who wouldn't – we will have them scoped by facial recognition, and then they will be trying to jump the police instead. I can't have you at risk, babe, so please remember to arm the system. Even if you are going out for fifteen minutes, please arm the system."

EZ gave her *oh this again* sigh and said, "I just don't always remember when I'm in a hurry, Quip. And, if I'm just going to the store for a few items that I need for a special meal for us, I simply don't see the point. We live in a nice area of the city, it's well lit, and while we don't know a lot of folks here, the ones we do know seem nice. We haven't had any trouble, so what is the big deal?"

Quip, sensing his point was going to be disregarded, responded, "Bad people come to nice areas because there be things of value, and women to be harvested in the biblical sense. You haven't forgotten that episode where you and that defense contractor Keith Avery got jumped and hauled away by those

Jihadist jerks. I nearly went crazy with worry about you. I couldn't bear it again."

EZ tried to placate. "My darling Quip, we got jumped in a poorly designed and ill-lit parking lot after a long work session. This isn't criminal-ridden Washington DC. We live in a nice, gated community here in Zürich that is well patrolled. However, just because you are so insistent, I will make an effort to set the system when leaving."

Then with a mischievous smile, she coyly added, "Heck, I'll even stop flashing cute guys on the mass transit system if you're THAT concerned, sweetheart!"

Quip's mind became locked into the naughty imagery provided by EZ, but before he could say anything, she moved in close to him and seductively caressed his neck and asked, "You know it is only really naughty, flashing on the mass transit, if you're not wearing any panties, right?"

Quip took a quick breath and firmly stated, "You know, there are just some things that must be experienced firsthand, or eyed, as the case may be. I'd be willing to grade this naughty session you have described, but I dare say, we don't need to go all the way to the mass transit to extract the full impact of your demonstration. Besides, there may be extra credit involved after the demo. What do you say, gorgeous? Or, rather, can you show me, gorgeous?"

EZ grinned and said, "Actually, I was hoping for some naughty exhibitionist tendencies from my man. Tell me how you ran naked through the university campus on a dare that one night after too many brewskies, hmmm? Or, better still, can you show me?"

Quip brightened up and asked, "Would you like to leave the curtains open again so the neighbors can grade us like that time when we first moved in?"

EZ just smiled and pushed Quip over into bed.

CHAPTER THIRTY

No Holds Barred

The moonlight gently illuminated objects scattered along its deepening path. Juan mentally noted how much more lovely the moonlight would have been if the bars to his cell window were removed. He was tired and sulked as he listened, yet again, to Jesus talking in his sleep.

It was the same topics over and over again. Jesus was carrying on about top heavy waitresses carelessly brushing their breasts across his head while he was trying to negotiate silver commodity trades on a trading floor before the last bell. Juan had learned that if you had the bad manners to wake up your dreaming uncle, he would then recount the dream and spin it into a more fantastic yarn than what he had even dreamed about. His tedious recounting really made Juan miss his Julie.

Suddenly Jesus sat up in his cell bunk, blinked a few times, and then asked, "Was I dreaming again? Boy, let me tell you about this one!"

Juan made a sour face, which the light from the moon captured, as he blandly replied, "You mean this pair? Uncle, I may have to listen to you talk in your sleep, but I don't want to hear about your bra-less dream girls doing demos again, so drop it."

Jesus rolled back a bit as he positioned himself to sitting and stated, "My, we ARE in mood, aren't we? There is nothing wrong with a little recreational dreaming to fill in the gaps of missing female companionship now, is there? Anyway, that was not the interesting part. I dreamed about that slimeball Paulo from the CHARD group who took my earnest money to get me into the copper commodities trading gig."

Juan gave Jesus his *oh really* look and said, "Tell me, uncle, when did this valuable commodities broker, whom you gave your earnest money to because you trusted him, become a slimeball? If he was a slimeball before the money changed hands, then one has to wonder if he wasn't a slimeball all along. Perhaps you went from naïve to foolish with one transaction."

Jesus, who was clearly sulking while he stared at Juan, finally offered, "The information Paulo was offering from the CHARD group had a bit of insider trading flavor to it, nephew. He was telling me to short the commodity pricing, not go long. You can't recommend that unless you know something."

Juan looked puzzled as he asked, "If he was giving good insider trading information, then why were you upset with him?"

Jesus, a little miffed, responded, "Because when I saw my investment go up in value, I wanted more action, dummy. We did it on copper futures, and I really wanted to play in silver for a bigger gain. It really ticked me off that he had vanished. I mean, here is a gravy train with biscuit wheels, which I have access to, and the guy up and vanishes. And to top it off, as soon as I start making inquiries, I get picked up on suspicion of foul play in his disappearance." Then more loudly in case the walls had ears, as it is in most small Mexican towns, Jesus added, "In the process I am incorrectly identified as some notorious drug dealer named Jesus. I tell you, nephew, life just isn't fair!"

Juan lowered his face, appearing to look over the tops of his glasses if he had worn any, and quietly commented, "He was a slimeball for vanishing with his insider trading information and all your future profits? You are right, how thoughtlessly inconsiderate of the man. And just for the record, you really are…"

About that time a guard opened the cell block door and led in a well-dressed man holding a briefcase who looked very intense but solemn.

As the guard stopped at the cells, he stated, "Looks like you two boys have a visitor. Says he's your lawyer." Juan's heart skipped a beat but he said nothing. Looking at both incarcerated men, the visitor commented, "Gentlemen, I'm glad you are unharmed from this ordeal. I hope you were not too inconvenienced, but this was the only way to protect you while we sorted out the death threats against you."

The guard wrinkled his nose at the lawyer's statement as though he was unable to comprehend why this was a safety measure for these two prisoners.

Jesus was very confused and had no idea who this lawyer might be, or why the man was adding death threats to an already sour situation. But Juan gave Jesus the high sign not to say anything.

Juan launched into character with what he hoped was the plan. "Damn, it's about damn time you showed up! How about getting us out of here, so I can thank all of you and your innovative protection of us from that half-crazed lunatic we got sideways with!"

The lawyer's face screwed up a bit as he rubbed his hand across the back of his neck, as if weighing his options. He replied, "The good news is you were saved with the bogus identification we established for you, but the bad news is I need a little more time to unwind the great cover we built. Oh, which reminds me…" The lawyer then opened his briefcase and casually took out an almost impossible to buy, exquisite bottle of the fine Don Julio tequila. From the corner of his eye, the lawyer saw the look of greed in the eyes of the guard who was now fixated on the tequila.

The guard was mildly reluctant to accept at first when presented with the bottle, but the lawyer conveyed his view of the ethics of the situation and offered, "No, you don't understand. You have been guarding my employer's son and brother while we chased down the perpetrators who were trying to kill these two. My employer wanted to show his gratitude to each of you fine officers of the law. Therefore, I have brought each of you your own bottle of this fine tequila in appreciation. This is not a bribe."

With the ethical issues clearly resolved, the guard accepted the bottle, then promptly broke open the seal. He gently caressed the custom-made bottle and tasted the fine distilled liquid and nodded with a grin as he gratefully acknowledged the gift. Before the lawyer left to deliver the gifts of appreciation to the other on-duty guards, he gave a quick wink to Juan and Jesus. Jesus looked longingly at the bottle but maintained his silence. Juan helped as they struggled to keep the confidence game in play under the watchful eye of the guard.

NMX ↓ -7.50
CMX ↓ -9.33
HCC ↓ -3.30
SOX ↓ -7.74

The conference call had been going for several hours with others coming and going, but Carlos, EZ, and Julie had been on the whole time and they were beginning to tire. After everything had been set into motion, there was nothing left to do but wait on the open conference bridge.

Carlos smiled as he offered, "That was some mighty fine cross tower cellular location of our wayward lamb, being as it were."

EZ smirked as she responded, "I don't think of him as a wayward lamb, but more of an Üφ⊤Ż𝝹, to use your Yaqui Indian term. Anyway, it keeps my skills sharp since he is always helping me to exercise them. However, let's be accurate here. It was you who taught me how to do this in the first place!"

Carlos politely offered, "It's always gratifying to see the student surpass the teacher, madam. You found him faster and with less attention than I could have, so again, well done. Now all we have to do is wait until the party is over."

Julie, tired of the admiration exchange, interrupted, "Are you two finished patting each other on the back? We still have the extraction to complete with someone on the ground who doesn't do this for a living. I would prefer we celebrate later, okay?"

Carlos puzzled a little at her comment. "Julie, everything is moving according to plan. Why the harsh comment?"

Julie, still irked by the whole scenario, snarled, "Manuel is out of his element and only doing this as a favor. I hate to think I alone have to make good on it. We should have waited until I could get one of my team there instead of Manuel, the photographer by day, bogus lawyer by night. He is a nice man who is helping us out with something that never should have been. If anything happens, that nice man…"

Carlos interjected, "Perhaps you don't understand how Mexican police work, sweetheart. I'm pretty sure you have worked all over the world, but I have a bit more expertise with these people. I've worked with enough of them to know that no matter what kind of ethics training or police academy training they may have gotten, I've NEVER seen one of them refuse an expensive and rare bottle of Don Julio.

"How do you think Juan and I navigated the police in our old business model? Now, you need to trust me on this and let Manuel do something nice for you and the family. I promise he won't be looking for anything more than bragging rights to say that he helped a lost flame. He knows that a hot smooch, coupled with a grope and feel, simply are not on the table!"

Both EZ and Julie's faces erupted into a grin almost at the same time. Then they both asked in their most disappointed voices, "It's not?"

Both ladies snickered as Carlos rolled his head toward the ceiling and proclaimed, "Women." Then after a loud sigh, he added, "I love 'em because they are."

CHAPTER THIRTY-ONE

A Pirate at Heart

LJ had mapped out a plan with a focus on South American shippers at the request of Takeru. The outbound shipments of crude and other natural resources he was increasingly familiar with were lower there than in other parts of the world. He planned to strike bargains with six different organizations in South America before he went to Asia. This operation was taking much more planning than usual and he found he enjoyed the challenge.

With the help of Takeru's *Counterfeit Latin American Identification Manufacturer* software, coined CLAIM by LJ, he was able to create six different identities that included passports with stamps and visas, untraceable credit cards with sufficient limits to use once and never pay, and background details to pass the scrutiny of any individual agency of a sovereign South American country. The critical factor was in using each identity one time and destroying it before moving to the next, if needed. Each of the identities was marked with the country of use and secured in the undetectable false bottom of his carry-on.

Fortunately, LJ was a master at locating bathrooms away from any surveillance cameras, to transform himself into someone different. All his years of being a changeling served him well in this venture. Not only did he want to escape detection by the border guards as he moved between countries, but more importantly, he needed to beat the SABOTAGE program. He was certainly not able to modify his size; however, he could seem smaller, less imposing, and be ignored with the various disguises.

Deplaning at Quiriquire Airport in Venezuela, he passed through customs with ease as Ronald Roper, a contract specialist for Brayker Farming Equipment out of Alabama. He sort of liked the way the glasses made him look like a professor. Ronald was a great identity for this first meeting. He picked up a friendly taxi driver that spoke English and could take him to Carúpano, where his first meeting was scheduled. Carúpano, since colonial times, was at the door of the Caribbean. Its traditional exports included timber, sugar, cotton, coffee and even cacao. The local rum was hardly an export as the locals and tourists drank the majority of the produced product. LJ planned to sample a bit during this meeting with Rafael Perez. For LJ, the history of pirates throughout the Caribbean suited his current ventures.

After reaching the local bar and grill, Martinez, LJ paid the taxi driver well to wait in Carúpano while he met with his contact. LJ walked into the bar and searched for his contact with a timid look. Not quite panic stricken, but with the persona of someone who was clearly a tourist with no idea where he was going next. Fortunately, Rafael spotted LJ almost immediately and welcomed Ronald Roper to his table. Rafael called for rum, which was quickly brought over by a very pretty girl.

Rafael said, "From our conversation, I gathered you wish to lease two or maybe three of my cargo ships. What I did not understand is if this request includes crews as well?"

LJ, in true character, reassured, "Mr. Perez, my understanding is that a minimal crew can manage this kind of vessel. So, yes, I would like to include the crew for each. Now, I know I am from Alabama, and just a glorified bookkeeper, but I did my homework, so don't try to take advantage of me. I will need their food provisions and services for six months."

Rafael grinned and ran his hand down his scraggly beard. Though his hair had met scissors recently, he wasn't a well-kept man. He was slim, toned, and strong with a look that indicated he descended from a family of pirates. Rafael assessed whether this black businessman could be any threat. The man was big enough, but he looked slow and intelligent only in the book sense, not the street sense. He needed the money, and the three ships he had hadn't been earning their keep in almost a year. He drank his shot of rum and ordered another for them both, along with some local cuisine, before he continued.

"Sir, I can see you are an experienced businessman. I can provide crews of ten for each of the three ships and will include their provisions in the overall rate. For you, sir, the cost is a mere 99,000 Venezuelan bolívar per month for these fine vessels, along with men I trust."

LJ smiled the way he always did when he knew someone had been completely taken by his cover and thought he was a push over. If Alisha had seen him, she would have immediately recognized the signs of anger just under the surface. He drank his rum and ate a few bites of the snack with appreciation. LJ smiled and asked, "Rafael, can we step outside, and you can point out these vessels in the marina for me, to see if they are worth the nearly ten thousand US dollars per month you're asking? And isn't the wage rate for crew members here close to 50 VEF per day or 5 USD? I want to make certain I get my value."

"Of course, Mr. Roper," agreed Rafael. "These are good boats and you can inspect them further if you want."

"I'm sure we will get to that, Mr. Perez, if our negotiation continues."

They both rose, and LJ seemed to grin like a kid in a candy store. Rafael offered to precede him out the door. They circled around the building to get the best vantage point of the docks, and Rafael raised his arm and indicated the three boats flying the flags of its registry in Malta and the orange and black of his company, Perez.

"Those boats, according to my research, can be easily manned in calm seas by three men. Son, why would you suggest over three times that number. Do I look that dumb?" LJ's voice was calm, but his face and eyes were darkening.

Rafael was in his element, or so he thought, as he grinned and remarked, "That, sir, is a misconception started by men who do not know the seas or this vessel. These crafts will hold your cargo, albeit drums or cartons, with a hold that has surprising space from stern to aft. Perhaps you don't realize the real value…"

LJ snapped and quickly pinned Rafael against the wall by the neck as he suggested, "Stop with the bull crap, you pirate. I done tol' ya I did my homework. There ain't no need for you to lie to me.

"I want a crew of three for each with their modest provisions, at a rate of 25,000 VEF per two months and not a penny more. I will be adding a captain to each of the vessels to make certain my organization's interests are top of mind. How does that sound, Mr. Perez?"

Rafael had seen his life briefly pass before his eyes and was lucky his bowels had not released. He immediately recognized the precarious state of his life as LJ released him onto the ground, still pressed against the wall. Catching his breath and recognizing he was not only beaten, but lucky to still be breathing at all, Rafael offered a weak smile of defeat and quietly remarked, "That is an acceptable offer, Mr. Roper. Sounds very reasonable. I will get the crew and ready the vessel for your inspection, sir. I meant no offense, just trying to make a decent living."

LJ clapped him on the back and replied, "I appreciate where you're coming from. My daddy would expect the same of me.

Let's go finish that fine rum inside and complete our paperwork.
You do take credit cards, right?"

NMX ↓ -7.50
CMK ↓ -9.33
HCC ↓ -3.30
SOX ↓ -7.74

"Honey, I think this is going to work out swell. Did you get any
blip over the last twenty-four hours at all?" LJ had phoned Alisha
when he thought she would be alone and able to speak to him.

"LJ, there has been nothing. Takeru received your message on
the secured line yesterday and actually tried to find a break in
security. When I asked if you should continue on this path, he
merely nodded. I think you did good, sweetums. Now, should I
send those three men you identified to your location?"

LJ smiled and replied, "Send them along. I will leave them a
message at this hotel, as we previously discussed, and move on
to my next destination.

"Honey, I did get a special gift for you yesterday and shipped
it to our apartment. I think you are going to really like me filling
up your belly button and then lapping up the contents in that slow
way that seems to get you all gooey. If you really like it, I can
also think of several other places we might experiment with."

Alisha thought hard for a minute, realizing she should know
what this gift was. The idea of LJ kissing or licking her though
was so very distracting. She quickly reviewed his itinerary and
things they really liked and exclaimed, "Rum! Oh my goodness,
you got some local rum, didn't you?" Her mind was flashing
on all the ways she loved to drink rum. For her it was far more
effective than tequila.

LJ chuckled and replied, "I sho did, sweetums, and I can hardly
wait to see you. I gotta go and I'm on a roll. Save some for us,
honey."

CHAPTER THIRTY-TWO

Better Let the Ego
Leave the Building

Stalker had completed his briefing on the conference call, placed the call on mute, and sat back to listen to the discussion. After a few seconds of dead air, he became concerned, so he took the phone off mute and queried, "Um...are you folks still there? Did I put everyone to sleep with my monolog?"

Otto and Quip chimed in to re-assure him. "Oh no, you're fine. We had you on mute so we could have a sidebar conversation."

Then Otto continued, "Mr. Hughes, what we are thinking is that we need to install a couple of computer routines on Mr. Tomkins's work PC to capture everything he is doing and echo them out to another storage drive, which can be isolated from everyone else except us. I hope you won't take offense, but this DMO group is so clever that you might miss some event or transaction in background processing that is key to solving this puzzle. You just standing behind Mr. Tomkins, taking notes or photos of his screen and keyboard activity, may be a wasted opportunity, particularly if you're detected."

Quip quickly added, "The DMO blackmailing Mr. Tomkins likely has a technical tripwire rigged, just for such a contingency. I would expect that Mr. Tomkins's PC is probably infected with its own self-serving monitoring software, looking for someone to try just this kind of trick.

"We wouldn't be surprised in the least if the video camera of the PC is under cloaked control by the DMO to observe their extortion victim. It would be easy to capture such a clumsy counterattack of you watching everything over Mr. Tomkins's shoulder."

Jim nodded his head and replied, "Once we lose the element of surprise, the game is lost. Well, I'm glad I talked this through with you, gentlemen. It certainly sounds like you know your craft. I thought about bringing in some of our techno spooks from my office, but that tends to take weeks rather than hours. Also, someone this sophisticated might be watching for extra eyes to specifically engage in countermeasures. What can I do to help from this end?"

Quip stated, "We would like to get you a self-installing encrypted package. This is easily transferred to a USB drive and then plugged into the PC while it's booting up.

"Now, let me reiterate, the machine must be rebooting BEFORE you install this package. The risk of detection will be greatly reduced if you do it that way. We will ship it to you via that nifty email encryption service you use for your private communication with Mercedes."

Jim sat blinking and considering the last statement before he asked, "Uh…how do you know about that email encryption service?"

Quip grinned from ear-to-ear. "Oh, we like to look in places people don't want us looking in. It's sort of a hobby, like social media, only it takes a little more effort to 'like' it."

Otto quickly interjected, "Mr. Hughes, there are many conversational threads that give us leads to our next destination of interrogation. But, rest assured, once we had ascertained it was your alias of *Boop-Oop-A-Doop,* we scrubbed your emails from our systems."

Jim dropped his head down in utter embarrassment. He couldn't decide if it was the fact that his supposedly secret email channel to Mercedes had been uncovered, or that his pet phrase inspired by a 1930s cartoon character had been clearly identified with him.

Otto and Quip chuckled slightly at the silence from Jim Hughes on the call.

Finally, Quip innocently asked, "Mr. Hughes, are you still there, sir?"

Jim frostily responded, "I had you on mute while I was having a sidebar conversation with my now-humbled ego."

NMX ↓ -7.50
CMX ↓ -9.33
HCC ↓ -3.90
SOX ↓ -7.74

Stalker was still sulking about how much of a rookie he appeared to be in front of Otto and Quip after the call. He was still chiding himself when his cell phone alerted him to a new incoming phone call that he did not recognize.

Glumly he answered, "Jim Hughes's answering service. Leave money and I'll make sure he spends it foolishly. Your turn."

The voice smirked at the dejected greeting and said, "Funny! You said to call if I came up with anything and I did. Hello, tall, dark, and unobtainable, this is Claudia. Are you taking calls or just playing sympathy cards?"

Jim immediately went into high alert and responded, "Claudia? Okay, I'm a little surprised, but it must mean you believed me when I asked that you call me with any new information. I don't know why, but for some reason it sounds good to hear your voice, ma'am."

Now it was Claudia's turn to be somewhat sullen as she flatly stated, "Alright, back it down, mister overeager! This isn't a social call, trying one last time to derail your commitment to the real lady in your life.

"The answer to the next obvious question in your mind is, yes, I've grown a conscience since our last meeting. I did some digging into the irregularities we talked about. You might as well know that it ticked me off to be called a butter babe who no longer understood the numbers of the trade. I started out in this industry believing I was going to be the best analyst they had ever seen. You called it right when you suggested that my ethics had slipped down into my...well, it stung. Call it a sobering moment in my career. I mean, here was someone working to solve a people problem, and all I was doing was...well, you got the rest."

Jim smiled and commended, "Welcome back to the right side, Claudia. What do you have for me to help us win this contest?"

Claudia smiled, and it came across in her voice as she offered, "Your lady, she is a very lucky lady to have you.

"Let me tell you what I found. When I started here, I tried to meet and greet everyone I could to help make my impact here more significant. I have stayed in contact with many of them. After our discussions, I started reaching out to visit with them and see what was going on. Almost without exception, they all sounded and acted polite, but somehow withdrawn, almost fearful.

"For the ones that *would* speak with me, the difference in personality was quite pronounced, but only if you knew them from before. When I say before, I am willing to say that something has changed them and I saw it. I'm telling you, something or someone has infected these company representatives. They are not who I knew from before."

Jim nodded and asked, "Can you send me a list of these people? Uh, but don't tell them you have done so, or alert them of who I am, okay? This keeps your hands out of it, and I get the element of surprise. Are we in agreement?"

Claudia smiled a devious smile and asked, "What am I to be given for important recon, hmmm?"

Jim smiled and replied, "Why, I add more ethics points to your character, ma'am."

Claudia clucked her tongue in annoyance and accepted, "Oh, gee thanks. How underwhelming, but not unexpected... again. Good evening, sir." And she disconnected the call with some measure of contempt.

CHAPTER THIRTY-THREE

Saving Time Without Pushing Your Luck

It was almost mid-morning before Jacob queried, "What happened to the new AA, Laurie? She should have already been back to tell us when we would get our info and when we could speak with the detective."

Petra looked out of the meeting room doorway and caught sight of Laurie stomping back to her desk with an exasperated expression on her face. Petra said nothing but motioned to Jacob with her eyes and slight chin movement, indicating Laurie was back at her desk. Petra resumed her computer file recovery efforts.

Jacob gave a bewildered look to the ceiling, frustrated at the time wasted. He was about to go out and see Laurie when she popped her head into the room for the needed update.

Straining to keep her annoyance in check, she stated, "As a Yank, you were probably expecting a prompt, jolly response from one of London's finest detectives that he was only too glad to drop everything and personally deliver a full report. When I finally got through to the detective in question, Mr. John Davies, he listened for almost eight seconds before he gave me a response to convey to you.

"Do you understand the significance of the statement, *Bugger off, Yank*? And that was the part of the conversation that we in polite society on this side of the Atlantic can repeat."

Petra did a mock indignant look and calmly reached for her cell phone. Smiling, she looked for a number in her contact list, then casually remarked, "Well, perhaps we were going about this the wrong way. Thank you, Laurie, that will be all for now."

As the cellular call got put through to the intended party, she greeted, "Hello, Bruno, this is Petra. Are you in the middle of something?"

Jacob smiled broadly at the impending storm about to hit.

Two hours later, Laurie popped into their meeting room again, but this time she appeared flabbergasted by the news she had been told to convey. After a few false starts at trying to speak, she finally blathered, "Detective John Davies is here. He is asking to please speak with you. May I bring him in now?"

Jacob was lightly chuckling as Petra innocently replied, "Why of course, you can bring in the kind detective. We would deem it an honor to meet with him."

The detective entered the room looking almost contrite. He held his hat in his hand and with some difficulty managed to introduce himself. "I'm Detective John Davies, and I'm here to offer all manner of assistance in your investigation. I'm hoping you can assist me in mine."

He looked over the standing couple and quickly sized them up as no nonsense individuals. After a moment he conveyed, "I rather expect you are Ms. Petra Rancowski, in the company of Mr. Jacob Michaels. Where can we start?"

Petra, completely into her professional character, innocently responded, "Detective Davies, I am pleased we could meet and collaborate. First though, can you provide me a good working definition of the phrase *Bugger off, Yank*?"

Detective Davies closed his eyes and dropped his head. Then they heard a quiet sigh of regret before he quietly asked, "Why didn't you say who you two were when the administrative assistant called? Now I've got everyone from the super on down in my department in an uproar because Interpol called asking for some inter-agency cooperation!"

Then he added, "I am more than ready to cooperate in any manner. To prove my statement, here is the accident report on Roslyn Burchfield."

Petra smiled politely and handed the report to Jacob, who acknowledged the folder of documents, but didn't bother to open it before he placed it on the desk.

Jacob asked, "Detective, what did you find on her phone? The report is a little unclear. There should at least have been a picture of us on there, if you could get into it."

Now fairly agitated and struggling to keep his anger under control, Davies shot back in an accusatory manner. "You've already gotten the report off our systems? Our so-called 'secure' systems? Why then the elaborate charade of having me come down here with it? What's the matter, don't you have a printer here?"

Jacob smiled as he clarified, "It's tidier if it looks like we got it from you with full cooperation. Our Interpol connections provided a secure copy only a short while ago."

Detective Davies, seething with indignation at having been completely outmaneuvered, stated, "Then you must already know that her damn cell phone was completely crushed by the bullet train. While you both may be a master magician in the data world, I am confident that you won't be able to decompress any files or photos from this new slim line model. And I do mean slim."

Jacob studied the angry detective a moment, then politely offered, "It's a shame about her and the phone. I'll bet there would have been some great forensics to be gathered from that device. You know, there are many government agencies, especially in the defense contract arena, that won't let you bring any cell phone into the building if it has a camera. Funny thing here is that Roslyn was taking a storm of pictures, which included ones of us, so she could put them in her scrapbook.

"Like many young people these days who take so many pictures, you want to store them someplace where you can annotate and arrange them at a later time."

Petra picked up on the line of thinking and quickly added, "You would have uploaded your precious pictures to a cloud service where they could be downloaded, categorized, and sorted for…"

Jacob smiled as he finished the sentence. "…use in distorting the oil commodity pricing level. Detective, may I recommend that you quickly locate her cellular provider and search the cloud service for her account. I believe there might be information stored there which could help both of our investigations."

Detective Davies studied both of them as he pulled out his phone to make a hurried call back to his colleagues at the station. While waiting for the call to connect, he offered, "The next time someone asks me to do something for them, I will ask if it is going to help with my investigation or not, BEFORE I tell them to bugger off. It will save me a lot of time that way."

NMX ↓ -7.50
CMX ↓ -9.33
HCC ↓ -3.90
SOX ↓ -7.74

At the hotel later that evening, Petra read the text on her cell phone. "Jacob, they are ready for us to join the conference bridge."

Jacob came in and sat down near the USB speakerphone attached to the video-enabled PC and offered, "Hi, all. Quip, thanks for the electronic report on Roslyn. And you were right, they were ticked off when they learned the report was finessed from their systems, even though I left the trail pointing elsewhere. Thank you, and thanks to ICABOD, for the skillful extraction. Any luck finding Roslyn's cloud service account, and, more importantly, was there anything in it?"

Quip responded, "We know which service provider it is. We have not located anything yet, but it shouldn't take us too long."

Jacob continued, "My suspicion is that as she took screenshots of the on-premises computer screens, then she uploaded what they wanted. After which she likely returned the input demands into the system with her own account. She was using a legitimate account for work in an appropriate work area. The only problem was that her work was adding to the oil pricing problem.

"There is a high probability that the people she worked for or with wiped everything as fast as they put it into this temporary area. I'm hoping that some of the cloud provider routines captured at least some of the data before it was erased. Let us know if you have any luck, Quip."

Quip responded, "Were I you, I wouldn't stop your sleuthing activities waiting for us to find something. It's a lot like a female's hindquarters. The larger the target the more time you have to spend trying to explore all of it."

Jacob gave Petra his incredulous and appalled look at Quip's outrageous statement. Before Petra could read Quip the riot act, Jacob jumped in and interrupted, "Uh, Quip, my sensitivity training would not allow me to make such a callous observation of the fairer sex, nor allow me to even agree with such a coarse statement. Since I don't remotely have that frame of reference to draw upon, are you suggesting that you do?"

Startling Quip, EZ's voice plunged into the conference call as she demanded, "Do you want to explain yourself, buster? Help me understand YOUR frame of reference for that comment!"

With a vacant look on his face, Quip offered as an aside to the video conference, "As the unwitting male steps into a maelstrom of his own making, you are there."

Thoroughly amused, Petra speculated, "I think that's probably a wrap for this call. Good thing Jacob has exercised his sensitivity training so promptly, but it occurs to me that your evening may be a bit more spirited in its dialog, Quip.

"I can assure you all, Jacob's sensitivity training is going to be well rewarded after we disconnect. ICABOD, since Quip will soon be offline and indisposed, can you please continue to prowl for our necessary information?"

ICABOD politely offered, "Yes, Ms. Petra. I too sense the imminent demise of Dr. Quip, based on the voice tones and speech patterns of Ms. EZ. Allow me to point out that I have resisted all of Dr. Quip's efforts to teach me these male clichés and have consciously steered clear of any coarse renderings of females.

"Aphorisms, like *she is forty axe-handles across the rear end,* simply do not belong in my data banks or sentence structure in my communications with the team."

Quip was visibly trembling on the video feed and unable to speak.

EZ's voice firmly soothed, "Honey, why don't we let these nice people go about their evening work, so we can...talk, hmmm?"

Before anyone could agree with ending the conference call, Quip's image quickly went dark from the video call.

Before the voice connection disconnected, Jacob added, "Let us know if you find anything, ICABOD. And good work not succumbing to Dr. Quip's vulgar platitudes."

ICABOD responded, "I will do so, Jacob. But can you comment on the use of axe-handles to calibrate or grade a female's..."

Before ICABOD could finish his statement, Petra manually disconnected them from the conference bridge.

Petra smiled at Jacob and said, "Let's not push your luck or your resolve to be a sensitive man, okay?"

CHAPTER THIRTY-FOUR

The Long Way Home

It seemed very dark outside the small window in the cell. Likely one or two o'clock in the morning, Juan thought. Someone, hopefully Manuel, had lobbed a stone in through the barred windows, alerting Juan. A moment later he appeared at the cell door, quietly fumbling with the keys. Juan nudged Jesus and roused him from his gentle nap. The snoring from the guards echoed down the hallway. Manuel was struggling to get the right key into the cell door as he tried to control the shaking of his hands. Though Juan knew they were lucky Manuel had done so much, he wanted to make certain they could escape.

Juan held out his hand and quietly recommended, "Manuel, let me do this, and you keep an eye on the outside door. We'll be out in a moment."

Manuel looked relieved as he turned and tiptoed back out to the front. Juan easily slid the key into the external hole and turned it quietly, releasing the door. He looked at his uncle and placed his fingers to his mouth to verify their silence was to be maintained. Jesus nodded, then stood and stretched to work out the kinks so he could walk with ease when they needed to move.

Jesus had told Juan earlier that he walked far slower than when he was young. He had claimed his lifestyle of drinking cocktails on the beach while lounging all day had left its mark, not that he was an old man. Juan had laughed at the time but had noted the issue to Manuel on the phony papers he had signed earlier, hoping he might secure some sort of transportation after they escaped the cell.

Juan led the way out of the cell and down the hallway to the front door with Jesus closely behind. It was fortunate that there were no other detainees in the other cells. All three guards were harmonizing in a symphony of snoring after consuming all the tequila. Juan located his phone in the desk drawer and was delighted it still had a charge. They went to where Manuel waited at the door. From the cell, Juan had thought the night was very dark, but the moonlight that seemed to illuminate the street worried him a bit. Fortunately, there was no noise from anywhere down the street, nor were any lights visible to suggest the good people were awake. So far, the first stage of the escape was working as designed.

They exited the building and held close to the shadows, walking with as low a profile as possible. As they rounded the corner of the block, they heard a small dog yipping further down the street. They all froze. Juan and Manuel strained their eyes to see any movement up ahead. The dog quieted. They waited a few more minutes to ensure the silence continued, then continued down their path as directed by Manuel. The slow tedious walk was made longer by the resting Jesus required. He really struggled with walking to the point that Juan finally suggested that he carry Jesus piggyback style.

After reaching outside what were likely the extended boundaries of the small town an hour later, Juan found a couple of rocks for them to sit upon. Jesus scrambled off and sat on one while the other two men sat very close so they might talk. Manuel passed each of them bottles of water which were rapidly consumed. They all scanned the surrounding area, looking for any movement which might indicate a person was tracking them. The area was a likely spot for drifters and robbers to use for resting for the night. The only movement was a coyote looking for a late-night snack, pointed out by Jesus.

Manuel whispered, "Around a quarter of a mile from here, I parked a car. I wanted it far enough away that starting it would not wake anyone. It's not too much further."

Juan looked at his uncle, who appeared to have aged significantly since their escape. He quietly asked, "Uncle, can you walk just a little bit further, perhaps if you hold each of our arms?"

Jesus was a very proud man who, despite all his bravado, had always made his own way even when it was considered by some as dishonest, or worse. He had once been feared and a force to be reckoned with when he ran his portion of the drug business in his corner of Mexico. He raised his head and pulled up his chin, then replied, "Of course I can make it, nephew. I just thought it was always better to ride if one was being offered. Let's get a move on."

They stood, Jesus with a bit of assistance from Juan, and headed down the dirt path. The night was quiet, and their footfalls could be heard but were not desperately loud. Juan knew they needed to be on the road to the insignificant airfield before sunrise. From the cryptic messaging in the papers he had reviewed, a plane would be waiting for them. He suspected that his brother, Carlos, and their old business partners would be their transport. Juan mused that would certainly take him out of the frying pan and directly into the fire, as it were. Those guys were always being tracked by the federales.

A short time later, a small car slowly became visible. It had seen better days, but as long as it started, no one was about to complain. Jesus seemed to believe the backseat was his new bed as he entered and stretched out. Manuel drove and Juan navigated from the passenger seat.

"The road should be up here on the right," announced Manuel.

Juan located their position on the map and their destination. He had been to this air strip before and knew that, for a few pesos, their passage would be unstopped and unremembered. Then he turned on his cell phone and sent a quick text to Carlos.

En route to air strip. Jesus is with us. Thanks bro.

A few seconds past while Juan entered the coordinates of the air strip into his GPS. Manuel had a phone charger which he handed to Juan. A few seconds later a tone indicated an incoming text.

I am having you brought here to Brasilia closer. Text JAC she is worried.

Juan frowned; he had so hoped his wife would miss this little fiasco, and they could laugh about it when he saw her and swooped her into their bedroom. She always seemed far more understanding when he was holding and kissing her. Hopefully she would forgive him for getting caught.

Honey, on my way to see Carlos. Then I will come home. Love you.

He sent the text and then made certain Manuel made the next turn. Juan and Manuel had spent many a night together when Juan had worked for Lara, flying lovely models about the world for her fashion shoots.

"Manuel, thanks for coming to rescue us. Your use of tequila was brilliant. You didn't happen to leave any in the car for our trip tonight, did you?"

Manuel chuckled and reached under his seat. He extracted a small bottle and passed it to his friend. "Glad we made it out so easily. I was worried. This is not my normal evening activities. Carlos was hesitant to call me. Lara was none too happy that I was recruited. Women worry, you know."

Juan groaned, took a small sip, sighed, and commented, "Really, we have Carlos, you and me with my Uncle Jesus on this, as well as my wife and Carlos's...um, significant other? What a mess. Why I bet..."

Just then he was startled by a tap on his shoulder from the back seat. A quiet, yet commanding request then came from Jesus. "You were going to hand that back here, right, Juan?"

Juan chuckled and passed it back, "Now you can't have it all, uncle. We are sharing, don't forget."

Seconds later he passed the bottle back to Juan and blatantly stated, "Sorry, son, there must be a hole in that bottle. And, since you are going to be flying us out of here as the pilot, you didn't need it anyway."

Before Juan could get angry and react, the cell phone chirped with an inbound text.

I am so relieved. I am going to try to meet you in Sao Paulo. Twins love you. I love you. Yell at you later, promise

Juan read the text and smiled. He just loved make up sex with his beautiful Julie. An hour or so later, they arrived at the airfield, and Manuel bid his goodbyes. Juan was not familiar with this pilot, but he did work for Carlos's old business partners. A very quiet man. Big on pointing, grunting, and absolute denial of anyone touching anything in the cockpit of the small but fast plane. Juan settled in and closed his eyes. It was going to be a very long flight.

NMX ↓ -7.50
CMX ↓ -9.33
HCC ↓ -3.90
SOX ↓ -7.74

Carlos had driven Juan and Jesus from the airport to Thiago's house. He explained this was where Jesus could stay for a while, as well as Juan, until Julie arrived. They fell into an easy conversation like they always did when together. Time and distance had never been much of a barrier between them.

Lara descended upon them as she ushered them into the house. She took Jesus in hand and escorted him to a room with a bathroom attached. The two of them had met previously at Julie and Juan's wedding, so there was no awkwardness between them. They treated each other like family. As they walked away, Jesus asked, "My dear Lara, has that no-good nephew of mine asked to marry you yet?"

Lara laughed and replied, "No, Uncle Jesus, not yet."

The rest of their conversation was lost as Carlos took Juan to the kitchen where he pointed Juan to a chair. Then he retrieved a plate of food for Juan and grabbed both of them a cerveza.

"Glad you are here and safe, bro," started Carlos. "I was worried, with you in Mexico. You should have left the old man." Carlos ran his fingers subconsciously through his raven black hair.

Juan took a drink of the cool cerveza and chuckled, "Just like you would have done, right?

"How mad is Julie, do you think?"

Carlos made a slow smile and replied, "Not nearly as mad as EZ or Quip. Quip actually seemed a bit exacerbated, though he finally helped some to locate you."

Juan hung his head and mumbled, "Really, them too. I will never get out of the dog house at this rate. Oh well. I need to explain what Jesus told me about how he ended up in Mexico. It is quite a story and leads me to believe that he might be a target of something bigger."

Over the next few hours they had migrated to Carlos's work space. Juan related everything that Jesus had told him. Carlos looked up some of the information, and they assembled the story they would discuss with Quip.

CHAPTER THIRTY-FIVE

Were You Ever There?

The plane finally landed at Ministro Pistarini International Airport in Argentina and taxied up to the gangway. After an excessively long delay, the doors were finally opened so the passengers could disembark. The incoming passengers to Argentina were funneled toward the gauntlet of customs and security checks before seeing daylight or getting to any ground transportation. LJ chuckled to himself as he waved goodbye to his flight, which he had rebranded as *Adios Airlines,* since he resolved never to fly them again.

At all three checkpoints the security teams tore everything apart looking for U.S. currency, which was illegal to own rather than the government-issued pesos. At each stop he had to make, he strategically lightened up his unchecked bag when each security team would confiscate one of the bottles of fine Kentucky whiskey that LJ brought with him. It was all part of his ploy to ease through security with hidden U.S. greenbacks that would allow him great bargaining power for the ships he wanted.

At each checkpoint LJ would go into his usual routine of grinning. He was almost like an opossum as he showed off his gold-encrusted toothy grin, which was so infectious and disarming to others. Then he would strike up something of a conversation, and invariably the security lead ended up with an unopened bottle of whiskey, and LJ was quickly on his way.

After passing through the third security checkpoint, LJ chuckled to himself and under his breath said to no one in particular, "Those right friendly boys are going to be downright mad when they finally sample that regular old tea that I swapped for the whiskey."

The calmness of the terminal was quickly replaced with the chaotic pandemonium just outside. Cars came flying into the curb like skaters on ice at a hockey game. Locals were pleading for assistance from the incoming passengers for anything at all, like at a swap meet. The doomed look on the faces of these local beggar children and adults was enough to make even LJ feel ashamed for being so well off.

LJ had researched in advance and learned that the local elected official boasted that inflation had been tamed, but it was still at 36%. The black market was still trying to get U.S. dollars due to the currency needs of people trying to conserve their wealth. Being caught trying to move your Argentinean pesos into U.S. dollars was considered a crime against the state and came with prison sentences. The trouble was everyone was doing it under the radar for the most part, so the law was largely ignored.

Everywhere LJ looked it was the same. People, desperate to make ends meet, were accosting every traveler who came out the gates to try and buy their U.S. currency so they could make it through to the next week. In some cases, even with the quick hands of the young pickpockets, it appeared the currency exchange might only make it until the next day. The trouble was that a traveler had to bring cash in with them to do business because the Argentinean government had slapped a 30% surcharge on any credit card transaction done using foreign or international-based credit cards to help stop the outflow of U.S. currency. The surcharge had the same effect as throwing high octane jet fuel into a fire.

LJ finally saw his name on a large piece of white cardboard being held by what looked like a well-tailored chauffeur wearing a driver's hat. LJ grinned and had to force his way through the crowds of pleading people.

Once there, he asked, "You do speak English, right?" The chauffeur nodded. Then LJ boisterously announced, "My name is Simon, and I wants to go to the fair. I've got my wares for this fare which don't include no apples. And don't be thinking I'm a Simple Simon."

The chauffeur, not quite sure about the mental state of his fare, slowly rotated his head downward to the right, all the while keeping his sight on LJ.

LJ laughed uproariously and slapped his knee. In over-the-top high spirits, he then offered, "You know, I've been using that greeting all my life, and you're the first person I've seen look at me like I'm crazy. But I'll let you in on a little secret. When I was born, my mamma was all set to name me after her grandmother, Simone. But when the doctor caught me he said, Mrs. 'Ongree, you best be using a boy's name, so she dropped the last letter. Well, here I am, Simon 'Ongree."

LJ studied the chauffeur for a few moments during the brief silence and then asked, "Did you misunderstand when I asked if you spoke English? I'm going to be mighty put out if I told you my best opening introduction, and you don't speak no English."

With only a slight trace of an accent the chauffeur responded, "I speak English fluently. Times are hard now here in Argentina, so there is little mirth in our daily lives."

LJ rocked back a little but offered, "Judging from how you speak, I'd be willing to bet that your English is far better than my Spanish, young'un. I'm sorry about how hard things are here in your country. I can see it in their faces. I can feel the tension. What the poet Thoreau would have called 'lives of quiet desperation', only there ain't nothing quiet about this place."

As they walked towards the limo, LJ seemed a bit reflective on the turmoil swirling around them and offered, "This place and all these tragic people remind me of those last days of evacuating all our military personnel out of 'Nam. That was a sight. People pleading with the chopper pilots, offering their life savings to just get over the fence and onto a gun ship." LJ nodded his head as he allowed the imagery to sink in, and then, just before he got in the back of the limo, he grinned and said, "And I was never there!"

The chauffeur sighed as he closed the door, now realizing it was going to be a long three day assignment. About that time, he could hear his passenger hollering from inside the car.

"Son, you know of any good eateries around here? After nine hours in the air on Adios Airlines, old Simon is 'Ongree." Again, LJ laughed heartily, being completely immersed in his new persona.

LJ was a little put out but managed to keep a civil tone during his response. "Mr. Javier, we've been talking – no, let me re-state that. We've been arguing for the last three hours, and we ain't no closer to an agreement than when I first got here. And you haven't even offered me some refreshment. I came here directly from my ghastly Adios Airlines plane ride. I didn't stop to call on anyone else but you, 'cause you said 'I'll cut you a deal.'

"Well, if you don't have any refreshments, I will just open one of my Kentucky tea bottles and re-hydrate myself. Since you might be thirsty too, I'm prepared to share some of my delightful beverage. Do you possibly have some glasses, Javier, or is that something else you are short on here?"

Javier was obviously thirsty, but his pride held him back from an easy acceptance. LJ could see that the tough times had taken their toll on Javier and that he had been given strict negotiating parameters to maintain. LJ smiled as he found two semi-clean coffee cups and poured up the sweet Kentucky tea for them both. LJ handed the other cup to Javier and toasted.

"To better dealing." LJ lightly sipped the beverage and then asked, "Javier, how is yours?"

Javier's look of surprise said it all as he politely sipped the golden beverage and discovered its true nature. The look of surprise was quickly replaced with a broad grin as they both silently acknowledged the beverage was the Kentucky whiskey that had been swapped for tea.

Javier took a casual accounting of the bottles that LJ had with him in the open bag. After draining his first cup of whiskey, he remarked, "You know, Mr. 'Ongree, I didn't realize just how thirsty I was until you offered to share your Kentucky tea. In my country, when someone is generous in their sharing, our cultural heritage demands we reciprocate in kind. I'm of the opinion that the limitation on the offered contract terms was, shall we say, not generous enough. I would like to re-open our discussion.

"I would like to point out, our discussion might be greatly enhanced with another round of your fine Kentucky tea. However, this time, I'm quite sure two nice glasses can be used to comple-ment the presentation of your proposal."

With that invitation, Javier promptly produced two exquisite crystal tumblers that brilliantly highlighted the beautiful color of the amber beverage that LJ was pouring up.

Once the crystal tumblers were filled and each man was resting comfortably, LJ gently opened the discussion. "Javier, I am a man who has come a great distance to charter four of your oil tankers for a private venture. I want a crew of three for each, with their modest provisions, at a rate of 300,000 ARS per two months and not a penny more. I will be adding a captain to each of the vessels to make certain my organization's interests are top of mind.

"Further, my IT group has a couple of software routines that need to be loaded into the on-board computer systems to ensure my cargo is correctly accounted for. It's not that I don't trust you, it's, well…it's that I don't trust anyone. I'm sure you understand."

Now down to the bottom of his second glass, Javier reflected, "It is a harsh world, and I don't blame you for caution in your dealings with others. I must confess that my trust only goes as far as my next glass of your fine Kentucky tea, kind sir."

Javier politely extended his glass for a refill that LJ only too happily obliged by promptly filling it to the brim.

Javier savored another sip, then stated, "I sense that you have done your homework in bargaining for oil tanker charters. However, you must understand that our Argentinean peso is dropping daily against all other currencies, especially against the U.S. dollar. By the time we finish your second bottle, I will need another 90,000 ARS just to keep up with the USD to ARS exchange rate.

"I suspect you already know that, since all of our creditors are non-Argentinean, they insist on payments in dollars, not pesos. Even if I can get the pesos changed into dollars, I still need to find a way to pay them so the government doesn't take their excessive cut. It is a very large problem."

LJ smiled and offered, "Ma dear Javier, who said anything about paying you with pesos? I know the exchange rate issues you folks have here, so I showed up to negotiate in pesos of course. For the right deal, I am prepared to pay in good old U.S. green-backs. I don't rightly have the full amount in U.S. greenbacks, 'cause I couldn't bring all the needed cash through airport security. But, as a show of good faith, instead of the full 21,000 dollars and change, I am putting down 10,000 U.S. and the rest in pesos so you get the full amount. How does that sound?"

In an effort to help seal the deal, LJ moved to refill Javier's glass to the brim again.

Javier smiled lovingly at the full glass of whiskey and responded, "Are you taking the other three bottles of Kentucky tea with you if I agree, or will they be left as your security deposit?"

LJ grinned broadly and stated, "I was hoping you might accept them as my gift for teaching me about your cultural heritage."

LJ held his glass over for a toast to consummate the deal with Javier, who promptly obliged.

"Kind sir, I believe we have a deal."

CHAPTER THIRTY-SIX

Incomplete Backgrounds

Jacob had been reviewing the data from one machine to another. He was still waiting on the cloud service information. Laurie, whose attitude towards Jacob and Petra had changed since the incident with Detective Davies, had grown too eager to learn about his work. He suggested to Petra that she take Laurie out for a drink and dinner to see if she might convey any information as a part of girl talk. Petra was effective at getting people to open up while sharing almost nothing on her part. It was an art form. He had already made arrangements to go out with Mike to create the converse male bonding time.

Mike peered his head around the doorway and suggested, "I am ready to head out when you are. There is a quiet little pub within walking distance where we can get a good pint or any beverage you want. As this is a week night and reasonably early, we will have the place mostly to ourselves until around nine or ten this evening."

Jacob acknowledged, "Sounds good to me. Let me shut down my laptop and meet you at the elevators. A change of scenery would be welcomed."

Mike, with no change of expression, turned and walked away. Jacob noticed Mike's shoulders were hunched over and there was no spring in his step. He thought for a moment while he loaded his laptop into his backpack. Mike was forcing his behavior. It seemed a little too pat. They met at the elevator, timed so that the doors opened immediately.

The elevator was empty until they both entered and stood to their respective sides. Jacob chuckled and said, "I always like a snappy elevator. Never find that in New York, would we, Mike."

"No, not at all."

Mike led them to the pub and was greeted by name. He introduced Jacob, and the burly host shook hands as if he'd just found a long-lost cousin.

"Lads, take the booth in the back, and one of the girls will bring your drinks. Mike, I suppose you'll have your double shot of Bushmills neat. And you, lad, what's your preference?"

Jacob smiled at the jovial manner of the host and replied, "How could I not ask for a Guinness?"

Mike grinned and agreed, "Perfect, Adam. But make it two each and tell the girls to keep them coming.

"Come on, Jacob, I will show you the way."

Mike ambled down the aisle toward the table and loosened his collar after he sat. He looked around and noticed no other patrons in the area. Mike took the seat that would provide him with the best view of the incoming patrons, leaving Jacob with his back to the inbound flow.

Their barmaid showed up with a cheery smile and their drinks, which she placed in front of them correctly. She winked at Mike and grinned at Jacob. "Mike, I'm Sally and I'll be serving you tonight. Jacob, I presume you are pleased with your visit to London so far."

She rested her hand on his shoulder a bit too long and looked at him wistfully before she realized he was simply not looking back. She smiled, shrugged her shoulders, then said, "Simply raise your hand, gents, and I will bring another round." Sally turned with a quick swing of her hips and a view of her cleavage shifting and walked back toward the bar.

Mike raised his first glass toward Jacob and announced, "Cheers!"

Jacob almost had his glass raised to acknowledge the toast when Mike tossed back his first drink. He closed his eyes for a moment then raised glass number two, meeting Jacob's in midair.

Jacob withheld his surprised look and stated, "Cheers!" then raised his glass to sip the creamy liquid.

Mike raised his hand, and Sally quickly returned with two more for Mike and another for Jacob.

Jacob grinned at the cheery barmaid and suggested, "Sally, I can tell you right now this is my limit, but you keep 'em coming for Mike, please. I am treating the lad this evening, so whatever he wants is fine by me."

Mike requested, "Sally, my dear, bring me back another pair and a basket of your fresh chips if you please. My friend here needs a bit of food to soak up the alcohol, so he can have another in a little while."

Then he let loose with a roar of laughter at his joke and tossed back his third double. He grinned as the liquor took effect, increasingly turning him into a very happy person. Jacob could almost see the emotional weights dropping off Mike's shoulders. He began to tell Jacob stories, more jokes really. Each one becoming increasingly disjointed and nonsensical. Jacob had learned long ago that when someone was going down the road of drinking and talking to just let it go.

A couple of hours later and several sheets to the wind, Mike began to get a little morose. First, he was sad about Roslyn. Then it was his family and how he'd let them down over the years. He was still coherent, but Jacob could tell he was well on his way down. The words were mushed together and delayed in some cases, but it was getting interesting.

"Why, after boarding school and doing so well, my folks put me into a European university. I was to be the shining star and take over all the global oil drilling businesses run by my three uncles."

He held up a glass and continued, "I had been drinking with a couple of my buddies, and we did a really stupid thing to one of our professors. My buddies were so much smarter than I was, it wasn't surprising when they left me to hold the bag."

Mike shook his head as if the image of that event was playing like a movie in his mind. Then he looked really angry as he almost yelled, "And then those two asses decided to make me the patsy. Heck, I was thrown out of the school without as much as a second chance. I called my closest cousin and he insisted I was such a disappointment that he basically tossed me out of the family."

Mike nursed his double number ten as he slowly started to close his eyes and lean more onto the table. He was holding himself up, but just barely. Mike added, "I vowed I'd kill those two so-called buddies, after I became a success. I bummed around for a couple of years, tried to get my degree in Texas after I expunged my European stint from my files. I finally finished school and made a success out of my life. Now, I feel lost without her…"

Setting down his glass, he moved his arms onto the table and laid his head onto them, with tears running from his eyes and a soft moaning like that of a wounded animal coming from his lips.

Jacob thought how best to try and comfort this rather disappointing human being but quickly decided to let Mike's emotions simply drain out onto the pub table. After all, he thought, self-pity was as good a tonic as anything he could offer at this stage.

NMX ↓ -7.50
CMX ↓ -3.33
HCC ↓ -3.30
SOX ↓ -7.74

Half an hour later, Petra ambled to the back table and slid in next to Jacob. She looked over at Mike and said, "As they say in this part of the world, Mike is really into his cups now, isn't he?"

Jacob grinned and gently kissed her cheek. "He is that, my dear. I can assure you this is my second. Would you like a white wine? Then we can discuss the success of our divide-and-conquer strategy."

Petra scooted a bit closer. Sally arrived and asked, "This must be the reason you refused to flirt with me, Jacob. Miss, he is one straight arrow. Does he have a brother?"

Petra chuckled and replied, "If you are calling him Jacob, then please, call me Petra. No brother, sorry. May I have a white wine, please?"

Sally warmed right up and smiled in her most cheery way as she replied, "Call me Sally. White wine it is. Coming right up.

"Jacob, Mike here seems to be done all in for the night, which is fairly standard for him. Where is his girl though? Um…oh yes, Roslyn it is. She usually helps navigate him out to a black cab."

Jacob looked at Sally with sadness and explained, "Roslyn was killed in the tube accident that was on the news. Mike is really broken up about it. I was just letting him have a shoulder to lean on."

"Oh, that is just sad. But I can tell you, Roslyn was always talking bad about him after he passed out. She'd sit here for a good while and then call someone, telling them she was sending photos. I figured she was trying to get him fired or something. Not a nice woman, in my book. Sort of a cow in nice clothes, which was a shame for the nice clothes. But enough of that now. I can't speak ill of the departed.

"Let me get your wine, Petra, and you two can have a visit. He won't be waking up any time soon. You let me know if I need to get Mickey to help you get him to a cab when you're ready to leave. You are still picking up his tab, right?"

Jacob nodded and she scurried off.

Petra asked, "Did you learn anything new, before he passed out?"

"I did. He has a past that is not in our information sources. I have ICABOD trying to dig up some details, but it will be a while. Don't have much to go on. And you, my dear one, any luck?"

"Our Laurie got the job from a referral by a company out of South America, Char or Chair. Hard to tell, her slurring was so bad, once she finally opened up. I think it is safe to say she's a plant. She said she was instructed to take photos of the computer screens at certain times from a distance and send the pictures to a mobile number. She gave me the mobile number and then passed out. I could not unlock her cell, so I plugged it in and asked ICABOD to track it to see if the data is uploading to her cloud service."

The wine arrived. Jacob raised his glass, "Cheers! To our finding a trail we can actually follow."

"To us!" Petra smiled and looked at Jacob in that very special way, which she knew was what he liked.

CHAPTER THIRTY-SEVEN

Trust is Such a Rare Commodity

The last time he and Henry had spoken, he'd had the distinct impression that his friend was not playing straight. Roundhouse needed to either get back to work or make a real effort to find work in a different field. He sure didn't want to worry Mildred any more than she already was. Sticking close to the house to wait for a phone call was ridiculous. He paced, then Mildred groused and told him to go do something. This was the first time in a very long time that anything he wanted to do cost money. Money, he didn't want to waste even on a game of bowling. Mildred was very loving and supportive, but having him underfoot was not in her routine. It was just different from a two- or three-day break until he had another trip out. And it was putting a strain on their relationship.

Today when she had suggested he leave so she could clean, he had taken a long walk to the park and thought about stuff. What was it Henry had said that didn't sit well? He tried to replay the conversation, but he'd been so angry at the time, part of that discussion was just gone. Roundhouse had been distracted by two boys playing catch in the park when it finally hit him. Henry had said there was a discrepancy in how many trips he had made. At the time, Roundhouse had clarified his trips. Thinking back on it now, replaying the conversation, he might have misunderstood. Could Henry have thought he messed up his trips? Surely Henry knew him better than that.

He took out his cell phone and called the office.

Henry answered right away, though there was no warmth in the tone of his voice as he asked, "Roundhouse, how are you doing, man? Having a good ol' time with that pretty wife of yours? I only have a minute, buddy, what can I help with. You did file your unemployment claim, right? I don't recall it coming by for approval, but I'll make sure it clears quickly."

Roundhouse frowned and searched his memory again. Then he hopefully asked, "Are you back at work, Henry? That must mean things are getting better if they brought you back in a dispatching role. Why, I can be at the train yard in an hour and ready to go anywhere you say, man. Mildred will be happy to get me gone, so she can clean." Then he paused and backed up mentally to the start of the discussion.

"Unemployment filing. You asked about that, didn't you?"

Henry sighed and then replied, "Roundhouse, I am back at work trying to help with the books, not as a dispatcher. Go file and it'll come through fairly fast. I'll make sure it's approved." Then, feeling a little uncomfortable and not wanting to lie to his old friend, he said, "Hey, Roundhouse, I gotta go back to work. File the claim. I'll try to call you soon." Then Henry disconnected without a goodbye.

Roundhouse looked at the phone in utter surprise. Never in their long years of knowing one another had they ever ended a call like that. Usually a joke or chuckle, but never a 'try to call you soon' comment. It felt like being dismissed, which simply made him mad. He tried to call back, but the phone had apparently been turned off as the call went to voicemail. He turned and stomped back to the house and muttered, "We'll see about this!"

By the time he returned home, his temper was almost in check. He wanted to pack and get out of the house without raising Mildred's suspicions. He went up to their bedroom and got out his go bag. Like always, it was packed and ready to go.

"Mildred, honey, good news," announced Roundhouse. "I may have a train, if I can get up to Fort Worth. Just spoke to Henry. Seems like he was trying to give me a heads up."

Mildred smiled broadly and said, "Honey, how wonderful. Your bag is ready, of course. Call me when you catch a train, sweetheart. I knew they couldn't work without you for long.

"I told you they would sort out the issue of the number of trips they thought you were taking. Why, during my postings on social media, one of the friends of a friend of Lucy in Wichita said her husband had been laid off out in Tennessee for not reporting the coal production correctly, which she swore was a lie. You recall Lucy, I'm sure. She is the first cousin of Wade Masterson, who went to school with me.

"Anyway, there are several different discussions going on about what is or is not being reported right. I think the government wants to use this as another excuse to raise our taxes. Somebody's pockets are getting lined with someone else's work, mark my words, honey."

He smiled at her loving support, then she leaned into him to give him a hug. Suddenly feeling the love and support of his wonderful wife, he picked her up and soundly kissed her while he spun her around. She was the best part of his life, and he hated to mislead her. He set her down, and her eyes were shimmering with joy.

"I will call you as soon as I get to Fort Worth and get assigned to a train. Promise."

NMX ↓ -7.50
CMX ↓ -9.33
HCC ↓ -3.90
SOX ↓ -7.74

Driving for almost six hours hadn't improved Roundhouse's mood. On top of the drive with all the inept drivers on the road, he'd left his CDs at home, so the fading in and out of radio stations was also majorly annoying. Several attempts at reaching Henry by cell phone had been unsuccessful. At least when he pulled into the parking lot there were spaces open. Roundhouse parked with an attitude then barreled into the main offices in Fort Worth. He caught Henry totally by surprise as he stomped into the office area.

Stalker, monitoring the calls and screens per the agreement with Henry and Tomkins, knew the man was both determined and very angry. A combination which Stalker wanted avoided for the time being. Like all men, Stalker did a rapid comparison, should it become necessary to help defend anyone. Stalker was fit and trim, but this man matched him in fitness and appeared a bit taller and heavier. He felt he could take him, but Stalker wanted to avoid this sort of confrontation. He remained on high alert as the man closed the ground on Henry.

The look on Henry's face wasn't fear but utter amazement. He stood almost toe-to-toe but a half a foot shorter and many pounds lighter. "Roundhouse, what are you doing here? There's nothing here for you!"

"Henry," shouted Roundhouse, moving menacingly closer toward Henry's nose, "you said the trains were doing too many runs. That some of us engineers were pushing the loads without authorization. That is a flat out lie, I tell you. It's messed up, man. Wyatt in Wyoming said he was closing the mine because they couldn't sell what had been out of the earth for months. The surplus was piled up outside the mine.

"I would never do any unauthorized extra runs, nor would any of the folks on our trains. We've been in this for too long to want to take the chance on not running a train. It's all most of us know, man. How could you, or anyone else, think that?"

Finally, Roundhouse stopped and stared at Henry, their noses almost touching. Small or big, neither of these two were going to give in. Tomkins came out of his office and stopped in his doorway, wondering exactly what had occurred and what should be done. Then he recognized the man.

Tomkins quietly stated, "Timothy Standour, right?" Tomkins walked forward with a pleasant look on his face but no smile. When he was fairly close to the two men that hadn't even flinched, he struck out his right hand and continued, "Nice to meet you. You may not know me, but I am Mr. Tomkins. How 'bout you take a seat and we discuss your concerns like civilized men?"

Stalker watched this scene unfolding and had to give each man credit for being a standup guy. Roundhouse turned his gaze toward Tomkins and stepped back. Henry eased up some and also backed up.

Roundhouse took a breath, turned slightly toward Tomkins and shook his extended hand. "Yes, sir. Most folks just call me Roundhouse. I don't want to take a seat, thank you, sir. I just drove for hours and standing feels pretty good.

"I wasn't trying to bust in on your day, but Henry and me have known each other for a long time. Something's up, and I feel I have a right to know some of the details after all my years of service."

Tomkins tilted his head to one side and considered the comment. He acknowledged Henry with a slight incline of his head before he responded, "Well, Roundhouse, that makes sense to me. Why don't you and Henry take a walk, grab some coffee, and talk it out. I am sure Henry can answer your questions. When you men are done, come on back and I'll have your check ready for you."

Both men turned to Tomkins and looked a bit confused. Then it dawned on Henry what was needed. He called over to Stalker, "Mr. Hughes, why don't you join us? Roundhouse tells a great story. I promise he'll make you laugh. Heck, he'll probably invite you home for dinner."

The three men walked outside. Once clear of the front of the building, Henry turned to Jim Hughes and said, "Go around back. Tomkins was saying he was being checked on. Something must be up with the monitoring. You go around, and we'll keep going."

Henry could see the puzzled look on his face but flatly stated, "Roundhouse, just shut up for a while and stay with me on this. I'll explain what I can. Come on!"

CHAPTER THIRTY-EIGHT

I Wish I'd Said That!

Juan accepted the early morning cerveza from Carlos with a smile and said, "Thanks, bro. I think I'm almost ready to relate this story about Uncle Jesus's CHARD dealings to Quip and let them use their computer resources to find out what happened."

Carlos sipped his own cerveza, nodded and said, "You know, doing just that might make a good start toward rebuilding the trust you and I lost with Quip. He and EZ seemed a little angry about me calling you, like we had slipped back into our old lifestyles. Besides, it would be good manners to say thanks for having EZ help me locate you. I suspect it caused more than a little ruckus between them."

Juan complained, "You know, maybe we should just get the piggyback rider down here to be on the call. He can help explain his ill-advised business venture!"

Carlos cautioned, "I don't think Uncle Jesus needs to know any more about our business or who we relate to than he already thinks he knows. Let's just keep it to you, me, and Quip on a call. If he wants EZ in, then fine. Actually, you should probably ask to have her on the call to properly say thank you."

Juan looked at Carlos and loudly admonished, "If we are going to talk to Quip and EZ, don't you think that EZ is going to tell Julie? Then I will be yelled at again for not looping her in so she could hear it as fresh as the rest of them. Let me get one more cerveza down to steady my nerves before we get on the call. It'll be fun to let the beatings begin!"

Carlos studied Juan a moment and then grinned. "You say that like it's a negative thing. I mean, after all, you were the clumsy one who got caught here. Let's get them on a call all together so you can admit being a rookie in this sleuthing game."

Juan became livid. "Let me play this back for you. Oh, Juan, dear me, I've become little Carlos Bo Peep who has lost my little sheep Jesus, and I don't know where to find him.

"Ah hell, what we should have done is left him alone 'cause he would come home wagging his tail behind him."

Carlos studied Juan for a moment and responded, "While I've always liked that nursery rhyme, I don't see the relevance of it to our situation. You don't have to lead off groveling by saying your next lesson in detective school is on how not to get caught when going undercover. Just admit to being modestly incompetent, and I'm sure everything will be fine."

Carlos and Juan had grown up together. They each knew exactly how to completely bait the other's ego in such a way as to set the stage for a real live fist fight. The one fight in their youth was enough for each to remember never to do it again. Juan was afraid of Carlos and his temper. Carlos was glad of it. Each of them respected the other, and even though they could taunt each other to the max, no one else would have dared.

Just as their tempers were reaching seething levels, a charming voice admonished, "Boys, boys. What have I told you about your testosterone levels going unchecked? Do I need to send you to your rooms to cool down?"

Carlos glanced at Lara standing in the doorway, then returned his stare to Juan. After a long moment, he replied to Lara, "I was just apologizing to Juan for the mess I got everyone into. I wanted to thank him for all his detective work and say that I am very proud of my younger brother. I was very worried for his safety and that my sordid past flared up, engulfing him when he least expected it."

Juan smiled at Carlos like he always did when Carlos accepted all the blame for something Juan had done.

Then Juan asked, "Hand me another cerveza, and let's get the team on the call. I can't wait to blame all this on you!"

Lara rolled her eyes at the outrageous comment from Juan.

Carlos gritted his teeth and groused, "We should have let you rot in jail a little longer. Maybe you might have learned your proper place in the universe!"

After studying each other for a few moments, they both blurted out simultaneously "Naaaah!"

```
HMX  ↓  -7.50
CMX  ↓  -9.33
HCC  ↓  -3.90
SOX  ↓  -7.74
```

After everyone had joined the call, Juan opened the conversation. "Thanks for joining. Let me begin with a very large thank you to EZ for helping to geo-locate me in an extremely low-tech jail cell in Mexico. Madam, you have my gratitude.

"Next, let me offer something of an explanation. This will quickly lead to an apology to all of you involved in this assignment and could be used as an excellent MBA study course in near fatal incompetence.

"Our Uncle Jesus went missing. Carlos suggested that I could nose around looking for him with fewer eyebrows going up due to our CATS team endeavors. I know some of you might think we had slipped back into our old past life, but I can promise you that was not the case. I am not looking to go back to where I came from, only forward with my wife Julie and our twins. I'm pretty sure that Carlos is on his life's glide path with his remarkable Lara.

"Perhaps you believe us, or maybe you don't, but I hope that you will accept our explanations and perhaps one day will allow us back into your extended family."

The conference call attendees were all quiet and didn't seem to know what to say in response.

Finally, in true character, Quip offered, "Juan, can you go over the part again about being a jerk in all this?"

Since EZ and Quip had joined on the same phone, EZ was able to turn her head to aim her withering gaze of astonishment and annoyance at Quip.

She curtly stated for all on the conference bridge to hear, "Just when I think I will no longer be appalled by yet another outrageous statement, you set the bar even higher! Oh, I know, Quip, let's try something different for a change, shall we? How about graciously accepting the apology being offered and perhaps indicate that a little more time might be needed to get past our unsettled feelings in this matter?"

The conference bridge was quiet with Quip now on the spot. Without missing a breath, Quip offered, "Juan, I'd like to accept your explanation. While the apology is appreciated, I don't feel it is necessary. I would like a little time to work through my feelings in this matter. However, I would like to go on record as saying, if I go missing, I would want you hunting for me."

Juan grinned and solemnly promised, "Quip, I would do that for you. If nothing else, you would have someone in the next cell to talk to."

Juan's sense of humor never failed to disarm everyone, and the riotous laughter that ensued proved it.

After the laughter subsided, Juan continued, "Well, now that we have that behind us, there is some unfinished business tied to Jesus's disappearance that doesn't make any sense. Quip, I was hoping we could discuss it on this call. Would that be alright?

I am pretty sure Julie, you, and your computer resources could help us with this puzzle."

Quip immersed himself fully into character and responded, "You have a puzzle that needs unraveling? That's what the Quipster does best. Fire away, my boy. Fire away and fall back."

CHAPTER THIRTY-NINE

Stand Up Like a Texan

Near the office was the makings of a small town, both quaint and safe. The main street, covered sidewalks on either side, had old and new specialty shops as well as a renowned diner that most everyone favored. They found a booth at the back of the diner to slide into. The waitress handed them each a menu followed by a quick smile. Before she could walk away to give them time to review the menu, Henry ordered a coffee and Roundhouse ordered coffee and a burger with fries. With the straight drive through, coupled with missing lunch in total, Roundhouse was hungry. He was also highly agitated, which also made him hungry. The waitress smiled and retrieved the menus. Seconds later she returned with two cups of coffee, along with creamer, then vanished to check on her other customers.

Roundhouse glanced out the window, taking in the scene. People walked along the sidewalk, some obviously business people going to or from their offices, a few kids collected near the ice cream store patiently waiting to order their treats, and moms pushed strollers or held toddler hands. Roundhouse had been here many times and frequently enjoyed the square at the end of the street, which sported a park area for walking, playing, or simply sitting. He often went there if he was waiting on his train. He reflected on a life that appeared to be quiet and enjoyable for those he watched. After a few minutes of stirring the caffeine nearly out of the coffee in his cup, he turned to Henry.

"Henry, what is going on here? I realize I barged in and disrupted everything, but I suspect there is a lot more going on than just my little issue of getting laid off. We have been friends for a long time, so I will respect your wishes if you cannot tell me, but maybe I can help," offered Roundhouse.

Henry looked at his friend, shrugged his shoulders, and finally replied, "It is the craziest thing I've ever been involved in. I'm not even sure how to explain it. It seems like it started several months ago when the coal supply started to increase and the pricing began to decrease. Our company transports so much of the coal in the United States that we typically have a great view of the pricing. There are a defined number of places where coal is mined and then distributed to the various buying entities. Like all commodity markets, the rise and fall can be seasonal, but can also shift as technology changes. All monitored, all watched, and all understood.

"When the pricing begins to drop, every party in the chain, from producers to buyers, begins to position to either protect themselves or take advantage of the situation. In the case of our rail transport, we can control the number of cars and trains that are available because we are the logistics of getting product to market. As you would expect, things are measured and managed logically from one end to the other. Then the numbers started to look distorted. It looked like more product was being shipped than produced, but the result was the prices dropped substantially further."

Henry looked around their immediate area and, lowering his voice, continued, "As the supply was reportedly increasing, the pricing for coal couldn't find the bottom and that launched anxiety trading, driven purely by emotion. No one wanted to take a futures position any further than twenty minutes, which continued to drive prices down. Basically, the damn system was driven by fear, and the fear was supplied by the system. Then the foreign nationals panicked and began dropping their prices to stay in the market, which only helped the supply problem get worse.

"I heard one foreign coal rep say they needed currency, any currency, to make their debt service, so they were willing to take less than what it cost to mine the coal. That action punished the market even further, which forced our domestic producers to cut back and idle their mines. It has become an economic feeding frenzy that I don't see can be stopped. "

Roundhouse shook his head as he tried to process what Henry was suggesting. "Henry, I am not the number whiz you are, and all this global economics stuff you are covering is making my head hurt. I know that what you are suggesting is that nothing is adding up like it should. But, with all the moving parts, how do you find out where the weak links are?"

Henry looked really sad and explained, "This is where it gets crazier, if that's possible. Tomkins seems to be one of the issues, but it appears to be because his family is being threatened. The other man you met, Mr. Hughes, is trying to find out where that threat is coming from as well as find out how the other numbers are being changed. Mr. Hughes put some monitoring programs on the computers to see if it's like a virus."

"Henry, what can I do to help? Should I take Tomkins's family back home with me to keep them safe until it gets sorted out, because I can. I know Mildred would be good with my making the offer. Heck, we could get all of Cut 'N Shoot on board with protecting a family."

Henry rubbed his chin and thought about that as an option. He had not done any real detailed discussion about the family, other than knowing they were safe. He knew Tomkins was willing to help as long as his family was safe. Perhaps it was worth pursuing.

"You don't think your sweet wife would mind having another family under foot? It sounded to me like Mr. Tomkins didn't think he had any options. But I think it is worth a try. Why don't you call her to be certain it is okay? Then we can invite him for coffee and we can discuss the possibilities."

The men finished their coffee and Roundhouse his burger. While Roundhouse went off to call Mildred in private, Henry ordered them more coffee and the peach pie fresh out of the oven. The pie and coffees had just been served when Roundhouse returned to the table grinning. He sat down and looked at the French vanilla ice cream as it melted onto the golden-brown pie crust. The men inhaled the scent of the peaches and perfectly flakey pie crust. Taking a small amount of the glorious aromatic pie onto their forks and into their mouths, they both sighed in unison.

Roundhouse swallowed and stated, "That is some fine pie. I hate to admit it, but it could give Mildred's a run for her money.

"I did explain to Mildred a little about the situation going on, and she was relieved that in fact I was as innocent as she had proclaimed to all her friends that would listen. Taking on the family was approved wholeheartedly, the sooner the better. She wanted to know if you or I were at risk, and I assured her we weren't.

"If I call her back she will come get them, or I can simply bring them home. I suspect, in the ten minutes since we spoke, she has all manner of community support with a safe place, round the clock guards, food, and whatever is needed already arranged.

"Let's get Mr. Hughes and Mr. Tomkins over here and outline our plan. The sooner we get agreement on a plan, the sooner we can take the threat away from whoever these people are."

Henry decided it would be best if he went back to the office and wrote out the idea rather than call. He reasoned if the computers could be a problem then the phones in the office could also be a problem. Roundhouse leaned back with a sense of pride that he might be helping in this situation and earning a bit of credibility back so he could get back to running trains.

A short time later, Henry returned with Mr. Tomkins in tow. Henry sat down and ordered another coffee for himself and one for Mr. Tomkins. Mr. Tomkins acknowledged Roundhouse and shook his hand, but seemed unsettled. In his hand was a piece of paper that Roundhouse snatched. He opened it, read it, but gave a puzzled look to Mr. Tomkins. Roundhouse gave a bewildered look to both men and then removed his cell phone from his pocket. After he found the contact he sought, he two fingered a text that seemed to go on and on. A few seconds later he received a response.

Henry said, "Mr. Hughes said he'd be over in a few minutes. He needed to place a quick phone call to verify some text information he'd received. Tomkins here wanted to get a cup of coffee and take a little break with us."

"Great to have you, Mr. Tomkins. I know how busy you are with all the trains being brought back to their home stations. I'm sure we will get some more orders, and I am here to help in any way I can. Heck, I can even load and unload if needed," suggested Roundhouse.

Mr. Tomkins replied, "I know the work reduction is tough on our people. I think for a couple of weeks if you could be a courier for messaging, we could find a way to pay you and reimburse your expenses. Would you be interested in that type of work, sir?"

Roundhouse looked pleased as he nodded and agreed, "Sure, I can do that. When do I start?"

About that time, Mr. Hughes walked in looking very anxious and concerned. He walked up to the table and sat down next to Roundhouse. The waitress smiled and brought over yet another cup of coffee and refreshed all the cups.

Jim Hughes leaned over toward Roundhouse and, in a quiet voice, asked, "Does your wife have a lot of friends that use social media?"

Roundhouse nodded and quietly replied, "Well sure. She has friends all across the country. Why?"

Jim Hughes shook his head slightly, as if he'd hoped to have been wrong. "Apparently, she lit a fire under hundreds of her closest friends, and the issue of corrupt number recording on coal transport has gone viral. The only thing missing, fortunately, are the names of the folks here that are threatened. I recommend you go pick up your new charges and get out of town, now!"

Roundhouse looked horrified as he could barely wait for Jim to get out of the booth. As Roundhouse was trying to intercept the social media damage his wife had launched, Tomkins sat looking defeated and motioned for calm from everyone.

Each man looked to the other for clues about Tomkins's emotion when he finally said, "Gentlemen, I cannot leave nor will I abandon my family. This…situation is my doing, and I can't just run, letting others clean up my mess. I was…I am afraid. But if one doesn't stand and fight, with the intention to make things right, what sort of man does that make me?"

They all looked to Jim Hughes, who smiled and quietly offered, "Sounds like a Texas attitude to me. Gentlemen, you all have a hand to play in this, but please run your ideas through me before we have anymore false steps. Agreed? We still have family at risk and economic chaos staring us in the face. We have to put the wheels back on the train, quite literally, and I would like very much to move to my next destination knowing things are in proper play and under control here."

Tomkins, Henry, and Roundhouse all sat nodding in quiet reflection.

CHAPTER FORTY

My Louie to Lean on...

After some prodding and coaxing, Carlos had acquiesced to make the trip with Lara, especially after Juan had recovered and joined them. Carlos had alerted Andy he would be off for a few days but available by cell. The flight was uneventful, and the hotel lobby was modern and decorated with beautiful artwork, exotic carpets, and French fabrics. Their penthouse suite on the top floor had a stunning view of Rio de Janeiro, along with a private pool and full services.

Lara reaffirmed, "Thanks, honey, for doing this meeting with me for Papá. The dock area can be a little rough, not to mention creepy, especially for a woman alone. I just want to handle the meeting with this buyer and get us out of there."

Carlos puzzled and asked, "I thought you liked Rio. You have an entire line of lingerie named after it. Plus, we have a really nice hotel to stay at while we are here. You shouldn't let the armed security personnel at the door and on each elevator detract from our stay here."

Lara responded, "It is like a lot of big cities. Marketed to sound like the most exotic and fun place on the planet, but the city is mired in crime, due in part to so many tourists who make it their prime destination. We also have to go to the grimiest area of Rio to make our meeting at Porto de Rio de Janeiro. I'll just be glad when this is done, that's all. Then we can enjoy the accommodations. I certainly wouldn't do it without you."

Carlos smiled, took her in his arms, and reassured, "Well, not only do you have me, my love, but also my trusty Louisville Slugger walking stick that I procured from that secondhand store in New York. I still chuckle now and again when I remember how the owner called out to me and boldly stated that he could help with my limp. Then he proceeded to hustle me to purchase this walking stick. It has served me well, though."

Lara grinned at the story. It always came out a bit differently with each retelling. "You've always had a fondness for that walking stick, Carlos. I'm glad it has good memories for you."

"I will also point out that it was and still is a formidable weapon, as those two Asian thugs found out. Yes sir, we have nothing to fear as long as I have you!"

Carlos took a more serious tone as he asked, "Now if you want, I can ask Juan to join us for the meeting if it will make you feel better, honey. Then you would have two men to escort you."

Lara somewhat apprehensively remarked, "No, I don't think we need to add Juan. I'm glad the hotel was able to give us the other suite on this floor. Fortunately, this is not the height of the season here. I was hoping Julie might make it."

Carlos offered, "It sounds like she might be sending someone else in her place, based on the slamming of doors and muttering under his breath the last time I saw Juan. But, okay, you and I can go do this meeting, get some boats into service, then we can come back here and smooch…naked of course."

Lara tried hard to give Carlos her *oh really* look but broke into a broad smile and agreed, "You know, I might like coming to Rio more often if business casual is going to be pursued for afterhours meetings."

Carlos smiled as well, then absentmindedly asked, "What is the buyer's name? The one we are supposed to be meeting with?"

Lara, though somewhat distracted, responded, "Rogers, his name is Holland Rogers."

HMX ↓ -7.50
CMX ↓ -9.33
HCC ↓ -5.90
SOX ↓ -7.74

Carlos and Lara got out of the cab and Carlos paid the fare. He insured that the same cab driver would return for them by giving him an extra 100 Brazilian real. In Brazil's big cities, like Rio, one didn't get into any cab unless you knew they were properly contracted and approved. And a good cab driver always deserved an extra tip, especially in this part of the world where it could mean your life.

As they meandered down to the dock offices of Thiago's company, where they would do the negotiations with Holland Rogers, another cab pulled up and a large black man got out.

This man loudly proclaimed, "Son, you did some of the finest urban combat driving I've ever seen. This ol' boy been in 3D games that didn't get my pulse going the way your driving did. And, to top it off, you didn't hit nothing. Of course, that woman carrying her offspring in that crosswalk will never be the same.

"Now, can I count on you to come pick me up too when my negotiations are concluded? I mean, riding with you is better than a rollercoaster ride at the state fair."

The cabbie grinned, understanding some of what the tourist had said, and quickly took the 10 real tip in exchange for his business card with a phone number on it.

All the commotion from this man's exit from the cab got noticed by Carlos just before they entered the dock offices. As Carlos let Lara through the doorway first, he studied the large man momentarily and then quickly stepped into the offices.

With a very odd look on his face, he flatly stated, "Babe, my Yaqui Indian senses are tingling madly. Let's hold back a second so I can get a better..."

Lara's concern grew as Carlos pulled out his phone and dialed an important contact that immediately connected. "Juan, I need you here at the docks to support Lara. I know this ship charter representative, I think, and my Yaqui Indian senses tell me something is very wrong. I don't want this guy to see me. Hurry, please!"

Lara, somewhat alarmed, questioned, "Carlos, what's wrong? I've never seen you like this. Don't leave me alone now. Juan is fifteen to twenty minutes away and judging from the blustery arrival up on the street, that obnoxious character is most probably the charter rep wanting to negotiate!"

Carlos quickly sized up the situation and offered, "Alright, here's what we will do. Have the office manager greet the bellowing charter rep and state that you are running late. Then, let's duck out the side entrance and wait for Juan to take you in to meet with him. I want to watch from the shadows but not let him see me. Now let's be clear, work with him just as if he is a legitimate charter rep, but I want a photo of him if you can get it to my phone. Got it? I'm going to try and get some photos too, but yours will have better resolution."

Puzzled, Lara responded, "I'll see what I can do, but I don't understand…."

Carlos interrupted her with a reassuring kiss, and they quickly looped the office manager in on what had to happen to achieve the desired sequence of events. Then they both slipped out the side door discreetly, carefully keeping their faces away from the man as well as the entrance into the building.

Fortunately, Juan was already dressed and mobile for some personal business, so it was easy to get there in under eight minutes to support the situation. He had the cabbie drop him close to where he spotted Lara and Carlos.

After a quick payment that dismissed the cab driver, he turned to Carlos and asked, "Okay, so what's so important?"

Carlos, eyeing his cane, lowered his voice to tell both of them, "When I was in New York City looking for you and working undercover as Dakota, I developed something of a limp.

"Well, as I moved past this secondhand store, a rather large affable black gentleman came over to me and hustled me to buy this cane from him. He also promised to buy it back once I got over my limp. I never returned to the store, but I believe this is that same man."

Juan studied Carlos a moment and asked, "You want us to help you get your money back from him?"

Annoyed by Juan's humor, Carlos flatly replied, "Let me pose the obvious question here. How can someone go from being a secondhand junk dealer on the seedy side of New York City to being an international traveler chartering oil tankers in the span of a couple of years? Convince me that my tingling Yaqui Indian senses are wrong."

Juan sighed, then looked at Lara and confirmed, "His Yaqui Indian senses don't tingle unless something's wrong. Why don't you and I go down to meet and greet Mr. Whatever to see if we can discover what's going on?"

Juan offered up his arm as a proper escort and Lara accepted it, swallowed hard, and they both moved to enter the dock offices. Once inside, introductions began between the three of them. Lara began and, after introducing herself, gave an intro for Juan, her legal counsel.

LJ, into his new persona of Holland Rogers, went into negotiation mode. "Howdy, young persons. I know you were told that a Mr. Holland Rogers was coming calling, but my friends and acquaintances always just call me Jolly. As a 20-year veteran of oil tanker chartering, the people across the table from me start calling me Jolly Rogers. Pirate first class. Har! Har! I always get a kick out of that story by way of my introduction to folks!"

Juan studied this skilled character a moment and said, "Mr. Rogers, if you have indeed been in this business 20 years, you must have seen a lot of peaks and valleys in the price of oil. I bet you have a boatload of stories to tell, quite literally."

Jolly flashed his big toothy grin and stated, "You know I do, young feller, but let's save the stories of the good old days for another time. My schedule is kind of full, and I'll bet yours is too, so let's get down to business, shall we?"

Lara asked, "Where is the rest of your group? We were told that there would be six people in attendance."

Jolly smiled and offered, "Those would be my operations folk and I don't rightly need them here for the negotiations. They will be along directly, if we can come to terms."

Lara smiled politely, but Juan reached down to retrieve his phone and glanced at the screen.

In a tone which made him seem moderately inconvenienced, Juan stated, "My apologies, sir, but they just sent me a text that we need a quick photo of you for the temporary security badge. The security badge is required to board and review the ships. We take security very seriously here in Brazil, so I'm sure you understand."

Jolly rocked back a bit but said, "I don't know that I like that idea, but I'll make you a deal. I'll let you take my photo for the badge, but I want this beautiful Brazilian lady in it with me and a copy of the photo for my scrapbook. When you are rough on good looks like me, you need some proof that you can be a ladies' man. Whaddaya say?"

The look of absolute panic on Lara's face spoke volumes of terror.

Smiling with the grin of a crocodile, Juan boldly stated, "Sir, you should also know that I am her bodyguard and brother to her jealous husband. I will need to be in between you two in the picture to avoid any unpleasant repercussions. Otherwise, I will be, as you Americans say, *on the hook* for her safety. Are we in agreement?"

Lara, a little more emboldened with Juan's statement, gently maneuvered in between the two men and suggested, "Oh, I don't mind. However, it will make a significant cost impact to you in the negotiated price, Mr. Jolly Rogers."

Jolly howled at Lara's bargaining tact, then inclined his head and said, "They are going to be mad at me for not driving a hard bargain, but, ma'am, you're alright. Bring on the camera, but don't you be trying to flirt with me while we are this close, Miss Lara."

The office manager came over and quickly took several shots of Jolly and left without saying a word. He did wink knowingly at Juan without anyone else the wiser.

Then Lara suggested, "Let's talk about charter price, duration, crew costs, and, most importantly, currency. We are a multinational corporation, so all of our transactions are in U.S. currency, not the Brazilian real, Mr. Jolly."

He smiled and politely stated, "That's just as well, as I couldn't carry enough reals through to pay for the charters anyway. However, I do have a few IT requirements that need to go along with the transaction."

Lara responded, "Yes, so your email stated. I believe we can accommodate your needs with the reasons why. I would expect that you already have a price in mind, so I suggest that we begin there."

CHAPTER FORTY-ONE

My Friend, My Lover, My Betrayer
...The Enigma Chronicles

Mike Patrick was nearing his breaking point. The strain of the conference call without the buffer Roslyn normally provided was taking its toll on him psychologically. It used to be that Mike enjoyed corporate combat and the verbal back-and-forth of the game, but now it was just an exhausting exercise for him.

The verbal onslaught felt like it had been going on for hours, while, in fact, they were only twelve minutes into the one-sided discussion. Mike was so worn out from the verbal barrage that he was about to put his head down on his desk and just dissolve when Marge roared, "Dammit, Mike, don't you dare disengage from this conversation.

"Now, where are we in fixing this pricing freefall? I see where our competitors in the Middle East haven't backed down one iota of production, and we are still in an alleged oversupply. I'm watching the American oil producers fold up like cheap lawn chairs and leave the picnic because the fireworks show is over. I'm certainly all about playing oil production chicken with our competitors from the Middle East, but not if this is a rigged game like you keep saying. Tell me what you've got so far."

An emotionally sapped and physically exhausted Mike Patrick rolled his head to one side so he could respond with all his remaining strength. He explained, "Marge, I've brought in two of the best data forensic people in the business to help find what is being tampered with and where. Roslyn was working with them all the way, until she was killed in a subway tube.

"You know, you get a little behind in your work when your trusted adviser suddenly gets killed. So, yes, I feel a little tired at the moment, but I haven't given up."

Marge was only modestly taken aback by the news of Roslyn's death. She had no practice in offering condolences or even a polite regret to the bereaved Mike. She offered, "Well, that's a damn shame, and at such a critical time for this company too.

"I knew she had feelings for you, especially since you were banging her like a loose screen door in a hurricane. Mike, you need to pull yourself out of the emotional morass you seem to be in and get this situation under control. Do I need to come there and help, or can you soldier on with Roslyn's replacement and these two computer geeks?"

Mike slowly rocked back into his chair, thoroughly awash with disgust and contempt for Marge. He sarcastically responded, "Marge, thank you for the warm sentiment that easily betrays your humanistic side in regards to Roslyn's passing. Perhaps one day your eulogy will cheer and inspire others just as you have done for me today."

Marge uncharacteristically took the sarcastic statements without losing her temper. She stated, "Oh come on, Mike. You and I have been over tougher ground than this, and we are still on top of our game. We've beaten others out of their promotions, side-stepped those grand jury investigations, and cleanly pinned those racketeering charges on our competitors. We will beat this thing too. But I need you back in the saddle, cowboy. Let's get this thing under control, and I'll buy you a nice tattoo in Roslyn's honor. Now can I count on you?"

Mike, with a fatalistic smile on his face, offered, "Yes, Marge, you can count on me. I feel ever so much better after your pep talk. I am all ready to jump back into the fray. I'll get back to you with the best news I can get."

Marge beamed as she responded, "There's a good lad. Keep your pecker up and talk soon."

After she disconnected from the conference call, Mike absent-mindedly stated to the phone, "Bitch!"

HMX ↓ -7.50
CMX ↓ -9.33
HCC ↓ -3.90
SOX ↓ -7.74

Petra was the first to be distracted by the commotion in the outer office. Even though the door to their working conference room was closed, Mike Patrick's voice easily penetrated into their work area.

Petra glanced at Jacob, who remained focused on his computer screen but commented, "Yeah, I hear him too. Unless I miss my guess, it sounds like we are about to have an unscheduled meeting with him."

Petra got up and almost made it to the door before Mike barged right through it into the room. Petra stood between Mike and Jacob, who was still facing his screen at a ninety-degree angle to the seething cauldron of emotion being emitted from Mike Patrick. Jacob sensed that Petra was on high alert and that she wouldn't back down from Mike even though he was twice her size. He knew she was always a consummate professional, but she would always stand her ground any man trying to bully her. It had cost her dearly in a similar altercation with Sönders, the director of the Werewolf Clan, and Jacob wasn't going to let that happen again.

To help diffuse the situation, Jacob turned toward Mike and stated, "It seems like the triple espresso shots you told me about certainly have your metabolic heart rate in overdrive. Where can I get one, and how much are they?"

It was enough to pull both of them back from the brinkmanship exercise they were about to launch into. Petra was still in a guarded mode.

Mike calmly offered, "Oh good, at least you two are working as expected. No one seems to know what's become of Laurie. I thought she might be in here. I see that is not the case, but since I've interrupted anyway, perhaps I could have a status report, Jacob."

Jacob knew it had irked Petra to no end that Mike was speaking to Jacob even though Petra was standing between them.

He suppressed his smile and responded, "Mr. Patrick, you should understand that both Petra and I have updates to provide you. We sense you are under great pressure to get to the bottom of this, which is why you have our team's top two professionals. I'd like to begin the briefing, sir, if you will take a seat after closing the door."

Mike, now in control of his temper, acknowledged Petra with a nod of his head and closed the door. Petra had returned to her seat as Mike took a seat across the table from the two of them.

Jacob began. "We have been digging into your computer systems. All of the regular ebb and flow of data is as it should be. That surprised us at first, since we expected an outside breach from somewhere, but nothing could be found. I've looked for rootkits, false credentials, unexplained escalated admin privileges, bogus virtual servers coming and going at inappropriate times, unexplained encrypted traffic on your network. Nothing. I was beginning to think I had lost my data forensic skills."

Mike's puzzled look telegraphed his thoughts before he asked, "You mean you can't find anything? Nothing is wrong?"

Jacob allowed his smile to set the stage for the next statement. "Actually, we modified our approach and began looking internally for the culprit. This was where we began finding things that did not add up, so to speak. The culprit wasn't on your data network where we could see tampering evidence but was working through a parallel network to extract data using a multimedia-enabled cell phone to take pictures and upload them to their cellular carrier's cloud service. There, they were shared with the next stage of the information laundering effort."

Mike, not completely understanding what he was being told, shook his head. Then he commented, "Okay, so someone took pictures and uploaded them to their photo page. These were then shared with a few hundred of their closest friends. How does that help with what we are trying to fix?"

Jacob furrowed his brow and explained, "The cell phone photos of the production numbers for your firm are the high runners of this data export exercise.

"You would recognize that what can go out can also find its way in, yes? So, if information is going out, then it is logical to assume that new bogus information is being sent back. But that is where we, or rather I, got stumped. What was found on the cloud service provider account was encrypted data. We found that the cloud service provider had a mirror site in region, and even though the MACDORS were scrubbing the account regularly, the other site retained the telemetry of the main site. The cloud service provider must have thought they would be dealing with some really dim bulb customers. So, in the event that someone called up crying that they had accidently deleted their files, the provider could restore them in minutes."

Mike, engaged but confused, flatly asked, "Uh, MACDORs? What the hell is that?"

Petra, joining in the conversation, said, "*Malicious Acting Characters Deserving Ostracism and Retribution.* It's how we like to refer to the bad guys within cyber space.

"For the encryption problem, I've been trying to break it so we could see the material coming in. This MACDOR is very clever in that he didn't use linear programming to encrypt his messages but rather elliptical encryption algorithms, which are infinitely more complex. They don't yield very well to primitive cracking techniques like brute force password attacks. I am sure you probably don't care how I broke their encryption cypher but we can report that we have opened the file, and Jacob can now read what is being sent into your environment."

Mike's mouth was slightly open, which only enhanced the dumbfounded look on his face as he blandly stated, "You know, I understood several words that you spoke, young lady, but can I get the abridged English version of how this might somehow be good news?"

Jacob stepped back into the conversation flow as he clarified, "Mike, once Petra had broken the encryption algorithm used to send and receive traffic of important data, we could then see how your number reporting was being poisoned. We saw the doctored production numbers being sent to the cloud account as though it was a mailbox delivering the next installment of number tampering."

Mike brightened up and sought some clarification. "I just heard you say that someone was moving information in and out, undetected, using a cell phone, and that is how our oil reporting numbers were being altered. What I haven't heard was who?"

Jacob and Petra exchanged quick but uneasy glances. Almost as if Jacob had lost the invisible coin toss, he quietly stated, "Mike, it was Roslyn. It was her account."

CHAPTER FORTY-TWO

Anybody, Everybody, but in fact Nobody

...The Enigma Chronicles

Carlos hoped that Quip's facial recognition program wouldn't take too long. Carlos had used his phone to ship the photo off with a quick text to Quip, hoping that he would get a fast turnaround on perhaps the true identity of Mr. Jolly Rogers. He had also texted Juan to ask that they try and stall the negotiations as much as possible so they could plan their next move. He didn't want this character to get away before they figured out who he really was.

Carlos was a little startled when his phone went off with an inbound text message from Quip. The message read:

Can you talk?

Somewhat puzzled by the text, Carlos scanned the area he was in and, deciding it was safe, dialed Quip's number.

Quip quickly answered. "Boy, you sure can pick 'em. Remind me to have your Yaqui Indian senses captured to disk so I can upload them to ICABOD at the next earliest convenience."

Carlos, fairly confused by the remark, asked, "Quip, what are you talking about?"

Quip dryly replied, "Juan had texted me that you were having a Yaqui Indian moment and that I ought to be standing by. He was right of course, but what none of us knew was how crazy your Yaqui Indian moment would be. Geez! Well, let's get down to it, my friend.

"I might as well admit it; I don't know who this Holland Rogers really is. I mean, there is a great case to make that what you have identified is a paranormal entity with no end to his cloaking ability."

Carlos was beginning to sense a real problem unfolding before his eyes and asked, "You say you don't know who he really is? What do you know? Anything?"

Quip studied the output on his computer screen for a moment and then flatly stated, "To begin with, he was identified in New York as the secondhand shop dealer, just as you indicated. Turns out he was also buying contract software from our old friends, the D-Team, for what was probably some hacking operation. Then he turned up in Atlanta at the airport as a chauffeur at one point and then as a medical technician at another. Then there are some fragments of his mug in the Helsinki-Vantaa Airport. Oh, and he also had a brief respite as a barbeque entrepreneur in Moscow. I like that one the best.

"This guy can be everybody, anybody, but in fact, is nobody. We've even got some near matches of his mug in Argentina just last month, but in no two places can we match the same name or passport to his face. We got his face, but apparently he doesn't want anyone to know who he really is."

Carlos was taking all this in and trying to process all that Quip was telling him. After a few seconds he asked, "Do you really think you can program ICABOD to hunt like a Yaqui Indian?"

Quip rolled his eyes and responded, "I might suggest that since you have a bead on him now, it might be a good idea to not let him out of your sight. Maybe with a little more input we can figure out who he really is. If you lose him, we may not be able to catch him again. Since he may already know and remember you, the next best option would be to have Juan track him."

Carlos nodded and stated, "That is probably true, but as we all know, Juan doesn't tail suspects very well. I think we'll have to use plan B to track this guy."

It was now Quip's turn to be puzzled as he asked, "Uh…plan B? What's plan B?"

Carlos smiled slightly as he replied, "Why, one hides in plain sight, of course."

NMX ↓ -7.50
CMX ↓ -9.33
HCC ↓ -3.90
SOX ↓ -7.74

Juan was still puzzling over the text message from Carlos when Lara came over near him and quietly asked, "How much longer do we need to keep up this charade with the Looney Rogers? After we are done with him, I've got to take an extremely hot shower and burn these clothes to get his proximity off my skin."

Juan thought for a moment and then commented, "Lara, I need a diversion that will give me a reason to try and work for the Looney Rogers. But I can't go ask him for a job if I still work for you. Carlos wants this guy tailed and…well, it needs to look good."

Lara studied Juan for a moment while Mr. Jolly Rogers was otherwise distracted inspecting the ship's bridge. Lara pulled Juan in close to her but then began to struggle enough to gain Holland's attention. Once she was under his full gaze, Lara pushed Juan away and, with a smart slap across his face, stormed, "I've just about had all of your pawing I can stand. Being a bodyguard doesn't mean you get to squeeze the fruit to see if it is to your liking. You're fired, and I want you off the premises right now!"

Juan studied her a moment with his hand on his face where she had clocked him. He turned to leave and caught Jolly's eye before he left the bridge. After Juan had left, Lara became noticeably calmer and almost smiled as she said, "I'm sorry you had to see that, but I've never been the kind of lady to tolerate inappropriate advances. Let us return to my offices and finish up our negotiation, shall we?"

Jolly, curious about the events that had just unfolded, asked, "I know it's none of my business, but wasn't that bodyguard the brother of your husband? Don't you want to call your husband and get your story in first? I'm pretty sure those two are going to talk. Well, in my experience, you'd be best served by having your story in first."

Lara studied Jolly a moment and then strolled over so her face was close to his and firmly offered in a low agitated tone, "You're right, Mr. Rogers, it's none of your business." She curtly moved out of the bridge and down the gangway to the shipping office.

CHAPTER FORTY-THREE

You Have to Earn the Right to Wear the Pants in the Family

...The Enigma Chronicles

When Quip arrived home to their comfortable flat, he was greeted with the aroma of garlic, onions, and salmon. The music was a nice medley of jazz, which he knew EZ played when she was trying to relax. Quip recognized he'd been a little pointed during a couple of recent conversations, which EZ had mentioned when she grumbled on their way to bed last evening without so much as offering to scrub his back in the shower. The shift in their routine had him worried. Perhaps this delicious smelling meal spoke to another new beginning. This living with a woman was a real challenge at times, but he loved her.

He set a bouquet of flowers on the bar, watching her focused on stirring. He had certainly learned that sneaking up behind her to nuzzle her neck when she had hot spoons or knives in her hand was a poor idea. She only had to burn him once for him to earn that lesson. She set the spoon in the holder on the stove and turned. He grinned and she almost smiled back.

"Honey," Quip said, "it smells wonderful in here. Whatcha making, sweetheart?"

"Don't sweetheart me. Sometimes, Quip, the things you say are, well...I don't know, more suited to the locker room when you were ten. They are so childish and borderline mean. I wasn't kidding earlier when I suggested you sleep on the couch.

"If my feelings are no more important than what you have suggested over the last few conversations, then go snooze with ICABOD, if he'll have you. Even he knows you are over the line. I'll have you know that my derriere is still the same size as when we met. If anything, a little more toned because I walk more here than I ever did in the States.

"However, since you have commented, all our meals are going to be fresh, healthy, and no more chocolate in this house, at all. You got that?"

Quip, rarely finding it hard to generate a smart retort, realized he was on dangerous ground. No chocolate would be a problem. But he also refused to be bullied in his own home.

"I am going to put these lovely flowers, which I brought home for the most beautiful lady in the world, into a vase. Then, I am going to set the table so I can taste what you have been working so hard on. After that, if you are still angry, darling, then I'll help you put sheets and a blanket on the couch for you to sleep on tonight."

The look of outrage on her face was priceless. He reached into the cabinet and pulled down the glass vase and filled it with water. She stomped back to the stove and stirred like there was no end in sight, but uttered not another word. He schooled his features and carefully got out all the table settings and placed them the way he knew she liked them. With the flowers on the table, he cocked his head to one side, then remembered the candles.

"Do I have time for a fast shower before the magnificent meal is ready?" he sweetly inquired.

"Yes." she replied without turning her head. Then she added, "Do you want to open the wine before you shower so it can breathe."

"Of course, sweetheart."

Quip made quick work of the wine and set it on the table and added the appropriate glasses. Then he went for a fast shower. He figured he must have made his point since she had not raised a knife, and she was close to several.

He smiled as he recalled how delightfully feisty, she was and pondered the wonderful things he would do to her later tonight to hear those unbridled pleasure sounds from her swollen lips after kissing her senseless. He would simply take her clothes off and kiss her from mouth to toes and everywhere in between. He fantasized about the way her breasts became so firm, with nipples that begged to be mouthed and sucked. EZ would pull his head so he would get even closer and please her more. Then he would trail down toward her toes and become distracted with her very warm core and how she was always so wet, so ready. He looked down to see how ready he was for the evening activities and grinned. He might be ready, but she still needed the romance side, especially after he had reaffirmed that he wore the pants in this family, even if his goal was to get hers off.

He quickly shut off the shower and toweled off. Dinner first and then hours of pleasure for both of them. He ran a comb through his hair and put on some comfy shorts and shirt. Wiping down the walls and hanging up the towel completed his chore. He turned to leave and whistled a tune, the plan firmly in his mind.

As he reached the main room, the music was still playing, though noticeably quieter, the lights were dimmed and she was seated at the table. The dishes were on the table and she reached up and lit the candles. He loved how the light reflected off her fiery red hair.

"Honey, it smells even better than when I first walked in. Thank you, again, for making wonderful food for us to share."

He poured the wine for them and raised his glass toward her. Their glasses touched and before he could make his toast, EZ firmly stated, "Sweetheart, if you ever try to lord it over me again, that you are the 'man' and I am the mere 'woman' in this relationship, I will short sheet the bed and find creative ways to use…well you just wonder about that part, mister. I am just as important as you are. You aren't serious about us, or you wouldn't make those hurtful comments. If you don't think so, I can be gone on the flight in the morning back to Atlanta. So, cheers to that."

Tears were running down her cheeks as the fury in her statements made her shake. She stood and walked over to the windows to stare at the evening lights.

Quip was beside himself. This was not the evening he had planned. Perhaps he had been a bit arrogant and heavy handed earlier. But he never expected her to cry, or worse, threaten to leave. He loved her.

He walked toward her with a close eye on her hands in case she decided to take a swing. He was reminded of wise words he once heard. When in doubt admit you are wrong and take your licks. That was what he had done with his major boondoggle in college with Tuck and Mike T., and it had worked.

"EZ, honey, don't cry. I'm sorry. You know off-the-cuff comments are how I am. You're right though, I did go wayyyy too far. I can learn. Honest, I can if you help me." He wrapped his arms around her, and she leaned into him with the shudders that signaled the end of the crying stint. "I don't want to fight with you, EZ. I want you to come back, and let's enjoy this wonderful meal you worked so hard to make. The smell of the food is almost as erotic as you are, my sweet."

"Quip, you really think that, or are you saying these things just because you're hungry?"

"Oh, no doubt about it, I am hungry. Hungry for you. I want to enjoy dinner and celebrate us staring into your green eyes can seeing highlights of the candlelight off your hair. Then I want to set the date for us to get married a month from today, anywhere you want."

EZ's eyes got as big as saucers as she smiled and hugged him, then bounced up to wrap her legs around his waist. She exclaimed, "Really, a month from today?"

"EZ, I don't want to ever feel like we could walk away from one another. I want to build a life with you. I will make mistakes and say things, but you have to know I love you. We will have fun, I will make you laugh, and you, my darling, can knock sense into me when I deserve it. I, in turn, will have my way with you, or you can have your way with me. Curtains open is always an option. Let's set the date in a month and do this."

She nuzzled into his ear. "Yes, oh yes, Quip. I love you so very much. I want to belong to you forever."

NMX ↓ -7.50
CMX ↓ -9.33
HCC ↓ -3.90
SOX ↓ -7.74

After a very romantic and erotic night with Quip, EZ was luxuriating in bed. They had spoken about some of the plans for their wedding, and Quip reassured her that anywhere she wanted for the wedding was fine. He agreed they should have the family involved, with Jacob and Tuck standing up with him. He said he would reach out to Tuck later today and alert him. He suggested she work out the details and let him know any things he needed to handle.

He had left for work early, and it dawned on her through her sleepy haze that a month was hardly any time at all. Heck, she didn't know if he wanted an engagement party to tell his family. She jumped up and grabbed her phone. She had to tell someone.

Moments later when Lara answered, EZ squealed, "Lara, I want to beg a favor from you, but don't tell anyone yet. Quip and I are ready to get married, with the date a month from today. I am not certain where yet, but I think on my family farm in Georgia. Quip said anywhere is fine with him."

Lara sputtered and squealed with excitement to match her friend and then rapidly asked, "How can I help, EZ? Did you want me to be in the wedding, or just tell someone? Does Julie know yet? Or Petra, Jacob? Do you want to have a shower, I would love to do that for you. This is so exciting. Did he go down on bended knee? I know you already had a ring. Emeralds and diamonds, right? Lovely, simply lovely."

EZ interrupted, "We haven't told his family yet. I am going to ask him if he wants to have a special call or dinner or…I don't really know. He wants his friend Tuck from Australia who he went to college with, and Jacob, specifically, to stand up with him. I know he would want it balanced with the ladies that want to be in it. It is such short notice.

"A shower would be lots of fun, but the time is so short, that might not be possible," she commented with a bit less enthusiasm.

Lara declared, "Anything is possible, my dear EZ. We'll make this so special! I have goosebumps thinking about how fun this will be, a whirlwind wedding."

"I know, Lara! Actually, that was why I called you first, I guess. Do you have time to perhaps create a wedding dress for me? I know it is crazy short notice, but I love all the clothes you design, and your wedding fashions have been one exclusive per year. I want an exclusive with lace, satin, fitted nicely. You know, to show off the shape but still leave something for the imagination."

"Wow, the ideas are already popping in my mind, EZ. With your lovely shape, long legs and gorgeous hair. Oh, hair…down or up? I need to know if you want a veil or perhaps just flowers.

Georgia is very pretty, lots of flowers, right, and peaches too. Your bridesmaids, do you want peach for your color or green to match your ring?

"I can do your dress and dresses for your bridesmaids. The men, how do you want them to be dressed? I moved you to speakerphone and am drawing like mad. Hopefully with a few details from you, I can send over some examples later today."

"Lara, I knew I could count on you. I think hair down, Quip really likes it down and curly. Flowers in the hair would be so nice, almost like a crown. I think I do want it on the farm. Peach-colored bridesmaid dresses and tuxedos for the men. Maybe light peach shirts, but I want to ask Quip, he might not like that idea.

"Would you stand up with me, Lara? It is crazy short notice and you've offered the dresses. It seems like a lot. Plus, I would love Julie and Petra to be with me. I think Julie's twins would be adorable as flower girl and ring bearer. What do you think? Daddy would love to give me away, I know. Su Lin, hmmm. What about Su Lin, should I ask her?"

"Okay, don't get too ahead of yourself. Su Lin will do what- ever you want, but she might want to stand next to Andrew after he hands you off. How is he feeling, by the way?"

EZ took a breath and calmly stated, "You are right, I need to slow down. Daddy says he is feeling great, and he looked good during our most recent video call. He's eating better, and Su Lin dotes on him. Apparently, they do most everything together. Even though he is still working, I think Carlos is doing the bulk of the work, except for his older customers. Last time we spoke, his doctor removed him from all his medications. As long as he keeps eating right and exercising, he will be great. I think Su Lin and Daddy are actually getting fairly serious. They really are great together."

Lara chuckled, "Alright, I am going to get these drawings done and send them to you. Would it be okay if we get a little advertising mileage out of this too, or would that upset you?"

EZ replied, "With all that you are offering to do for me, sure, get some advertising out of it. Friends help friends. I am so excited."

"I know, me too. Talk soon." Then a bit more seriously, Lara added, "Thanks for letting me know, EZ. I am so very happy for you and Quip."

CHAPTER FORTY-FOUR

Who Said It Should Be Fair?

...The Enigma Chronicles

In the African savanna, it is said, nothing is more dangerous than a wounded Cape buffalo. They are normally ill-tempered animals anyway and always more than a match for three to four attacking lionesses. More than one well-armed but ill-famed hunter has lost a contest in the bush with a wounded Cape buffalo who has been pushed into a thoroughly crazed and angered state.

The data forensics that Petra and Jacob had just delivered to Mike Patrick had launched him into an emotional state similar to a wounded Cape buffalo. Petra and Jacob shot uneasy glances at each other trying to comprehend the wounded animal's next move. While Mike's movements were like a slow-motion recording, Petra and Jacob were the highly animated motions at the opposite end of the filming spectrum. Mike's heart rate was not just high, but at a level close to detonation. His features were all flushed, his vision clouded by his rage, and his mouth no longer able to contain his saliva, which ran down his chin giving him the look of a rabid animal. Even though both Jacob and Petra were accomplished martial arts practitioners, the picture facing them was terrifying.

Mike mouthed almost coherently, "I'll kill you for that accusation. I...I cared for her! She would never have betrayed me."

Petra and Jacob moved into their respective positions of a fighting stance in the modest conference room. Mike still lunged clumsily in an effort to tackle both of them. Petra hit first with her curled fist straight into his solar plexus, which slowed him down but made him angrier. Mike might have taken out his anger on her if he hadn't been stopped cold with a frontal kick from Jacob that caught him right under his chin. The action had halted the charge and spun Mike into the corner. There, Jacob wrenched his arm back behind him, forcing Mike's head firmly into the wall with a heavy thud, which must have been heard on the other side of the wall.

The contest was over as quickly as it had begun, only Mike was no longer the raging Cape buffalo. Jacob gently tugged on Petra's arm to get her to move back in case he erupted again.

Once she was back a safe distance, Jacob, still breathing heavily, asked, "Mr. Patrick, can we talk now? I wasn't prepared to do any sparring with my customer on this trip, but I cannot let you take out your hostility on my partner, who is also my lady. We both understand your feelings in this matter, and it is perfectly alright to challenge our statements. However, before you lunge at either of us again, perhaps you should see what we have unearthed so far.

"Do I have your assurances that you will control your anger during this exchange? If not, we will be on our way."

Mike, trying to get his breathing under control as well as reel in his temper, slowly rotated around in the corner to face them. Still seething, bleeding from his nose, and with one eye swollen shut, he actually seemed satisfied with the beating he had just received. Somewhat smirking, he offered, "You don't have a damn thing. She loved me…she proved it on several occasions, so you couldn't possibly get me to believe she was the one rigging the numbers. You do a little computer mumbo-jumbo, and you think you've got it all solved. You may have beaten me in this little exercise, but I'm not done yet. I didn't get to where I am by letting some kids smear my woman's name after she's..."

Mike's voice trailed off, and now tears were added to the other fluids running down his face.

Petra began to pull on Jacob's arm to coax him to leave. Jacob resisted and flatly said, "You, Mike, I thought you were a hard nut to crack. You really didn't see this coming, did you? Well, I'll make you a deal. Let me show you our proof points per our contract, collect our fees, and then we will be on our way."

Mike sneered, "Like I said, she was in on all my decisions, and I paid her well. There was nothing she didn't get or couldn't have. You are wasting your time, as well as mine."

Jacob began to feel sorry for the arrogant and delusional Mike Patrick but refused to leave without sharing the truth.

Jacob commented, "Okay, I get it. You don't want to believe the computer traces of the photos being uploaded and new material being sent to her. I found an exact correlation to the received photos with that information being input into your systems, data cell by data cell with her user ID. But let's be generous here and offer her the benefit of the doubt, shall we? I mean, someone else could have gotten her user ID and password, then sat at her PC with the exact same TCP/IP computer address that is specifically reserved for her in the DHCP scopes, and keyed in this bogus information, during regular business hours when Roslyn wasn't at her terminal. By the way, it would require Roslyn to have been away for at least four hours at a time not to catch the real perpetrator."

Mike smirked and, wiping some of the blood off of his mouth, exclaimed, "Okay, let's say that. What else you got, bright boy?"

Jacob hesitated a moment, not knowing what his next statements would do to Mike, but finally asked, "If none of what I told you is true, then can you explain her stock purchase activities? Or, should I say, her short selling activities? More specifically, the short selling of ePETRO stock? I checked to see if she was an officer of the company, which would have thrown up a red flag in the securities trading arena. Oddly enough she wasn't even listed as your trusted secretary or administrative assistant. Mike, the short selling of stock with insider information is strictly illegal in every market that I know of. Someone has to know that it is insider information."

Mike's face turned ashen, and stuttering to make his point, he shouted, "That's not possible! Are you fabricating material now to justify your accusations? This is just more lies on top of the other lies!"

Jacob continued, "It did take a little digging to find the stock shorting activity because she was clever enough to use another person's name and identity, her aunt I believe. The one in the nursing home that Roslyn has the power of attorney for."

Jacob calmly handed over the stock trading history with Roslyn's aunt's name, government number, and nursing home address to Mike for his review.

Jacob added, "Quite a lot of trading gains in her aunt's name which should amount to some rather large tax consequences, I should think, but there doesn't seem to be any provision for paying the looming tax bill since the trading gains are being re-routed as fast as they are realized. I'm pretty sure that the aunt is not going to understand any of this, based on her current mental state, so at least that is something of a blessing."

Mike's temper began to reengage as he read through row after row and page after page while Petra and Jacob looked on.

Jacob waited a few moments before he proposed, "You know what is odd? She spent a lot of time and effort to camouflage her trail here in the UK. However, she sent all her fairly well-hidden profits to an offshore bank in the Cayman Islands, without using an alias. It took a little convincing of the bank president to discuss her activities with us since they have very strict bank secrecy laws there. I guess she was counting on that. After I explained that they were harboring monies from a securities fugitive, they quickly came around.

"They also felt justified in, ah…retaining a penalty fee for misrepresenting herself. The rest will be re-patriated to the UK where, most likely, the funds will have more penalties extracted. You will want a full accounting for your bosses, I suspect."

Mike, only half listening to Jacob, kept leafing through the printout, partially expecting the output to magically change.

"Oh, and one other detail here. Apparently when the funds were repatriated, a young man showed up asking about his weekly stipend for managing the property that Roslyn had acquired not too long ago. He didn't seem to offer much in the way of iden- tification, other than a claim to be the cabana boy for Roslyn's property. Word is, he caused quite a ruckus when they denied his money requests on her behalf." Jacob supplied a copy of the property deed that displayed only Roslyn's name on it.

After several minutes, Mike quietly put the report on the table and painfully helped himself up so he could stand. The final pieces of evidence had proved their point, and it had hollowed Mike out from the inside.

Jacob almost felt sorry for Mike as he consoled, "It is bitter knowledge to share with you, Mr. Patrick. I promised you we would get to the bottom of your issue, but we never promised you'd like what we would find."

Mike studied both of them. After a useless effort to make himself presentable, he left the room without saying a word.

CHAPTER FORTY-FIVE

Up, Up, and Over, Roger

Juan waited down the block from the shipping offices for Mr. Rogers to finish the negotiations and leave. Juan had been in contact with Julie via text to alert her as to the possibilities of his hooking up with this guy to keep him under surveillance. Her response had clearly indicated she hated the idea, but she really didn't have an alternative plan. She insisted he keep her in the loop and included Carlos in that text to avoid any misunderstanding. Carlos had suggested Jolly Rogers was one man they wanted to keep a close eye on, based on the findings he related from Quip.

A grinning Mr. Rogers exited the office building with a swagger in his step, suggesting the deal had been finalized as he'd wanted. He called someone and paused under a tree to complete the conversation. Juan suspected it was business not pleasure as the man was very attentive to the conversation, almost intense. Juan waited until the conversation was completed and Mr. Rogers was headed toward him, obviously to meet his cab.

Rogers spotted him, grinned, and said, "Son, you really messed up a sweet deal back there. I would agree that Miss Lara is a beautiful lady, but your brother's wife! That is just messed up, like something I might have done years ago. I guess you are just a young pup with no better sense. Har, har, har!"

Juan looked chagrined and responded, "Sir, I would have to agree with you that it was foolish, but she is a flirt and a half. I think it was more for the office manager she feared was spying than anything she didn't want. You know how some women are, not worth the time of day at all. Now though, I am without work in a country with the economy spiraling in, and I wondered if we might share a ride back to the airport.

"I presume you are going to the airport, if your negotiations were successfully completed. I need to take a trip to Chile or Argentina to try to hook up with one of my part-time piloting jobs. Making money is seriously needed here in South America, as you can tell. Piloting pays far better than this lousy bodyguard stuff anyway, plus it is way more fun. There is nothing like the freedom of taking a bird up and going anyplace you want. No one to mess with you. Sorry, I do go on. May I join your cab ride, sir? I will, of course, pay half."

LJ thought about what he had heard and studied over what the problem with that might be. Not able to find a downside, he said, "I don't mind at all, young man. I will even pay. Heck, for me it is nothing but a bidness expense. You wouldn't happen to speak Spanish or Portuguese, would you? I have one stop I want to make on the way to the airport, but this driver was only tracking on a part of my conversation, I think."

Juan chuckled and replied, "I do speak Spanish well and some Portuguese. However, sometimes these drivers know more about what you are saying than you think. You know, they learn most of their English listening to rock'n'roll music. I will certainly help you. No need for you to be taken advantage of, sir."

They waited in companionable silence for a few minutes with Juan staring at a group of young kids playing a game with rocks and sticks. Their pants were well worn and shoes clearly had holes, but they seemed to ignore all of that to just be kids.

LJ watched where Juan was watching and finally asked, "Why are you staring at those young'uns like that?"

Juan moved his head to look LJ in the eyes and replied, "I grew up like that. Too poor for decent shoes or clothes, and no ball or glove until my uncle took me in. I'd guess someone of your success wouldn't understand what it is to be so very poor. Most of these kids are lucky if they get a meal a day."

LJ turned away and shook his head. "We have poor areas in the US of A too." Then a few minutes later, he seemed to want to change the subject so he asked, "How long you been a pilot? And do you have a current license?"

Juan replied, "I have been flying small and large aircraft for right at fifteen years. These days, I only fly private planes, any size though. I have flown all over the United States, Mexico, South America, some in Europe and the Caribbean. It is lots of fun. I even had this job where I flew these pretty models around for their photoshoots. Boy, there were some benefits in that job!"

LJ grinned and replied, "Now you're talking. So what was that like?"

Before Juan could respond, LJ's phone rang. LJ looked at the screen and said to Juan, "I gotta take this, young man. If the cab shows up, hold it for me, okay?"

"Sure, no problem."

LJ stepped away and seemed to be in a lively two-way conversation, though Juan could not make out any of the words. Juan did consider how he might make this guy ask him to help. He decided the best way was to show how great his language skills were. A few minutes later the driver arrived, and Juan spoke to the driver briefly and handed him some cash to seal the deal. LJ finally finished and returned to the car.

LJ asked, "Where were we? Oh, now I recall, you were going to tell me about them models. Let's do that on the ride to the hotel for me to pick up my bags and then to the airport. I also need to stop at the bank and get a wire transfer I was just sent."

LJ turned to the driver and tried for five minutes to convey the route he needed to take. The driver looked confused and kept holding up his arms in confusion or shaking his head and saying 'no comprende'. This went on for at least ten minutes, and LJ saw the time on the meter was already running.

"Juan is your name, right? Can you explain to this man in his language what I needs to do? Now I am afraid if this keeps up, I won't get to the airport in time."

Juan faced the driver, gave him a wink and smile as he conveyed the request in perfect Spanish. The driver smiled and nodded, then opened the door for his two passengers. He continued to chatter until the car entered onto the freeway, at which point Juan had replied for the driver to watch the road and let them continue their conversation.

Juan said, "Hey, I am sorry that took so long, but after he realized I could speak Spanish, he had to tell me about his kids and family. He was so glad to have someone during the day that he could speak with for a change . He said the tourists were always pushy and rude, not that you were. He is taking us to your hotel. I will wait in the cab while you check out, unless you need my translation support. I doubt it as this hotel chain typically staffs multilingual people to accommodate the tourist."

"I can do the hotel and the bank just fine. If you can keep hold of this cab, that does help. Now about those models, details, young man, I want details."

Juan regaled Mr. Rogers with wild stories amassing every story any of his pilot friends had ever told. It had them both laughing by the time they pulled up to the hotel. The driver insisted on being paid for this leg of the trip, though Juan said he would stay with the driver to make certain he did not take off. Mr. Rogers returned with suitcases in hand and a grin. He looked a little different with gold teeth showing that Juan hadn't previously noticed. He'd also changed his shirt and added a Panama hat that not only mushed down his hair some, but gave it a fringe effect that completed his hairstyle change.

Juan arched his eyebrow after the man entered the cab, and they took off toward the bank near the airport.

Then he asked, "Mr. Rogers, you look a little different. That is a great shirt, sir."

LJ grinned, flashed the golden teeth, and stated, "I do like this shirt, and the hat makes me look important, doesn't it?"

"Yes, sir, it does indeed."

At the bank entrance, Juan again stayed with the cab but successfully captured a photo of Rogers with his phone in the reflection of the bank window. Fortunately, there was a lovely woman nearby which he would use as his excuse for taking the shot, if it came up. Mr. Rogers returned half an hour later with a soft leather satchel, like an old-fashioned doctor's bag. He carried it closely and, after getting into the car, placed it under his feet.

LJ asked, "So, did I hear you mention you needed to get to Chile, young man?"

Juan replied, "I did. There is a chance I can get a three-day job on a charter plane. It is for one of the places I sometimes do part-time flying for. Is that where you are going?"

"I could go there and do some quick bidness, but I was really thinking of chartering my own plane. I am so tired of customs in these South American airports, and I just want to get in, get out, and go to my next destination."

Juan thought for a moment and replied, "There are three charter plane companies at the Rio de Janeiro–Galeão International Airport. I have flown for both NetJet and PrivateFly, and they keep their equipment in good working order. No fun flying if the plane has issues. Now you should know that I have flown enough with them that I can be your pilot. That means we will only have to pay for a co-pilot, which will cost less. But let me choose the co-pilot. I hate flying with someone who can't find a destination airport and turns into a map thrasher in the cockpit!"

LJ roared with laughter and, nodding, said, "That sounds fine, then. Why don't you call them and see if you can rent one from either of those places. Then you can fly me to Chile and then to Panama. Chile will be an overnight trip, and I'll make the hotel arrangements. Panama might be a couple of days, and I will make the hotel arrangements. I'll cover the charter costs, hotel, your food, and give you five hundred US dollars per day. But I ain't paying top dollar for no map thrashing co-pilot, so we need to be driving a hard bargain with these folks. Comprende?"

Juan looked pleased with the arrangements and responded, "Wow! That is great, just great, and solves two of my problems. Let me see if one of them has planes available."

LJ added as an afterthought, "Make sure we get something that is comfortable. I don't want to fly in one of those low flying bug-smashers that takes a shoehorn to get into. This old boy is too large for a small plane, and, well, I can afford a little luxury at this stage in my career."

With that Juan dialed Julie and asked in Spanish if she had a plane available like it was NetJet on the line. It took a few minutes of rapid speech for him to convey at a high level what the plans were without saying too much in such close quarters, in case this man knew more Spanish than he let on. On the back end, Julie worked her magic and arranged, not only for a plane with NetJet, but that their operative Mercedes, who was already in Rio, would meet them at the airport and be the hostess for the flights. Julie had a little more trouble convincing the NetJet people that all they wanted was a junior grade co-pilot, but in the end she won out in her bargaining. She would coordinate getting the food on board as well, making certain the co-pilot was totally attuned with his MP3 player in case Juan needed him to avoid any unwarranted eavesdropping. Juan was sincere when he thanked the person on the call, which LJ obviously understood.

"Sir, I think we are set. NetJet has a nice aircraft for us, and I was able to negotiate the price down due to my being the pilot. They agreed to a junior grade co-pilot but insisted on one of their attendants for the crew, which I said would be okay. She will be with the plane in each country and help facilitate the local customs areas. I was told she is very efficient as long as you have passports.

"If it is the one, I am thinking of, I've flown with her before. A real cutie with brown curly hair and big brown eyes, roughly a meter and a half tall, with well-placed curves. She speaks four languages. I think her name is Kitty, though the person on the phone said Caitlyn." Juan grinned, knowing that Mercedes was all that and more.

LJ cocked his head to one side and roared with laughter. Then he collected himself, flashed his teeth, and responded, "I think we're going to get along just fine."

CHAPTER FORTY-SIX

Forgetting Something?

Quip had been exuberant when he arrived at work. He was filled with a sense that today he could solve anything. He had called Tuck and told him the news about the upcoming wedding, as well as requested his standing up for him. He'd been a little worried when Tuck had promised he would have a wonderful bachelor party two nights before the big day so Quip could recover. Knowing Tuck as he did, he wondered if two days recovery time would be enough.

Returning to his current work focus, he decided to have ICABOD assemble commodity data from a new perspective, one that included twice the timelines previously considered. Coupled to that data gathering process change was the facial recognition for the recurring black man who appeared in several unrelated incidents, including those Carlos had brought to light. All this data was parsed together for Wolfgang to review with Otto and possibly Jim Hughes. There was a nagging suspicion in the back of Quip's mind in all of this that he should recognize, but it was just out of reach.

ICABOD commented, "Dr. Quip, you have previously stated that sometimes when things are out of reach by your mind, you need a distraction. Is your upcoming wedding not enough distraction for you to pull the data you seek from your memory?"

Quip replied, "Sometimes it works for humans in that way, yes. Other times the specific memory might remain out of reach until some catalyst helps it resurface. For the time being, I think the path of looking at the data from this viewpoint and adding relevant associated data will help us find those that are manipulating the pricing issue. My thinking is that we need to layer on additional but unlikely threads of activity from unlikely sources that are impacting our basic observations. I suspect we are not interweaving all the relevant parts to this equation, which is why we keep asking, 'What's wrong with this picture?'

"But let me change gears on you. Say EZ has suggested that perhaps my routine commentary might be a bit harsher these days. How would you evaluate that comment, ICABOD?"

"Dr. Quip, I am still learning the subtleties of humor, so my commenting on that would not be insightful. Those aspects of human humor which trigger feelings would logically differ from one being to another as well as to the same being at different times. I have noticed in many cultures females sometimes seem illogical in their responses if they are under stress, in love, or overtired. EZ is obviously in love with you or she would not have agreed to a wedding within such a short time frame.

"You do have a very quick wit and a ready retort to most statements, especially when you and Jacob are working on a problem together. Jacob has become quite adept at rapid responses as well. But I also observe that you tend to stay too long in a jesting mode while everyone else has changed their emotional gears to be in another state of mind. Perhaps there is a saturation point of humor or jests that you have not quite grasped when dealing with others."

Quip absentmindedly replied, "Yes, of course. ICABOD, you have learned how to avoid responses. Well done! Now let's get this data assembled. I am completing some modifications to the data collection and sorting I want done. It may take a while to complete, but interim summaries are desired, with the caveat that those will be revised as more data is reviewed.

"I need to text Jacob and let him know about the wedding too."

HMX ↓ -7.50
CMX ↓ -9.33
HCC ↓ -5.90
SOX ↓ -7.74

Lara had sent several different wedding dress designs to EZ since her return from Rio, with the most recent design being the one EZ had replied was absolutely the one. It was a different style than what Lara had started with, but it captured all the lines of a woman and still left a lot to the imagination.

Lara smiled to herself as she called Marcia Sanchez, her advertising and marketing expert.

Marcia was a traditional Brazilian beauty in her own right at just over 1.7 meters. Her frame was slight, with her dark auburn hair coiled in a perfect twist with a few wisps curled near her forehead. Her espresso brown eyes were large and observant. Her mouth had generous lips coated with lipstick the color of a fine merlot, which today matched her dress. One of the reasons Lara enjoyed Marcia so much, outside of being excellent at her job, was her immediate grasp of any situation.

Marcia entered and asked, "What can I do for you, Lara? You sounded excited on the phone."

Lara nodded and pointed to the drawing that was up on the easel in her office. Her corner office at Destiny Fashions had floor to ceiling windows which allowed the natural light to fill the room. Colors seemed richer in this room, so she would often have the fabrics she wanted shown in here at several times during the day to see the colors in every light. Marcia approached the drawing and then moved to catch it from different angles.

After a few minutes of studying the drawing, she announced, "Lara, this is really lovely. And the samples of the ivory-colored lace and satin seem perfect to my untrained eye."

Lara laughed and replied, "Untrained! Hardly. You may not be an artist, but color and textures are definitely your strength.

"My dear friend, Eilla-Zan Marshall, is getting married in a month. She has agreed to this design for her dress."

"Lara, it is a beauty. I presume that she is the lady in the photograph next to the drawing. Her red hair is extraordinary and vibrant. A month is a short time to build a campaign. Who is she to marry?"

"She is marrying the brilliant Dr. Quentin Waters. They are to be married in Georgia. I am waiting for the date, though we don't want to publish the date or details of the location exactly. They are fairly private. His family has been involved in several philanthropic causes associated with European families impacted by the Nazis, as well as scholarships for future technology engineers."

"How exciting. Is it one of those fabulous whirlwind romances, or have they dated for some time?"

Lara smiled as she recalled, "They have dated for some time. She and Carlos actually work together. She is so smart, and her father has this well-established telecommunications business. I don't have a photograph of Quip, but he is very handsome and they look well matched. She wants tuxedos for the men and ivory shirts. Apparently, he did not find favor with the peach color she suggested. I am going to work on the bridesmaid dresses next, and I get to be a bridesmaid."

Marcia crowed, "That's delightful. Our own Destiny Fashions leader is creating the one-of-a-kind dress and will be in the wedding. That is exciting. Who are the groomsmen, do I know any of them? I bet they are famous."

Lara shook her head and answered, "Not really famous, at least I had not heard of them. One I know quite well, Jacob Michaels, who does some computer programming, I believe, and the other is a David Tucker, currently residing in Australia, who Quentin went to graduate school with. I think. I have no idea what he looks like, but you know those Aussies are all gorgeous.

"Anyway, I think I want to also do a custom bridal lingerie from this design, which we could sell, if you think we can build a campaign from that. I would not want to sell another of these dresses of course, but for the more romantic I think we could do the lingerie line in several pastel shades. I could have a few samples by the wedding. I have a few ideas that I will get on paper later today and into the design team for some samples. I am also going to ask my friend Julie to see if she has any contributing ideas. Eilla-Zan currently works for Julie, doing unified communications work. Julie contributes design ideas sometimes but doesn't want her name used."

Marcia nodded and replied, "I knew that. Julie has been to a couple of the on-site photo shoots, right? She has the most captivating smile. No problem, her name will not be used anywhere. Any other particulars, boss?"

Lara shook her head even as she picked up her drawing pad and started sketching like a mad woman. Then she stopped suddenly and looked up as she stated, "No, I think you can deal with it. I have this idea I have to capture. I trust you to take care of it, Marcia. Let me know if you need me."

CHAPTER FORTY-SEVEN

Retraining Old School Data Soldiers

Quip stated, "I mean, to hear you talk, Wolfgang, this sounds like some sort of GEPS. What I'm hearing is that we are getting fresh chaos being injected into our regular stale chaos."

Wolfgang puzzled a moment and asked, "GEPS?"

Quip, always pleased when an acronym pulled a listener up short, cheerfully replied, "*Global Economic Perfect Storm*, or GEPS. I often quote myself to enhance the mystic of talking to me."

Wolfgang studied Quip while wondering if he or Quip should be forcibly volunteered for the first Martian space colony, beginning immediately, for Wolfgang's psychological preservation.

Quip interrupted this thought process. "Wolfgang, we know that ICABOD has been over-running your buffers here of late, and it occurs to me that we are doing this all wrong. You should not be reviewing, assimilating, or correlating what ICABOD is assembling. We need him to do that while you review his threaded analysis. I don't want to watch you age before my eyes due to something our fabulous AI computer can do.

"Now, Jacob and I have crafted a voice-activated program that will allow you to alter collection parameters. It will let you ask for cause and effect, while retaining the right to distort the results with *what if* scenarios. I would like to help you test drive it as soon as you're ready, but please stop this last century analysis. This process you are doing borders on Franciscan friars copying manuscripts."

Wolfgang gave a sigh of resignation and acknowledged, "Yes, you are quite right. I've been foolish to try to do this analysis with my own brainpower. I must admit that it is terribly inefficient. Plus, I would like to better use our good friend ICABOD to process these huge data mines to find our culprit. When can we start? And, more importantly, what manuals do I need to read before we can use the program?"

Quip just stared blankly for a moment before returning to the conversation and offering, "Uh, Wolfgang, I program ICABOD so there are NO manuals to read in order to work with him. He is programmed to build the needed data program changes, based on what results you are hunting. You state out loud so he can hear what you're thinking and where we should be prowling. Then it is his job to go fetch the relevant data, shift it against the query parameters you want cross indexed, and distill appropriate answers to be modeled further. Think of ICABOD as a genie, where you speak your command and your wish is granted. Is that any clearer?"

Wolfgang shook his head, looking amazed, and acquiesced, "There is so much to learn. So how about a tutorial then that I can watch and take notes from?"

Quip was nearly undone with the question and was about to respond when ICABOD offered, "Wolfgang, I anticipated such a need, so why don't you and I go through the tutorial that we have built while Dr. Quip finishes up his other issues? I believe the tutorial will only take fifteen minutes and will be time well spent. Is that agreeable, sir?"

Wolfgang brightened and replied, "Yes, of course. Quip, leave me to this learning session, and we can reengage later for the in-depth explanation you obviously have in mind. Thank you both for your efforts to bring this old school data soldier into the 21st century. And Quip…I really am not planning to volunteer you for Mars colonization, just so you know."

Quip smiled to cover his puzzlement and allowed his eyes to trail off of Wolfgang. He tried to make sense of the statement while conducting a speedy exit from the room.

```
NMX  ↓ -7.50
CMX  ↓ -9.33
HCC  ↓ -3.90
20X  ↓ -7.74
```

Hours later Otto stuck his head into Quip's work area and stated, "Oh, you're in here. With the system being so slow, I figured you were re-indexing your porn collection. But since you're not, any ideas of why the system is DSS?"

Quip, wide-eyed and pretending innocence, offered, "Otto, I promised not to do that anymore. Besides, the last sequencing rendered a very agreeable orientation of well-proportioned ladies in a suitable progression of…"

Otto raised his hand to halt further details of how Quip's subject matter had been arranged. Otto asked, "Alright! If it isn't you, then why are we DSS processing?"

Quip, unable to go any further in the conversation, complained, "Okay, I have to know. What is DSS processing?"

Otto grinned and replied, "Why, *Dog-Sled Slow,* my boy. I know we are going to get there eventually, but I don't want my muscles to atrophy while waiting for my routines to complete. If it's not you, then what is Wolfgang working on?"

Quip, also aware of the slowness of the system, suggested, "I left him a couple of hours ago with ICABOD to run through a non-existent tutorial. Why don't we go see where they are in Wolfgang's reeducation?

"Oh, and Wolfgang has offered to rescind my being sentenced to a Martian penal colony. So let's not try to upset him any more than what he already is."

It was Otto's turn to be uncomfortable with what he was being told. He wisely didn't ask for further clarification.

Once they arrived in Wolfgang's work area, they were greeted with a most unusual sight. ICABOD's endless rows of racked blade servers were all either rapidly pulsing their respective blue lights or in an orange steady state on the front panels. Wolfgang sat with his eyes closed in a lotus position, as if he was in a trance, but he was making rapid fire statements that seemed to be executed immediately by ICABOD. They watched in astonishment as more and more blade servers began to go from flashing blue to solid orange with every sentence uttered by Wolfgang.

Alarmed at the data center's condition, Quip frantically asked, "Wolfgang, what are you doing? I left you with ICABOD for a modest tutorial, and I come back to see what looks like digital Armageddon in my data center!"

Trying to get a handle on ICABOD's runaway processing effort, Quip loudly stated, "ICABOD, whatever you are doing, bring it to a halt and cap the processing event you are executing. I don't want to have to sponge up your core processors!"

Startled, Wolfgang opened his eyes and took stock of where he was and the condition of the systems tottering on meltdown. He sheepishly stated, "Uh, I'm sorry, gentlemen, and ICABOD. I didn't mean to overamp the system with iterative commands that spawned multiple cascading threads to explore. But dang, what a ride!

"I mean, you think out loud, ICABOD runs with it until the answer comes back, and then we take that response to query along another line of thinking. Then, and I really like this part, you can take and compare two apparently dissimilar linear sequences and look for parallelisms between them. Then I added others to see how they intertwined!"

Wolfgang enthusiastically added, "ICABOD, you did some great broken field running in the data processing of my requests. Was I pushing your processing limits too far? This new program is intoxicating, but I don't want to damage your processing abilities by trying to analyze too much. Quip is absolutely correct to question my use of resources, pursuing this line of thinking."

Quip, very interested in their line of thinking, asked, "ICABOD, can you recount the multiple query threads you two have assembled, so we can see at a high level where we are, please?"

ICABOD responded, "Certainly, Dr. Quip. After you left, Wolfgang and I began our tutorial starting with some free form questions he wanted to resolve. Our journey began with the simple question 'Can world commodity prices be manipulated to not conform to regular supply and demand pricing?'

"Our supposition was, if commodity pricing can be manipulated, then how? If commodity pricing can be distorted, then why? It was at this point our data sets started to get rather large to try and capture the dependencies and the cascading outcomes. Once we had some why issues on the table, the ultimate question came up of who?"

Wolfgang was very animated at this point as he suggested, "Quip, this program is fantastic. I was so used to putting figures into spreadsheet columns, I wasn't capable of seeing the benefit of ICABOD's processing power just by speaking out loud. Sorry for my exuberance, but I've gotten further in a few hours than all of my efforts of the past two weeks!"

Otto and Quip cast uneasy glances at each other as Wolfgang offered, "Okay, I see the looks you are giving each other. Let me jump to some interesting results, since you seem uninterested in my freshly developed skillset. I know we have more to examine, but we now understand the game plan of the DMO.

"We have focused primarily on oil and coal because of the planet's energy needs. Our analysis shows an inter-correlation with government-issued bonds, commodity pricing, the local job market relative to the host country, tax revenues and social programs relative to the producing countries, and civil unrest when governmental promises are not met.

"In each scenario we ran, each country was destabilized financially and economically by dropping the underlying commodity price. When that happened, loans and debt instruments of the sovereign country were disrupted because the price of the collateral commodity was no longer enough to guarantee the note. We noticed a lender tolerance of 20% loss, but as the loss drifts past 30% on its way to 40% down, the lender tolerance vanishes. Additionally, collateral was demanded at the same time tax revenues were dropping, which strains the social programs that each commodity-producing country has in place.

"Businesses retrench, resulting in layoffs, which further depresses the tax revenues, and people quit spending. That puts downward pressure on inflation upon which every government counts upon. Again fewer revenues, strain on social services, all of which puts pressure on existing governments, setting the stage for destabilization or just the collapse of governments."

Otto, fully on board with the DMO's trajectory, asked, "What then? Time for a new governmental entity, or just fresh chaos on top of our normal stale chaos, to quote Quip."

Wolfgang became very intense as he postulated, "Basically, the model predicts a government overthrown in favor of another entity promising to fix everything. The DMO steps in just like the Nazi party did in the elections of 1933, when everyone had given up and had nothing left to lose. And, since the DMO has rigged the commodity pricing to their advantage, they can reverse the downward spiral and make everything wonderful again. People go back to work, social services resume, and the DMO now controls the government. It doesn't take much imagination to see what the new world order would be like once these criminals get into power. It is a scenario which has played time and time again."

Everyone was quiet for a moment until Wolfgang quietly offered, "In all the modeling we worked through, gentlemen, we saw no way to stop the falling dominoes that begins with falling commodity prices. Once it starts it cannot be stopped.

"At this point we know the game plan, but I must confess, we don't have a handle on this DMO's identity yet. Whoever they are, they have not yet stepped up to take control in these targeted countries. However, let me plainly state, all of these countries we have looked at are targeted. The numbers prove it."

CHAPTER FORTY-EIGHT

Some Things Can't Be Helped

The last couple of days had been filled with fun and plans for the wedding. The families had been delighted with Quip and EZ's announcement for the wedding as well as its location at the farm in Georgia. From the European side, Haddy was busy setting up travel for the family and friends to get everyone into Georgia four days in advance to allow for the respective bachelor and bachelorette parties that everyone wanted to attend. From the Georgia side, Su Lin and Andy were busy arranging for the catering, making certain the guests actually staying at the ranch had rooms, and hiring a car service to pick up all the guests for transport. Though it was to be a relatively quiet wedding, the guests' travel was inbounded from so many places.

ICABOD had reminded Quip earlier that he needed to make certain to get David Tucker's flight arrangements to Haddy for the coordination efforts. Quip finished up the final touches on the modifications to the data sourcing programs he wanted to get into place and placed the call to his buddy. It had been several years since they had all been at the barbie Tuck had hosted, and Quip was looking forward to more outrageous stories with his friends.

Quip went into the smaller conference room to gain a little privacy and placed the call. Tuck actually answered the private line himself. "Hey, Quip, I was just about to call you."

Quip coolly replied, "Good, you have the flight information I need, and will you be bringing that pretty lady who was at the barbie? I want to make certain we have the correct private accommodations for you. It takes time to arrange for sound-proofing, you know."

Tucker heartily laughed, then commented, "Yes, I am bringing my darling Mavie. Now you best reel in your imagination, mate. She is a real lady, and I won't have you embarrassing her with your crass commentary. You have a lady too now, so that knife cuts both ways."

"Now, Tuck, you and I both know that ladies who favor us have to know we talk trash a lot. But we are totally sincere in the romance department, or we'd never be seen with them in public."

"Don't *now, Tuck* me, Quentin! The real reason I was about to call you is to tell you to knock it off. I am tired of your little I-Spy game because it is creeping Mavie out. I told her it was probably on account of your fear of what I am planning for your bachelor party, but she thinks you are over the top in the invading-our-privacy thing. Thankfully she is just as good at covering her computer tracks as we are and spotted the early signs. We've been through a lot together over the years, but in this matter, I don't want to play. I'm telling you, knock it off now, or you can stand up by yourself!"

Quip looked at the phone and then swapped it for a video call. Then he checked his computer data and time to see if he had worked longer than he thought. When the video image of his friend was clear, he noticed that his face looked sincerely angry. Quip was confused at the conversation and even angry as he looked straight into the camera and replied, "Look, Tuck, I'm not certain what you are referring to by the I-Spy game. I am really busy with work, and the wedding is an all-consuming thing but something I thought you'd like to share in. If you don't want to stand up, fine by me, but don't accuse me of something I'm not doing. And, yes, we have been through a lot together, but I'm actually offended that you would accuse me of something so juvenile. I do enough on my own to get blamed for without taking on other stuff, and this other stuff you are describing isn't me!"

Tuck was taken aback and studied the image of Quip on his screen. Then he rubbed his chin in thought before he suggested, "Alright, Quip, let me start over and ask. Have you and your clever computer skills been trying to follow me around? Mavie is living with me and continues to see things that are odd in our technology-driven home. Most recently, she thinks the behavior is like someone is watching or, more precisely, prowling."

Quip looked very concerned as he carefully answered, "Tuck, I honestly don't have the time or any reason to spy on you and your girl. Frankly, it is a little creepy that you would even consider that as an option. It begs the question, why would you and Mavie think it was me at all? I haven't seen you since the barbie, and we don't have routine conversations."

Tuck nodded and replied, "You're right, mate, we don't. But it started the day after I agreed to stand up at your wedding, and you had called me back to say where it was being held so I could book flights. It seems like every single time I get hooked up with you on something, one or both of us get into hot water. I figured you were concerned about the party I am planning for you, which, by the way, will be a doozy!"

Quip shook his head in denial and stated, "I am not doing anything, and I know the rest of my team, like Jacob, are far too busy to mess with you. It must be something else. You want me to help find out what?

"I didn't know you automated your home. I have the refrigerator, security, and climate control automated, but EZ drew the line at what she considers the invasive stuff. Even on the security,

EZ doesn't get the part about setting it to 'On' when she leaves the place."

Tuck thought for a moment and responded, "I will investigate a little more on my own, but if it gets any worse, I may call for help. In the meantime, I will send the flight information to our encrypted place. Talk later, mate."

Quip disconnected the call and returned to his normal work area. He made a notation to follow up in a day or two with Tuck. After they resolved this current commodity issue, he would do some additional investigation. He was uncomfortable with what Tuck had said. Then he resumed his work, reviewing the interim data summaries.

```
HMX ↓ -7.50
CMX ↓ -9.33
HCC ↓ -3.90
SOX ↓ -7.74
```

It was extra late when Quip returned to the flat. He'd called EZ to say that he would be late and to not wait on him for dinner. He frowned at the light being out in the entrance hallway when he opened the door, so he reached around and turned on the light in the living room. He figured EZ was already asleep and decided not to wake her for something so silly when he could fix it. He walked toward the kitchen, turned on that light, and at the far end of the room he opened the small utility closet. He rustled around for several minutes and extracted a new light bulb. Then he turned to head back to the hallway, shutting off the kitchen light.

He turned into the living room, surprised to see the hallway was lit properly. He rubbed his eyes and looked again. Sure enough, it was functioning correctly. The weariness of the day overtook him and he yawned. Then he decided he was simply overtired and needed to get some rest. He turned off the light in the living room and went to the bedroom. EZ was curled up in bed with the sheet sliding off her wonderfully naked body. He loved watching her while she slept, especially if she was dreaming, as that caused her to protrude through the sheets as well as sometimes talk or mumble. She was so pretty.

After making short work of a shower, along with his other nighttime rituals, he carefully slid under the sheet and gently pulled her close to him. Her body, sensing his presence, pressed into him, spooning in a way that reminded him of how well they fit together. He stroked her side and hip with a feather light caress, not wanting to wake her but wanting to feel her skin respond.

After a few minutes of his gentle ministrations, she was awake enough to respond in kind to his touches. Her body quickly warmed and responded. She moved, turning her face to him and kissing him in welcome. The quiet groans and whimpers told him she was not opposed to some sleepy lovemaking. He stroked her core and felt her heat and moistness increase as he kissed her mouth, neck, and then down to her responsive breasts. She pressed into him as he touched and handled her just the way he knew excited her to the point of release.

Through her ragged breathing and increasing excitement, she begged him to join with her, which he willingly obliged. He filled her and felt her tighten around him as he thrust into her with increasing urgency. With a free hand he teased and caressed her in between his thrusts until she moaned her release, taking him with her into the perfect end to the day. They remained joined until their breathing recovered, and he shifted her under his arm.

She wiggled in closer to him and in her half-sleep mumbled, "Hummm, that was lovely, sweetheart. I so enjoy your coming into bed so insistently."

Quip whispered back, "I love it when you sleep with everything accessible. It makes me want you even more."

"Good, let's keep it that way after we get married. Hey, can you wake me up early? I want to talk about you taking the movement sensors off the lights in here. They aren't working properly. I also forgot to set the alarm when I left this morning, in case you have a program watching that too."

And with that, her breathing indicated she was headed rapidly back to deep sleep. Sadly, Quip was now fully awake.

CHAPTER FORTY-NINE

Ah, the Lifestyles of a Jetsetter

The travel toward Chile was uneventful, and LJ, still posing as Holland Rogers, enjoyed endless flirting on the flight with the attendant he called Kitty. He commended her attention to details and prompt responses to his requests. Her endless ability to twist and turn at the appropriate time to avoid Mr. Rogers grabbing anything on her person became almost a game.

Mercedes, playing the role of Kitty on this flight in support of Juan, was tiring of the dodging. It did, however, afford her ample opportunity to capture some covert photos of the man at different angles. As a member of Juan and Julie's CATS team, she brought her skills learned while in the employment of a United States three letter agency.

When this assignment concluded and they returned home, she could just imagine the pillow talk they would be having. Those elements of her job and personal life were keeping her from backhanding the man. He looked big and competent, but he completely disregarded and underestimated her, like most of her opponents. She grinned at her advantage but still went to grouse at Juan.

Making certain her charge was still buckled in and absorbed with a snack and onboard movie streaming, she knocked at, then opened the cockpit door. She nodded to the co-pilot who was obviously jamming out to music coming into his earphones with the air guitar as his instrument of choice. The only time he needed to pay attention was during take-off and landing, unless Juan requested a change.

"Boss, I need to have you keep on the seatbelt sign. This guy is a jovial piece of work, and I swear…"

Juan flipped on the fasten seatbelt notice then looked at her and stated, "You will be totally professional and maintain the cover we have so carefully created. He is not a trusting soul, and I would hate to have to return to square one. Got it, Kitty?"

She furrowed her brow and scrunched up her nose but nodded agreement. Mentally, she regretted telling Juan how much she liked cats.

Juan continued, "Now make the announcement that we will be landing in twenty and get his passport from him to expedite customs. He should be okay with that request, as I filled him in on the process at the airport in Rio. Then ask where he wants the next leg of travel to go to so you can make certain the provisions are available. He had indicated Panama, but let's get that confirmed please. Lastly, tell him that I want to speak privately with him before he deplanes."

When she raised an eyebrow, he grinned and added, "I will tell you all, Kitty. Now get back there and make the appropriate final preparations for landing. And, yes, I have advised Julie of the current plan."

Kitty sauntered back and advised, "Mr. Rogers, sir, we are getting ready to land. I need to collect these items and tidy up the galley." She picked up the tray and sweetly smiled as she asked, "I need to also get your passport so I can push us through customs. May I get that from you when I return, sir? The pilot stated you do not wish to be delayed. There is also a car ready and waiting to take you anywhere you need."

She started back to the galley and provided a nice going away view. LJ loudly yet appreciatively commented, "Miss Kitty, if you keep walking like that for me, I will provide more than just my passport if you want. You are such a purty little thing."

She looked back with a smile and then returned quickly with her hand out. He took her hand between both of his and grinned, the sparkle of his gold teeth catching the light. She was about ready to insist he release her when he said, "You have been so sweet. My mama would just hug you. I want you to be a part of the next leg of our trip, you sweet thing. As much as I would love to try to steal your heart, my heart belongs to another that I am seeing tomorrow. So will you stick with this plane, Miss Kitty?"

Mercedes grinned and affirmed, "I was hoping you would ask. Where is our next destination, sir? And I still need the passport, please."

LJ released her hands and grinned as he handed over his passport and said, "I want to keep it a surprise, but my white hat came from there originally."

She plucked the passport out of his hand and smiled. "I will take care of this and look forward to the next journey we might have together. Oh, I almost forgot, the pilot would like to speak with you privately before you deplane."

They landed easily and taxied to the gate area. Mercedes deplaned with the co-pilot and took their paperwork to the Chilean official. LJ stood up with his satchel in hand, and Juan approached him.

LJ grinned and stated, "That was one fine flight, young man. You did fine, and that purty little thing served real nice. As soon as I get my paperwork back, I will get to my meeting and could be finished in a few hours. The three of us could have dinner and take off early in the morning, if that works for you. I presume the co-pilot stays with the plane, right?"

"That is correct. The co-pilot remains with the plane all night. It was one of the requirements.

"I'm glad you enjoyed the flight, Mr. Rogers. I need to file the flight plan for that next destination tonight, if you want to leave early. I will see if our attendant can stay with us, if you like."

"I already asked Miss Kitty, and she agreed. I will take care of her room at the Ritz-Carlton in Santiago, just like for yours." He chuckled, "But she has her own room, Juan. I saw how you was eyeing her."

"What can I say, she is easy on the eyes but not as pretty as those models I have traveled with. Later, I will regale you with the stories from my time in Acapulco when this redhead, Rita, I think her name was…well, for later.

"They speak mostly Spanish here, Mr. Rogers. Do you need me to go with you to help translate? I did verify the car is present."

LJ thought for a moment and then nodded. "Yeah, I think that would be best. You come with me and you can do that flight plan later. Miss Kitty can check in to her room after she finishes up her duties here. We are headed to Tocumen International Airport in Panama. Is that a long flight from here at Santiago?"

"No. It should be less than a seven hour flight, depending on weather. It is an easy flight plan to do, so no worries. Since we are still waiting for our papers, I will do the flight plan right now and also arrange for refueling, to have us ready to go. This company does some standard maintenance checks here as common procedure, though she flew like a regal bird."

Juan went off to finish the flight plan, and LJ waited inside the plane for the paperwork. He quickly placed a call to Alisha to update her on his whereabouts and upcoming plans. He promised to meet her tomorrow, hopefully with a plan on what to do with the pilot. Right now, he liked the kid, and his piloting skills were excellent. Best flight he'd had since he landed this job.

He even hinted to Alisha they could take a vacation together and use this pilot.

NMX ↓ -7.50
CMX ↓ -9.33
HCC ↓ -3.90
SOX ↓ -7.74

The meetings had gone well, with LJ securing a few more storage containers and one small vessel for sea transport. He'd only had to use half the Chilean pesos in his satchel, so he'd exchanged them for US dollars, which he could use in other places. The only downside of the visit into Chile had been the continued view into the poverty and economic struggles that the local people faced. It had upset his digestion to the point that he limited his dining intake. Not a common event for LJ to say the least.

They had laughed and enjoyed several stories that they all knew were filled with lies before retiring for their early flight. Juan and Kitty made certain they had no interaction other than to comment in front of Mr. Rogers that she would get to the plane early to make certain the food was on board. Since he'd wanted to leave so early, she had promised to fix fresh fruit and omelets as their first meal and a surprise for the second one.

The flight had taken off on time, and the omelets were better than promised. Mr. Rogers had some mimosas which helped keep him in a jovial mood. Even though he teased her incessantly, he hadn't tried to grab at her again. She chalked that up to her telling him over dinner of the man she was saving herself for who hardly knew she existed. It had been an almost sad tale that ended with LJ offering to have a discussion with the man if she wanted.

They landed, and the customs process was even better since Alisha had greased the way from their home base. Takeru had enough power and influence, even though the source was not identified per se, to make certain no detaining or searching took place.

Mr. Rogers stated, "I set up rooms for you and Miss Kitty, Juan, at the Crowne Plaza. I have some acquaintances here I will be staying with. Not certain what the next trip will be yet, but I want to keep you and Miss Kitty on retainers, along with the aircraft for at least two days."

LJ figured the credit card he'd previously used to charge the plane would simply allow the extension. He handed Juan some of the funds he had converted in Chile and asked, "I think this will hold you and Miss Kitty for a few days. I held the rooms on my card for you. The plane should just continue to rack up the charges. Har, har, har, not certain if my expense budget will hold too much more of this without more permission. Now, don't you worry, I was just teasing. I will see you both tomorrow night for dinner at the hotel to discuss our next trip."

"Mr. Rogers, Spanish is the primary language here as well. Are you certain I can't help you?"

"You have done a good job as a pilot and translator, but I think I am good. If I need you, I will find you at the hotel or call your cell phone."

LJ took his paperwork and wandered across the terminal with Juan following closely, yet in the shadows. Juan watched as Mr. Rogers met with some woman waiting by a car and gave her a hug and kiss. Juan continued to snap photos with his phone until Mercedes was next to him with their belongings.

CHAPTER FIFTY

The Eyes Have It

Following the evidence review on his former administrative assistant and lover, Mike had been working steadily for two days from very early morning until well after the rest of the staff had left. He rarely spoke to his team outside of Laurie, who had finally resurfaced yesterday with a story about taking care of an ailing family member. Mike had her distribute work assignments to the rest of the staff. Otherwise, business seemed rather quiet. Though the price of oil had not risen sharply, it also seemed more stable at the moment. Three days of flat pricing did not make for merriment in ePETRO's London offices.

Laurie was far mousier than the flamboyant Roslyn in dealing with the office and staff. It was fairly clear that the staff did not miss Roslyn in the least, and any mourning previously displayed had been for the benefit of the boss. Since the evening out with Petra, Laurie had avoided Petra and deliberately turned around if it appeared they might cross paths in the office.

Petra had been able to verify that Laurie used the same cloud service provider for her cell phone that Roslyn had. ICABOD had trapped the data which had been uploaded since Laurie began working at ePETRO, and Petra was still trying to overcome the encryption on the files. Petra was focused on the screen, and her fingers had been flying across the keyboard in a steady stream of keying, which had continued for the last five hours.

Jacob interrupted, "Petra, how about we take a break and get some lunch or at least some tea?"

Petra waited for a long time to respond and then distractedly mumbled, "Humm, whatever you say…busy…"

Jacob could easily relate to the focus needed for her work, as it was similar to his work in tracking the IP addresses the data had traveled along. Some of that had been found in working through the data details with the cloud service provider. It was a long, tedious process to track all the hops the data had made, and at this juncture he had four possible end points he had confidence in.

He was getting hungry and knew that she needed a break. Petra, like him, worked better when she was well rested and well fed. The last two nights they had returned to the hotel and wolfed down a meal before falling into bed, asleep almost as soon as their heads hit the pillow. Other than a fast breakfast of toast and juice, neither of them had eaten. Though he knew Petra had been upset by Mike's response to the overwhelming evidence that Roslyn had played him, her breaking this encryption and reading the file would not change what they both knew. Laurie was a plant put in place to continue with Roslyn's mission. Who put her in place was what they needed as much as what data was transferred.

He got up from his chair and walked over behind Petra's. He began gently rubbing her shoulders, immediately feeling the tense muscles. The gentle kneading had the desired results when she closed her eyes and almost purred.

"Jacob, that feels amazing."

"Well, my dear, you are very tense, and it is time for us to get up and walk away for a bit. Sometimes we get better perspective when we walk away, get refreshed, and then come back to things. You know that, right?"

"I do. It is just that it feels like I am getting very close to solving this. I hate to walk away. Ah, you know how it is."

"I do, Petra, but I know you, and I know we need to force ourselves to take breaks at times. This is one of those times."

Petra chuckled as she saved her work and turned off the machine. "Alright, honey, I get it. Your stomach alarm sounded."

"Before we walk out of here though, let's spin up that other program instance and see if we can catch a snoop while we are out walking and eating. I promise tonight I am going to work out with you before and after dinner."

Jacob looked up in surprise, and as he was completing her request of the special program they had crafted, he arched one of his eyebrows and replied, "I will hold you to that statement."

She laughed a bit as she stood and gathered her purse and commented, "Oh, I do hope so. Counting on it actually. I am kind of hungry, now that you mention it. Perhaps fish and chips."

Jacob finished setting up the machine, and they both made a good amount of noise as they were leaving. Laurie was speaking to the receptionist in the front entrance as they headed out.

Petra glanced at Laurie and smiled sweetly as she said, "Laurie, you look like you are feeling better today. We are headed out for a bite of lunch. I would like to chat with you today, though, if you can fit a time into your schedule this afternoon."

Laurie looked surprised but quietly responded, "Yes, of course. I will leave a time on your keyboard, Miss Petra."

"Great, Laurie. See you later this afternoon."

The weather in London was unusually lovely today with mild temperatures and even sunshine, which was not a common occurrence. Petra and Jacob decided a nice walk to a little place they'd eaten fish and chips at before would permit them to take advantage of the nice day as well as stretch out the kinks. They had left a bit later than the normal lunch crowd and were delighted when they were immediately seated in one of the few window seats available. The waiter gave them the run down on the specials of the day, but they both smiled and opted for the outstanding fish and chips.

"Jacob, this is such a lovely, quaint little place. I love the homey atmosphere, and the service is so friendly."

"Yes, it is a nice place. It is so very British, isn't it? Everyone outside looks so happy to be enjoying the day, even the stiff upper lipped businessmen look pleased. Of course, it is Friday. That might have something to do with the upbeat spirits as well."

Their tea arrived along with a couple of small scones with clotted cream. This was the other reason they both enjoyed this venue. The small scones were just enough to take the edge off, and yet not enough to fill them up. They sat quietly munching the tasty treat and watching the people passing by outdoors. The rest of their section of the restaurant cleared out, and the tables were quickly serviced and reset, likely for supper. A scant thirty minutes later a refill on their tea as well as the piping fresh fish and chips arrived.

After the waiter had left, Jacob asked, "Do you think it has been long enough to turn on the scanner?"

Petra nodded as she took out her phone and logged into the program. Even though they had not been watching the entire time, everything was being recorded to replay later for evidence. As she watched the screen, a slow smile emerged on her face. She set up the device holder so they might both watch it like a standard movie.

Petra offered, "We can look back later, but I think the program is working like a champ. I really like the added value of a picture of the user in front of the machine in the viewing window. Nice touch, honey. She seems to be doing a nice job of keying and then using her photo application. Some habits don't change, even from person to person."

Jacob finished chewing his bite of fish and concurred, "I know. What I want to know is where is the information going and who is manipulating it. That is the real problem."

"I agree. The program notified our team to start tracking the data from her device, right?"

Jacob nodded as he savored a piping hot chip, dipped in fresh mayonnaise. Then he added, "Yes, my darling, just like we discussed. Now enjoy your meal and remember to please save your strength for the promised workouts later this evening. I believe I will be more than ready for you."

Petra chuckled and replied, "Yes, dear, I am sure you will. But we will need to go back and have a meeting with our little snoop first."

```
NMX ↓ -7.50
CMX ↓ -9.33
HCC ↓ -3.90
SOX ↓ -7.74
```

After they returned from lunch, Petra and Jacob resumed their activities. They had reviewed the portion of the recording which confirmed what they had seen before Jacob shipped the file to Quip. Predictably, after the nice lunch break, Jacob had been correct in that it took only a very short time for Petra to finish breaking the encryption on the files. For his part, Jacob had reduced the number of likely end points for the data transfers to three. The hope was to isolate the end point of the transfer with what occurred today.

Shortly before the time Laurie had indicated they could meet, Petra asked, "Are you and I doing any speculation on what her reasoning or excuse might be?"

Jacob looked up toward the ceiling, thoughtful for a moment, then replied, "Nope. A consummate liar will say anything, and I simply don't want to waste time wondering. We could, however, do a fast game of rock, paper, scissors, best two out of three, on who gets to back her into the corner. Or I could just defer to your expertness in the game."

Petra chuckled, then turned as the door opened, and Laurie entered.

"Excuse me, is now a good time to talk?"

Petra replied, "Certainly, Laurie, come on in. I was just saying to Jacob how much fun we had the other night, you and me. He was asking for some of the details about the number you called to share the photos you had taken. Can you explain the details to him? I would hate to misrepresent the processes you are following or who is telling you to follow them."

Laurie's eyes got wide and panic flashed across her face. Tears rolled down her face as she sputtered and gasped for a breath. "My mum is so ill. This job is all I have to take care of her. She requires so much care, medicine, and I am all alone."

That much was true based on what they'd been able to turn up on Laurie so far with only a cursory search. That, however, did not mean it was the truth. This kind of background was easy to build. Heck, Julie could build this sort of background in between changing diapers on the twins.

Petra prompted, "I understand that, Laurie, but how did you get this job?"

Laurie sniffled and wiped her nose on a well-worn handkerchief she had been wringing out between her hands. "I signed up with a part-time agency several months ago. I had not heard anything at all from them until the day before I started here. They called me at home that evening and said I was to report to Mr. Patrick. The voice on the other end of the call gave me my orders of what I was to do and when – from the moment I sign onto a system, what screens to photograph, and the numbers to send information to via text. I was informed these were the job requirements, per the boss.

"They did not seem too hard, just time sensitive. I have always been great at keeping schedules. I presumed the boss, being Mr. Patrick, would know everything. The morning I started work he looked up the fulfillment email sent by the agency. Nodded at me. Provided me with a quick view of my desk, logon information and the like. That was it."

She began weeping again, then paused and remarked, "Every evening when I leave, I tell him I completed the tasks for the day, just like I had been told by the woman on the phone. However, Mr. Patrick barely acknowledges my comments, outside of raising his hand in dismissal from his office. It's like he doesn't hear me or doesn't care."

Jacob interjected, "What was the reason you were not in the office yesterday then?"

She looked up with red eyes and a swollen nose and answered, "It was my mum's day to go to the doctor. My orders were to phone the woman if I ever had to be out, which I did. She was understanding and told me to look at the computer today to fulfill my tasks and not to worry about the boss. She would take care of making certain it was not a problem as long as I stuck to the job and didn't tell anyone what I was doing."

Petra furrowed her brow and asked, "Did you phone her from your cell phone?"

Laurie nodded.

Jacob shook his head, feeling a bit nauseous for what he was going to suggest, and said, "Okay, here is what you will do until one of us tells you to stop..."

They outlined her new job rules in addition to the ones she had been told when she took the job. Neither Jacob nor Petra thought it would take more than a few days to run through the various numbers and track the data flows through the cloud service provider. Jacob also noted this provider might be worthy of a closer look at the data being stored.

CHAPTER FIFTY-ONE

Change in the Wind,
or Just on the Mind

LJ greeted Alisha warmly, almost too warmly for the streets of Tocumen. They both laughed as she inserted her arm into the crook of his arm and guided him toward her vehicle.

"Honey, I am so glad you're back. We have much to discuss. I think it might be time for us to find new work."

LJ patted her arm and soothed, "Now, sweetums, are you overreacting to the good director again? I had a good set of negotiations and lease plans with several different folks and, with your help, had two of the crews launch their vessels, aligned to the timing requested by the director. I figure at the team meeting on Saturday, in the cave room reminiscent of a bad horror film, I will be touted as the man to emulate. Right? He has not had any negatives or misgivings you might have seen, has he?"

"No, honey, I think you are the best of the leads in the field. The guy on mergers and acquisitions has missed a couple of real good deals, and I heard grumbling about those. I was told to stay close to him during the meeting and watch for his signals.

"He just makes me queasy most of the time I am around him. The darkness, aside from the lights of the computer screens, plus the silence outside of the drone of the machines, is getting to me. I get so tired of the mode I have to work under that when I get back to our place I put my earbuds in and turn up the sounds."

They reached the car and LJ took the driver's seat while she slid into the other side. He started the engine and jumped as the music blared inside the closed car. Once he got his heart under control and his breathing back to normal, he turned down the radio and laughed. She laughed right along with him and leaned over for another kiss.

LJ commented, "Sugah, we got a few more weeks of this, the bonus after this round to be determined during the meeting, and then I'll find us an exit strategy.

"I want you to help me think of a way to get the sword out of there. I gotta tell you, I want that beautiful *katana* so bad I even dreamed about it." He chuckled and added, "Ah course when I dream about it I am sitting on a throne, and you are serving me, wearing your hair a bit wild and just a pair of high heeled shoes in a ruby red color that matches your nail polish and your signature red lipstick perfectly. Hmm huh, you know what happens next, don't you?"

Alisha howled with laughter and said, "If I don't, I'm sure you'll provide details later tonight. You know I only have the window to pick you up that he gave me, and as usual the time factor he provided will be enough if we don't pull over to the side of the road and act out your fantasy. See what I mean? He is way too controlling."

LJ thought for a minute as he guided the car over the mountain roads, closing in on the compound, which was mostly underground. With its own generator below ground and well water supply, the only modern technology visible was the camo-painted satellite dish, which signaled the end of the road. He knew other elements were above ground but never took the time to worry about those aspects of Director Takeru's business.

LJ was in the final few miles when he replied, "He is that, sugah. He truly is that. On this trip I also found out I may be a mean, disreputable SOB in for every buck I can get, but in all my years I knew that my home country was something special. These deprived places that I am traveling to are even worse than the projects in New York where you grew up or my own town, with me on the wrong side of the tracks. But, look at us, we've done okay rising above our economic station. I never ended the life of anyone that wasn't already corrupt. I think the director wants to crush the economy of every country, including the US of A, and I didn't see that possibility when I found us this gig.

"Yeah, sweetums, we'll be leaving as soon as we collect our money and me that sword. Yes siree, you, me, and the beaches of our choice."

Alisha leaned in closer and patted his arm until they arrived at the compound entrance where they both resumed their business personas.

CHAPTER FIFTY-TWO

Readying for the Ready

Quip rolled in last to the video conference room and picked a video camera spot close to Otto but facing Wolfgang. The conference session went live almost immediately with Jacob and Petra sharing a single camera. Julie had been asked to join to brief the team on Juan's sleuthing activity. Jim Hughes was the last to join but only with an audio connection. As usual ICABOD was there as well, but with no video camera required.

Otto opened with the usual pleasantries and asked for updates and/or requests of each to help drive their individual tasks.

Quip seemed a bit distracted but began, "Julie, the stream of photos Juan has been getting on our mystery man are quite interesting and almost useless. I mean, this character is obviously up to something, but he is a ghost with no reliable background to leverage a real discovery about him. Even his voice patterns that Juan captured in those conversations lead us to no less than eight different identities.

"Then, the photo of the large lady our mystery man met in Panama also produced multiple personas all over the damn place. First she is in Atlanta, then Finland, then London... geezers, she turns up everywhere, but she's from nowhere!"

Petra puzzled a moment, then abruptly asked, "When did you find her in London, Quip?"

Quip casually stated, "We found a video trace of her going through customs about ten days ago. Why?"

Petra and Jacob exchanged hard glances at each other, and Jacob answered, "Because that was about the same time that Roslyn had her accident in the tubes here in London. Any chance of ICABOD trying to get some proximity images of those two together? You know that London has the most video cameras per capita in the world. I would find it very interesting if you could find some images of them together before Roslyn's death."

ICABOD acknowledged, "I will begin the video hunt to see if those two can be placed together, Jacob."

Petra continued, "We have uncovered the information mule that took over for Roslyn and have our cloaked routines in place to capture all the telemetry. However, I have not yet been able to break the encryption algorithm they use to mask their communications. I've never seen anything quite this good, but with ICABOD's processing muscle, it is only a matter of time before we can decipher everything."

Otto, wanting to restrict some of the more sensitive information from Jim's understanding, intercepted the call and asked, "Jim, I'd like to hear from you at this juncture. We need more traction from your efforts.

"Now, I'm not suggesting that you aren't providing great information on the bogus oil and coal reporting scams being run. However, we are going to need to capture all of them before we run out of time. Can we have a status report and know of your needs?"

Jim was aware that he had only one major breakthrough and that was only because the R-Group was on top of the source throttling the bogus number reporting. He offered, "I've got a list of probable players here in the U.S. If each one requires the same level of effort to terminate…well, my progress is simply too slow to deal with this many bogus reporting points. I just can't get to them all, do the G-man badge routine, persuade them to join our cause, and then ride into the sunset. Folks, there has to be a better way."

Quip smirked as he responded, "Jim, why don't you give me that list so we can do a collective search and destroy on these bogus end points all at once. We have a few tricks up our sleeve that should cut this task down to size and still let you ride into the sunset."

Julie added, "Jim, once you turn that list of shell companies over to Quip, I have an idea that you could help with in our discovery in South America, if you're up for it."

Jim, somewhat intrigued by the statement but also a little miffed by the challenge of being up for it, tersely asked, "What do you have mind, JAC?"

Julie grinned and responded, "We've got this unidentifiable rogue character running around buying or leasing oil tankers at the very time when no one else would go near them in this market. Almost like he is running on a different playbook, and I want to understand why.

"My Brazilian sources said he spent a lot of time on the ship's bridge and in particular, with their on-board computer systems. If we can get a peek at that system …uh, using your G-man badge, perhaps we can get a better idea of what he is really up to.

"Sorry, if I made it sound like you couldn't handle it. It is a little out of your jurisdiction, so no offense meant."

Jim chuckled slightly and responded, "None taken, JAC. With this then, let me drop from this call, folks, and check in with my management about giving you the list. JAC, can you give me the particulars so I can head out and try to add some value here?"

Julie smiled and said, "Yes, Jim. I will call when I get this all teed up, sir. Best."

After Jim dropped, Wolfgang broke in at that moment and stated, "Jim's information is good. We will use it accordingly, but understand we can't simply pound these suspect sites based on our suspicions. Even if these are bona fide rogue shell reporting companies, we certainly can't terminate them all at once. This problem didn't happen overnight. We certainly can't solve it overnight because of the world chaos it will create."

Petra interjected, "Wolfgang, there are people suffering from this mess, with governments globally about to collapse. We can't just take our sweet time unwinding it. The faucet of bogus information needs to be turned off!"

Quip quickly offered, "Petra, I tend to agree with you, but only if we had nailed this jerk's buttocks to the floorboards with a heavy gauge nail gun. You know the kind, with the 16 penny nails used for framing. I had a friend let me try it on him once for ten Swiss francs. It worked really well, but the stitches cost more than what I paid him." Then in a reflective moment, Quip mused, "We don't talk much anymore..."

Otto rolled his eyes in a thoroughly appalled state and said, "Let me paraphrase the crass Quip statement. We can only discuss how to put the commodity buy/sell system globally back online once we have a complete handle on our adversary. We should assume that, unless the DMO is completely neutralized, it will only resurface somewhere else, only craftier."

A somewhat indignant Quip flatly stated, "Well, that's what I said."

Otto sensed the video conference attendees were ready to move back into their structured work and stated, "I think we all have more to do on this project.

"Julie, you are going to work with Jim on the shipping angle.

"Petra, you and Jacob are still working on the encryption that is used to deliver the bogus values into the commodity numbers.

"Wolfgang, you've got more work to do on the financials, but you are kind of at an impasse until we can discover who is behind all of this.

"ICABOD, you are going to try and find the large mystery lady that may have been in London at the same time of Roslyn's demise.

"And lastly, Quip, you are going to attend the *CANDY* meetings."

Quip tried to keep his curiosity under control but finally insisted, "I have to know! Candy meetings?"

Otto suppressed a smile and replied, "*Crass Announcements Needing Discipline or Yelling* at. I promised EZ you would start your two-year program tonight. You already missed the morning session."

CHAPTER FIFTY-THREE

Graphics Make All the Difference

Lara had been hard at work on the bridal wardrobe since she had returned from the tanker lease negotiations. Carlos had been working with Juan and Julie to follow that strange Mr. Rogers and had told Lara to focus on the wedding. He had also asked her not to discuss Mr. Rogers but keep it happy and light. When she asked if Juan would be back in time for the wedding, he'd assured her Juan would be there. He had even set up her video conferencing system for this call with a smile and a kiss, promising more in-depth adoration in the near future.

She was delighted that her team had the samples completed this morning in the graphical program. Her goal for this discussion was to get approval from EZ and her bridesmaids so the final garments could be completed. To make this as real an experience as possible, Lara was using her new 3D graphic modeling software. This software permitted her team to create a rendering, mathematically accurate to their size and shapes, for the bride and the bridal party. The team had added skin tones and hair color for each of them to make certain EZ would have a perfect visual, as if the ladies were all shopping together.

Destiny Fashions had recently revised their version of this leading-edge software, and Lara felt this was a great way to test it. So far, she had only used it to set up the appearance order for her models in fashion shows, as a way to advise the models on which features of a garment should be highlighted as each of them walked. The software had also been used to brainstorm her visions for print ads. Lara found this software allowed her to optimize the actual fashion construction time, as well as make certain the rendering matched to her design vision. She hoped it would continue to give her a competitive advantage and reduce time to market for her fashions.

Lara had decided to try using it when EZ asked for a call with all the ladies so they could see the designs. EZ had said with a tone of sadness that she wished they could go on a shopping spree together and get insights from everyone. The idea of showing drawings and the fabric samples was good, but this was far more than what EZ was expecting. Lara ran through the animated presentation one more time and was very pleased. She dialed into the conference call and added in the high-definition video aspect.

EZ had already opened the conference and smiled as Lara joined. Within minutes Julie, Petra, Mavie, and Su Lin had joined. Su Lin was in charge of the final flower order, so the colors were critical. She had sent over some photographs that morning of the flowers currently in season in Atlanta.

EZ grinned into the screen and said, "Thank you all for joining me. I know everyone is busy, and we are all so far apart. I am getting very nervous about all of this even getting done. By the way, I am loving all the sweet engagement gifts you have all sent. Really way too kind. I will be sending thank you notes soon, with pictures of where they are placed. The latest one was a shimmering silvery glass vase. Really heavy and perfectly suited to our living room décor, but somehow the messaging was missing. Quip suspects it is from older family friends that simply forgot the enclosure. He figures we will find out who when we have the after-wedding party here later. No more though, please, and no wedding gifts. These are all too much, honestly.

"Maybe I should just run to Las Vegas with Quip and keep it simple? It would make all of this so much easier for you all."

They all could see the tears shimmering in her eyes. Su Lin confidently stated, "Little one, it will all work out well. Your father is so excited about hosting this and walking you down the aisle. You don't want to disappoint him and take this honor away from him, do you? He has told me more than once that he is hoping he can do it without tripping over his big feet!"

They all laughed, the tension eased, and EZ really appeared happier.

EZ beamed as she continued, "We all know one another except for Mavie. Mavie is coming with David Tucker, one of Quip's best men. Mavie, these are the best ladies a girl could ever call friends. I am so glad you agreed to be a part of the party, virtually now and in person in Georgia."

Mavie looked at all the pretty faces of the group. Her pretty smile and nearly white-blonde hair looked lovely against her tanned skin. Her bright blue eyes were almost the color of the sky. With her pretty Aussie accent she replied, "Very nice to meet you all. Petra, I recall you from the barbie. Nice to be included, EZ. I must say I was honored to be asked."

EZ added, "Welcome, and I think we are ready to look at the designs. Do you want me to turn over control, Lara?"

Lara nodded, took control of the conference presentation, and interjected, "I have a real treat for you all! At least, I hope it will be. I wanted to show you what the dresses should look like finalized, unless you collectively ask for changes."

Petra said, "Lara, the wedding is so close now, I am certain changes won't be necessary. Right, ladies?"

All the ladies nodded their agreement.

Lara ignored the feedback as she brought up the framework of the screen and announced, "EZ, I am going to show these garments in the order I think you will want them in the wedding. Anything you want to see changed or modified, including the order, will be noted.

"The flowers that you will see are rendered from the photographs Su Lin sent to me, and she would like your final decision on those as well. Here we go.

"First up, we have the twins in their toddler versions of the wedding party attendants."

The screen showed an immersive 3D video of the twins proceeding down the pathway at the farm in Georgia. Juan Jr. was balancing a soft, peach colored satin pillow that looked like it held two rings as he walked straight ahead with his eyes firmly on the goal of the arch. Then Gracie followed, sprinkling flower pedals, and stomped in the same direction as her brother in her beautiful peach colored dress.

Julie laughed, flashed her megawatt smile, and said, "Oh my goodness, Lara, it's like we're really there. You really captured the determination and focus of my toddlers. I love the way they look alive. I want a copy of this to share with Juan. Please don't show them arguing, will you?"

Lara chuckled and replied, "There won't be arguing in this program or on the day. Is the length of the dress good? And the shoes, should they be peach color or white? We can get them dyed if you wish."

EZ grinned and clapped her hands as she replied, "Unless Julie wants it shorter, this looks great to me. White shoes are just fine as long as they are comfortable."

All the ladies chimed in and agreed they were adorable.

Then Petra said, "Okay, fashion-designer-techno-geek, I want to see the bridesmaids, then the groomsmen. All at once though, rather than walking out, or we will be here for hours.

"I am not sure about all of you, but I poured my glass of champagne here. Cheers!"

Petra held up her glass in a toast and was pleased that they all had received the same message earlier and raised their glasses in unison.

Lara smiled and reached over to make a quick change in the program. She was planning on how to thank Carlos later for making her side pallet of drag-and-drop icons so she didn't have to fumble at being a techno-geek. The immersive program brought in all the depth of the area, and then the bridesmaids all appeared in their peach-colored tea-length dresses. The bodices for each of the dresses was specifically suited to the individual's generous or modest cleavage, including Lara's. None were too revealing, and all the lines of the dresses made them look particularly lovely.

EZ caught herself a couple of times trying to reach into the video to touch. Of course, it didn't hurt that they were all young, healthy, and very lovely women. Each of the hairstyles would likely change, but all looked fabulous as they suited their facial structures.

A collective "Ahhhhhh" sounded across the conference call. Then they were speaking on top of one another.

"I love my hair!"

"I look so thin. The color is fabulous with my skin!"

"The skirt length is perfect for dancing."

"Oh, boy, am I going to dance his socks off in this dress."

EZ smiled broadly and exclaimed, "Lara, these are fabulous! I love the way all the flowers are different for each one. The animation, the depth, and the modeling of not just the dresses, but the people too, is astounding. If you all have no objections, I think I would like the different bouquets for each of you."

Unified nods across the screens were clear. No objections were voiced.

"Now me, please. I can hardly wait to see what you have done, Lara. I love this software. It is like we are really all together. I can just taste the champagne and hear our laughter as if we are changing in a bridal store."

The screen changed, and the groomsmen appeared with their black tuxes and white shirts. The only splash of peach color came from their boutonnieres.

The collective "Ahhhhhh" sounded again.

Petra remarked, "I can see that Jacob needs to get a haircut, but boy, does he look, well, yummy!"

Julie added, "They all do. I like it if you do, EZ. I think this is so very exciting, even virtually. What an advanced view. I think this will really catch on in the fashion industry, especially for weddings being put on with friends coming in from all over. Great use of graphic software, Lara."

EZ nodded and agreed, "I love it all, Lara, and this view is perfect. I feel so much better. We might actually pull this off, ladies. Now me?"

Lara shook her head. "Not yet, EZ. I created something for Su Lin and your father."

The scene changed to the petite Su Lin and Andy, with her barely reaching Andy's shoulder. Andy was in a tuxedo that matched the groomsmen, and Su Lin was in an elegant dress of ivory with black roses at random intervals. Su Lin nodded approval, but tears welled up in her eyes preventing her from speaking.

EZ nodded her approval again too as she said, "Nothing needs to be changed, Lara, other than we all need to be together for this celebration. Su Lin, you look so elegant. Oh, Quip needs to get his hair cut too. I am totally getting excited. Now me?"

Lara nodded, and the screen cleared and displayed EZ in the beautiful dress she and Lara had discussed. It rendered well on her 3D body with her fiery hair all shining and flowing. Lara had selected a mix of all the flowers for the long bouquet clasped in her hands. Her smile was radiant as the figure of Quip appeared in the tuxedo matching the rest of the men, except for the multicolored boutonniere in his lapel.

Everyone was so engaged in the presentation, no one noticed that Mavie was having trouble on her end and couldn't make herself heard. Mavie's video was slightly distorted as she asked, "What did you say, EZ? You broke…"

Seconds later Mavie was showing fuzzy on the video, but there was no audio. Petra typed into the screen.

Mavie, is everything okay, we lost your audio?

Mavie looked at the camera, almost fearful, and raised her hands in confusion. Then the screen went black as she was disconnected.

Petra was concerned but did not want to raise too many alarms for the ladies. She sent a quick text to both Quip and Jacob to check it out.

Petra smiled and commented, "I guess it must be happy hour in Sydney. EZ, are you happy?"

EZ was beside herself, smiling with delight and nodding agreement to everything. She said, "Lara, this is so perfect. Thank you so very much! I wouldn't change a thing.

"Su Lin, I hope you can make the flowers look just like this.

"No one shows this to Quip, right?"

Lara shook her head and added, "No, of course not. Now for the last part. Julie, are the kids away from the monitor?"

Julie looked confused, and then an idea hit her. She rubbed her hands together and got a gleam in her eye. "They are playing outside right now. Now we get the male stripper?"

"No, now we get the bride's lingerie show!"

Six barely-there outfits appeared on EZ to represent the planned six days of honeymoon.

"Woohoo, you go, EZ."

"You'll never get out of bed again, girl!"

"My dear, he will be captivated."

EZ grinned and said, "Yes, he will. Thank you, Lara, this was the best. See you ladies in Georgia. I'm getting married!"

CHAPTER FIFTY-FOUR

The Details are Totally Absent

There was no sound outside of the intense staccato of his fingers hitting the keys, as if he was chasing the characters across the screen in search for his life. His face contorted with what might be construed as desperation, severe grief, or significant retribution, should anyone have been around to see. It was late, and the only thing visible was the movements on the screen and the variations of screen brightness, highlighting his skin with blotches of muted color. No colors could be discerned in the shadowy background of the room, in his hair, or in his clothes, just the random highlights as his fingers dictated the direction of the cursor on the screen. The reflection of the screen light off his eyes emphasized their hollowness and the intensity of his work.

The assignment he'd laid out for himself was nearly finished. He wanted this to be the most complete, perfectly executed program he'd ever built. Even though the physical location was unknown to him, the research of the building plans, network connections, and real time tests looked to be coming together just as he'd planned. A few more keystrokes and, regardless of whether he ever returned to the programs or not, the programs would execute with a continual and accelerated precision. It really didn't matter the outcome as long as the journey was long, painful, and life-threatening, with no hope of terminating the inevitable.

He paused in this one area and checked on the standing routines already operating, which controlled so many different areas of his power base. The investments were doing well, and several locations would be failing soon. Not only was he a brilliant programmer, but his ongoing study of human behavior also allowed him to force changes, like pushing cattle toward the branding iron. Planned well, executed flawlessly, this final project had taken him years to prepare as he remained undetectable and, as far as he could see, invincible! This was not only about his ability to control people, places, and things, but to remind himself he cared for nothing and no one anywhere in the world.

He returned his focus to the current project and glanced at the time to determine how long he could continue. The others would be arriving soon, and he needed a bit of rest, though not much, as he'd discovered over the years. A few more strokes on the keyboard and his face assumed the inscrutable look of success. He powered off the machine, plunging the room into total darkness. Using practiced moves, he exited without a sound.

NMX ↓ -7.58
CMX ↓ -9.33
HCC ↓ -3.90
SOX ↓ -7.74

Quip arrived at the operations center a little earlier than usual because EZ had some wedding plans to discuss with the ladies. He was a bit miffed he had been unable to do all the things to his lady love he'd woken up thinking about. She hadn't really denied his adoration but hadn't done the lazy languishing lovemaking they both enjoyed. He wanted to marry her but at this point looked forward to the wedding being over. They had looked at the engagement presents received, and he had dutifully helped to place them at appropriate spots around their apartment. He even hung the original impressionist painting Wolfgang had sent. It was amazing, and EZ loved it.

He hoped his early arrival would move the yardstick forward, as the team needed to resolve this whole commodity issue, and fast. Too many situations were beginning to take on the look of a momentous economic collision course. Giving the Americans the lead, via Mr. Hughes, and providing them with the proper data had been the right decision. He had protested it at first, but upon reflection, the case Otto and Wolfgang made was correct. Though all the team members of the R-Group were permitted opinions as long as they could substantiate them, he should have looked at the bigger picture. He would make certain that Hughes had everything he needed with all the support they could provide. And the costs for this effort would be part of the invoice to Eric's team.

He was almost finished reviewing the overnight stats and summaries provided by ICABOD when his screen alerted him to an inbound call. It showed from Tuck, which made it really late in the day for him. Perhaps he'd changed his flight and wanted to make certain to tell him.

Tuck's image appeared on the screen, and he looked odd. Quip greeted, "Hey, Tuck, how goes it. Bar time at your house. EZ loved the crystal lovers figurine you sent. Thank you."

"Don't even try it, Quentin." Tuck, looking like he would try to tear Quip apart if he were within reach, shouted, "I told you before to stop messing around with my home and my girl. Mavie was all upset when she got disconnected from the call with your wife-to-be. It's so not funny and, at this point, it's cruel."

"Tuck, slow down there. I told you before I'm not doing anything to you. Besides, to be honest, I'm far too busy trying to wrap up a project so I can get married. I am working like 16 hours a day, plus being the dutiful fiancée! Can you lighten up a little?

"Now, what exactly happened, and maybe we can figure it out together. If you want me to check out some things, I am happy to do so because you're obviously stressed. Once more, I have done nothing to you. I swear!"

Tuck shook his head, and one hand wiped his face as if gathering himself. "Okay, I just wanted to be certain you weren't playing any games. I didn't really think it was you, but I'll be damned if I can figure out who is messing with my house and my life!

"It started this morning when the coffee pot decided to brew with the top open and the pot not centered on the base. Coffee spewed everywhere, which of course Mavie walked on with her bare feet. Then she remade the coffee, poured us each a cup. When she went for the cream, the entire refrigerator was over-heated and the cream, along with everything else, was ruined. Of course she cursed a blue streak at me, and I was late to work while also getting to clean the mess up.

"She got home before me with groceries in hand to replace what had been ruined. The hand scan keypad that we use reli-giously took ten tries before it remembered her, but not before she threw the grape juice at the door in frustration. We had a white door before that. She brought in the groceries, checked the refrigerator temperature and put the groceries away. Of course, she pushes on the front pad to see the inside refrigerator temperature like, every half-hour now, or makes me.

"She went into the home office to talk to your fiancée and others that were on the call. The noises I heard made it sound like a happy sheila kind of call, so I was making plans for the rest of my happy satisfying evening, when all of a sudden she screamed. I tried to go in to see what the matter was, but the damn door won't open. I kept trying to get the knob to release, while she screamed my name over and over. Finally, I break the door open with my foot. I rush in, and she's pointing to the screens in the office which are all showing pictures of rats.

"Mavie has this horrible fear of rats that goes back to a time she'd fallen into a pit of rats. It made the news here for days. She was lucky to survive, but the embedded fear obviously still exists. I gave her some relaxants and finally got her to sleep."

Quip was watching his friend with mouth open. Here was the guy who could spin a story even faster than he could, but this didn't look or sound like a yarn. "Tuck, it sounds like your automated smart house of the future took a left turn to go through The House of Automated Misery! Would you like me to conduct a bit of review from your data logs and see if I can find anything?

"You remember, Jacob. He's amazing with discovering cyber fingerprints, if you would rather, he do it. Let me get him on the line, please. I don't want Mavie to be afraid to live in her own home or feel targeted for anything. I respect you two far too much to do anything close to this."

Tuck agreed and Jacob was conferenced in. Jacob was allowed remote access and spent a couple of hours reviewing Tuck's files, logs, and programs. He found trace evidence of previous unauthorized remote access, with the timing for that access outside of either Tuck or Mavie being in the house. With Tuck's permission, Jacob set up some cyber traps to catch any future intrusion but not alert the intruder. Quip promised he would keep an eye on the systems.

Then Quip set up ICABOD to start mapping all the strange issues with his own flat, going back to the lightbulb in the hallway all the way to this current incident at Tuck's. He wanted a linear view to cross check back to the files Jacob was reviewing. Quip finished up his work and headed home. He called EZ, but she didn't answer. Then he remembered they were meeting at Wolfgang's for drinks and dinner.

Upon arrival to their flat, he went inside. He suffered through the quickest shower ever since there was no hot water and changed clothes while trying to make the lights work properly. Since he was late, he figured that he would deal with everything when he got back. As he went to leave and set the alarm, he realized it had not been set when he entered. He set the alarm and left.

As Quip rushed over to Wolfgang's, he called EZ again, ready to read her the riot act about not setting the alarm. He had decided to add in a motion-activated voice command to remind her, going and coming, about the alarm. No way would he want EZ to be faced with something similar to what poor Mavie had been subjected to earlier today.

Then a cold thought flashed through his mind. Why were both ladies being targeted for this mischief at this precise time? The female anxiety was now his and Tuck's anxiety, and that was almost too coincidental. He was going to have to run some extra checks in the morning.

Quip's breathing stopped as he recalled the old adage, *all coincidences are highly engineered events.* And now everything in his world suddenly felt wrong. How he wished he had checked the refrigerator before leaving to see if it had been sabotaged as well.

CHAPTER FIFTY-FIVE

Keep On Thinking and Planning, or Just Do It!

LJ had provided the brief update the previous evening, using the preferred crisp bullets, after arriving at Takeru's compound. The only response had been a curt nod and dismissal with a wave of the hand. The next review would be at the upcoming meeting with the rest of the area managers. All would be staying within the compound as they arrived over the next two days. Alisha would be on enforcer duty, shadowing Takeru everywhere.

LJ had missed Alisha so much on this trip that he had planned to have endless mad passion when they had returned to their room for the night. Alisha had been just as stressed as he had been, which really put a damper on the passion. They had made love quickly to reconnect with one another and to reduce some of the stress. Alisha had finally fallen asleep, and LJ had watched her throughout the rest of the night. He avoided bothering her, knowing she would need to be in top condition to deal with the events and activities as they unfolded. He had been thinking of all the possible scenarios and stepped them out in his mind. Before she left this morning, he wanted to share his thoughts and get her agreement.

The digital timer on the radio toned, and quiet jazz began playing. Lights in the room automatically rose in brightness to simulate early morning daylight sneaking into the room. Alisha's eyes fluttered open, and she looked over at him and smiled. Her body naturally stretched and extended under the covers as she rolled onto her side, brushing up against him.

"Morning. You know, honey, I was just dreaming about you and me on that beach you mentioned. It would be so nice if we were on that peaceful beach with the breezes passing over us and real sun rising from the ocean. Ah, but we are not. We are still here in Takeruville with no margaritas."

LJ chuckled and grinned at the pretty picture that popped into his mind. "We are still here, but I have been doing some thinking since our latest discussions. I wanna talk, okay?"

Alisha nodded and rubbed the sleep from her eyes. Then she scooted up and leaned against a pillow. He did the same and pulled the covers up some to keep them both comfortable.

LJ suggested, "It occurs to me that we may not get the payday here we wanted. We are not in bad shape, between our two earnings and with what we have in our offshore account. I believe we could be comfortable, relaxing in the sun for one, maybe two years, depending upon which island we go to. Longer if we have just a little part-time work, maybe even a bar with bar-b-que, har, har, har. If that is good, we could leave right after the meeting with the rest of the members and simply not return. Go off the grid, as it were, and just run. But you and I both know that we would have to be looking over our shoulders from here on out if we do. I'm not sure I want to sign up to always be carrying a target on my back."

Alisha nodded but said nothing while she contemplated the scenario.

LJ added, "Or, we could stay to the end of this oil project I am working, get the extra bonus and take a vacation. Then disappear off the grid. Of course, that is assuming we get that far. There always seems to be a steady stream of new faces at the monthly meetings, so counting on cashing out at the end of the project may be just a heroic wish."

Alisha shifted under the covers, but it was obvious she was uncomfortable with LJ's musings.

"Both of us have remade ourselves and changed identities many times. I have the means to appropriate new identities. Hell, he might simply decide he has bigger fish to fry and not expend the effort, with all the other activities he has going on. He is scary and getting more self-centered each time I see him. Like you and me have seen before, that is never a good sign. Perhaps cutting our losses is the smart choice."

LJ stared off into space for a moment, then quietly considered, "And, for some reason, this oil and coal gig we are in makes me real uneasy. I mean, I learned early on how to con someone out of their money and have them thank me for it, but toppling whole governments and adding untold misery to those little ragamuffins I saw in South America is a little over the top…even for me. Not only that, but our home country is a target as well! I thought I could deal with it…but now I'm not so sure."

Alisha contemplated what LJ said and replied, "Frankly, honey, I agree with you. This is not a stable man. Heck, I didn't tell you last night, but one of the men coming to the meeting is already tagged with not leaving. He was skimming money off the top, and the director saw. It was done so poorly that even I spotted it right off.

"I know I have that fun activity to look forward to. The director is not a forgiving person, I don't think. He will hold a grudge unless we leave and dissolve our trail as we go. We have not misappropriated any money, and you have good documentation for every penny spent. But as you pointed out, that probably won't mean anything. When I saw him enter various amounts during your travels, it was within minutes of being spent, and you returned all the differences in the shortest time of anyone.

"The problem is, he thinks we all belong to him. When I went to London and took care of the tasks I had to complete, he made me keep my cell phone connected the whole time. One, so he could remotely follow the unfolding of the scene, and two, so he could make suggestions if needed. Control and checking in are his biggest hot buttons. Walking away without permission is a recipe for failure, unless we are very, very careful. Honestly, honey, I would like to go sooner than later. I'm all for packing up now and just going, but you decide. What about the sword you want so badly?"

LJ smirked and stated, "I don't even know why I want the damn thing. I only know that I do. Mostly, I want us to get out with a sizable payday as well as a chance to enjoy it. Listen to me, I sound like one of my marks who thinks playing a little longer will get him well. I knew he was only going to lose more. I've already lost too much! Even like last night, the hours I wanted to spend with you were not originally just to watch you sleep!"

Alisha smiled, kissed him, and promised, "Look, I'm in this because of you and for you, with no other consideration. If you wanna run now or later, we will just learn to watch over each other's shoulder so no one sneaks up on us. For right now, we have tonight to think on it 'cause nobody is arriving until tomorrow. We will return early and then play the rest of the evening, if you think you and your soldier can get up for that."

LJ pulled her in close and gave her a passionate kiss filled with great enthusiasm. He firmly stated, "Don't you worry, sweetums, I will be up for it. Now you get going, or you'll be really late. I am going to review our options and set a plan up to leave right after the meeting when the others go. If we leave after the meeting, then we will have a 30-day head start of becoming new citizens…somewhere."

Alisha scooted out of bed and looked over her shoulder with a smile as she moved to the bathroom to shower and get ready. She added, "Thank you, honey. I am ready to wake up on the beach with you. Plan good, sugah!"

After Alisha left, LJ made breakfast and spent the rest of the morning outlining his plan for their departure. He reviewed their money and moved a bit to one of the accounts he had set up. He was quite glad he never tried to skim a penny from the director. However, he had been careful to secure all bonus monies that were offered for meeting and exceeding the assignments. Outside of the one small misstep, he had collected on everyone. Alisha's bonuses hadn't been that much or very regular, but it all helped.

During his quick briefing to the director, he had mentioned the idea of a personal pilot, which the director hadn't frowned upon and had seemed to agree to the costs. However, if he wanted to show he was frugal with the director's expense account, he thought it might be prudent to have the pilot leave and then return to start shuttling the members back to their respective home bases. The inbound flights had not been an option for them as those plans had been set some time ago.

The only unresolved issue was the damn sword. He chided himself for coveting it, and at one point he had even talked himself out of it, but he simply couldn't forget that flashing blade resting on his shoulder. Finally, he resolved that if the sword was convenient to bring out, he would, but not at the risk of derailing their exit. He reminded himself that things wanted too badly end up owning you, and an old con man like himself should know better. Then he hit on the idea of swapping it out with a plausible substitute, which he hoped would remain unidentified for at least a short period of time. He would go into town later and see if he could figure out the substitute angle when he met with Juan.

```
NMX ↓ -7.50
CMX ↓ -9.33
HCC ↓ -3.90
SOX ↓ -7.74
```

LJ sent a note to the director on his plans for the pilot and the request to borrow the car to go into town. The response had been immediate, along with an attached list of supplies to acquire. LJ grinned as this would provide him a longer time period to be in town, looking for a substitute for the sword. At his request, Alisha had sent a photo of the sword. He would try to see if he could uncover any other options.

LJ sent a text to Juan that he would meet with him in the hotel and have lunch in the restaurant, but without Kitty. The drive to town was slow but uneventful. Traffic on these roads was mostly carts and walkers but usually only on market days. Today, it seemed like several walkers jumped in and out of the way. Life was slower here, and cars in general were too expensive for most of the farmers in this area. He found it odd that he had never before noticed the local poverty or the look on the faces of the thin children. It startled him slightly when he realized that he was actually feeling ashamed for what he was involved in and how it would punish these people even more.

At the hotel he found a handy parking place and proceeded to the restaurant. There was a nice view of the pool from the outside pavilion where he found Juan seated with a local beer already in his hand. The view of the tourists at the pool was close enough to enjoy the women but far enough to not be overheard. The big, wide palm blade fans turned at the perfect speed to keep the breeze moving. The music emanating up from the pool area was upbeat but not overpowering.

LJ grinned as he took his seat and said, "Did you have a nice evening and enjoy some of the local color? I understand the rum is even better than this cold beer."

Juan smiled and related, "Kitty and I had dinner here actually, then she went to bed, and I did twenty laps. I was so tired I don't even recall turning out the light in my room, but I did. This is a really nice place, Mr. Rogers. Thank you for the rooms. I feel like we need to get our flight plans in place. The plane is costing you sitting here, and that co-pilot watching it has complained twice to me this morning that he is bored. Of course, I told him that was a shame, so I put him to work washing and waxing it while we had time on our hands. It's the oddest thing, but he hasn't said anything since."

LJ smirked and said, "Well, son, that is exactly why I wanted to meet with you. Let's order lunch and see what we can do about building that plan."

The waiter took their order, and both men focused on the pool below as several of the lovely tourists decided to cool off with a bit of a dip.

LJ commented, "My, those are some lovely women, aren't they? I sho wish I had one of those pretty girls close by to see how pretty those tiny strips of cloth are that just barely cover what I can imagine! Har, har, har! Do you have a special woman in your life, Juan?"

Juan replied, "Not me. You might recall, I am in between women at present. And you, sir, are you close to someone special?"

LJ laughed heartily and replied, "Like the pirates I always remind folks of, I got a girl in every port."

The waiter interrupted as he brought their food and fresh beers. After he left, LJ continued, "I have one in this port who is quite the demanding sort, if you know what I mean. She always begs me to take her on trips with me. I hate to put her off, but every few months I need to sneak her away for a short trip to keep her settled, if you get my drift. She was really putting it to me even this morning, so I told her I would try."

Then looking a bit bothered, though Juan thought it was contrived, LJ added, "That is part of why I wanted to get with you."

Juan slowly took a sip of his cold beer and offered, "I can understand that. I would have thought you the type to keep a woman in her place."

LJ laughed while he nodded and said, "Yeah, but to keep her in the right place, sometimes you have to make 'em think they are winning, right?

"Anyway, I wanted to let you know that I spoke to my boss. He thinks we could use a pilot on retainer as it were, but not full time. The fee structure would be based on a per trip basis, but no constant trip schedule. For example, I have no travel, nor do any of my…uh, associates before Sunday. On Sunday I would want you here, ready to take a trip, though I am not certain of the destination yet. Several of my associates may need travel as well. Uh…did I mention the part about it being confidential travel?"

Juan sipped his beer and thought about the right response. He finally suggested, "It sounds like I might be able to take advantage of a request to fulfill a flight for an important customer of the owners of this aircraft we are using. It would help keep the revenue on the aircraft and take me off your credit card. The crew sitting idle is also costing you."

LJ replied, "Exactly my thought. You have a chance to do a flight but still be back here by Sunday. I would like to count on you for Sunday, or I will make other arrangements."

"No, sir, Mr. Rogers, I can make certain me and the plane are back here on Sunday, first thing in the morning. I won't commit to the other flight if I cannot be back here by Sunday morning.

"I think we could do some work together. If I cannot fly all the time, I will investigate ways I can fill my time. Perhaps even some more translation services if you need them."

His eyes wandered and settled on a particularly pretty gal exiting the pool.

LJ followed the direction of Juan's eyes and grinned. "Good! I will see you then, and I will text you late Saturday with the destination and number of passengers. I expect you here early Sunday at the airport and ready to go. And you can bring back Kitty if you want. She might give that pretty lady in the pool a run for her money."

Juan looked LJ in the eyes as he rose and shook hands. "Thank you again, Mr. Rogers. I will do what I can in getting Miss Kitty to join us."

CHAPTER FIFTY-SIX

So Much Data, So Little Time
...The Enigma Chronicles

Quip walked toward his work area in the operations center, past the glass walled area with all the processors captured inside. It was not as bad as the day when Wolfgang was learning the power of immediate data gathering and analysis, but the flashy, lighty things were definitely not in rest mode. As he sat in his customized chair, the screen lightened, and the 3D keyboard surfaced from the tabletop. He grinned and then frowned as he focused on the messaging on the screen. Reading quickly through the details and retrieving some additional summaries, he rapidly came up to speed with the current situation.

"ICABOD, you have been busy. Did that program Jacob shipped in help sift through the data?"

"Yes, Dr. Quip. I have been very busy. The program is helping to sift out the repetitive data being captured from the cloud provider sources. The other program Petra provided is allowing me to open the encrypted data before applying the sifting program. It is making the process more efficient by not gathering unnecessary yottabytes of data only to remove it later as a duplicate. That is making it much easier on our resources, even with the ability you added to create on the fly with virtual machines."

Quip grinned to himself as he thought about how much repetition was acceptable, depending upon the content. "Good.

Have you been able to do some of the correlations and analytics using Wolfgang's suppositions?"

"Yes, and the summaries are being routinely updated to him. He is able to isolate the financial transactions better and is overlaying them with the communication end points Jacob and Petra are tracking. It is taking up a majority of my processing power each time I go to a cloud provider to inspect the information and get through their security barriers. It is new ground for us. Once that is completed, it becomes a simple mining exercise like any other data source, including social media. Social media is still growing faster than even these cloud providers can gear up for. But the difference is in the real time data versus the longer term stored or historical data."

Quip hit some keys and inspected some of the summaries and located a file labeled QUOD. He tried to open the folder and found it password protected. He entered his top ten passwords, none of which worked, and the message flashed for the tenth time.

Insufficient password, try again?

Annoyed, Quip asked, "ICABOD, there is a file I cannot access. I believe that I was to have access to every file on your system. That was the design intent anyway. Did I change this policy?"

"No, Dr. Quip, you did not change the policy."

"Then why, ICABOD, can I not get into this file?"

"It requires a password."

Not one to resist a challenge or what he considered a gauntlet being thrown down, he tried a dozen more passwords with the same annoying result.

Insufficient password, try again?

It reminded him of the time when he was testing Jacob and making him jump hurdles but taunting him at each misstep. With that in mind, he decided to approach it from a different angle. "ICABOD, doesn't the word quod mean prison?"

"Yes, sir, I believe it does."

"Okay, then this file has to do with prison, right?"

"Dr. Quip, I am not in any position to make that level of determination. I am certain, like with many cases, there are extenuating circumstances, or at least that was what Jacob thought."

Quip grinned, then stated, "Okay, so Jacob is at the root of this issue. What is the password for this file about prison?"

"Dr. Quip, I am not aware of a file about prison."

Quip started fuming and opened a conference bridge while sending an invite to Jacob. A few minutes later, Jacob's image appeared with a smirk, and he asked, "Hey, Quip, what's up, or how can I help answer something for you?"

Quip looked very annoyed as he said, "I want to know how you blocked me from seeing a file and what the hell is in the file about prison."

Jacob looked genuinely confused and asked, "I don't know anything about a file on prison and can't think of a reason we would want to have a closed file about it. That makes no sense, buddy. Did EZ buy those cheap wine coolers again instead of your usual Beaujolais?"

Quip threw up his hands and shook his head. He was turning red with frustration until he finally did a screen share and super-sized the view. The image of the file folder labeled QUOD appeared. "This folder on prison right here, Jacob. It is password protected, and I cannot get to the contents. I have the admin rights to all the contents in this data center!"

Jacob looked and laughed aloud. After a few moments he gathered himself, and Petra slid into the video view as well with a grin on her face, barely suppressing a chortle. Jacob countered, "I put the files that were flagged from one of the searches ICABOD did in the cloud provider. There are two very old documents in there. The QUOD notation is not prison, Quip, but *Quite Unusual Old Documents*."

Quip closed his eyes and looked mortified. Jacob was American, not English. Quip was embarrassed he had not considered that before he jumped. Then he started to laugh, after which he asked, "Good one, Jacob!" Quip raised one eyebrow and looked confused as he asked, "What are they? And, more importantly, why did you save them with a password?"

Petra intervened, "I told him to protect them, until we could speak about them. With all the analytic questions Wolfgang is using to get information, we wanted to block this from view until we spoke with you.

"The contents are two letters from nine years ago based on the last save date of the file. The dates on the letters are a little older. And to make things a little more challenging, they were constructed with an antique application called *Wordy* running on an obsolete operating system called *Lame-OS*. I assume that it was named after the founder of the company. We would still be trying to decipher it if Jacob hadn't found a copy of it with its companion program *Invis-a-Calc* in the Museum of Obsolete Digital Artifacts, outside of Redmond, Washington in the United States."

Quip looked confused as he asked, "Okay, so what are they, and again why are they relevant?"

Jacob stated, "When ICABOD came across these, he and I were working on the data transfers that Laurie has been doing. He asked me to review the contents and provide direction. He said you were already at home. I read them and locked them away. I told ICABOD he was absolutely not to reveal the contents to anyone, as I would take care of it."

ICABOD added, "I am sorry, Dr. Quip, I was trying to maintain requested confidentiality from a valued team member."

Quip shook his head in annoyance at mostly himself before he responded, "All is well, ICABOD, and you did the right thing. So can I see the damn file now, Jacob?"

Jacob did a remote access to the file and opened it, allowing the first of two documents to be displayed on the screen. It appeared to be an old handwritten document, and the date at the top was ten years before. The thing that made Quip's blood turn cold was the opening salutation.

Quentin,
I write this following my dismissal from school. Due to the childish antics of you and your buddy, Tuck, I have lost the right to complete my semester and my family has disowned me. I recognize that you could care less about my education or family life, but I wanted you to know that even if it takes three lifetimes I will make certain that you and Tuck pay. I don't know how, when, or where, but I will make you two suffer.

For my side, I was foolish enough to think I wanted you both as friends because of your brilliant minds and ability to think on your feet. I no longer value those qualities in you, but will use them against you when you least expect it. I will be remembered for beating you and Tuck. Just wait.

Quip read it over again, flabbergasted at the content. He was looking at the screen, but his mind was clearly elsewhere.

Jacob waited a minute and then asked, "Do you know who might have written it? I went back through your school information but located nothing about a dismissal of any students, nor any trouble you might have been in. Nothing was on your record anywhere that Petra or I could find. This seems to be a letter that was photographed and saved from a hard drive. Likely, if this guy was this mad, the physical paper was not important, but looking at the file on a routine basis would have kept the fires burning. I suspect he copied the image into this old software to somehow preserve the sentiment from when it was written.

"We thought it relevant because of the issue going on with you and Tuck recently. The only correlation between those events and this file is the social media blitz about the wedding that Lara sent out with your full name. When did you gain your nickname? Petra could not recall."

Quip was still stunned at the content and the old memories it stirred up in him. He gathered his wits and replied, "Oddly enough, Tuck gave me the handle after we graduated. I liked it and it stuck. My full name is so formal and uptight, I found the shortened version suited me. Even my grandfather thought so.

"I recall the incident, and it was not our best shining moment in school. The guy that wrote this was an Asian kid that Tuck and I took a liking to. A really smart kid, who studied all the time. He said once he was the hope for his family, and he needed to prove himself in school. He did too. He was in the top five all the years at university, just like Tuck and me. We jostled in classes from one position to another but were all high achievers. The difference was Tuck and I also liked to have fun. We'd party hearty and apply our learnings to strange situations to see the outcomes.

"The one referenced here specifically involved stock manip-ulation and convincing a professor that his entire life savings were swallowed up by the market trading in Europe. Of course, it was all contrived and based on computer modeling. Great model that was. It has spawned many directions over the years for building and creating the algorithms in much of ICABOD's foundational programs. Funny, this incident was actually the reason I brought the idea back to the family to have technology inroads committed to preservation, like with the family values."

Jacob and Petra looked at each other until Petra asked, "It sounds like it had a profound effect on you, and I want to hear the entire story soon, but what is his name?"

Quip mused, "Tuck and I tried to find him once our three-day suspension ended, but he was already gone. The office staff said he had taken his transcripts and resigned from school with no forwarding address. His name was Yamato, I believe. We called him Yammy, or more fondly Mike T., as he wanted to blend into the European scene.

"What about the other document? How is it different?"

Jacob answered, "It is no different, other than Tuck replacing your name and visa-versa. Tuck must have only used his nickname in school. We think this is why yours and David Tucker's households are being targeted. He must have continued his schooling and gained many proficiencies. He could be a challenge to get rid of, but we should be able to locate him.

"I need to finish the review of Tuck's place, as he finally completed the access credentials I asked for. Once that is done, I want to get with you on our next steps. How about you alert Tuck, and we will work on it with your new information. It is your call on whether to tell the others."

NMX ↓ -7.50
CMX ↓ -9.33
HCC ↓ -3.90
SOX ↓ -7.74

Following the team meeting, Jim had decided to take a more active role in discovering the group behind this commodity trading number manipulation. He reviewed the data from all the current sources as well as the termination points for the data being pulled from Tomkins's machine and several of the others Claudia had helped him access. There seemed to be a common location which begged for a bit of personal inspection.

Otto and Quip had been very much in favor of his taking an active role, especially as he could use his U.S. credentials to penetrate some areas which would help with future prosecution. Eric wanted to make certain that the U.S. government be involved in investigating any irregularities in the numbers before it became an international incident. But they also wanted to make certain the profile was low.

Jim recalled that Julie had received a text from Juan that he needed to leave Panama for a few days and was heading back to Brazil. She suggested Juan fly Jim to wherever he needed to travel to help maintain a lower profile. Quip, always one to take advantage of an opening, agreed. Juan was routed to Texas and would pick Jim up later that evening. For the first time during this mess, Jim felt he was making progress and getting closer to the source. He had a few things to wrap up before he could head for the airport.

CHAPTER FIFTY-SEVEN

Several Maids for Milking...

The late evening of the night before had amped up their passions, and the ensuing sleep had been quite deep for them both. It was still very early when the text message Alisha received on her phone shot her into instant alert status.

Again, now...

Alisha wanted to ignore the text and pretend that she never received it. LJ was still deeply asleep. She studied the message for a few moments, trying to get her annoyance under control, when she finally admitted to herself that there was no way around it. She made a sour face and then took a deep breath before quietly getting out of bed, so as not to awaken LJ. Alisha hastened to dress quickly and leave before LJ could intercept her. She didn't want to explain it to him, and since they were leaving in a couple of days, she told herself LJ never needed to know.

Alisha picked up her usual accoutrements for the exercise and made her way to Takeru's inner sanctum. As usual, the monitor was the only thing providing any illumination to his area outside of the blade server lights and one small desk lamp. She moved quietly and slowly up to where Takeru was sitting in his silk robe and stopped. Like so many times before, he was almost fully engaged in the screen output, except this time this appeared to be a live video feed of two people. She simply assumed it was some Internet porn that he had been watching.

Without moving his gaze from the screen, Takeru rotated his captain's chair around so she could have full access to him. With full clinical precision and no emotion, she moved his robe aside and took his manhood in each hand to deliver what he had texted for. As usual, she gently oiled his erection and male pair to begin the gentle but insistent stroking that would bring him to climax.

On this occasion, she briefly looked up at the images on the screen to find what Takeru was so aroused by. There was a male and female in a frantic scene of anxiety and fear. This was no sexual voyeurism on his part as she'd expected. She struggled with her own anxiety, or possibly fear, in that he was enjoying these two people's torment in a situation that they obviously had no control over.

As the tormented people struggled with their situation and their fear grew, Takeru became more aroused, and Alisha, sensing her chore would be over quite soon, quickened her stroking pace. He delivered a full charge into the moist cloth Alisha had brought for clean up as a part of the standard operating procedure. A short, low moan, with a slight shudder, were the only clues he gave to indicate that she was done and could now leave.

Without a word from either of them, she gathered up the standard session items and quickly left the area. Her training as a nurse had allowed her to move through the session with clinical efficiency, but she was still shaken by the cold, cruel session demanded by Takeru. As she walked back to her room and LJ, she hoped he would still be sleeping so no explanation would be required.

As she absentmindedly washed her hands for the third time, she wondered why Takeru would want to watch people being tormented. Did he know them, or was it some site on the Internet he visited? It seemed more likely, if he actually knew them, he would have simply ordered a hit.

Alisha smiled as she watched LJ sleeping. They had discussed leaving as soon as possible and without the sword, as LJ hadn't been able to find any sort of replacement. Now, she was so unsettled by the Takeru session, she quickly showered and changed clothes so she could go outside and clear the vulgar session from her mind. If LJ woke up he would be in an amorous mood, and that was the last emotion she wanted to deal with after the summons from Takeru. Alisha quietly closed the door and went out, knowing she couldn't wait to leave this place, this job, and be away from Takeru. The potential payoff, she had agreed with LJ, though for different reasons, simply wasn't worth it.

NMX ↓ -7.50
CMX ↓ -9.33
HCC ↓ -3.90
SOX ↓ -7.74

Takeru sat motionless at the large mahogany table as the associate members of his organization filed in. It was an unspoken rule that Takeru always showed up last, so everyone was a little surprised and somewhat fearful of being late to the meeting. The low light conditions and dark mahogany wood used throughout the room made the air seem somehow more oppressive. Takeru's icy, intimidating manner made all the attendees uneasy.

No one wanted to speak before Takeru opened the proceedings. However, the mood in the room was such that it fanned everyone's anxieties, coaxing more fear internally the longer the silence continued. Alisha stood behind him as always, Takeru's only visible enforcer. As a female enforcer, she was untried to them, and they had less fear than when the associate over the oil commodity stood in that position. Alisha had learned how to echo Takeru's icy silence, and the associates sensed that something was up. They weren't wrong.

Takeru always began the proceedings with little or no pleasantries, but this time he jumped right to what was on his mind.

"LJ, can you address the data reporting problem we have with the commodities trading reports?"

Alisha became alarmed and filled with dread but struggled to contain her breathing and heart rate. She sent up a silent, terrified prayer that she would not be directed to execute LJ as the next targeted associate who had failed. She could barely contain herself as she shot a horrified look to her man. LJ coolly returned her stare and stood up to address the issue.

A long moment passed before LJ calmly offered, "Director, I have discharged my role faithfully in the establishment of the shell reporting companies and put into place all the computer equipment you indicated was required. Once I had done that, you charged me with altering the computer systems on selected oil tankers in and around South America. This too was completed. I have been completely focused on my new assignment and have not been involved with the commodity reporting infrastructure. I had assumed that my replacement, Manpreed Summa, had the situation under control. It was verified by you as working correctly when I handed it over to him.

"Do I need to reengage in that area to repair a problem? You have but to ask, my director, and I will shift my focus immediately."

The turbaned Indian associate who had been smirking and had expected to see LJ dealt with was now choked up with terror and unable to challenge the issue.

Manpreed finally managed to bring himself to a defensive mode and argued, "No, that's not true. Things have stopped working in the reporting cascade from almost all of our shell company data terminals, and it's his fault. The only one reliably working is our newest agent in the UK. At least she knows how to follow instructions and report correctly!"

Alisha breathed a very quiet sigh of relief that her target was not going to be LJ, but obviously was going to be Manpreed.

Alisha was quickly able to put herself back into character and watched for the subtle signal from Takeru in the reflection of the darkened mirror on the table.

Manpreed was now desperately pleading his case and maintained, "His data infrastructure is fatally flawed. Thus, it is endangering our operations. The commodity numbers are returning to normal, and all attempts to reprogram the terminals are being thwarted against all my efforts. It's almost like something is controlling them, director, and..."

In the mirror, Alisha saw Takeru cut his eyes up to her. She closely watched as he cut his eyes over to Manpreed, signaling the termination order. With the signal given, Alisha moved swiftly behind Manpreed. She looped a garrote over his head and pulled it tight around his windpipe while driving her large, powerful knee into his back, forcing him down onto the mahogany table. Even the most hardened associates were dumbfounded by the horrific sight of Manpreed's arms flailing wildly in an effort to halt the attack or get some breathable air. The grim execution took no more than a few minutes but was clearly emotionally draining for the audience. Even LJ was a little disturbed by the spectacle.

Finally, after the victim had given up his greatest gift, Alisha, still holding the garrote ends, dragged Manpreed's lifeless body out of the meeting room.

Takeru calmly stated, "Failure here has its own reward in this organization."

Takeru let the harshness of the statement sink in before he added, "LJ, now that our South America plans are in motion, I want you to pick this problem back up and cure it. Return all the milking maids for the commodities reporting project to production status. Also, the reporting agent in the UK that Manpreed bragged about has also failed our expectations. That loose end needs attention, now."

Everyone witnessed Alisha's return to the room to again stand behind Takeru. After another extended pause, Takeru blandly asked, "Are there any more failures to discuss for this meeting?" No one dared to respond, so he added, "Tomorrow you will each outline your plans for the next 90 days of activity to meet the goals on the envelopes in front of you. LJ, you will be first."

Takeru rose to leave with Alisha following close behind.

CHAPTER FIFTY-EIGHT

Is It Anchors Aweigh or Not?

Jim had provided the list to Quip and Otto with the full understanding that they would be following the data to the endpoints. He suggested they leave Claudia out of the equation, but if needed Jim would reach back to her. This list, coupled with the data Quip had trapped from Mr. Tomkins's machine, allowed a faster connection to the sources. In a quick follow up conversation with Otto and Quip, Jim felt confident the time needed to complete the search and destroy efforts would be considerably reduced with what Quip had in mind. Faster, more elegant, and with deeper analytics, but only because of the foundational work Jim had completed to date.

Jim briefed Eric on the progress of the commodities investigation. The team modeled several scenarios on how to rectify but none stood out as viable. Sadly, each mockups suggested the timing would be critical to avoid a horrible economic impact in the U.S. There was also potential impact for other countries, but Eric reminded Jim to continue to focus on the primary objective. Eric had agreed to Jim's traveling and flashing his authority until the locals pushed back to the edge of creating an international incident. With the friendly countries on the list, he was vectored on, neither of them felt it would be a problem. They kept it very low key with only portions of the modeling distributed to the teams under Jim.

Eric approved the rough scheduling Jim and Julie had outlined. It seemed quite logical that there was a link across the
commodity trade issues by a group or groups of people focused
on this specialized market. The fluctuations that had occurred
recently were beginning to illustrate a pattern which Julie said
Wolfgang was mapping and analyzing. Julie had arranged for
her husband Juan to fly Jim to the planned stops and help guide
him as needed. Eric knew the private plane she had arranged
would be a bit pricey, but it would ensure Jim could go into these
places quickly and efficiently with minimum suspicion aroused.

Jim called Eric for his final update when he was en route to
Dallas Love Field to board the private plane after a fast check
out from his hotel. He hadn't wanted to waste another minute in
achieving a solid lead on the instigators of this mess. Breezing
through security with his federal identification, he proceeded to
the area reserved for private aircraft customers. Juan was casually leaning against the steps to the aircraft and he grinned as he
watched Jim approach.

"Jim, you finally made it, man. I was beginning to wonder
if I needed to send out a search party, until I remembered you
were one of those G-man types who can find anything, anywhere.
Right?"

Jim chuckled and said, "Yeah, except I couldn't find time for
lunch before I got here. I hope you have a snack on board."

Juan clapped Jim on the back and gestured him to proceed
up the stairs. "Jim, I have many things on board this aircraft that
you might enjoy. You can fold a map, right?"

Jim paused and looked back at Juan. "Fold a map, well, yeah
sure. Why would you ask that?"

Juan replied with a smile, "I don't think you are qualified to
fly, but I listed you as a co-pilot. In all honesty, I am hoping you
can at least fold a map if needed. Oh, and we do have a flight

attendant, Miss Kitty, to help with that food service and safety part."

Jim's face held a look of confusion as he nodded and then finally turned around, continuing up the steps. He entered and saw the beautifully appointed plane with its inlaid varnished wood embellishments, camel-colored leather seats with wrap-around arms, and flat screen television on the wall. The surround sound music was at just the right volume.

"Wow, Juan, you sure know how to travel. All this luxury and a Miss Kitty too. No kidding!"

Just then Mercedes stepped out of the galley to Jim's left and grinned. Not missing a beat, Jim said, "Ah, you must be Miss Kitty. I can be Marshal Dillon if you want, ma'am."

Juan laughed loudly as he closed up the plane and headed toward the cockpit. "I think that is all I want to know on that subject. You two have fun. I am going to finish the checklist and get us out of here. Next stop will be Brazil.

"Hey, Miss Kitty, if I need you, I will call."

Jim pulled Mercedes into his arms and soundly kissed her. Then he lessened his hold and looked her in the eye with a mixture of wonder and passion. "No wonder I haven't been able to reach you. Hanging around with flyboy here."

Mercedes coyly smiled and replied, "Yep, we've been busy. Julie set this up, so you need to thank her later. Come on, buckle up, my dear. Once we are in the air we can…"

Jim interrupted with a leer. "Join the mile high club? Boy, I have missed you."

Mercedes laughed as she fastened her seatbelt in the seat next to his. She took his hand into hers, gently stroking with the tips of her fingers. As the engines revved a bit with Juan positioning for takeoff, she sweetly offered, "Not on this flight. We need to get our plan outlined and see if we can find the bad guys. Sort of like what we use to do. No fooling around, though."

Jim squeezed her hand and replied, "Yes, dear. But later that will change."

Mercedes replied, "Oh, I hope so, Marshal Dillon. How do you know about Marshal Dillon? You hardly ever watch television and definitely aren't old enough for that one."

"I saw it once on the History Channel, and my dad said it was great!"

Once in the air and leveled off, Juan turned off the seat belts sign. Mercedes took him some food and a beverage and then served Jim. Mercedes explained what they had been up to and what she had learned from Julie. With Juan and Julie as her bosses, she was able to bring Jim up to speed on her side. Jim explained the goal of the first stop was to check in on the leased tankers which were apparently still docked at Porto de Rio de Janeiro.

"Part of why this was suspicious is the crew for the leaser, Mr. Holland Rogers, had arrived a week ago and was supposed to already be headed out to some destination. They had not moved according to the port master, yet the ship itself had been reported as on the water and has arrived in two ports, so far, to pick up cargo. Something that was reported one way yet visible in another is what I am checking on, with the full backing and approval of the ship owner."

```
HMX  ↓ -7.50
CMX  ↓ -8.33
HCC  ↓ -3.90
SOX  ↓ -7.74
```

Jim and Juan arrived at the Port Master's office in Rio, and he showed them the logs he had on the tankers in question. These tankers were docked at the far end, out of his line of sight, but the nightly rounds which were recorded by hand had shown the tankers had not moved. Jim verified the slip numbers and confirmed his permission from Thiago Bernardes to check on the ships.

As Jim and Juan walked toward the tankers, Juan said, "It all looks quiet, so we'll play it nice and easy like you wanted. I will back you up."

Jim nodded and proceeded up the gangway to the ship. With the gangway in place, they both knew the ship was not planning on taking to the sea any time soon. They arrived at the top of the gangway and a scruffy looking character approached from the far side. He had a swarthy complexion, tall and skinny, and looked like he had not shaved or bathed in several days. Jim noticed no sidearm on the man.

The man arrived and stopped. Speaking English with a Jamaican accent, he said, "Mon, sorry, we aren't looking to add to the crew. You can go along now."

Jim smiled agreeably and replied, "That is good. We weren't looking for work. Already have a job. Need to speak to your man in charge, possibly the captain."

The man cocked his head to one side and questioned, "Why would you want the captain?"

"I think it's better if I tell him. Would you like to tell him we are here?"

The man chuckled. "Alright, I am the captain. Captain Franks, that is. I am in charge of this vessel. What can I do for you?"

Jim looked him over as if unconvinced by the statement. He finally stated, "Great. My name is Jim Hughes. I want to go to the bridge and review the ship logs. The owner of this vessel, Mr. Bernardes, is concerned about some maintenance that was needed which may have been forgotten before your firm took over this tanker. He had hoped you were still in port to allow me to review the status and report back."

Franks looked over the documents Jim provided. Satisfied that it was a valid reason, he seemed unconcerned as he nodded agreement and led them toward the bridge. They passed one other crew member who hardly gave them notice.

Juan casually asked, "Where is the rest of your crew? It seems quiet."

Frank replied, "They are below decks resting up until we leave."

Jim asked, "Are you leaving port soon?"

Franks replied, "Hopefully tomorrow. We are waiting on orders to where to take our 40,000 tons of oil now."

Jim seemed interested as he responded, "40,000 tons! Wow, it must be a full load on this vessel."

Franks smiled and nodded. "Yep. Once we get our orders to move this to our next port, I expect my bosses to be delighted."

Opening the door, Franks announced, "This is the bridge, gentlemen. The logs are right here."

Jim replied with a thanks and picked up the logs. No one else was on the bridge.

Juan interrupted, "Excuse me, Mr. Franks, can you point me to the head. Even the slight rocking has me unsettled, if you get my drift."

Franks laughed and replied, "Right this way. Sometimes it takes a while to gain your sea legs. Be right back, Jim."

Jim edged toward the computer console and quickly found the USB port. He inserted the thumb drive and with a few keystrokes loaded up the program he'd been given. Edging back over to the table, he finished his review of the logs just as Franks and Juan returned.

"Captain Franks, I think you are okay for leaving tomorrow, if needed. There was one problem with a missed maintenance, as the owner suspected. The maintenance can be arranged on the lifeboats this afternoon. I will call for it on my way off the ship. It won't take too long, and Mr. Bernardes apologizes for the inconvenience to you. You can let your boss know that a small refund for the time will be provided to cover your time in port for this oversight."

As they waved from the dock, continuing on their way off the pier, they observed Captain Franks place a call from his cell phone.

Juan placed a call from his own phone and when the call was connected said, "Trace all of the calls now!"

EZ replied, "Triangulation from the tanker and end point identification in progress. I will forward you the information when the verification and length of call are determined."

Juan disconnected the call and looked at Jim as he asked, "Did you get the program in place?"

Jim grinned and replied, "I did. That boat is riding really high in the water for having a full load. You'd think the deadweight tonnage line would be close to the 52,000 tons max for this Panamax vessel. Look at where it is against the markings on the hull as we pass. I doubt there is anything in the tanks.

"I just hope the check on the ships in Chile goes this easy."

Juan asked, "Panamax vessel? I'm not up on my tankers. What does that mean?"

Jim laughed, "Sounded smart, right? Actually, it is a term for tankers that can go through the Panama Canal safely. Mercedes told me when she was briefing me on the tankers we were going to look at."

CHAPTER FIFTY-NINE

Get Sharply into Focus, Team

Amazingly Quip opened the video conference call on time. He stated, "Well, it looks like we are all here and everyone appears to be themselves.

"Petra and Jacob, can you update us on the ePETRO state of affairs? You two had a new mole surface there, and you had some encryption breaking efforts going on to work backwards into the source as a sort of *Digital Dumpster Diving* effort that I like to call DDD. Also, what is your analysis of Mike Patrick? Is he animal, mineral, vegetable, criminal, or just plain incompetent?"

Jacob and Petra gave each other quizzical looks. Jacob promptly responded, "Uh, can we have Otto lead the call instead of you? Sounds like you are having errors writing to disk, likely due to the pending ceremony with your betrothed."

Otto stepped into the audio portion of the call and said, "Thank you, Quip. How about you let me take it from here? I want to first update you on what we have to date, so you can understand where your efforts fit in, alright?

"First, we have Jim Hughes traveling to Brazil to help us trap what we expect are bogus reporting programs on the chartered tankers. He has the tools to then disrupt their falsifying efforts.

"The shell corporations in North America, we have verified, have already been throttled, and their reports are being brought back in line, but this effort will take some time. Now that timeline may be disrupted if the DMO stays in the wind. If this DMO senses the positive strides we are making, he will most likely unwind everything we have in play, unless we get to him first."

Quip hastily offered, "Yeah, that's what I meant."

Otto rotated his head to give that quiet down look that Quip needed now and again, before he continued, "We need a clear target so we can preempt any more commodity price tampering that will lead to toppling multiple governments with catastrophic consequences.

"Is Mike Patrick the target source, or is he just a bystander who is just really too close for comfort? This Laurie person seems to be your best lead, but she is, by your classification, an information mule whose only value is to lead us to the source. Any new breakthroughs or fresh insights that we can work?"

Jacob promptly responded, "We don't believe that Mike Patrick is our DMO. While he is certainly not an ethically or morally pure example of what humans should be, he is basically being used as a pipeline. We found that his first admin and her replacement admin are both functioning as information mules for another organization.

"Petra and I have essentially given him back his company to operate, but we have confiscated his reporting rights and installed some guardrails. Only ICABOD can do the reporting for ePETRO for the next three months, with an option for another three months if we need to go slower.

"As the team had previously pointed out, we can't cure the commodity trading information overnight, but we can't trust him to do it correctly in his current state of denial. Basically, we own his network until such time as we need to return it to him."

Petra added, "I am able to decrypt most of what is going through, since it can't be too tough for the modest encryption capabilities of the admin's cell phone. However, so far I haven't been able to penetrate the service group Laurie works for."

Wolfgang stated, "We have seen anonymizing servers for digital communications before, but this is the first time I've seen evidence of analog anonymizing services providing the same functionality.

"Jacob and Petra, what you have discovered is like a 1-800 service for cloaking the operations from the intended targets. It appears that instructions come in from one side and are dispensed through another media, creating a discontinuity between the issuer and the director or operative. Julie, what do you make of this?"

Julie offered, "As always, Wolfgang, you see the complexity threads before the rest of us, with the exception of ICABOD, of course."

Quip cut his eyes around and flatly asked, "Sooo, still shining up to ICABOD, huh? I thought you had broken that off. Are you two still an item?"

Otto raised his eyes to the ceiling and sighed before he suggested, "Can we stay focused here, please?"

Julie asked, "Pet, can you get me to the location where the information disappears? If this is an analog cloaking routine, then there has to be physical people taking the digital material, converting it to another media and shipping it out. I think my team might be better suited to doing FOTSTMAG work."

While everyone nodded in agreement, Quip's brain was locked in neutral trying to decipher FOTSTMAG, but finally, with defeat resonating in his voice, he loudly admitted, "Okay, I give up! What is FOTSTMAG?!?"

Julie was smirking, but before she could respond, ICABOD calmly offered, "Dr. Quip, FOTSTMAG is shorthand for *Feet-on-the-Street-to-Meet-and-Greet*. Julie's team has demonstrated this advanced technique on more than one occasion. This skillset, which they have clearly perfected, is an excellent complement to our digital resources and almost essential in dealing with…"

Quip, not only embarrassed but now annoyed that he was both unaware and being lectured, flatly stated, "Okay, fine. That will be enough. We are supposed to be trying to figure out how to stop this DMO from destroying our civilization, but you and Julie seem to be rehearsing your comedy routine to apparently take it on the road. Can we stay focused here, please?"

Sensing that Quip needed to be refocused, Petra asked, "Quip, you and ICABOD were going to hunt for the mysterious black lady that met our mysterious oil tanker charterer in Panama. You indicated that she had also been in London at about the same time that Roslyn met with her demise. Did you and ICABOD dig anything up on her? Was it simply a coincidence, with no bearing on our case?"

Quip quickly snapped back to the meeting and with an open palm slap to his own forehead said, "Oh, I almost forgot. ICABOD, bring up those videos we unearthed from the UK Transit Authority and let's run them in order as we discussed."

Quip quickly assumed the role of an announcer trying hard to become a teacher and stated, "We have several different video feeds from the underground station cameras, but, geezus, the poor quality of these made it nearly impossible to get a single useful image."

Jacob asked, "Then it is just idle coincidence that our Panama lady was in London at the same time Roslyn was killed? No proof, just a dead end...uh, so to speak?"

Quip rocked his head back and, feigning mock indignation, offered, "The bobbies wrote it off, but we took a different approach. Which is to say we approached it from every angle. There were no less than five, count them five, video feeds, and all of them capturing crappy, grainy, and blurred images of everything on the platform that day. Part of the reason for the poor quality of the videos is not only are they last decade's analog cameras, but the dust and vibration cause them to capture everything in poor crud quality.

"However, I asked ICABOD to take video feeds from each of the cameras and stitch them together for a 360 degree picture to see if we could get something useable out of the individual feeds. He even added in the camera from the train that is focused on the door and that helped to create a *Point, Place, Panorama, and Pictorial of People on the Property* or P[6]. You guys judge the results."

ICABOD opened a video window in the whiteboard session area of the video conference window so that everyone could watch the playback.

Julie was the first to comment. "The video feeds now actually look like the black mystery lady from Panama. Oh wow, it's too bad we can't hear what she is saying, but with all the noise just getting a decent picture puts us way ahead of the game!"

Quip, now sporting a very smug, self-serving smile, stated, "Oh, so sure you are of what cannot be done. ICABOD and I have been augmenting the facial recognition software to now include lip reading, or mouth miming, as an enhancement to the program. Listen to what she is saying to get the crowd of people to let her move behind her intended target, Roslyn."

ICABOD boosted the video whiteboard window so they all could hear. "Excuse me, I'm a nurse trying to reach my patient. Excuse me, I'm a nurse trying to reach my patient...."

Quip then added, "Look how everyone defers to her request so that she is right behind Roslyn with the train just entering the station. We lose a lot of the clear video from the platform, but swinging around to the train-side video...."

Julie gasped and announced, "Look, Roslyn is there in the first video feed, but in the second the only person in the frame is the black lady in the nurse's uniform. First Roslyn is there and then she isn't.

"The times you show on the video whiteboard match exactly when Roslyn fell under the train, except that we now know she was most probably pushed. ICABOD and Quip, you've done it. Do the bobbies have this?"

Quip fell silent, contemplating his next statement for almost a minute. "No. Since this is almost like a photo editor but for videos, I don't think the bobbies are going to be interested in our highly engineered video composite because no judge would accept it in a court of law.

"Let's set that aside for the moment and let me tell you what we did with our enhanced video image of our mysterious black nurse."

Quip continued, "We managed to capture a modest arm gesture like she was pitching a softball, which was probably Roslyn's cell phone, and then we lose track of our mystery lady on the platform. We reasoned that if this was an ordered hit then we should expect to see our mystery nurse making a quick exit back to her home turf. We suspected that the nurse uniform was probably part of her disguise and that she would discard it in favor of another one which would make it even harder to catch her on an exit strategy. Turned out that it was easier than we expected, thanks to ICABOD."

Jacob puzzled and asked, "How do you mean easier?"

Quip again grinned and said, "She may have been excellent at changing costumes, but she didn't remember to change her signature red lipstick. Let me shorten the story at this point. We tracked her mouth miming and red lipstick all the way through multiple airports to reach her home destination of Panama. Thus, we have a high confidence factor that Roslyn was an ordered hit and that the enforcer who executed it is in Panama, schmoozing with our other mystery person. High probability that this is where you want to begin your search for the DMO and the analog anonymizing service."

Julie, appearing a little unsettled, quietly stated, "We already have two people there, Quip, Juan and Mercedes. And if this mystery lady has done what the video composite showed and is partnered with our mystery oil tanker charter gent, then I have two people at risk again."

A thoughtful Otto added, "With Jim Hughes heading that way as well."

CHAPTER SIXTY

I Scream, You Scream,
eh You Know the Rest

They were all seated at Heladería la Fontana near the Chacalluta International Airport in Arica, Chile. The food was reasonable and the ice cream renowned. They had window seats and could enjoy watching people and listening to the quiet conversations from other tables without being too close. For a Saturday afternoon it was very quiet, and they wanted to have a local meal and discuss the next stage of their travel. The food was served quickly by Chilean standards, and they were left to enjoy it in peace.

Juan seemed a bit distracted, uninterested in the overflowing freshly prepared fruit salad, and he kept looking at his watch. "You both know I committed to the man, Rogers or whatever his real name is, to be back in Panama tomorrow morning. The flight time is under six hours, so we should be good if we leave by 4am, though I am qualified to fly at night. Do we have all the provisions, and did you set up the refueling before you met us here, Mercedes?"

Mercedes provided an indulgent smile as she replied, "Yes, boss. For the third time, it is all taken care of. I even paid one of the local guys to watch the aircraft, so would you relax." In an effort to enjoy the respite from their almost non-stop flying, she turned toward Jim. "Jim, I have heard enough about the plane, how about you regale me with your tales from the adventures of the day. Please don't leave out any details. I am on my lunch break after all. Right, boss?"

Juan acquiesced and ordered them all another round of iced tea. He thought the tea here was even better than what Julie made, which was saying a lot. It was not a celebration meal, but a way to sit all together and make plans once they heard if any progress had been made from what they had done here and in Rio. Julie had spoken briefly with Juan, and she suggested that Panama was looking more and more like a key area for the data traffic on the commodities. It was starting to look like there were some significant efforts being made to mask all transmissions going to and coming from that area. The transmission captures EZ had worked out with Carlos on the communications signals were beginning to uncover some of the source points. It was to their advantage that Juan had flown Mr. Rogers to his latest destination. Julie promised she would update him later. What wasn't clear was what should be done once they arrived in Panama.

Jim patted Mercedes's hand softly and related, "Just like we planned, Juan and I went to see Joaquin Fuentes. He was the man Mr. Rogers met with and Juan had helped with translation, when the deal on his tankers was made. The tankers were still in port, just like the ones in Rio. Fuentes was more than willing for us to go have a look since the thugs onboard had blocked his attempts to board. Even Fuentes's crew of four, included in the contract, had not contacted him to report their status as requested. He traded the approval for me to board without alerting local officials for a status on his friends. That and the hundred Chilean pesos Juan added to sweeten the deal.

"We walked toward the slip the tanker was moored in. It was sitting further in the water, so something was obviously in the cargo tanks. We made a side bet whether the cargo was oil or water. When we looked up, these two burly men were blocking the top of the gangway. Juan insisted we hurry up the gangway anyway, so he started hollering at them in Spanish. What was it you were saying to them, Juan? It really got their attention."

"I just told them that this big guy with me was a high-ranking member in the federales, and he had the authority to hold the ship if they refused to cooperate. Jim speaks a little conversational Spanish, but this was the fast and seriously colorful side of the conversation.

"Jim insisted they let us see the cargo hold, based on his authority, as he flashed his badge out so it perfectly reflected the sun into their eyes. He called them some really impressive names when they refused. Then he pushed one of them out of the way so hard, he slipped and crashed onto the deck. The guy banged his head against the foundation of the railing and knocked himself out. I got the other guy in an arm lock behind his back, and we marched toward the first container."

"Juan is really scary in a fight, Mercedes," continued Jim, "and I was glad he was on my side.

"The deck was a mess, the guy was a slob, and if it had been my ship I would have been pissed. It gave me the idea to pause at the lifeboat we were passing. I picked up the tarp on the lifeboat and rooted around until I located the dry seal container and removed it to the deck. I grabbed out the flares and tucked the first aid kit under my free arm. I gestured we should continue to the hold. We opened the hold, and it smelled like old fish, not oil.

"Juan asked him with a bit more pressure to the arm, close to the breaking point, and still the man said the cargo was oil. So I went over and opened up one of the tanks and stuck in the flare. The guy didn't even break a sweat when he told me to go ahead and throw it into the tank."

Both men started laughing, and Juan added, "Yeah, but he sure did a dance when I pushed him forward, and Jim bounced the flare off his grimy pants. The guy did a reasonably good tuck and roll, trying to put out his pants, until he finally jumped into the tank and then yelled for us to help him out. Har, har, har!"

Jim continued the story. "The men that had gathered, also disgusting, gave us a wide berth as we then went to the bridge and added the program to the computer. Luckily, the crew of the owner were tied up on the bridge, likely to help with the messaging and if they did have to sail. We untied them and suggested they hold the others and call the authorities in the morning.

"Oh yeah, Juan, where is my two hundred bucks?"

Confused, Mercedes looked from one man to the other. She asked, "Two hundred bucks for what?"

"I said water on the bet!" Jim crowed.

Just then Juan received a text message on his cell phone. It was from Julie.

New information confirms oil tankers data transmissions terminate in Panama. Haven't pinpointed the spot yet, will soon.

Juan showed the message to Jim and Mercedes, and they both nodded as they finished their food. Mercedes had just ordered ice cream for them all when Juan received another text message.

Alright pilot, need you on the ground, gassed and ready by sun up. Hotel arranged for you and Miss Kitty. We need food for two. Confirm you will be here and text me upon arrival.

Juan replied 'confirm' and showed the text to Jim. The ice cream cones were retrieved as Juan paid the check at the front. Jim flagged a taxi down, and they proceeded to the airport.

NMX ↓ -7.50
CMX ↓ -9.33
HCC ↓ -3.90
SOX ↓ -7.74

Once they arrived in Panama, the three of them checked into a different hotel but still near Tocumen Airport. Juan had called and canceled the reservations made by Mr. Rogers. Jim simply did not want to be where anyone expected them, and no one protested his logic. They had spent several hours in Juan's room on a call with Julie and EZ, receiving updated information about calls being made between the ships and a location in the hills far from the city.

The only things visible, even from the satellite images Jim was able to secure with the help of Eric, was farmland. A few heat signatures indicated cattle spread out and some humans. The land in that entire area, close to 4,000 acres, was owned by a family trust known only as YT, Ltd. Eric was researching for more details, but this effort was on the back burner as it appeared the land had never been developed. He suspected it was a tax write-off of some sort.

After staring at the images for over an hour, Mercedes finally spotted what appeared to be a possible antenna or dish, well camouflaged in the terrain. It was odd that there was no real heat source, but she speculated it could be underground, or perhaps it was simply a misshapen water tank. In that area there were some fresh water streams, so the water tank idea was discounted. They tried to find a road that would reach the area and agreed they needed a four-wheel drive vehicle if they planned to go there. Julie arranged for a vehicle to be at the hotel within the hour if it was needed. If not, they would simply leave it. They returned to the plane and hauled all the weapons and equipment together that Juan and Mercedes had secured before they had picked up Jim in Texas. They pretty much had every contingency covered.

During the final conference call, a plan was finally completed. Much to her dismay, Mercedes would stay at the hotel and monitor the radios and phones. It made sense because, if everything really came undone, she would be able to reach out to the authorities with a viable story of being deserted by the pilot. Jim and Juan would drive into the area before dawn and hopefully see tire tracks to help them reach the geo-coordinates provided by EZ. If that failed, they hoped to spot the vehicles used by Mr. Rogers, as well as the female who had picked him up at the airport. They had several options of action, depending upon the scenario that unfolded.

Though everyone expected the names to end up phony, Holland Rogers and Alisha Jones had been confirmed through Panama customs officials as being in-country. According to Julie, Alisha had arrived not too long ago from London. Her face, as it turned out, was in all the airport video footage. The plan was to hold them until Jim determined where they would go, based on what they found. Jim cast an eye at their armaments, and while he felt reassured that there wasn't anything they couldn't handle, he really wanted answers from the mystery persons.

CHAPTER SIXTY-ONE

Said the Spider to the Fly
...The Enigma Chronicles

Jacob had completed his review of David Tucker's home remotely through a secure tunnel into the Tucker home network. Not only did Jacob find several areas that had been easily compromised, but he also found what he thought was the source of at least the video problems. He was unable to easily determine where the signal originated from and if it was a bidirectional transmission. He suspected there was a timer or motion sensitive trigger. His review of the home network had taken place while Tuck and Mavie were not at home.

After a couple of conversations between Quip and Jacob, Jacob had written a tracking program to get to the source location. They considered the source location to be passive until some sort of event occurred. The program was to be loaded onto the home network by Tuck or Mavie when they returned home.

Quip called his buddy Tuck on an encrypted voice communication line. Tuck took the call in a public library on their landline. "Hey, Tuck. Jacob has completed the review of the network and the endpoint devices you have connected to it. There was some suspicious code added to your television, possibly via your cable Wi-Fi connection."

Trying to sound upbeat, Tuck replied, "But that cable Wi-Fi has been in place for quite some time. It connects several items throughout the house so I can access the app on my cell phone and control my television recording. I've even got it to control our outside watering program. You only get one day a month, and I don't want to miss it."

"I totally understand, buddy, but it also leverages the rest of your IP network to connect your security pad, refrigerator, every video screen, alarm system, and twenty other endpoint devices. How do you like those eight flat screens for showing the game in every room, or do you have different channels playing on different screens?"

Tucker sighed and made an annoyed snorting sound, then he commented, "You know I have eight flat screens? I can certainly see where that would be a problem. Jacob did one hell of a review of the network and devices." Then, with a resigned sigh, he asked, "How many security gaps did he find, and are they fixed? I owe you a bundle, no doubt, Quip."

Quip replied, "I am not going to charge one of my best friends for something like this, though a beer or something at my bachelor party would be okay. I want to track how the control is occurring and from where. I don't want Mavie or even EZ having to worry that someone is nosing around. That is why we set up all the security we both have.

"The problem is you have old and new technology. Like me, you hate to throw something away when it still works. Some of the older items, like the television in the den, have potential for security gaps. Jacob found a remote command program that looks like it can turn on the video and do a send and receive. In other words, it can watch what occurs in the room even if it is not on for delivery of a program. Most of your devices, and mine as well, are intelligent devices but are expected to be running in passive, not active, modes. Somehow those switches in a few of the devices can be run in active mode with the right programming overrides.

"The net net is we suspect somebody is watching you. Toward that end, I want you to go to the secure dropbox we previously used and download the program in there called CRABYONE. When you get home, load it onto the office laptop where Mavie was on the call with the girls planning the wedding stuff. Then I want to see if you and Mavie can do an award winning performance of yelling at each other, regardless of what occurs on the screens throughout the house. It could come up with rats again or anything that might unnerve you. You need to tell each other in advance it is not real. We need to track the signal."

Tuck hesitated before he said, "Do I need to involve Mavie in this? It sounds awful."

"Tuck, you read that letter we uncovered. If this is a revenge gig against you and me, we at least know why this is coming at us. If this is just someone else messing with us...well, let's just say we need better groupies who are after our bods.

"It's possible it could be bad, though Jacob has neutralized anything he identified as potentially dangerous to you. The bad guys will think the doors are locking and trapping you, like before. That cannot happen now though. Only the monitors and flat screens can be controlled for content. I would explain to Mavie that whoever this is seems to enjoy the voyeurism part. We will track it back to the source and then continuously loop the video we will be making at the same time. I will signal that you can leave while we sanitize the rest of the house."

Tuck said, "Alright. I will see if she will go along, but the guy might still try to do something to me, right?"

"Agreed, he might if it's our old running buddy looking to get even. The trouble is we are not completely sure. Even though we found that digital archive where we were nosing around, the truth is digital junk stays out there long after the event. Social media statements or even text messages fired off in anger float around in the ether long after everyone forgets why it was important at the time. I mean, it could be an old enemy of EZ's, and she is out to get anyone involved."

"Yes, I get it, but most sheilas don't get revenge in this way. Oh, and before I go start the plan, which should take me about an hour to signal you that we are in place, what the hell does crabby one mean? You know I hate it when you do that, man, and it will bug me if I don't know."

Quip laughed and replied, "Why, it means *Crash, Rot and Burn You Overrated Network Eavesdropper*, of course."

NMX ↓ -7.50
CMX ↓ -9.33
HCC ↓ -3.90
SOX ↓ -7.74

Quip arrived back home late at night after what he considered a very successful day. Not only did they get a real lead on the source of the problem, but Tuck's house had been made more secure than ever before. Tuck insisted that he keep Quip under contract for the next two years at a minimum to monitor the security efforts at Tuck's home and business. Quip soundlessly opened the front door, and the house was bathed in darkness. He was annoyed that the hallway light was still misbehaving but was way too tired to deal with it right now. Quip knew his way around in the dark.

At the archway to the living room, he stopped as he spied a faint red glow. The glow was a stream of light, almost like a laser, which started on top of the coffee table and appeared to be moving systematically around the room. Then it stopped. He kept still and watched until it appeared again, then after about 30 seconds stopped. He walked toward the table where he thought the light originated. The only thing he saw was the table, a couple of congratulation cards, and the vase. He walked to the kitchen and turned on the light. He poured a glass of water and sent a text.

> ICABOD, something is happening in the flat. Check and see what is connected please. Text only.

Several seconds passed before there was a response.

> Dr. Quip, I have scanned everything. No breaches, nothing that should not be on your network, sir. What is happening?

Quip thought for a moment, then replied.

> There is a strange red light emanating from the vase on the table in the living room. A new gift. Can you video the room using the night vision setting?

Time passed and Quip mulled over the possibilities.

> Dr. Quip, I was able to record an event. I am evaluating it. It seems that the device has wireless connectivity, but not to your network, which is why it was missed.

Quip grew immediately angry and concerned. He shook his head and ran his tongue across his teeth before he clucked it as he typed:

> Where is it getting its signal from then?

The response was immediate.

> It seems to have a built in solar power battery which is why it is running, and it is connected to the open network from the apartment above.
>
> ICABOD, can you cut off its transmission?

Several seconds passed, then the reply.

No, Dr. Quip, it is random, and I cannot shut down the upstairs tenant's Wi-Fi.

Quip considered his options.

Order a car out front. I am packing up EZ and sending her to Georgia early.

We will track the signal from the upstairs Wi-Fi to the source if it takes all night.

Yes, Dr. Quip. There is no immediate danger, but I don't know what the laser is capable of yet.

Keep working on it, ICABOD.

CHAPTER SIXTY-TWO

Returning to Sender

When Takeru's machine froze and stopped responding, he was immediately consumed with unadulterated panic. The screen went black and the keyboard no longer echoed his keystrokes. His heart rate had skyrocketed so that it was the only thing he could hear. His breathing was on the verge of hyper-ventilation. Though he repeatedly pounded the keyboard in a desperate effort to regain control, nothing would respond. He began alternating between shouting at the screen and whimpering at the lost output, followed by begging and then slapping the monitor. Nothing would bring his system to life, and that was now bordering on life threatening to him.

Finally, the dark monitor began to pulse as though it was receiving impulses from deep space, until finally words spilled onto the screen:

> So how does it feel to be attacked in your own crib, man?

Somehow Takeru's terror ratcheted up significantly as his inner sanctum was penetrated and his life's blood was now poisoned. Again, the keys would not respond to his fingers or to pounding with his fists. Then the screen displayed:

> I have your video and audio controlled. Show me your anguish at being vulnerable to me.

Takeru shouted "Who are you? Get out of my machine!"

Alisha had come into the room after hearing the shouting, not knowing what to expect. She saw Takeru first pleading, then screaming orders at the screen. She was terrified by the emotional display of Takeru and so stood dumbfounded while the show was in play.

The screen again taunted:

> Oh that's right you can't see or hear me. Would you like to know who is busting your chops, Yammy?

Takeru was wild-eyed, in emotional overload, and barely able to stand from his outbursts, but shouted, "You...you're just a hacker who got into my network through some stroke of luck. But I'll find you and crush you for this insolent attack. You will rue the day..."

The screen displayed a familiar face that nearly caused Takeru to collapse.

"Hi, Yammy. Long time no miss, but thanks for reaching out to me and Tuck. I see your myopic view of the world hasn't changed, but boy, what you couldn't do with some anger management courses.

"Now don't tell me, let me guess. You are the Üẁ̂T̄Ż̂Ӂ who has been hosing up the world commodity prices, am I right? Just like you did with that poor professor that had to be institutionalized after your little prank. How much jail time did you get for that little stunt you tried to blame on Tuck and me?"

Takeru was so livid with rage he didn't notice Alisha moving closer to his prized sword. He shrieked, "Liar! You two cooked up that gag and got me to program it for your amusement. You two should have gone to jail, but all you got was a slap on the wrist. My family disowned me and even took away my name, you bastard! I swore I would get even, and I will."

With a puzzled look on his face, Quip innocently asked, "Uh, is this your idea of revenge? It looks like I'm in *your* knickers, not the other way around. I now own your system, and I believe you now work for me. Isn't that deliciously ironic?"

Takeru simply could not take any more and grabbed for a gun in his drawer and emptied the clip of 9mm rounds into the monitor, abruptly ending the taunting. It took a few minutes to bring himself under control and again become aware of his surroundings. Even though the area was still somewhat dark, he saw that he was quite alone. He noticed the stand was empty of his beautiful *katana* sword. His anger rose to a controlled pitch as he shoved another clip in the weapon and marched out into the data center.

CHAPTER SIXTY-THREE

Getting Married and the Emotional High

EZ rushed into the arms of her father just past security in the Atlanta airport. He held her tight as she sobbed against his shoulder and gently patted her back.

"There, there, it will be okay, little girl. Let's get you home and settled, then you'll feel better."

Andy hoisted her modest carry-on as they exited the main building. He guided her toward his pickup and opened the door for her. As he walked around to the other side, she dried her eyes and appeared almost back in control when he turned on the truck.

"Daddy, I just don't know what I will do if he doesn't get here soon. I am angry and worried at the same time. It's just not fair! I've waited my whole life for this man, and some idiot is trying to take him away from me. The big lug sent me on my way with a quick hug and kiss. I tried to call him when we landed, but the call went straight to voicemail."

Andy scowled a bit at the idea of his Eilla-Zan being distressed, then filled her in on some additional details. "When we get to the house, you can get with Julie and get some clarifications. And those kids of hers, my goodness they are adorable. Su Lin is totally in her element showing them the animals and taking them under her wing. You'll be amazed at how much she has changed for the positive.

"Otto and Haddy arrived late last night along with Wolfgang. When Quip sent me the text regarding your arrival, he'd said the only reason you were coming right now was that everyone else had already left. Lara is here as well, so if things weren't okay, do you think they would be here? And me, I get you an extra day, which I have no intention of being sorry about."

EZ nodded and reminded herself that all these people came all this way for her and Quip. She needed to be pleasant and trust that all would be fine. Quip had just rushed her out of the flat so fast. She had no idea what was in the suitcase he threw together while she dressed for a long flight. Thank goodness she flew on a private flight. He had arranged for her to get a massage as well as some delicious food on the flight. The flight attendant, Cathy, was so attentive and sweet. She did go on about how much she had enjoyed Petra and Jacob on a flight not too long ago. It was almost like flying with family. She had exactly nothing to be sad about, she realized. Quip would always keep her as safe as possible. It was one of those things she loved about him.

"You're right, Daddy. I'm sorry I had a minor meltdown. I will enjoy the time. I am so glad we are having the ceremony here.

"Have David Tucker and Mavie Lewis arrived yet?"

"No, they will be arriving in the morning. I have a car picking them up, as we had for everyone else. I love you, sweetie. Glad you are feeling better. There are a few finishing touches we need your approval on. The weather will be very nice and the company even better. Where are you two going on your honeymoon?"

EZ chuckled and said, "Quip has been so busy working on this project of his that he has not decided, as far as I know. I may have to do some shopping, depending on the final destination. I had to leave in such a hurry, I packed almost nothing."

"No problem, sweetie. That is the easy part. Now walking you down the pathway without blubbering might be the biggest challenge."

A short time later they arrived at the farm and EZ felt the joy of returning to her childhood home. As she scrambled out of the truck and went in the front door, she was greeted with hugs and squeals from Julie, Lara, and Petra. The laughter and warmth of her truest girlfriends was exactly what she needed. The ladies ushered her outside to the patio where the kids were playing in the pool with Jacob and Su Lin, who were playing like children as well. Otto, Wolfgang, and Haddy rose and gave her a hug while Lara got a glass of wine for her.

EZ exclaimed, "Petra, I am so surprised to see you and Jacob here. I thought you would be tied up in London until tomorrow evening."

"We got it all wrapped up and thought we would surprise you.

"You are going to love this. Su Lin arranged for a spa day for all of us tomorrow. I foresee manicures, pedicures, and possibly hair styling in our near future. I need a haircut before your big day. Plus, I understand you need to be pampered, per your soon-to-be-husband."

Julie flashed her renowned smile and announced, "We are also going to plan your honeymoon. Apparently Quip called Juan and said he was on the hook for planning the honeymoon as he owed Quip a favor. Juan called and said he, Jim, and Mercedes had a few things to finish up before they could be here.

"You will be delighted to learn Quip was successful in tracking the source location for the network terror your house and David Tucker's house were facing. I am so sorry you had to go through that. They don't have the persons apprehended yet, but it turns out Juan is very close to that source, so it should be soon. Quip was going to complete the security efforts at your house and said he is sorry about your new favorite vase."

EZ looked up and furrowed her brow, somewhat confused. "What happened to our new vase? I still have not determined who the generous gift giver was. I can show you a picture, I think, on my phone."

Julie and Petra both laughed, then Petra said, "I think that is one picture better in the trash, EZ. The vase actually contained a very sophisticated access point, transmitter, and wireless device, with a camera, which was at the heart of the trouble inside your flat. It had a solar power ability amplified through the glass. The silver waves and such were acting like antenna used to boost the signal and do bidirectional data sharing.

"Quip said having it embedded into the base of the vase was ingenious. He had to see it up close and take it apart. The only way to do that was to break the glass. I can show you the pictures, but I think you can just be happy it is gone. Quip still wonders where it was made but said he'd save that until after the wedding."

EZ looked relieved and added, "Does that mean he will be here soon? I am glad. It was a pretty piece but not a gift from my family, so it doesn't count anyway. Amazing chain of events brought on by our engagement."

Julie replied, "He will leave day after tomorrow, still in time for the big day and of course his bachelor party."

EZ smiled at everyone and said, "Now we can start the celebration daze!"

CHAPTER SIXTY-FOUR

The End, So Final

LJ moved quietly through the data center, looking cautiously for Takeru. He turned a corner into one of the server rows and found Alisha. She was crumpled on the floor in a growing puddle of her own blood but still breathing. He scooped her head up into his arms and tried to raise her into a sitting position.

This activity brought her around to consciousness, and she smiled at him. Unable to raise her arm to touch his face, she croaked, "Ah, that's my man. I'm here to tell you that my performance review with Takeru didn't go the way I had envisioned." She chuckled slightly and then coughed, half-heartedly spitting out some blood.

In a small voice, little above a whisper, she added, "I got it for you, honey. I know how much you wanted it. It's in our special hiding place. As smart as he is, he would never have thought to look there for it."

LJ's eyes were glistening and swollen with tears as he admonished, "Now there, save your strength, baby. You shouldn't have provoked him by taking it. We are going to fix this, I promise you. Let me get you to a hospital, then I will deal with Takeru the way I always deal with psychotic bastards!"

Alisha smirked and, shaking her head, replied, "Honey, I am a registered nurse, and I know what my chances are. I was the foolish one, because I thought I had a little more time to play out the charade. But instead, he pumped me two times before I could get to him, not like you would pump me two times." She lightly chuckled at her own humor.

LJ was sobbing at the pending disaster of his beloved Alisha, but he was unable to speak. Alisha begged, "LJ honey, can you sing that gospel hymn that I love so well? You know, that one done by Lonnie Lupnerder. I just loves the way you sing it."

LJ was so panicked and scared that he couldn't even make any sound other than keening Alisha's name over and over.

Alisha started soothing with a halting voice. "It's alright, LJ honey. It'll be alright. I just wish we had more time…"

Alisha coughed up more blood and seemed to be drifting away from LJ as he cried wildly at their lost chances and poor future. Alisha's body finally relaxed, and she spent her last breath into LJ's face. She was gone.

NMX ↓ -7.50
CMX ↓ -9.33
HCC ↓ -3.90
SOX ↓ -7.74

It took a while for LJ to come to terms with the fact that Alisha was gone. He pulled himself together as he gently rested her head back on the floor. He got up, still watching her, almost as if he expected her to pull back from the nether world. The only sound was the hum of the machines which increased in volume as he started to plan his next moves.

He walked over to the special hiding place Alisha had spoken about. Verifying that he was alone, he reached into the rack of servers and pulled out the much-coveted samurai sword. Though it was more than 106 centimeters long from end to end, it had slid easily into the area where no one looked or cleaned.

Takeru's great grandfather had worn it while in the service of the Japanese Imperial Army during WWII. LJ had heard the story of it being a treasured family heirloom for generations. With the defeat of Japan in 1945, all military personnel were disarmed, and all weapons confiscated, which was a crushing blow to Takeru's family. At one time, the family had the signature on the tang authenticated to a mid-range swordsmith of the mid-1800s who had been considered moderately successful in his time.

Takeru had told LJ the stories from his youth about how the sword had been stolen from the confiscated weapons storage area in the 1950s and sold to an American Air Force pilot on leave from the Korean War. Takeru had vowed to retrieve his ancestral sword and had finally tracked the sword after years of hunting for it. After all those years, the family of the Air Force pilot had needed to sell it for money so they could make ends meet. Luckily, they had been ignorant of its true value and had let it go back to Takeru for a fraction of its worth.

The restored black lacquer case, with its red star bursts embedded in the finish, and its carefully rebuilt handle wrapped in strips of leather made an impressive display. As LJ drew out the blade, it gleamed in the low light of the computer room. He admired the 76 centimeters of carefully forged steel that ran from the *tsuba* to the tip of the sword, easily classifying it as a *katana*. LJ admired the simple elegance of the weapon but was pained to know that his Alisha had died trying to steal it for him. He drew a deep breath, sheathed the magnificent weapon and went hunting for Takeru.

LJ didn't have to look far into the office area, where Takeru was frantically searching for the only thing on the planet he actually cared about. Takeru smiled as he drew a quick bead on LJ.

LJ looked fierce as he asked, "You looking for this?" Holding the sword slightly in front of himself, he suggested, "You know I'm holding the sword here, so if you shoot, your precious weapon will be shattered before you get one into me. I would submit, director, who has the drop on who?"

Takeru swallowed hard as he weighed his options without showing any emotion. "Throw me the sword and we'll call it even."

LJ snickered at the feeble offer but nodded his head in agreement. Takeru almost broke his chiseled features into a smile as he realized he was going to get his prize possession back unharmed. He lowered his guard just enough for LJ to pull off the scabbard and toss it to Takeru, causing a brief moment of confusion.

The brief distraction was almost enough as LJ swung the lethal instrument in an overhead arc while his other hand grabs the sword handle and brought it down with all his might. The motion caught both hands of Takeru under the powerful slicing motion. Takeru got off one wild shot before he stood, staring down at his hands and part of each forearm lying on the floor. LJ staggered backwards, as the one shot found and then left a fleshy hole through him.

Time seemed suspended as both men struggled to remain upright.

"Tell me, director, just how much computer programming can be done with no hands? And, now that I think about it, just how you gonna hold your beloved sword?"

LJ would have laughed uproariously if he hadn't been in such pain from the bullet wound. LJ slowly made his way over to Takeru, who was still standing but in complete shock. He pushed the bleeding man into a handy computer chair, then bound him with some tie straps left on the floor. LJ didn't have much trouble with Takeru as his shock was deepening with the continual loss of blood. LJ avoided the overspray from the stumps as he completed his task.

Takeru sat unmoving in the chair with his eyes glazing over. LJ dispassionately stated, "Now that is right fittin'. I'm gonna watch you bleed out just like I had to watch Alisha bleed out. But don't worry. I won't leave until it's done, so you take your time, Director Takeru."

LJ looked around the area he was in, distracted by a low hum. Even though his pain was growing worse, he grinned broadly and loudly stated, "Well, lookie here. Inside your office cabinet must be the anonymizing servers you use to cloak these here operations. Unless I'm mistaken, those are the firewall sentinels. Why don't we just turn those bad boys off and let the Internet beat a path to your door."

CHAPTER SIXTY-FIVE

Down...

Jim and Juan moved fairly rapidly towards the compound in their semi-attack vehicle. The rental car agency didn't have much to choose from, and they didn't want to waste time looking for a low mileage rental from the current decade. Jim wanted a good range of fire so he sat in the passenger side after removing the glass window with the butt of his rifle.

Juan drove as fast as the wreck would go but still kept an uneasy eye on Jim as he casually asked, "Does your mother know what you do for a living? I mean, breaking out car windows so you can shoot easier?"

Jim slightly smirked and offered, "Yes, she does, and her name is Eric of the agency. Can we go any faster? The messages being relayed must mean its show time. I want the goods on these bastards!"

Juan, always cool under pressure, jested, "Does that mean no stopping for donuts?"

Jim just cut his eyes over to look sideways at Juan before he refocused on the road. A few minutes later, their GPS began to indicate they were close to their target, so Juan slowed a little as they crested a small rise. Up ahead they saw a one lane bridge with another car heading at them just as fast, trying to be first for the bridge.

Jim hollered, "Crank it around to block the bridge with me facing that car so I, and Matilda here, can do some waltzing with them."

Juan, unable to think of a better plan, responded, "You got it, gunny!"

Juan scuttled the car up to the bridge and easily blocked it in a T-fashion so the oncoming vehicle had only the options to ram or stop. Unfortunately, the driver exercised a third unforeseen option.

Mercedes was still angrily throwing rocks at having been left behind to watch the action from afar while the men got to have all the fun. She'd called Julie to provide an update and had failed to conceal her annoyance in the short conversation. Still working off her mood, she heard the push-to-talk radio barking at her. She stopped and ran to hear the message. She picked up the PPT and asked for a repeat of the message. A voice finally responded with a very short message.

"Man down..."

CHAPTER SIXTY-SIX

Half-truths are Also Half Lies
...The Enigma Chronicles

The lighting in the room was muted but still seemed blazingly bright to the one eye LJ could open to look around with. Slowly, he took in his surroundings, noting the low frequency beeps just overhead and an IV in close proximity with a tube running down to his arm.

After taking all his surroundings in, he remarked openly to the empty room, "Leroy, the good news is they didn't send you to the lower regions of Hell for your time spent on earth. As many times as I've been through the good book, I'm pretty sure Hell didn't have all the health care equipment I'm seeing plugged into me. I doubt this is a substation to get me better before descending into Hades, nor a pause on my entrance into Heaven."

About that time, a voice he found familiar offered, "Ah, there you are. Welcome back, umm...Leroy, not Holland, right?"

With a great deal of effort, based on his large size and injuries, Leroy rolled over to see Juan grinning at him. As Leroy tried to straighten up in bed, he became acutely aware of his pain, to the point where he groaned and yelped a couple of times as he strained to get somewhat comfortable again.

Again, Leroy surveyed his own personal real estate and weakly stated, "Feeling somewhat poorly and not really up to much socializing at this point, my friend. Any chance you can fill in some blanks for me? I'm guessing that I ain't dead. But the way I feel, that might be changed for me at any moment."

Juan studied Leroy for a moment and commented, "We couldn't very well let you stay in that car that went over the cliff, could we? I'm sorry about your female companion, but you shouldn't have tried to go out with her by deliberately avoiding the one lane bridge out of the compound."

Tears welled up in Leroy's eyes as the memories of the last act in Takeru's data center began flooding back into his mind.

Leroy didn't fight to hold them back as he asked, "What has happened to my Alisha?"

Juan took a deep breath and consoled, "I'm sorry about Alisha. We didn't find a lot on her, or you, for that matter. We did arrange for a very nice cemetery lot and monument for her final resting place. I think you'll be pleased with what you purchased for her."

Leroy smirked and admitted, "I expect that means that all my money now belongs to you and for whoever you work. Just as well. That nest egg was going to be for us, but now that she's gone..."

Leroy's voice trailed off as his gaze stopped on the red cement cast on his left arm. He exclaimed, "My arm! What's happened to my arm? And, more importantly, where is my Rolex? I loved that watch so much that I called him *Rollie*. Don't take that too!"

Slightly chuckling, Juan approached the hospital bed. He stated, "Your left arm was crushed in the tumble over the cliff. You need to start wearing your seat belt, mister, if you aren't going to stay on the road."

Then Juan took out the Rolex from his pocket. He slipped it onto Leroy's right hand and fastened it. Leroy beamed.

Juan continued, "We pilots crave excellent timepieces. This watch did catch my eye. I know that sometimes, in situations like this one, an excellent timepiece doesn't always make its way out with the owner. I wanted to make certain this one did.

"I've been told that you are going to need a lot of therapy to get that left arm back into working order. Therefore, you might have to wear Rollie right-handed for quite a while."

Leroy smiled at the watch, then refocused on Juan, ready to hear the consequences he expected for his past misdeeds.

Juan offered, "With regards to the matter of your nest egg, I suppose some organizations would be rather put out by the financial and economic damage your team was instigating. In some places, all would be confiscated to rectify and to help make amends.

"For your portion, let me suggest, that is not the way we see it unfolding. We are annoyed but not vindictive. We consider your nest egg under our control, and it will not be confiscated."

Leroy was taken aback by the comment. He slowly was coming to grips with the idea and asked, "You're not taking my money? Kind of implies that I need to do some favors for you to work off my indiscretions. Is that about it?"

Juan chuckled slightly and remarked, "You know, the good thing about dealing with a slippery character like you is that you catch on quick. For all that we have teed up for you and, how does one say it…managing your nest egg, we need you to help manage someone for us.

"It might seem like a glory assignment because you need to sit on a beach with him and suck down FCDs while ogling, I mean, keeping an eye on, the waitresses. Of course, he can't know you are there to watch him, as well as keep him out of trouble. Then, to make sure you don't get into any more trouble, we'll throttle your funds to help discourage any, umm…new private enterprises. Do we have a deal?"

Leroy grinned from ear to ear as he responded, "FCDs, as in fruity chick drinks, on a Caribbean beach? Har! Har! You wouldn't be pulling my leg now, would you, son?"

Juan grinned as he replied, "I think that about covers it. We will monitor your progress and have you moved when the time is right."

Leroy nodded before he announced, "You're alright, pilot man. Agreed. Hey, thanks for my Rollie. I appreciate that more than you know."

A brief silence passed before Leroy asked, "Well, you been purty straight up with me on things, but uh…did you find my sword? Do I get that back like Rollie?"

Juan wrinkled his brow a little before he said, "You know, it's a funny thing about weapons like that. The police are always so possessive of murder weapons that you really can't get them to relent. The fact is, a sword wasn't found in the wreckage. While there is no wonderful weapon to be had, there is no incriminating evidence either. I guess things always balance out in the end, wouldn't you agree?"

Leroy nodded fatalistically and said, "Yeah, I see your point. But if it should ever turn up again…"

Juan smiled and finished the sentence. "Then I'm sure it would have a good home if we could get it to you. Say perhaps in two years, give or take?"

Leroy grinned from ear to ear.

Juan's phone chirped a familiar ring, so he left Leroy to take the call in the hallway. Once outside of the room, he answered. "Hi, honey. It's okay to talk. I just briefed him on his role."

Juan listened for a few seconds and answered, "Yes, we recovered the material requested by Quip. He has access to the systems until midnight, when Eric and his team take over.

"…yes, honey, we will be leaving here in the morning, all three of us. Quip will be there sometime tomorrow, I think.

"Yes, sweetheart, I will work on the honeymoon plans on the way home...

"Yes, honey, I love you too. See you soon."

NMX ↓ -7.50
CMX ↓ -9.33
HCC ↓ -3.90
SOX ↓ -7.74

Jesus whistled a merry Lonnie Lupnerder tune while Carlos watched with apprehension from the doorway. Jesus finished packing and turned to face Carlos.

Carlos studied Jesus for a moment but before he could say anything, Jesus insisted, "Nephew, I don't know how to thank you and your friends for getting me out of that stupid jail. If you ever need anything, you just let me know. I'm off to parts unknown, with the only requirement being they serve FCDs with top heavy waitresses. I am about ready to go now!"

Carlos offered a smile as he stated, "Uncle, I'm so glad you understand things. As a matter of fact, I do have a small request to make of you."

Jesus smiled and patted Carlos's shoulder as he said, "Fine, my boy, fine. Once I get to my next beach, we'll talk. How's that?"

Jesus picked up his bag and moved to leave, but Carlos stopped him.

"Perhaps, Uncle, you need to hear this discussion from me now, rather than later. It has been determined that you shouldn't be allowed to, umm...manage your own funds. As a consequence, you will be on a monthly stipend to operate within certain parameters, beginning immediately."

Jesus dropped his bag, his eyes burned with anger, and he bellowed, "Let me get this straight. Not only are you calling in a favor right this minute, but you're confiscating my money as well? I didn't agree to this!"

Carlos calmly responded, "Actually, you did agree to this when you went rogue and had to be broken out of jail, by folks doing a favor for me. Juan got sideways as well. You owe me and the people who got you out. They aren't confiscating your monies forever, they're just going to throttle the flow so you cannot run amok again."

Jesus backed down a little but was still angry. "Okay, so now I get it. What are you going to hold me for? What exactly do I need to do for you so I can go about my life, huh?"

Carlos gave a wry smile and suggested, "I need you to watch and keep track of someone while he orders FCDs from top heavy waitresses on a beach in the Caribbean. Of course, he can't know that you are there to keep him in line."

Jesus gave Carlos his ultimate incredulous look, then flatly asked, "You want me to do what I wanted to do on a beach anyway? Boy, you astound me sometimes. Of course, I volunteer for this dangerous assignment of spending my own money and watching someone. I don't have to pay his way, do I?"

Carlos offered, "Basically, you need to ride herd on him and not let him run amok while you behave yourself in the process."

Jesus grinned and agreed, "It doesn't sound so bad. Being under house arrest with all the food and adult beverages I want. Plus, I get a new friend to enjoy it without jail bars. Not a bad gig, actually!"

Carlos nodded. "That's a little straighter than how I was going to say it, but you grasp the concept correctly. I want you safe, and my friends have agreed to manage your funds for you, so no more unsanctioned investment exploration. You will be cared for with the funds we set aside for you. I need you to keep an eye on this character so he doesn't go rogue again. Comprende?"

Jesus smiled and said, "Yeah, alright, I get it. When do I start?"

Carlos smiled and replied, "That depends. Are you thirsty yet?"

CHAPTER SIXTY-SEVEN

Problem Solved...

Quip reached over to hold this beautiful, vibrant woman who was joined to him and made him whole. Her eyes were closed as she was in that sleep that some people grab near the end of a flight. Even with the recent refill of champagne, he was not going to rest until they were tucked away in their promised honeymoon suite – wherever it was they were being taken. He knew it didn't matter as long as they were together for the next two weeks.

His mind wandered back over the events of the previous day. The twins rushing down the walkway toward him with smiles of delight. The beauty of the bridesmaids that somehow paled when EZ appeared, radiant with her crowning cascade of hair, almost floating on the arm of Andy. He grinned when he recalled Andy looking scared to death as he marched forward.

The simple five minute ceremony was almost too long from his perspective, and he wanted the party to commence. The dancing, drinking, and laughter went on for some time. He'd caught snatches of conversation on how well the job had been completed when he was near Otto, Wolfgang, and Thiago. Wolfgang promised he'd keep close watch as the shell company network was removed, with oil and coal commodities returning to the real norm rather than the one Yammy had manufactured. Tuck and he had spent a little time talking about the sins of their past, but far more about their next business venture. Tuck had some great ideas that seemed like a good expansion for R-Group to consider, especially as Tuck had no idea of the breadth of what Quip or the family did.

All the people that attended the celebration enjoyed the event and were taking their own holidays or returning to the workday. EZ pointed out that the ring on Su Lin's finger was new and was certainly covered often when Andy held her hand. The speculation was short lived when they danced endlessly together. Andy's endless patio had been turned into an open air dance floor with a disc jockey who had access to every song requested, even the waltz that sent Otto and Haddy gliding across the floor. Carlos and Lara looked beautiful dancing together. EZ speculated they really should marry.

When the music ended and they'd changed to travel clothes, Petra and Jacob made certain Quip and EZ were at the car and handed off to their travel companions with hugs and encour-agement to relax and have fun, things would be covered. Quip knew things would be covered, or ICABOD would alert him, no matter what.

A tap on the shoulder aroused him from his musings as he looked up into the face of one of his best friends and her mega-watt smile.

"Hey, Quip, we are about ready to land. I need your glass, please. Juan says that the blindfold will only be necessary until we are at the hotel and he tells you the plan. I, for one, think you and your pretty wife will really have fun, so stop worrying. Would I let anything happen to you?"

Quip grinned and responded, "Of course you would, if you thought you could get away with it. This whole deal seems really silly though." He glanced over at EZ to make certain she was still dozing. "It just seems crazy that one part of Yammy's crazy plan might include a residual analog factor, which might possibly be running amok. You are positive that Tuck and Mavie are not going to be affected?"

"From the review of the detailed plans Takeru had in his system, which have been reviewed by Jacob, ICABOD, and my team, there is only a small possibility for you to have an impact, and none for Tuck. My team has it and is looking into it. This way, you get buddies to pal around with, a personal pilot, extra bodyguard for your bride, and an exciting honeymoon. Wait until later when Juan tells you how he came up with all this." She beamed and flashed her trademark smile again. "I get two weeks with my husband, too! In my book, Quip, it is a win-win."

Julie reached over and gently woke EZ, who nodded and smiled as the blindfold was placed over her eyes. She reached out and gave Quip's hand a squeeze, which lasted until they taxied to the gate. Fortunately, they were able to breeze through customs without the traditional process most folks follow, because of the private aircraft and great planning. Juan led Quip and Julie led EZ through to the waiting silver Lincoln town car. For this part of the journey, Julie planned to drive with Juan riding lookout. Juan plied his captives with champagne before he told the tale of the planned adventure.

Juan cleared his throat and began. "Once we get established in your suite, we can plan all the specific activities you will actually partake in. As you already agreed, you will each have one of us with you anytime outside of the suite. What happens in your suite stays in your suite." Distracted for a moment with images of his plans, Juan added, "The same goes for our suite too!

"Now, EZ, we all know that you are a thrill-seeker. You have parachuted, bungee jumped, and even done class V or VI white-water rafting. My hats off to you!"

EZ smiled slightly just below the blindfold edge and replied, "Juan, it is easy to take chances when you have friends who dare you or you just want to try something. I have had my failures, too, as you are aware. I just want to spend some lovely time with Quip, getting the most out of the time away from the office."

Juan patted EZ's hand for reassurance. "I know that, but you also want to experience this lovely place.

"Quip, you asked for some help in planning the perfect exciting trip for your bride. Though you have the unconfirmed story of bungee jumping with nuns, according to Jacob, you are much more cerebral in nature. Not that you don't want to have thrills – you simply take a different stance.

"I thought initially, I would review the activities that were considered for this trip, and while you are blindfolded, you can both use the rest of your senses to image what each of these might bring to your thrill level. If something was discounted incorrectly, you have but to ask and we will rearrange the activities. Again, though, you are not to wander around unprotected outside of the suite.

"Because I know that EZ is a certified scuba diver, we considered a lovely morning of swimming with the sharks. I found a cool spot that allows you to be inside a cage roughly 7 by 7 in the Pacific where you can be swarmed by up to a dozen sharks around their traditional feeding times, or bloody chum can be added from above to really get them in a frenzy. The last time the main provider of this thrill did the chum, one of the big males bent the bars by almost a foot."

Both EZ and Quip gasped at the image Juan was painting and Quip gripped EZ's hand a bit tighter before he commented, "Ah, I think that is a bit too much of a risk for my bride, and my scuba certification isn't current."

Juan continued, "The next consideration was bungee jumping since you both have some experience there. One of the most beautiful and terrifying jumps, it turns out, is out over the Nevis from a cabin suspended over a gorge near Queenstown, New Zealand. The eight second freefall is supposed to be almost as effective as any of the touted cleanse products on the market today. They say it is even more exciting blindfolded!"

EZ frowned and asked, "Juan, are you suggesting I need to lose some weight? No, I am glad you skipped this idea."

Quip's facial features looked tense as he verified, "You... ah, did skip this idea, right? And I am just about tired of being blindfolded, buddy."

The car stopped. Julie left, presumably to get the keys and check in. There were no sounds anywhere as the door opened and then shut. However, the fresh breeze which entered the car during this period had a hint of the sea along with distant tropical music. Juan suspended his story while he filled their glasses.

"I can hear what you are saying, man, but blindfolds applied at the right time and place can be very exciting. I figured you could do that in your suite all by yourselves.

"Then I considered sandboarding which is really snowboarding with different clothes on, actually a lot less. One of the best places for this is the Sahara in the world's largest desert, Erg Chigaga."

Quip laughed loudly, then commented, "Ah, come on, Juan. Everyone knows you can't build a ski lift on sand dunes, and I don't want to spend all my time climbing back to do the run again."

EZ added, "Wow, I would never have thought of that, Quip! Good one. No, Juan, not a good suggestion."

Juan chuckled. "How about parasailing near the summit of Angel Falls in Venezuela? They say the thundering sound of water dropping a kilometer from the golden façade of the steep cliffs echoes like a natural amphitheater. The five days of hiking over uneven terrain to get there is amazing. They say the updrafts should be enough to allow you to soar close to the falls for about five to eight minutes while you descend to the target landing area a few kilometers away. However, it can get a little tricky because the updrafts sometime swirl, which could take your parasail back into the falling water and will ruin your soaring and most probably the rest of your day."

Quip cocked his head to one side, and his mouth formed into a tight line while considering the possibilities. EZ gripped Quip's hand a little tighter as she held her breath, waiting for his response. Even blindfolded it seemed she could sense his apprehension. Just then the back door to the car opened, and the scent of the sea air along with the music in the distance infiltrated their cocoon. Another door opened, and the engine ceased, along with the air conditioning. The air became a little warmer and slightly more humid.

Juan studied the two and promptly stated, "I sense apprehension from you on this option, so I'm guessing a no vote to parasailing as well."

"Come on, you two," Julie encouraged. "Your room is ready and we will escort you inside." As she assisted Quip out and took his arm like a best buddy, she added, "We are close to removing your blindfold so you can begin your honeymoon adventure. You can pull your suitcase behind you, just follow my lead."

She made certain he had his suitcase and she had hers as they proceeded down a path toward their room, with Juan and EZ in a similar form behind them. Anyone who watched would think either two people were being kidnapped, or it was a game of some sort. Julie and Juan both nodded and grinned to those whom they passed. A few even gave thumbs up. Julie had obviously passed the word to the hotel regarding a wonderful adventure for their captives.

The path was an archway of vines and flowers which had grown over a long time. Both Quip and EZ inhaled deeply at the fragrant scents of tropical flowers. The sounds of the sea moving against the shore were increasing as they walked. The leisurely pace of their procession allowed them to explore with all their other senses.

Julie interrupted the natural sounds of the tropical environment when she asked, "So how much did Juan spill regarding your current destination, Quip?"

Quip chuckled. "Not much, only about the choices he took off the list. I sense we are not in Venezuela, which was his last suggested adventure, or we would be walking much faster and not in the open, like I suspect we are, due to the current unrest in that country. I am reasonably sure we are not in North Africa for the dune-boarding since I don't hear the faithful calling to prayer from a minaret. I don't feel any tanks being strapped to me so thankfully the swimming with the sharks is a pass-on experience as well. Between you and me, Jules, I am glad for that."

Juan and EZ both laughed, much closer to Quip than he thought. He decided to simply go with the flow. Julie stopped and the sounds of a key opening a lock were heard, along with some nearby laughter and conversation. They entered a room and the door was closed.

"Alright, you lovebirds, take off the blindfolds and feast your eyes on what will hopefully be your base for the remainder of your honeymoon," said Juan.

They both complied and gasped at the lovely surroundings. It was like they were on top of the world, and yet they could see endless water out of the floor to ceiling glass before them. The doors were open to a stone patio that seemed above the water line. The optics were both a sensation of height way above the water and yet a view of very blue water with what appeared to be sparkling diamonds dancing on the waves.

"Where are we?" asked EZ, as she took in the colorful surroundings of their suite. "It is so pretty." She turned to both Julie and Juan behind them. "This is amazing. I want to change into something suitable for the tropics and find the beach."

Quip nodded in agreement with a smile. He added, "Yes, honey, let's change, send these two to their room, and meet outside, in say, two or three hours after we test the sheets?"

Laughter ensued from them all.

Quip added, "This does look amazing. Where are we, and what is ahead of us?"

Juan grinned and wiggled his eyebrows toward Julie as he said, "We are going to be through the adjoining doors. I personally agree with the testing of the sheets. One can never be too careful.

"To answer your question though, right outside this patio is an area for cliff jumping or diving if you prefer. All you need is a swimsuit, good tropical attire as EZ offered, a bit of courage, and a willingness to take a calculated risk. We, my dear friends, are in Negril, Jamaica, with the renowned Rick's Café a short walk away up the cliff a bit. And if we don't want to jump, we can watch all the other crazies take the leap! The only real problem we will face there is the lap dance-loud music that they are famous for. But it is said that that's music to get your lady in the mood!"

Quip laughed and struck his hand out to a man who read him well. Then he commented, "This is the place to be! Now you two can get out of here. I want to mess with my wife alone."

"Fine, I am inclined to take my wife and explore our room. I will knock later to see if you are ready for the drinks and entertainment."

Julie and Juan took their bags and danced through the adjoining door. EZ commented after the door closed, leaving them alone, "You will take at least one jump with me, won't you, honey?!"

"Oh yeah!"

NMX ↓ -7.50
CMX ↓ -9.33
HCC ↓ -3.90
SOX ↓ -7.74

As soon as the call connected, she asked, "Are all the loose ends accounted for?"

With a slightly snarky tone, he responded, "Your proof of concept worked perfectly. His data center was wiped clean by the Scorched Earth program, but what a waste of resources. We could recover some of the equipment, then redeploy that data center in another operation. There was no danger of that data center being traced back to us."

Shaking her head and sighing, she replied, "They tracked everything back to him and that was what we wanted. Now he is dead, but the recent events are too fresh to be ignored if anything is disturbed. I've told you before, we operate the way the Russians think; leave nothing useable behind for your enemies. They used that philosophy to defeat Napoleon and then the Germans in World War II. The gear is wiped, but not inoperative. Therefore, whoever takes it, thinking it harmless as well as free, will be our tool, doing our bidding."

He shrugged in a way that suggested it made no difference either way to him, then he offered, "Our BANG zone technology should be sufficient to maintain our anonymity, based on the *Binary Analog Neutral Gapping* between our computer centers and our analog information mules."

She calmly reemphasized, "Once Takeru's data manipulation of the commodity prices was removed from operation, all our in-place bets had us ride a profitable tsunami that more than made up for the data center loss. It also cloaked our operations from people like that Jacob and Petra."

He nodded his head and, smiling with a little admiration, said, "They were good, weren't they? They broke down our encryption algorithms and quickly figured out how our AIM resources were being directed.

"Didn't I tell you he'd be good? I am glad I suggested that avenue. Are you still sure we can't use him and his cyborg sidekick?"

She sighed again, close to exasperation, and flatly stated, "Do you not see yourself hoping for the ridiculous? Takeru was easy to bring in and vector on our targets, because he matched the proper psychological profile. He hated his lot in life and wanted to extract revenge for living, which made him perfect for our purposes. He was emotionally susceptible to our way of thinking!

"These two people you admire so much cannot be trusted to work in our business model. Their flaw is that they believe in the greater good for humanity. Don't you understand, we would never be able to reach through that kind of thinking to bring them into our fold? They could never be trusted."

A little irked at being dismissed, he argued, "Oh, you mean like we could trust Takeru? The guy went off the reservation for his own personal reasons, which you never knew about or saw coming!"

She was enjoying the verbal sparring from an obviously substandard opponent when she caustically reminded, "Right! We could trust him to be self-centered, vindictive, and vicious. In other words, perfectly predictable and easily outmaneuvered in the long haul. He was not going to be a long-term player. Frankly, he did what I expected, only a little sooner than I wanted but well within our operational parameters.

"Besides, I really don't want them. I want into their data center resources, which is likely a supercomputer. By the way, good work convincing them that they should do all of ePETRO's reporting for the next three to six months. I do hope they will try to automate the reporting process, and then we will have a way in and the ability to potentially see behind the curtain. With these two attack vectors in play, we should be able to penetrate their organization. I want that supercomputer working for us."

Now growing tired of the conversation, he flatly asked, "Alright, so how much longer do I need to stay here at ePETRO playing this clown role?"

Sensing a little insubordination, she chided, "Mike, I'll tell you when you're done. You can't leave too promptly because of the reporting conduit that you have established with Jacob and his operation. It would jeopardize our digital hunting into their systems and look suspicious.

"And, by the way, the next time I put you in a role for a certain objective, I don't want you going native again. Roslyn was an AIM resource established to fulfill our purposes, not to be your banging babe. Got it? Don't make that mistake again!"

Fortunately for Mike, she couldn't see the contempt on his face as he replied, "Yes, Marge, I got it. Anything else?"

She gave a satisfied but cruel smile and stated, "No, that's all. I will start phase II so stay alert."

After Marge disconnected Mike absentmindedly barked at the phone. "Bitch!"

Specialized Terms
and Informational References

http://en.wikipedia.org/wiki/Wikipedia

Wikipedia (<u>wɪki' piː diə</u> / *WIK-i-PEE-dee-ə*) is a collaboratively edited, multilingual, free Internet encyclopedia supported by the non-profit Wikimedia Foundation. Wikipedia's 30 million articles in 287 languages, including over 4.3 million in the English Wikipedia, are written collaboratively by volunteers around the world. This is a great quick reference source to better understand terms.

3D graphic modeling 3D computer graphics are often referred to as 3D models. Apart from the rendered graphic, the model is contained within the graphical data file. However, there are differences: a 3D model is the mathematical representation of any three-dimensional object. A model is not technically a graphic until it is displayed. A model can be displayed visually as a two-dimensional image through a process called 3D rendering or used in non-graphical computer simulations and calculations, as in a software program. With 3D printing, 3D models are similarly rendered into a 3D physical representation of the model, with limitations to how accurate the rendering can match the virtual model.

Anonymize An anonymizer or an anonymous proxy is a tool that attempts to make activity on the Internet untraceable. It is a proxy server computer that acts as an intermediary and privacy shield between a client computer and the rest of the Internet. It accesses the Internet on the user's behalf, protecting personal information by hiding the client computer's identifying information.

Cloud Service Is provided from a vendor that offers cloud computing. Cloud computing is a type of Internet-based computing that provides shared computer processing resources and data to computers and other devices on demand. It is a model for enabling ubiquitous, on-demand access to a shared pool of configurable computing resources which can be rapidly provisioned and released with minimal management effort. Cloud computing and storage solutions provide users and enterprises with various capabilities to store and process their data in third-party data centers that may be located far from the user–ranging in distance from across a city to across the world. Costs for this is a pay-as-you-use model, also known by or as a service pricing.

Commodities In economics, a commodity is a marketable item produced to satisfy wants or needs. Often the item is fungible. For example, since one ounce of pure gold is equivalent to any other ounce of pure gold, gold is **fungible.** Other fungible commodities include sweet crude oil, company shares, bonds, other precious metals, and currencies. Economic commodities comprise goods and services.

DHCP scope Dynamic Host Configuration Protocol is the ability for a server to assign an address to be used on a network by any device. The DHCP server offers the "lease" of an IP address to the client, which the client is free to request or ignore. If the client requests it and the server acknowledges it, then the client is permitted to use that IP address for the "lease time" specified by the server. At some point before the lease expires, the client must re-request the same IP address if it wishes to continue to use it. The scope is the device's defined use of the address and the subnet.

Elliptical encryption algorithms or **Elliptic curve cryptography (ECC)** is an approach to public-key cryptography based on the algebraic structure of elliptic curves over finite fields. ECC requires smaller keys compared to non-ECC cryptography (based on plain Galois fields) to provide equivalent security.

Encryption In cryptography, encryption is the process of encoding messages (or information) in such a way that eavesdroppers or hackers cannot read it, but that authorized parties can. In an **encryption scheme,** the message or information (referred to as plaintext) is encrypted using an encryption algorithm, turning it into an unreadable cipher text (ibid.). This is usually done with the use of an encryption key, which specifies how the message is to be encoded. Any adversary that can see the cipher text should not be able to determine anything about the original message. An authorized party, however, is able to decode the cipher text using a **decryption** algorithm that usually requires a secret decryption key that adversaries do not have access to. For technical reasons, an encryption scheme usually needs a key-generation algorithm to randomly produce keys. Encryption can be done to any data, voice or video packet.

Enigma Machine An Enigma machine was any of a family of related electro-mechanical rotor cipher machines used in the twentieth century for enciphering and deciphering secret messages. Enigma was invented by the German engineer Arthur Scherbius at the end of World War I. Early models were used commercially from the early 1920s, and adopted by military and government services of several countries — most notably by Nazi Germany before and during World War II. Several different Enigma models were produced, but the German military models are the most commonly discussed.

German military texts enciphered on the Enigma machine were first broken by the Polish Cipher Bureau, beginning in December 1932. This success was a result of efforts by three Polish cryptologists, working for Polish military intelligence. Rejewski "reverse-engineered" the device, using theoretical mathematics and material supplied by French military intelligence. Subsequently the three mathematicians designed mechanical devices for breaking Enigma ciphers, including the cryptologic bomb. This work was an essential foundation to further work on decrypting ciphers from repeatedly modernized Enigma machines, first in Poland and after the outbreak of war in France and the UK.

Though Enigma had some cryptographic weaknesses, in practice it was German procedural flaws, operator mistakes, laziness, failure to systematically introduce changes in encypherment procedures, and Allied capture of key tables and hardware that, during the war, enabled Allied cryptologists to succeed.

Facial recognition program is a computer application capable of identifying or verifying a person from a digital image or a video frame from a video source. One of the ways to do this is by comparing selected facial features from the image and comparing it to a facial database.

Linear programming also call linear optimization is a method to achieve the best outcome (such as maximum profit or lowest cost) in a mathematical model whose requirements are represented by linear relationships. Linear programming is a special case of mathematical programming (mathematical optimization).

Party-line telecommunications A party line (multiparty line, shared service line, and party wire) is a local loop telephone circuit that is shared by multiple telephone service subscribers. Party line systems were widely used to provide telephone service, starting with the first commercial switchboards in 1878. A majority of Bell System subscribers in the mid-20th century in the United States and Canada were serviced by party lines, which carried a billing discount over individual service; during wartime shortages, these were often the only available lines. British users similarly benefited from the party line discount. Farmers in rural Australia used party lines, where a single line spanned miles from the nearest town to one property and on to the next.

Rootkits Is a collection of computer software, typically malicious, designed to enable access to a computer or areas of its software that would not otherwise be allowed (for example, to an unauthorized user) while at the same time masking its existence or the existence of other software. The term *rootkit* is a concatenation of "root" (the traditional name of the privileged account on Unix-like operating systems) and the word "kit" (which refers to the software components that implement the tool). The term "rootkit" has negative connotations through its association with malware.

Shell Corporation - Is a company which serves as a vehicle for business transactions without itself having any significant assets or operations.

Supercomputer a computer with a high-level computational pacity. Performance of a supercomputer is measured in floating point operations per second (FLOPS). As of 2015, there are super-computers which can perform up to quadrillions of FLOPS.

TCP/IP computer address Transmission Control Protocol and Internet Protocol is collectively the common Internet protocol suite in the computer networking model and set of communications protocol used on the Internet and similar computer networks. It is commonly known as TCP/IP, because these were the first networking protocols defined during the Internet's communication development.

USB Phone or **USB Speakerphone** Is a device which looks like a traditional telephone, but it has a USB (Universal Serial Bus) connector instead of a traditional telephone jack aka RJ-11. It may be used with most softphones (some equipped with speakers) and services (such as Skype).

Yaqui Indians Native Americans who inhabit the valley of the Rio Yaqui in the Mexican state of Sonora, Mexico and the Southwestern United States. The Pascua Yaqui Tribe is based in Tucson, Arizona.

Discussion Questions for
The Enigma Broker

Book Club Leaders … contact Charles and/or Rox to participate in a special meeting to discuss the book; the concepts; and the evolution of the series. We always encourage readers to post individual reviews on Amazon.com. And thank you.

In-person gatherings are possible if you are in the North Texas region. Otherwise, Zoom is always an option.

Group Discussion Questions

Did the ending pull you in? Did you want more?
- What was the best part of the ending?

- Did you have characters you felt sorry for? Which ones?

- What was your top takeaway from The Enigma Broker?

What do you think of Jacob's role and place inside the R-Group?
- Do you know anyone like him?

- Do you think that there are men committed to honesty in technology like him today?

- Do you think it's important for a man to have honor?

What do you think of Petra and Jacob's relationship?
- Do they work well together?

- Would you like to have them as friends?

- Where would you like to see them next in the stories of Enigma Series?

Who was your favorite supporting character?

- Why did you like them?

- Did you find them believable?

- Did they have relatable character flaws?

Do you think Takeru was a realistic antagonist?

- Did he get his just desserts or would you have liked something different?

- Have you crossed paths with a person like this?

- What would you do in a similar situation if you were called upon to act?

What risks did Juan take that should have been avoided?

- Should he have placed himself at risk?

- If you have seen him and Carlos in other stories of the series, do you like him better now?

- Was he a hero and why?

What themes surfaced in the story?

- Have you ever been in a situation where you needed someone to save you?

- Have you ever stepped in to save someone?

- Who could you count on if you received a digital threat?

Read a snippet from **Book 9: The Enigma Dragon**

the
Enigma
Dragon

BOOK 9: Award Winning Techno Thriller Series

Breakfield and Burkey

Control over one's destiny means having the right to fail. Failure is essential to the learning process. Sometimes success is best understood in terms of a failure. But beware of those who tout success from others' suffering. Success has a satisfying feel and taste to it, but it should not be gathered from the defeat or misery of others. Harvesting success from potential victims is why governments try to limit failures. Be not the victim of someone's success.

...The Enigma Chronicles

Old definition: drag·on 'dragən/ noun/A mythical monster like a giant reptile. In European tradition the dragon is typically fire-breathing and tends to symbolize chaos or evil, whereas in East Asia it is usually a beneficent symbol of fertility, associated with water and the heavens.

New definition: drag·on 'dragən/Specialized Term/ Digitally Randomized Analog Graphics for Off Net Sequencing

Locations and Primary Cast Members
CATS Team - Luxemburg
Julie "JAC" (Rancowski) Rodríguez and Juan Rodríguez – Owners of the CATS Team

Eilla Zan "EZ" (Marshall) Waters (CATS operation/communication headquarters in Luxemburg)

Supported by R-Group staff Quip, ICABOD, Petra, Jacob, Wolfgang, and Otto

Panama – (Data Center built into the mountain side)
Brayson Morris, member of the CATS team
Mercedes Field, member of the CATS team

Operations in Zürich - (R-Group Headquarters)
Eilla Zan "EZ" (Marshall) Waters, member of the CATS Team
Quip Waters, member of the R-Group
ICABOD

Singapore, Hong Kong, Istanbul
George Jones, member of the CATS team
Summit Hayes, member of the CATS team

New York, Washington D.C. - (Smart City)
Ernesto Gleen, member of the CATS team
Tyler Hebert, member of the CATS team
Jim Hughes, member of a US three letter agency
AIMs Penny and Jenny
Jamie Griffin, newest member of the CATS team

London, New York – (ePETRO)
Marge Barger, ePETRO executive
Mike Patrick, ePETRO executive
Steven Christopher

Iraq Interests
Kashan Nasr
Dabir Nasr
Achmet
Najih

North Korea Interests
Chung-He
Chung-Ho

Tracking Digital Betrayal

Beaten as he was, he could barely stand. Trembling fear was the only reason he didn't collapse in front of them. It was supposed to be a simple drop off, routine like the others, only this wasn't like the others. It was a trap, and he had walked into it only thinking about where to get his adult male entertainment that evening. It was evening now, but entertainment wasn't at the top of his list at this point, only surviving.

His captor snarled, "You were supposed to bring the package straight here, unopened! Did you think we would not notice, western dog?" The brooding man stalked around the prisoner once, then hollered, "Beat him again! I want to see him on his hands and knees whimpering, begging! His betrayal will earn everything we can deliver!"

Several heavy, flexible rubber hoses rained down on his shoulders, back, and arms which did indeed force him to his knees. The blows were designed to cause heavy bruising, swelling, and bleeding just under the skin, but not break any bones. The prisoner felt his strength dissolving under the pummeling.

Finally, through his sobs he cried, "I was phoned to pick up this package and deliver it here. Once delivered I would get a deposit into my account just like the other times. Someone must have gotten there ahead of me and tried to help themselves. I swear that is the truth!"

The captor demanded, "You think we believe you? How could that be possible when no money was missing?"

The prisoner was bewildered and sobbed as he asked, "What do you mean? If no money is missing, then why…?"

A new, confident male voice of authority, outside the circle of punishment, answered, "Because of the tracking device inside the package."

"You are all under arrest. Put down your guns and raise your hands over your heads. We are the…"

The man never finished his sentence as a short burst of an automatic weapon cut across his path. The bullets caught him just below his waist line, filling the area around his body with a blood rain. Gunfire then erupted from both sides. Men dropped to the ground and took cover behind the makeshift shield of those already dead. The body armor of the U.S. security troopers kept most of them from being killed outright, while the cruel captors weren't so lucky.

The gunfire ceased, almost as quickly as it had begun. One of the U.S. security troopers, after checking on fallen team members, went to see what the captive's status was. As he turned the captive over, it was obvious he'd been caught by a stray bullet in the fire fight and would never be able to answer any questions.

The trooper, in a fit of disgust, bitterly remarked, "Hell! After all that monitoring and tracking of this Muslim weasel, he had to go get himself killed before we could find out who hired him. Bastard! Running guns into my country to outfit a bunch of Muslim extremists! The only good news is that we won't have to feed and clothe him while he waits for trial."

A team member hollered, "Rogers, we are missing two insurgents! Looks like they slipped away during the firefight!"

Rogers quickly shouted, "Alright, men, let's pursue and trap them between the secondary line and us. Watch where you fire, since we have our people on the other side. Move out!"

Rogers continued, "Carl, you and Lee maintain a perimeter here in case they double back. Come on, people! With even two of these guys loose, they get a foothold to rebuild."

Carl finished dressing the wounds of a downed team member and stood up to check on the fallen suspects. Lee and Carl checked each body for some type of identity papers.

After checking the last body, Carl looked at Lee and spit before he said, "Here they are! Afghan troops who were brought to the U.S. for intensive counter-insurgence training by our Army Special Forces. They came in, earned some trust, then simply vanished. They had planned this all along. Suck up to the U.S. military in Afghanistan, plead for better training to protect themselves from the Muslim extremists and insurgents in their country, and all the while it was a ruse to get their military on our soil. Might have worked too, if we hadn't intercepted their cell phone calls. They were clumsy, and we got a lucky break digitally tracking them."

Lee shook his head and asked, "What I don't know is how they got all those weapons after leaving the Army compound. There were no weapons missing from the base, so someone must have smuggled them in anticipating this kind of scenario. It always seems like the bad guys have way more friends than we do."

Carl nodded his head but offered no response.

Lee and Carl both turned their heads in the direction of distant gunfire. They both hoped it meant the end or capture of the missing insurgents, but they couldn't be sure.

CHAPTER ONE

A Sneeze in Time
Will Make You Mine!

It had begun quietly enough with the group *Sequentially Nihilistic Efforts to Eradicate Zealots and Extremists*, or SNEEZE. Their charter was to destabilize a government, move a competing organization into the vacuum that was left, and then rule the country through the new proxy government. The process had been occurring little by little, one small country at a time.

An encrypted conference call opened with all high-profile participants present.

Without much of a greeting, the menacing Asian-accented voice demanded, "What happened to our operative? You assured this cabinet that his profile was ideal for the role, and our organization funded the operation. Now entire property contents are being viewed, it seems, by several competing governments. Tell us how we can look at this other than as a total failure on your part."

The calm female voice on the other end of the call soothed, "My dear comrade, there are two kinds of failure in our world. The first, as I expect is the way you are looking at the situation, is like a sports game where the clock has run out and your adversary has won.

"The second, as you should be considering, is for someone to think we have failed and that the acquisition of the data center is simply the spoils of war. We used our SEP routine and wiped the machines. That's what the *Scorched Earth Program* should do, except we left our signature code buried in the special purpose device driver chip, built into the motherboard. In other words, we expected this compromise to occur so that our competitors would bring our technology into their data universe, or as you would call it, their network."

The Asian man smirked softly and remarked, "I am educated and familiar enough with your western culture to observe that your actions frequently mirror Odysseus and the Trojan horse ruse he used to get the Greeks into the city of Troy.

"Instead of arguing semantics on the concept of failure, perhaps you should enlighten the cabinet on the real issue, the next stage of the plan. These plans within plans are becoming tedious as well as expensive. Our approach of subjugating entire populations in our other country conquests proved quite successful. We are beginning to question your methodology of exporting this to other countries. Frankly, the cabinet is weary of all this extra finesse you insist on engaging in."

Losing some confidence in her position, the woman looked anxiously at her male companion for a brief moment before she carefully delivered, "I would observe that we are trying to engineer events in these other countries for activities and processes you did not need to overcome in your earlier conquests. We are trying to move some more advanced countries and governments into a model like yours, but they still have more freewill that must be subdued in order to introduce our next step of transition. Without controlled chaos being precisely introduced, at the correct time, all we will do is instigate civil war.

"You claimed that you wanted the social infrastructure to remain intact. You indicated that food production was a high value item in these targeted countries and is a necessity to supplement your current shortfall. If all you want is mass carnage and civilization to return to the Stone Age, then simply continue to fund the Muslim extremists who are happy to destroy everything."

It was now the turn of the silent man next to her to shoot an alarmed stare at his counterpart because of her bold statement. The panicked look on his face was almost making her nervous.

It took a few seconds for the Asian on the other side of the call to respond, but finally he interjected, "We can see that you still retain that useless Western female tendency of throwing a temper tantrum when she doesn't have her views totally embraced by the other party."

She swallowed hard and in a thoroughly chastened voice replied, "I meant no disrespect to you, Chung-Ho, or to your cabinet. My organization is prepared to continue with our charter and will continue to cooperate with your team to reach our mutual goals. However, I would point out that we have a marked preference for our approach in this matter."

Chung-Ho smiled slightly as he firmly stated, "Ah, now that's more like it. Almost an apology, how classically Western of you. Your culture seems driven to point out deficiencies in others and then promptly offer to help the poor backward Asians. It is curious how your *help* always generates profits that flow in your direction.

"You should understand that we are not displeased with what you have brought us so far. This means we can be somewhat tolerant of your insubordination, but we assert that you leave that adversarial attitude somewhere else before joining a call with us. For now, you are permitted to disconnect from the call."

The large woman sat and drummed her chubby fingers, the office light bouncing off her jeweled rings, as she fumed post call. Her girth pressed against her shirt and jacket with sweat beginning to seep through the lower back area as she shifted in her chair to ease her tenseness. Her grey hair, though professionally cut to a medium, low maintenance length, lacked the shine associated with a healthy lifestyle. Her lips were outlined with a brown line and filled in with a deep red lipstick which drew the eye to her full cheeks and sagging jowls. Though sitting, she had a tall upper body with a total height that reached just over 1.8 meters to hold her close to 118 kilograms.

Her somewhat younger male companion struggled to suppress a smirk at her annoyance and finally stated, "Well done, Marge, at containing your feelings and maintaining a near perfect center during the discussions with his high-end ass."

She shot her minion a venomous look and assessed the poor specimen who faced her. Marge reflected on the man she had hired, who topped 1.9 meters, but now sported a pear shape which spoke of indulging eating habits. Mike Patrick's once thick dark hair showed highlights of grey and was shapeless even when combed. His rich baritone voice, once his major asset, seemed less commanding, especially when looking at his reddish nose and puffy complexion, a side effect of his continuous drinking.

In an agitated voice she stated, "Chung-Ho is so fricking smug after inheriting power over his country from his 'Daddy' and the nuclear technology we helped him get! We've built all his cyber assassin technology and trained his team of criminals on the subtleties of digitally pounding his enemies and even brought up that Muslim extremist scum into his Monday morning call for global destabilization. Now, we get treated like second class servants!"

Mike chuckled slightly as he suggested, "Well, I, for one, am glad you stood up to him and gave him a good strong listening to when he told you to remember a female's place. Of course, this might be best interpreted as no back-sassing."

Marge studied him a moment while grinding her teeth and in a strained tone offered, "At least he spoke with me, mister persona non grata! Did you hear ANY warmth in his voice for you, my dull friend?"

He rocked back in his chair, clucked his tongue, and in an annoyed tone flatly stated, "Well, it looks like the little ol' fat boy was right about western females throwing a temper tantrum when they don't get their way. But that's okay, I'm used to it. So, how about we plan our next move?"

CHAPTER TWO

Reality, the Alternate Viewpoint

The younger man practically shouted, "No, you're wrong! Their so-called greatest strength of ethnic diversity and religious tolerance is clearly their greatest weakness! They are a mongrel race of people with no unified voice! They grow their workforce by pretending to be a home for the oppressed outcasts while they are really skimming our intellectual and professional talent for chump change! That country is stealing our future by pirating our next generation of leaders!

"I say we leverage their weakness and pump in our freedom fighters to bring the fight onto their soil! I promise you they will embrace our refugees. Then, with them fully camouflaged among their civilians, we can launch an attack without fear of their stealth weapons dropping on us because they won't risk collateral damage to their own population! Maybe we can't win on our soil, but I am confident we can win on theirs!"

The older, scruffy bearded man took the insolent comments calmly with his facial features not revealing any reaction. This younger man was identical to how he had looked and reacted when he was twenty-five, way before the beard and wrinkles had punctuated his life experiences. He noted his young protégé's intensity was accentuated by his lithe frame at 64 kilograms of sinewy muscles, intense facial features, and closely cropped shiny black hair.

After the elder man mused a moment, he asked, "You think you have enough patience to plan something like this out? What you are proposing takes time and funding, using dedicated freedom fighters who risk being corrupted in their target surroundings before you are ready to strike. You have always advocated strike now, and strike fast. Now I hear you describing a lengthy planning exercise that depends upon our enemy accepting our freedom fighters with no hesitation.

"I would not expect our freedom fighters to be accepted and embraced in their target population with their weapons over their shoulders. Thus, arming them at some point in the future will be another effort which depends upon either regular communications or having them fully briefed on the overall project before they depart. The problem with both of those is that regular communications are easily traced and long-range planning is always subject to change. The fundamental flaw with your approach is that our enemy is always changing moods, politics, and directions, so an erratic foe cannot be counted on to cooperate with our plan."

The eager young man sensed a modest shift of some sort in the older man toward his plea. He wanted to see if this was due to some consideration for his opinion or only because he also knew him on a more personal level.

The young freedom fighter gently offered, "Sir, I sense some acceptance to my recommended approach to taking the battle to the enemy. I find it gratifying that you like my ideas on this matter. Am I allowed to continue my planning approach?"

Kashan responded, "I believe this council should explore all well-crafted plans, but understand, ideas are judged by their merit as either good or bad only after extensive planning and a flawless execution. When you show us that level of planning and forethought, we will then render an opinion of good or bad."

The comment irked the young freedom fighter but, keeping his anger in check, Najih stated, "We have transparent funding from a likeminded comrade. We have given you several proofs of concept that clearly demonstrate the viability of the approach, but you still deny their worth. I need to know why."

The older man smiled, not quite indulgent as he almost teased, "As the phrase is stated by our highland farmers who tend their animals, Najih, *even an old blind camel may find an olive now and then.* This council does not want to gamble on a few olives, they want the whole harvest in the grove. Return to us with the methodology of obtaining the whole harvest."

The smirks from the other attendees only added to his infuriated mood, but the young freedom fighter, Najih, only ground his teeth as he nodded upon taking leave of the council.

CHAPTER THREE

Advice for Guests,
Don't Stay Too Long

EZ said, "You know this is really unnecessary, Julie. You and Juan have been overprotective of Quip and me since we started our honeymoon in Jamaica. Plus, it's still continuing, with no end in sight. At some point, you need to stop mothering us so we can live our lives. Yours too. We aren't your children. Speaking of which, aren't you anxious to get back to Luxemburg, to Juan Jr. and Gracie, let alone your home and business? We'll be fine here in our flat."

Quip, growing a little annoyed, asked, "Uh, where is Juan? He isn't doing an electronic sweep on our flat, is he? I have had ICABOD sanitizing this quadrant of the galaxy on our behalf, so can you lighten up a bit? Besides, I don't want him finding our um…adult play room. It's been grand and loads of fun, but you guys need to disengage so we can settle into the newlywed thing here. Got it?"

Juan strolled absentmindedly into the living room, turning a piece of leather gear over and over in his hands, and asked, "Quip, I'm not sure what this device or garment does, or for that matter, who it's for. I mean, it's nicely adorned with metal studs and short chains, but can you give me some contextual clues about how…"

Quip snatched it from his hands and quite crossly demanded, "Gimme that! See, this is what I mean."

Juan gave some exaggerated winks and nods to Quip to assure him that he was actually in the know about what said item was used for, but could rely on Juan's discretion. This only served to further inflame Quip.

EZ sensed that Juan and Quip were on a collision course and promptly interjected, "Hey, guys, let's take this unwanted protection issue up again in the morning, hmmm? We're kind of tired after the trip, and I don't want us to come off sounding negative to your generous support. That will give you time to check in at home and time for us to digest what is needed and, of course, what is practical. Would that be alright?"

Julie smiled a knowing smile, nodded her head, and offered, "Yes, of course, darlings. Your point is well taken. Perhaps we have been a little too overprotective, and frankly, I would like to do our family thing too. Let's take off for the night. I don't want any risk of friction in our relationship."

Juan added, "Hey, it's just that we care about you. Plus, it has been our experience that just about the time you let your guard down, thinking everything is okay, that's when a secondary strike occurs. I'd like to propose that I stay engaged here for a while longer, just to be safe. Julie can head home and begin putting the pieces of our family back together. We all need to feel safe, and we are family."

Quip, a little chastened, nodded and said, "Alright, point taken. There is some logic in scouring for any missed clues before we stick a fork in this episode and call it done."

Julie queried, "EZ, are you alright with this?"

With a tired smile EZ nodded and added, "I'm sure this will all sound better in the morning. Now you scoot. We promise to keep a watchful eye open at all times."

Quip was trying to hurry Juan and Julie out the door, but EZ put her arm into the crook of Juan's and slightly held him back while Julie and Quip moved ahead of them to the door. In a low, mischievous and sultry voice, EZ asked, "Juan, do you really not know how the leather garment is used?"

Usually, Juan was the teaser in these situations, but the sensual undertones of EZ's question caught him off guard. With something of a stammer, he offered, "Uh, well ah, you see…that is to say… it is an unusual…article…that could be multi-purpose…well, I didn't want to seem like a novice in the uh…you see."

Suppressing her grin at catching Juan flat-footed, she politely offered, "Juan, it is used for a comprehensive workout." Juan swallowed hard and, trying to maintain some dignity as the conversation seemed to be sliding into an awkward area of discussion, lamely asked, "Oh, so is the…uh, garment for him or you?"

EZ, grinning like a Cheshire cat, mischievously offered, "Yes, it is. Both parties slide into it with the chains used to…"

Julie, grinning from ear to ear, stepped in to Juan's rescue. "Honey! Stop dawdling! We said we would go and leave them to their own devices. Besides, whatever you and EZ are discussing I want to hear about later because you are blushing profusely! Now come on."

Juan stammered a little more for effect and lamely protested, "But EZ wasn't finished with her side of the conversation!"

EZ grinned at both of them and innocently offered, "Juan, perhaps another time?"

After Juan and Julie had gone, EZ turned to Quip and asked, "What exactly is this used for?"

Quip broke out laughing and then finally said, "That, my dear, is the best gag gift I have ever seen. It is a harness for holding the back legs of a sheep while the shearer shores off the wool of the animal. The additional chains are to hold the shearer up but take the load off his back while shearing the sheep. I think it will be sometime before Juan goes poking around another newlywed's apartment, don't you?"

They both howled with laughter at their gag and antics with Juan.

After waking to a wonderful early morning lovemaking session, Juan and Julie lounged in bed and continued the previous night's discussion.

Juan reassured, "Sweetheart, just give me a few more days here with EZ and Quip to make sure they are not going to be targeted again. Then, I promise to be on a plane home to you and the kids faster than you can say, my wayward Uncle Jesus is safely at the beach now. Everything will be fine with me, but I don't want you to let your guard down."

Julie responded, "I know, but I feel a little guilty leaving you here going over the last details when I should be here helping."

Juan gently reminded, "Now don't forget that the team is all assembled and looking for direction, so it doesn't make sense for both of us to be here with no one driving the business. And you know how Juan Jr. and Gracie are if one of us is not there monitor on them. I mean, think of poor Maude trying to deal with those two growing terrors! We need you home now, and I'll finish up this business as quickly as I can. I promise."

Julie frowned at Juan and scolded, "The last time you promised me something similar, we had to hunt for your whereabouts and break you out of jail!"

Juan somewhat indignantly responded, "Hey, it isn't always my fault! But in the meantime, I need you to also promise not to get into any trouble. It could happen. Right?"

Julie smirked and retorted, "Moi? In trouble? Oh push-tush!

I'll be fine. I don't go courting trouble like you, mister accident prone!"

Juan reflected for a moment, then gently offered, "Honey, thanks for saving my backside so many times. If the tables ever get turned, I will be there hunting for you. I just hope it won't be like the time you drug me out of that dungeon in China. It would devastate me to see you that worked over. I will come for you whenever you are in trouble, even though I know it will never happen, okay?"

Julie mushed into Juan and, after a passionate kiss, quickly pulled away and hopped out of bed. She raced to the shower with Juan hot on her heels. They cleaned up after steaming up the mirrors in the bathroom even further. Julie dressed and finished her packing. Juan carried her suitcase as they walked outside to the waiting car.

One more passionate kiss and Julie entered the car for transport to the airport. As the cab pulled away, a stray tear got away from her eye before she could trap it.

CHAPTER FOUR

Round Two May Be a Tie

Even with the conversation only happening over the state-of-the-art speakerphone, the tension was vilely palatable in the room where the two of them sat.

Mike insisted, "I can inter-trade your oil because of this organization with no retaliation from the world powers. The infrastructure is such that, using the methods and procedures we put in place, you can get a fair and reasonable price for your oil, even while the world believes you are stockpiling these resources."

After a long pause, Kashan replied, "ePETRO is too close to the investigations of the U.S., with many of their number trying to infiltrate the thinly veiled enterprise."

Marge knowingly nodded in silence toward Mike as if her former predictions that he was in way over his head were coming to fruition. Mike ignored her and continued with the conversation exactly as he had planned.

Mike laughed loudly, then said, "There! That's my point exactly. If you think the web, you see is what they're watching, then we're very much hidden from view. Those tankers are simply decoys. Our actual live storage is at specific ports which are accessed only by our silent partners. The details and directions for the operations are conveyed by non-electronic means, period. In other words, we let them hear what we want so our efforts are not under a microscope.

"I'm not going to explain the details of my operations to you, but they are insulated from any outside hacking, prying, or any electronic means. There is simply no way to penetrate to the heart of the operation without the hundreds of feet on the street, which I control. Suffice it to say, we have embraced *Digital Eavesdropping Avoidance Through Analog Crowd Sourcing,* or what we refer to as DEATACS, to confound and confuse our competitors and potential enemies."

Mike remained silent, letting the words be dissected by his potential partner. Though he may have found the partnership distasteful from several aspects, he could not deny the fortune that he was building because of this relationship. Marge thought she knew about all of his holdings, but she was only aware of a fraction of his amassed wealth in the Caribbean banks. He glanced briefly at her and saw her smug *I told you so* look of disdain. She was as vicious as he was, but he was grateful that he at least didn't have the heavy sagging jowls that she sported. She was another person he couldn't care less about, outside of her being a means to his retirement. Marge thought her control over Mike was sealed when he lost his love, but she was so very wrong. He would never let her see how he thought until her last breath, which was something he hoped he could engineer soon.

The minutes ticked by until the silence was broken, and Kashan asked, "So, you are in charge of this operation, rather than that whale you publicly report to? We have no respect or tolerance for stupid females who should be at home servicing their men.

"In her case, it would take a desperate man to want to use that for service." Then he practically spit out the next comment. "Women are too stupid emotionally for serious business transactions. They turn red and then become too angry to even speak full sentences. It would lessen the value of our relationship if the beached whale was silently attending this call. I insist you assure me, Mike, she is not listening."

Mike glanced again at Marge to see the immediate effect that Kashan's words were having. He feared she would explode; she was so visibly angry. He reached over and placed the call on mute.

"Marge, you need to leave this room before you ruin this discussion. You know that it is for show and for our end game. Now leave, or I will be forced to end the call and apologize when I call back. He has to trust ePETRO, or at least me, in this arrangement. This, as you know, will weaken our position and my bargaining avenues. This is why we agreed, I am Kashan and his team's point-of-contact."

Marge struggled to gain her feet, her anger causing her to not lift her heavy body correctly from the chair. She was seething but, without a sound, left the room, surprisingly not slamming the door to the room next to his. Her office had an equally private entrance and exit, and he felt certain she would remain there until he briefed her on the remainder of the call.

Mike cleared the phone from the cradle and suggested, "Kashan, you are correct, of course. Even educated women should remain in their place.

"Now, Kashan, are we aligned with the goals for the next three months on the quantity of oil we can use for trade? If not, I have other contacts I will need to make to fill the orders I have waiting. I only reached out to you as we have the longest and most equitable business relationship."

"Mike, we have done business since you demonstrated we could remain out of sight and off the grid. You have stayed out of my side affairs and I out of yours. I don't trust you anymore than you trust me, but business works well between us. I will agree to the supply numbers discussed, with one condition."

The silence after that statement weighed on Mike, and he broke the silence before he meant to. "What is your condition, Kashan?" Mike realized his error in answering too fast and quickly added with a bit of humor in his tone, "The amount cannot change and still work with the cost models, unless you are petitioning to take less."

Kashan chuckled and replied, "You would wish, but no, that is not the condition. My nephew, Dabir, has completed his university education and now requires some real experience. I would like him to work in your London office for the next three months and learn the numbers side of the business. He would not need the intimate details, but rather operate as a standard office worker. He did well in his studies but wants to be close to his friends in London, and I need him to see how work is done in a Western business."

Mike thought about how much of the operation was centered in London and if he would be able to control the access to his information mules. He decided he could but mentally added that Marge could never be told of the fox in the henhouse.

"Kashan, I think that would be agreeable. When should I expect the young man? I would prefer taking care of the details of his addition to the staff personally, to avoid any confusion."

"Good, I will tell him to be there next Monday and ask for you. I will have him carry the signed contract so that we may proceed. But let me caution you not to discuss our business arrangements with him since he is not yet aware of all that concerns me and my organization, nor is he aware of my history of the lessons of fire I gained in the U.S. Agreed?"

Mike paused a moment for effect and said, "Agreed, Kashan."

They continued discussing some of the finer terms of the agreement before disconnecting. Mike was making notes to make certain he briefed Marge on the details when she barged into his office and stood by his chair until he was forced to rise and meet her eye-to-eye.

Marge seethed, "You little piss ant. You will not forget your place and what you owe me. I am in charge of this operation, and you do *my* bidding. Kashan and the rest of those assholes may think women are tools, but I can crush you in oh-so many ways. Don't you ever tell me to leave a room again! Do you understand me?"

Mike appeared to wilt under the piercing stare and nose-to-nose proximity. "Yes, Marge. I was only doing what we had agreed to. I am sorry if you feel I overstepped. I can quit if you prefer."

She stared hard and replied, "You may quit, when I tell you to. Now, get me the details on the final negotiations within the hour. I am leaving this godforsaken city and going back to headquarters tonight!"

Inside, Mike smiled at his good fortune as he nodded agreement to the request.

About the Authors

Breakfield – Works for a high-tech manufacturer as a solution architect, functioning in hybrid data/telecom environments. He considers himself a long-time technology geek, who also enjoys writing, studying World War II history, travel, and cultural exchanges. Charles' love of wine tastings, cooking, and Harley riding has found ways into the stories. As a child, he moved often because of his father's military career, which even helps him with the various character perspectives he helps bring to life in the series. He continues to try to teach Burkey humor.

Burkey – Works as a business architect who builds solutions for customers on a good technology foundation. She has written many technology papers, white papers, but finds the freedom of writing fiction a lot more fun. As a child, she helped to lead the kids with exciting new adventures built on make believe characters, was a Girl Scout until high school, and contributed to the community as a young member of a Head Start program. Rox enjoys family, learning, listening to people, travel, outdoor activities, sewing, cooking, and thinking about how to diversify the series.

Breakfield and Burkey – started writing non-fictional papers and books, but it wasn't nearly as fun as writing fictional stories. They found it interesting to use the aspects of technology that people are incorporating into their daily lives more and more as a perfect way to create a good guy/bad guy story with elements of travel to the various places they have visited either professionally and personally, humor, romance, intrigue, suspense, and a spirited way to remember people who have crossed paths with them. They love to talk about their stories with private and public book readings. Burkey also conducts regular interviews for Texas authors, which she finds very interesting. Her first interview was, wait for it, Breakfield. You can often find them at local book fairs or other family-oriented events.

The primary series is based on a family organization called R-Group. Recently they have spawned a subgroup that contains some of the original characters as the Cyber Assassins Technology Services (CATS) team. The authors have ideas for continuing the series in both of these tracks. They track the more than 150 characters on a spreadsheet, with a hidden avenue for the future coined The Enigma Chronicles tagged in some portions of the stories. Fan reviews seem to frequently suggest that these would make good television or movie stories, so the possibilities appear endless, just like their ideas for new stories.

They have book video trailers for each of the stories, which can be viewed on YouTube, Amazon's Authors page, or on their website, *www.EnigmaBookSeries.com*. Their website is routinely updated with new interviews, answers to readers' questions, book trailers, and contests. You may also find it fascinating to check out the fun acronyms they create for the stories summarized on their website. Reach out to them at *Authors@EnigmaSeries.com, Twitter@EnigmaSeries,* or *Facebook@TheEnigmaSeries.*

Please provide a fair and honest review on amazon and any other places you post reviews. We appreciate the feedback.

Other stories by Breakfield and Burkey in
The Enigma Series are at **www.EnigmaBookSeries.com**

We would greatly appreciate
if you would take a few minutes
and provide a review of this work
on Amazon, Goodreads
and any of your other favorite places.

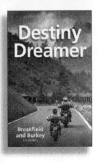

Other stories by Breakfield and Burkey in
the Heirs Series are at **www.EnigmaBookSeries.com**

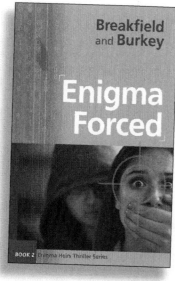

MAGNOLIA BLUFF CRIME CHRONICLES

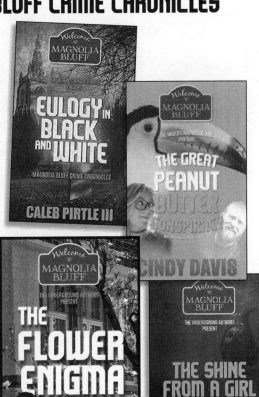

MAGNOLIA BLUFF CRIME CHRONICLES

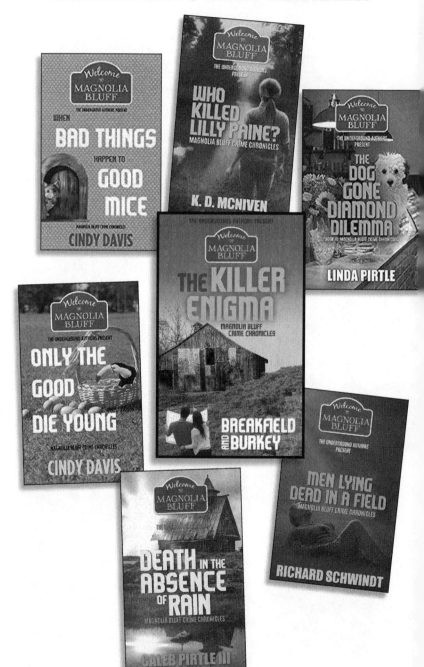

Made in the USA
Columbia, SC
16 December 2024

49694075R00257